Also by Therese Fowler

Souvenir

Reunion

EXPOSURE

EXPOSURE

A NOVEL

Therese Fowler

BALLANTINE BOOKS   NEW YORK

Published in the United States by Ballantine Books, an imprint of The Random House Publishing Group, a division of Random House, Inc., New York.

BALLANTINE and colophon are registered trademarks of Random House, Inc.

Library of Congress Cataloging-in Publication Data
Fowler, Therese.
Exposure : a novel / Therese Fowler.
p. cm.
ISBN 978-0-345-51553-7 (hardcover : alk. paper)—ISBN 978-0-345-52625-0 (ebook)
1. Parental overprotection—Fiction.   2. Fathers and daughters—Fiction.
3. High school students—Fiction.   4. Malicious accusation—Fiction.   I. Title.
PS3606.O857E97 2011
813'.6—dc22   2010048109

Printed in the United States of America on acid-free paper

www.ballantinebooks.com

2 4 6 8 9 7 5 3 1

First Edition

Book design by Karin Batten

*To my boys, who have to navigate a world fraught with challenges
and dangers I never imagined as a teen.*

*And to their peers, and their peers' parents,
who are trying to do the same.*

And, lastly, to the ones who weren't able to weather the storms.

Love that is not madness is not love.

~PEDRO CALDERON DE LA BARCA

ACT I

I would live in your love as the sea-grasses live in the sea,
Borne up by each wave as it passes, drawn down by each wave that recedes;
I would empty my soul of the dreams that have gathered in me,
I would beat with your heart as it beats, I would follow your soul as it leads.

—SARA TEASDALE

1

NINE HOURS BEFORE THE POLICE ARRIVED, ANTHONY WINTER stood, barefooted and wild, on the narrow front porch of the house he shared with his mother. The painted wooden planks were damp and cool beneath his feet, but he hardly noticed. In his right hand he held a fallen maple leaf up to a sun that was just breaking the horizon. In his left he held his phone. He squinted at the leaf, marveling at its deep blood-orange color, amazed and happy that nature could make such a thing from what had, only a few weeks earlier, been emerald green, and before that, deep lime, and before that, a tight, tiny bundle of a bud on a spindly limb, waving in a North Carolina spring breeze. He'd always been an observant person; he hadn't always been so romantic. Amelia brought it out in him. She brought it out in everybody.

When she answered his call, Amelia's voice was lazy with sleep. It was a Monday, her day to sleep a little later than she could the rest of the week. Tuesday through Friday, she rose at five thirty to get homework done before her three-mile run, which came before the

8:50 start of their Ravenswood Academy school day. At three
o'clock was dance—ballet, modern, jazz—then voice lessons twice
a week at five; often there was some play's rehearsal after that, and
then, if her eyelids weren't drooping like the dingy shades in her
voice teacher's living room, she might start on her homework. But
more often she would sneak out of her astonishing house to spend a
stolen hour with him. With Anthony. The man (she loved to call him
that, now that he'd turned eighteen) with whom she intended to
spend all of her future life, and then, if God was good to them, eter-
nity to follow.

Seeing Amelia and Anthony together, you would never have
guessed they were destined for anything other than a charmed future, and possibly greatness. Perhaps Amelia had, as her father was
fond of saying, emerged from the womb coated in stardust. And
maybe it was also true what Anthony's mother claimed: that her son
had been first prize in the cosmic lottery, and she'd won. They were,
separately, well tended and adored. Together, they were a small but
powerful force of nature. Love makes that of people, sometimes.

That morning, nine hours and perhaps five minutes before his
arrest, Anthony stood on the narrow front porch with a leaf and a
phone in his chilly hands. Amelia was saying, "I dreamt of us," in a
suggestive voice that stirred him, inside and out. He heard his
mother coming downstairs, so he pulled the front door closed.
Unlike the rest of his school's faculty, she knew about Amelia and
him; in her way, she approved. Still, he preferred to keep his conversations private. There were certain things even an approving
mother wouldn't want to hear. Certain things he absolutely did not
want her to know.

2

At 8:35 that morning, Amelia parked her car in the student lot and sat with the engine running, keeping warm until Anthony arrived as well. She was still smiling with her recollection of his words, spoken softly as she'd swum up out of sleep and into the day. He'd quoted her Shakespeare:

No sooner met, but they looked;
No sooner looked but they loved;
No sooner loved but they sighed;
No sooner sighed but they asked one another the reason;
No sooner knew the reason but they sought the remedy.

She knew the lines by heart. She had been Rosalind, he Orlando, in last year's school production of *As You Like It*. And while the lines were Rosalind's, about her cousin's love for Orlando's brother, this was, after all, *their* story, in verse.

No sooner looked but they loved.

Love at first sight. Amelia, sixteen when it struck, a focused high-school junior whose romantic experience with boys was tenuous and limited, hadn't believed it could happen to someone like her. But as with anything that a person dismisses and then experiences in full force—a hurricane, the Lord, a visit from a ghost—she was converted instantaneously. With her heart pierced as surely as Shakespeare's lovers' had been, she became Immediate Love's happy evangelist—quietly, though. Selectively, so that her father would not find out and ruin everything.

Whenever her most trusted girlfriends heard her talk about seeing Anthony across the stage at auditions, of falling for him before he'd even spoken a single word, the girls gravitated toward her like she was fire and they were chilled travelers of a hopeless, barren snowscape. Oh, to be loved. To *have* love, true love, not the pistol-in-my-pocket variety they were offered all too often. Or worse: the lurid, online-porn-fed ambitions of the most heinous of their rich-boy classmates, whose ideal woman was an oversexed Lady Gaga in fishnet and pasties. No. To be Amelia, who had *Anthony,* that was the dream these girls nurtured. Anthony was passionate. A noncon-formist. Perhaps best of all, Anthony was a secret.

They were sure Amelia's father, Harlan Wilkes, would kill her, or maybe Anthony, or maybe both of them, if he found out Amelia was not just dating someone he disapproved of but was, in planning a future with Anthony Winter, deceiving her father in every possible way. The girls talked about Amelia's risky love with dewy, faraway expressions, with smiles and sighs. They trailed Anthony like ladies of the court, always respectful of Amelia's claim on him but, at the same time, always angling to be the one he might turn to should anything ever go wrong.

Sitting there in the parking lot, Amelia watched car after car—many of them luxury models bought from her father's franchises—pull into the lot and park while the heater's air warmed her skirt-bared legs. Save for the pleasure of seeing Anthony, she didn't want to spend yet another day at Ravenswood. She'd been attending school there on the forested, esteemed campus since she was four years old. The buildings and grounds, the sports fields, the stadium, the teachers and staff, the classrooms, the gym—nothing seemed to have changed in all that time. There were new students every year, yes, but they were, for the most part, replicas of all the students who had come before them, and models for the ones who would come after. Amelia knew the word for her feelings: *ennui*. She knew the remedy, too: escape.

No sooner knew the reason but they sought the remedy. These days she lived that line, though it had given her trouble when they'd first been rehearsing the play. "The *remedy*," Ms. Fitz, their director, had explained, "for the *reason* for their sighs. Oliver and Celia are desperate to sleep together, so their solution is to marry the next day and scratch that itch, so to speak." What Amelia and Anthony plotted was a remedy for the pretty ribbon-wrapped life her father insisted should be her future—a future that didn't include anyone remotely like Anthony. No intellectuals of any kind ("Too much thinking, not enough doing," Harlan Wilkes was known to say). No tall, lean, black-haired young man with curls framing his heart-shaped face, a face that made one think, *Italian,* or possibly *Jewish,* or, depending on one's familiarity with the wider world, *Jordanian.* Anthony could be any of these, could play all of them—that, Amelia thought, was part of his brilliance onstage.

Kim Winter, his pale-skinned, ginger-haired mother and one of Amelia's favorite teachers, had lent only her hazel eyes; the rest of Anthony's features owed to his father's contribution, the only thing the man had contributed before running out on his wife and unborn son, claiming that he'd made a mistake with marriage and a bigger one with fatherhood. Fortunately, Anthony inherited his mother's capacity to soldier on—which is not to say Kim and Anthony were unaffected. When Anthony got moody he sometimes talked about how he would show his absent father how well he could do without him, how his father's rejection was no loss but rather a favor, as useful to him as the Andalusian heritage responsible for their looks.

His mother, native to upstate New York, where Anthony had lived until he was ten, was part Russian Jew, part Irish Catholic, part Canadian Quebecer, with a dose of Iroquois added in a few generations back. Heritage mattered, but it was not and should not be allowed to become everything. "*On est tous dans le même bain,*" she often told her French class students, Amelia included. We are all in the same boat. She also reminded them that "Borders are arbitrary, man-made things." And then there was the one Amelia liked best: "Question authority." That was the kind of adage Amelia needed, to help give her the courage to live her own life.

Anthony's mother was popular with the Ravenswood students, who signed up for her art or French classes even if they weren't especially talented in either subject. Amelia, en route to school for first-quarter parent-teacher-student conferences last year, had told her parents this. "It's not that she gives easy A's or doesn't assign homework. She's just . . . cool." This was a few weeks before Amelia met Anthony, at a time when she'd only heard him spoken of, sometimes in unfavorable tones. He'd started there as a junior, when Ms. Winter got hired on, and so he was a mystery to those who, like Amelia, had been there forever. Her fellow students weren't sure how to classify him; he didn't fit into any of the cliques. Not a jock. Not a prep. Not a stoner. Not goth. He was said to be smart, but quiet—not nerdy, though. More like the kind of guy you'd see in an Apple ad. His eyelashes were so thick and dark that even an innocent glance could seem sultry. The students couldn't peg him, so they disparaged him—the girls halfheartedly because, after all, he was *hot;* there was no other word for it. When Amelia finally did see him, love him, meet him, she categorized him simply as *Anthony*.

Driving home from the school after conferring with Amelia's teachers, Harlan Wilkes had said, "Nothing against you, Ladybug, but I don't see what's so special about that Ms. Winter."

"She seemed very nice," Amelia's mother said. She turned to Amelia, who was riding in the backseat. "I noticed she doesn't wear a wedding ring."

"She says she's keeping her options open." Amelia admired Ms. Winter's positive attitude about being single and hoped it would rub off on her. Yes, Amelia had been only sixteen at the time, and a long way from having to face spinsterhood (if they even called it that these days), but she was fairly convinced that no man would love her once her faults were known. She thought she'd do well to accept that fate. Some things just weren't attainable by determination and hard work.

Her father said, "Keeping her options open? At her age?"

"She's not that old. You're older than she is," Amelia said.

"And I'm married, and have been for twenty years."

"Well, I think she's great." That night Kim Winter had been dressed in wide-legged aubergine trousers and a cream knit turtleneck, with a vibrant watered-silk scarf tied around her neck. Amelia admired everything about her, including her style.

Her father said, "Sure, she's 'great,' if you think 'great' is being a single, middle-aged art teacher and making, what, thirty grand a year." He glanced at Amelia over his shoulder. "And you wonder why I'm pushing you to go to school for business."

She didn't wonder. She knew he simply didn't understand. His world, the business of selling import cars, was not about art or beauty or magic. He indulged her interests, true, but only because he viewed them as extracurriculars, no different than her running track, or joining Drama Guild and French Club. She would have to wait until she was on her own, independent, and then she'd live the life she wanted. She'd be privileged to end up like Ms. Winter if it meant she was doing the things she loved.

In the year that had passed since that evening, nothing had changed in her father's way of thinking. Amelia's thinking had changed, though, and once she turned eighteen in February, she

would tell her parents in exactly which ways. She'd reveal her plan
to move with Anthony to New York City, where they would both, if
they got in, go to New York University for drama, and at the same
time pursue Broadway careers. She longed to tell them now; it
pained her to keep her feelings and her plans a secret. She knew,
though, how they would react, and so the best strategy was to delay
until it became a fait accompli, an unchangeable fact.

Amelia saw Anthony's aging Mini Cooper trailing Brandt
Wilson's new Infiniti, and shut off her car's engine. Cameron
McGuiness, her most faithful friend since their first days of kinder-
garten, spotted her from across the lot and waved. Cameron knew
not to stop to talk in the morning, knew the few minutes Amelia
would have with Anthony before class were a precious commodity.
Amelia leaned her head against the leather-covered headrest and
sighed. Summer could not come soon enough.

Given his way, her father would see her married off on the
Saturday following her college graduation (from any top Southern
school, but preferably Duke) in a huge white wedding that included, of course, a ridiculously expensive white dress that would
be complemented by an engagement diamond so heavy that
she'd struggle to raise her left hand. A ring that would have been
presented to her some tasteful number of months earlier (meaning,
more than nine) by a twenty-first-century version of Barbie's Ken.
Ken would wear a tux he owned, bought with his substantial in-
come working in some first-rate white-collar field. There would
be no Broadway career, only Broadway tickets—a torturous scenario to Amelia, who imagined the gut-wrenching envy she'd
experience sitting in the audience watching other women live
out the dream she'd been too softhearted and obedient to pursue. Her future could so easily have gone that way, if not for
Anthony.

Amelia's smile, which had faded with the negative thoughts,
reappeared when she saw Anthony walking toward her car. He, with
his luxurious hair, his full lips, his quick wit, his quiet assurance, was

her savior. He'd made her believe not only that she should claim her future for herself when the time came, but that she truly would. Her father did not own her. No man did. Whatever she would do, wherever she would go, it would all be on her terms.

"Hello, beautiful," Anthony said as Amelia opened her door and got out. She smiled. The thrill of him, of his love for her, *her* and not someone else, someone whose childhood had not been spent hiding a shameful flaw, delighted her. He looked at her mouth in that butterfly-inducing way he had, a kiss without contact. *Safety first,* they often joked with each other. Officially, publicly, they were nothing more than good friends who shared a common love for theatre, sushi, and music. Officially, they were too busy to date—anyone, at all. "Plenty of time for that later," they always said.

Amelia imagined the kiss (his soft lips, the heat of his mouth), and said, "Can't we just run away?" She looked toward the Upper School, its pale stone edifice dazzling white in the morning sunlight. Teenagers streamed into the building, dressed in the uniform colors of navy and white and gray. The students were given some sartorial leeway: skirt, pants, or tailored shorts; collared blouse, button-down, tasteful knit shirt or golf shirt; crewneck, V-neck, or cardigan sweater—and in any combination of blue, white, or gray (except no white on the bottom between Labor Day and Memorial Day). But really, Amelia felt that requiring uniforms in the first place was a kind of tyranny. Free expression, that was what she longed for. Free expression of every kind.

"Who needs this?" she said. "We can get GEDs in New York."

Anthony gave an exaggerated serious nod. "Right, sure, the NYU admissions office won't see any difference."

"They shouldn't," she said. "If only we could stay there, after evaluations." They both had to audition as part of their application to NYU's Tisch School of the Arts. They'd set their appointments for the Tuesday before Thanksgiving, when they would be traveling to Manhattan with the Drama Guild. It was a chaperoned trip, but because they were seniors, they had blocks of free time to shop or roam or, as the case might be, fit in a morning at NYU. Anthony hadn't needed to hide his plan from his mother, and Amelia envied this. What good were all the privileges she'd grown up with when none allowed her to be genuine at home? How good it would be to live every day honestly.

"Seven months till graduation," Anthony said. "We can make it. Then nobody can bitch at us about being irresponsible or ruining our futures."

"You don't know my dad."

She had told Anthony all about him, of course, and Anthony had met him, briefly, a time or two, but she wondered if he thought she exaggerated. Harlan Wilkes the businessman, the offspring of Robeson County trailer-trash teenagers, a man who had pulled his own bootstraps up so high that no one in central North Carolina could think of imported automobiles without also thinking of his name, was known as bighearted and generous, fair and honest in all his dealings. And he was those things. He was also implacable, at least when it came to setting boundaries and providing guidance to his one dear, indulged, protected child. He fully expected Amelia to sail the course he'd charted for her. For the majority of her life, she'd let him expect it; despite her dreams, she had expected it of herself. Until Anthony.

Anthony said, "Well, okay, you're ruining *his* future either way. But let's make sure we don't ruin yours."

"Or yours."

Amelia imagined them headlining together at the Gershwin Theatre to a capacity crowd. Anthony was not the strongest tenor as Broadway tenors went, but what his voice didn't do he made up for with stage presence. He was a panther, lithe, sleek, sloe-eyed. In her view—a rose-tinted view, by any adult's standards—he would have no difficulty bewitching casting directors and audiences such that their ears would be persuaded to adore both his voice and him, much the way her mother's had been when watching Pierce Brosnan in the film version of *Mamma Mia!*

Anthony said, "Seven months."

"Two hundred and ten days."

"Give or take. Come on, let's get this one over with."

During second period, the entire Upper School attended character assembly in the auditorium. This month's trait was Trustworthiness. Amelia paid little attention to the serious, brittle-looking woman standing at the podium onstage, lecturing them on the value of trust. Who among them hadn't sat through this presentation multiple times before? More important to Amelia was her forgotten laptop, which, in her dreamy morning state, she'd left on the kitchen counter. She needed it for her fifth-period Earth Science presentation, a PowerPoint project that had taken her three weeks to construct. She texted her mother, asking her to drop the computer by the school ASAP, then sat there forming sign-language letters with her left hand, photographing them with her cellphone, and sending each picture to Anthony. She spelled out Y-A-W-N, and then K-I-S-S, while around her many of the other students were behaving similarly, texting complaints or jokes or making plans for where to go for lunch. No, they were not supposed to use their cellphones or any electronic devices during school hours, but they knew they could get away with it during assembly if they gave the appearance of paying attention. Even some of the teachers took out their devices to check email or keep up with the news. The stricter teachers would confiscate electronics used during class, and the school's policy was to hold all confiscated items until the end of the term. The school had received so many complaints, though, from parents who depended on having continual access to their children, that the policy went unenforced; devices, if taken at all, were returned at the end of the day.

Anthony wrote in reply: "—*es,*" and Amelia smiled. *Kisses.* On the heels of his reply came her mother's: *Hi. I'm in durham for a meeting.*

Will try to get it to you by lunch ok? Amelia wrote back, *K, thx.* The girl on Amelia's right, Bella Giordano, nudged her and hissed, "Braddock." The Upper School's headmaster was coming down the aisle behind them. Amelia wondered whether Anthony was right in thinking there was something romantic going on between Braddock and his mother. That, she thought, would be weird, but also nice; they'd make a perfect pair. Like herself and Anthony. Meant to be. Amelia pressed her phone between her palms and sighed. *Seven months,* she thought. *Two hundred and ten days, give or take.*

The waiting—for graduation, but more than that, for The Future—was exhausting. Every day was like treading water while waiting for a ship she could barely see on the horizon. Time passed so slowly that Amelia would swear the Earth had quit rotating—possibly at her father's request. Hardly a day went by when Harlan Wilkes didn't lament that *Next year at this time, you'll be waking up in a Duke dorm room,* which he didn't know wouldn't happen even if she did get in, or, *It's going to be way too quiet without you here,* despite her spending almost no time at home already, and his rarely being there when she did.

He wanted Amelia to be ten again, his adoring, adorable princess waving from atop the backseat of a Mercedes convertible as they inched through downtown Raleigh in the Christmas parade. He missed the preteen who'd been his steadfast companion in the "stable," helping him wash and wax whichever roadster they would take out for a drive that day. There were Bugattis, Triumphs, an Austin Healey, a Bentley, a Morgan, and a 1947 Rolls-Royce Silver Wraith, which he would drive only early in the morning on days when the roads were dry and there was no wind. Though Amelia had no genuine interest in the cars themselves, she'd loved listening to her father's stories of his childhood, of how poor he'd been, of how he'd dreamt of one day being rich enough to buy a brand-new Chevy truck. "And now look at us," he'd say, polishing the Wraith's black fender into a mirror that reflected his satisfaction and her proud grin. He had been the only man in her world then.

The phrase "Daddy's Girl" had been inspired by daughters like Amelia, who couldn't know that by simply growing up they were bound to break their fathers' hearts. Had Amelia known that a tough man could be fragile, too, she might have taken even more care to protect him.

3

THAT MONDAY, EIGHTY-SEVEN MINUTES BEFORE HE WOULD call the police, Harlan Wilkes left the office at eleven, planning to work from home for a while and then, if the weather held, get over to the driving range and try to get rid of the hook that, lately, was putting his score over ninety every time he played. Sheri would probably be out, as usual. He didn't keep track of her schedule, which was packed with activities ranging from fitness classes to volunteer work at Amelia's school, for their church, at the county animal shelter, and for the Red Cross. Harlan was as proud of Sheri, who'd come from the kind of Southern family he wished he'd had, as he was of his thoughtful, accomplished daughter. A lot of men's wives passed their days spending the money the men had worked so hard to make. Not Sheri. She'd been a decorator when he met her—hired her, actually, to turn his first house into something that looked like a home. She had a great work ethic. After Amelia was born, Sheri made a career of managing Amelia's life—playdates and school and camp and lessons and the like. Now that Amelia had shown that she was as capable as her parents and could manage her schedule admirably, Sheri found ways to give her time to others in need.

Harlan doted on his girls. Everyone said so, and he liked that they did. He was proud that he had, through a lot of hard work, long hours, and, early on, some amount of ass-kissing, gotten himself to a place in life where he *could* dote—on Amelia, on Sheri, even on their dog, a golden Lab named Buttercup. Buttercup was getting white around the eyes and muzzle, and a rabbit's presence no longer provoked her to do more than stand up. Still, he regularly gave her the choicest table scraps, and took her to work with him on days when he wouldn't be cutting out early. She was his best girl, in the simple and uncomplicated way that only a dog could be.

Everyone said, too, that Amelia and Harlan were a lot alike, in looks if not in talents. He was tall, as was Amelia, and both had dark hair with red tones that, in the sun, shone like the cherry wine Harlan had stolen from the Stop-n-Shop when he was a kid. Both had aquiline noses and expressive eyebrows, and light blue eyes that in Amelia's case were flecked with gold. Harlan's jaw was more angular, and his forehead was growing as his silvering hairline crept upward, but there was no mistaking whose child she was. Amelia looked so much like Harlan that Sheri often told the joke, "What did the blonde say when she found out she was pregnant? 'Oh, gosh, I hope it's mine!'"

Amelia looked like Harlan, but he always said she was like her mother in temperament: kind, generous, and forgiving of people's faults. Too nice at times, he thought, but he couldn't complain when he'd so often been the beneficiary of that attribute. Unlike Amelia, Harlan couldn't sing, and outside of the shower he didn't attempt to. Neither could he dance well, and he was no actor, that was certain. But his wife said he had the physique of a god—a minor god, she used to tease, in the days when the ideal male specimens were men like Stallone and Schwarzenegger. Amelia's physique, she said, was an angel's.

That Amelia was seventeen was the single thing that troubled Harlan, who was otherwise the happy master of his import-auto sales universe—six franchises now: Honda, Maserati, Toyota, Rolls/Bentley, Mercedes/VW, BMW, and still growing. Seventeen was worse than any of the previous -teens, being so close to the age when the law said she could make all her own decisions and take care of herself. This seemed to him a ridiculous idea. At eighteen, she'd need him looking out for her more than ever. It was lucky, he thought, that she understood this already. She listened to his advice, followed his rules, and thanked him for the trouble he took in making sure she had everything she needed (and most of what she wanted) in life.

His employees—from sales managers down to detailers, and every job in between—admired the relationship he and his daughter had. From what he'd heard, a lot of their kids were lazy or spoiled, willful, mouthy, and sometimes troublesome. Harlan knew of two who'd been busted for drug possession, a few who'd been charged with DWI, one who'd gotten pregnant at fifteen—a classmate of Amelia's, who had twins and refused to give them up. The father had been twenty at the time, and had been arrested for statutory rape. Harlan shook his head, thinking of it. What an ugly mess all that had been. Amelia had her moments—*Girls,* people often said with that telltale headshake, *they're prone to drama,* and sure Amelia sometimes was, too. Even so, even though she could be stubborn at times, he thanked God every day for his good fortune.

Harlan pulled into the driveway and parked under what their home builder had called a porte cochère, a sort of pass-through, bridgelike structure that divided the front yard from the courtyard, where the driveway continued on and branched into two. The structure itself was part of the house; "the bridge room," then-six-year-old Amelia had named it, upon seeing the house framed up. She'd been delighted that it led from the bedrooms wing to her playroom. They'd had both bridge and playroom done with long, arcing stretches of windows, and got a designer to make it all look like an old stone castle inside, complete with gas "torches," and cobble-stone in the walkways. Amelia's wide-eyed surprise and delight when he brought her to the just-finished house and led her to that space had just about done him in. At bedtime that night, he'd put his head against Sheri's shoulder and cried. In all of the forty-seven years he'd lived up till then, he had never been as grateful to a God who had first made him a skinny fleabag of a kid, effectively or-phaned by ignorant, good-time, teenaged parents, but then outfit-ted him with the grit and the wit to become such a man as the one who could do *this* for his own child.

Now he climbed out of his Maserati GranCabrio, and smiled at the resounding thump the door made when it shut. The last couple of years had been tough for high-end sales, but this car, well, this one got deep-pocketed corporate execs excited, eager to jump-start the economic recovery and look awfully good doing it. A fam-ily car, Maserati's first true four-seater. He drove it just so he could turn those prospective buyers' heads, get them looking for the showroom.

"Heh," Harlan chuckled, patting the car's hood. "A little better'n that piece o'shit Cutlass." His first car, bought with the first two hundred dollars he'd made, dealing pot. Amelia didn't know that part of his story; almost no one did. Building his empire by first sell-ing marijuana to his shiftless teenaged friends was information best kept to himself.

Buttercup greeted him in the back foyer. He squatted down to scratch her ears, and gave her a kiss on the muzzle. Then he dropped his keys on the counter, next to Amelia's laptop—one of those amaz-ing lightweight Macs, thin as a notepad. They'd bought it to help minimize the weight she had to haul around in her book bag. Sheri read some old Richard Russo novel where the teenaged daughter was overwhelmed by a too-heavy bag, and had gotten concerned for Amelia. Harlan wasn't much of a reader himself, but Sheri took a lot from books, and he admired that about her. As for the Mac, well, it was a slick piece of technology, and Harlan was all for that.

He grabbed a bottle of cold beer and took Buttercup outside, into the backyard. The maples, oaks, hickories, and sweetgums on and surrounding his two acres were in full November color. The beeches, always lagging, were just beginning to turn. What a difference between the seasons here and up in leaf-naked Ohio, where he'd just spent a week touring Honda plants. Truth told, he hated being away for such a long stretch. Oh, Sheri did fine without him. Amelia too. If he had to admit it, he'd say he was the one who got lonely and morose when he was away on business. Being away deprived him of his moorings. In a rental car, or on the sidewalk of some random city, he was just some random guy. He was, too easily, that mongrel kid who'd lived in a busted-up trailer, eating stale Cap'n Crunch and wondering when his parents would get sober and wander back home.

His cellphone rang and he answered, "Wilkes here."

"Mr. Wilkes, this is Parker Finch. How're y'all doing today?"

"Parker, my boy!" Harlan had been expecting the call. "Whattya have for me?"

"Well, I'm pleased to say that we're gonna be able to come through on the loan. With the securities you've pledged, the board is more than happy to front you the cash."

Harlan grinned. The country-and-western nightclub in which he was buying a stake was a dream that had its roots in his earliest days selling cars. Back then, after long hours spent selling nothing to nobody and despairing that he'd never get his business off the ground, he'd go knock back a few beers at a little country tavern run by a guy named Clem Carroll. Clem and Harlan passed the time talking about the nightclub Clem meant to open someday. They'd lost touch for a time, and then two years ago Clem walked into Wilkes Toyota to buy a Tundra, and to see whether Harlan had a taste for a beer and a go at co-ownership of that nightclub. Harlan had proposed that when Clem got up 70 percent of what he'd need for start-up, Harlan would front the rest. Now, that time had come.

Harlan asked Parker, "You do own a pair o' boots, don't you?"

Parker said, "You let me know when that club's open for business, and I'll show up wearin' them."

"Fair enough." And by that time, July most likely, Harlan would be ready to introduce Parker to Amelia. With Parker working out of the bank's Chapel Hill office and Amelia not too far away at Duke, they'd have a just-right arrangement for casual dating that, in due time, might well lead to the boy becoming kin. Harlan liked this idea a lot; Parker was exactly the kind of guy who would keep Amelia living the life she was accustomed to, the life she deserved. He was the kind of guy to keep Amelia from ending up the way Harlan's mother had.

After he got off the phone, Harlan put his fingers to his mouth and whistled the dog in. "C'mon," he said when she came trotting back. "Let's get us some lunch."

Inside, he took out a tub of potato salad, Sheri's special red-skin recipe, and sat down at the counter bar. With nothing more than curiosity motivating him, he opened Amelia's computer. A box appeared in the center of an otherwise black screen, awaiting a password. Of course she'd have the thing secured; if she forgot it at school or left it at a friend's house, she couldn't have other people messing up her files and such. He tipped the screen forward, almost closed it, and then pushed it up again.

B-U-T-T-E-R-C-U-P, he typed. Amelia loved the dog like the sister she never got, though not for lack of him and Sheri trying. Sheri had carried three more babies to near twenty weeks and had almost bled to death miscarrying the third, so the doctor said that was it, and tied her tubes.

Nope, *Buttercup* wasn't the password.

Thinking of Amelia's sense of humor, Harlan tried P-A-S-S-W-O-R-D. Not that either.

He rubbed his mouth, took a swig of beer, then tried C-U-R-R-I-T-U-C-K, the street on which their beach house was located, down on Bald Head Island. Amelia loved that house, could hardly wait for the day each year when they trundled out of here for the summer—

or, that was how it had used to be. This past summer she'd gone grudgingly, then moped around for days before settling in to the routine of island life. Harlan had been worried, but Sheri told him to let her be. "She's seventeen. It's lonely here. Dull, compared to her usual schedule and school. Her friends are her life."

Strike three. The Mac politely informed him that he'd tried to log in too many times without success, and to try again later. Harlan snapped it closed, feeling mildly embarrassed. Theirs was a household built upon mutual respect for one another and here he was, trying to pry into his daughter's personal stuff as surely as if he'd gone into her bedroom and tried to jimmy open a locked desk drawer.

Actually, he'd done that once, when Amelia was eleven or twelve—not because he was suspicious of anything, but because he wanted to know, really *know,* the little changeling she had become—from a combination, he thought, of puberty and getting closer to finally conquering the stutter that had been troubling all of them since near her fifth birthday. The drawer had held the treasures particular to girls of that age: pretty stones, pressed flowers and leaves, poems that she'd either copied out or made up; Harlan, with his meager high-school education, sure couldn't say. There was a playbill from their first trip to New York, when they'd seen *The Lion King.* Tucked into it was a carefully written list, at the top of which was, "Steps for Success." She'd come up with only three: *1. Practice singing, 2. Watch more plays, 3. Ask Daddy for his secrets.* And she'd followed that plan strictly; she was his girl, all right.

He opened the laptop again. The password screen obligingly reappeared, giving him another turn at bat. He stared at the rectangular box with its blinking cursor, trying his best to get into Amelia's mind. But that was the trouble, wasn't it? He couldn't get in, not really; that's why he was sitting here, a flush creeping up his neck as he steadfastly ignored the impropriety of what he was doing—trying to do. He rationalized that it was parental diligence to see what your kid was up to, and anyway, she'd never know he'd done it.

L-A-D-Y-B-U-G, he tried, his nickname for her. No dice.

L-I-M-E-C-I-C-L-E, her favorite treat. No.

Harlan leaned away from the counter and closed his eyes. What else was significant to her? Dance. Singing. Drama. He thought of the *Lion King* playbill, and of how Amelia, eight years old at the time, had been so entranced by the production that she spoke of nothing else on the flight back to RDU. "I w-w-want to be Nala," she'd declared in a soft, deliberate, voice, her eyes shining. Then, all serious: "Daddy, w-why does it have to be *k-king* of the jungle?"

Her stutter pained him. The doctors had no explanation for why it had started and why it persisted, and that pained him, too; he liked action, motion, progress. When they'd first gotten her a speech therapist, he'd told the woman, "Let's nip this in the bud," only to get a lecture about setting reasonable expectations.

Reasonable. Well, that all depended on who was doing the reasoning, didn't it? If he had followed a "reasonable" track all his life, he'd have spent the years struggling the way Clem had for so long. But he'd minded the woman's advice after Sheri pointed out that he knew less than nothing about curing a stutter.

On the plane that day he'd told Amelia, "It doesn't have to be, Ladybug, that's just a play. When you're a little older we'll go to Africa on safari, how's that? And we'll see lionesses for real— they're the ones in charge, i'n't that right, hon?" Sheri, sitting across the aisle from them, reached over and patted his arm. "Always," she said, smiling.

He'd expected Amelia to jump on the idea of taking a safari, but no. She'd sat back in her seat, curled her legs beneath her, and gazed out the window. Her dreams had nothing to do with Africa. Thanks to Sheri's indulgence, and thanks to older girls that Amelia had since met at singing competitions and in community theater who'd gone on to get meager jobs in New York plays, she was *still* dreaming. She kept up with these girls on Facebook and was always telling him and Sheri about so-and-so's latest whatever. This was why he made an ongoing, serious effort to direct her toward more practical pursuits, secure ones. He had to make certain that too much of what she'd inherited from his mother didn't come out and ruin her life as surely as his mother's dreamy, poorly considered choices had ruined hers—and nearly his own.

B-R-O-A-D-W-A-Y, Harlan typed, and then he hit ENTER.

"Bingo," he breathed, grinning as the screen became a field of wildflowers backdropped by blue sky. His pleasure would last a mere seven minutes, and that seven-minute span would be the last of it for a long time to come.

4

THE BUFFED, GLOWING FLOORS OF THE RAVENSWOOD HALLWAYS were aswarm with students hurrying to their lockers or pushing their way toward the cafeteria or the exit to the parking lot. Kim Winter stepped into the chaos with Brittany Mangum on her heels.

"But see, Ms. Winter, I really do actually know how to conjugate *dormir* and *venir,* it's just that I was up really late Sunday, studying, for, for my Algebra II test, okay, and so I was so-o-o tired by French, right, and I didn't even eat any breakfast that day, I mean, I know I should have, and I do, most days—"

"It was one quiz," Kim said. "You'll have chances to make up the lost points before term ends." Looking past Brittany, she spotted William Braddock at the far end of the hallway, near the stairwell entrance. He caught her eye and smiled.

"I know, I know," the girl said, flinging her straight brown hair behind her shoulders, "but see, my dad, he expects me to get all A's on quizzes—no excuse for a bad quiz grade, that's what he says, quizzes being easier than tests, right—"

"If I let you take it over, I have to do the same for everyone who did poorly." Which was most of the class. When the students traded papers and Kim had begun reading out the answers, groans came from every row.

"Okay, yeah. Strictly speaking, you would, right, to be fair—which is why we don't have to *tell* anybody. I'll come in after school, and—"

"Brittany. No. I'm sorry. Tell your dad you'll do extra credit—I have several opportunities outlined on Blackboard—and then make sure you do it."

"Please? Please please *please?*" The girl pouted charmingly, but Kim wasn't swayed. Based on what she'd overheard in first period Art Studio, she knew Brittany's Sunday night hadn't been occupied by math, but by Seth Herzog, her boyfriend, who'd hosted a big parents-are-gone party. What might Brittany's dad think of that? What might William Braddock think of it—and had he heard the tale yet? Kim glanced at him. His cheekbones still showed signs of his weekend sunburn, a reminder of their lunch date in a kayak on Lake Johnson. Might he be wearing the same aftershave he'd worn Saturday? Scent had a lot to do with attraction, though he could smell like dirt and she'd hardly care—

"Ms. Winter?" Brittany said.

"What? Oh," she said, turning back to the girl. "Nope, sorry. Now go on and get some lunch." The girl was too thin by far.

Kim watched William—admired him, really, as he bantered with passing students, until Debbie Marchek, the twenty-three-year-old newly minted teacher who taught German in a neighboring classroom appeared next to her, saying, "Is it just my students, or is there something in the air today?"

"What's that?" Kim asked, turning toward Debbie reluctantly.

"They seem to be a little out of focus, and I don't mean through my eyes, I mean, oh, you know, like they're preoccupied en masse."

Kim laughed. "That is the natural state of the teenager, have you forgotten?"

"Okay, yeah," Debbie said, "but it's more than that. Like the planets are aligned oddly or something."

"Hangovers."

"You're not serious. On a *week*day?"

"I know. Maybe we've been a little too effective in exhorting them all to 'seize the opportunities that come your way.'"

Debbie shook her head. "Wow. So I guess we have to report it, then?"

"Mm. I'll tell William during my planning period," Kim said, hoping she sounded suitably reluctant. "For whatever good it will do."

"I thought Ravenswood kids were supposed to be the smarter ones."

"What, just because their families are well off?" She raised her eyebrows in a way that said Debbie had a lot to learn. "But even if that were the case," Kim went on, "there's intelligence, and then there's wisdom. They don't always go together."

When she looked down the hallway again, William Braddock had gone. The pleasure of having seen him, though, remained.

Kim had spent much of her own sometimes-impulsive, sometimes-unwise adolescence in her parents' bookshop in Ithaca, New York. This was where she met Santos Ruiz Arroyo, a college exchange student three years older than the seventeen she'd been at the time. The bookshop was the stage for their early courtship, which lasted most of his junior year and then picked up again eight years later, when he returned to Ithaca to teach world literature to college undergraduates. He was arresting, the sort of man who displayed his passions publicly, lived them daily, and couldn't understand why everyone didn't do the same. Kim couldn't hide her fascination. He embodied the person she wanted to be, while he called her the yin to his yang. "You balance me," he said when he proposed, and she naïvely imagined that this balance would infuse them both, rather than lead to perpetual misunderstandings and frustrations.

Her parents, and the bookshop, featured strongly in her life again after Santos left her. *Left her*—that was far too mild an expression for what he'd done, running out on her ten days before she gave birth, for God's sake, while she was trying to figure out how she would reconcile the woman she had been before her pregnancy with the woman she would become after it, how she would be both mother and wife. Well, he'd resolved that for her one morning when he carried a packed bag into the nursery, where she was folding Onesies into a soft, expectant pile, and said in his unfailingly charming, knee-weakening Spanish accent, "I just can't handle all this, Kim." He pointed at the Onesies, at the crib, at the washstand that had, improbably, started the chain reaction that led to his pointing, now, at her belly. "I know I said sure, let's do it. I know I was a willing participant, but I've done a lot of soul searching, and now I know I'm not cut out to be a dad. Not much of a husband, either, right? You're always saying I play too much, I don't pull my weight. What good am I to you if all I want to do is escape? You'll be better off without me, you'll see."

He was right. He couldn't handle it, and she didn't want him— not as a husband and not as father to her child—*because* he couldn't handle it, and in that way she was better off without him. It had only taken her, oh, a crushingly miserable year or so, during which she'd doubted all of her instincts and second-guessed all her decisions, to come around to that viewpoint. Talking to a therapist helped, as did Anthony finally sleeping through the night (it was amazing what a full night's sleep did to improve one's mental health), and she was able to see that to hold on to her anger and self-pity was to give a selfish man control of her life. A selfish *absent* man, who'd sent divorce papers and a note saying he was returning to Spain, love and best wishes to her, he knew she would be a fabulous mother.

Left her, though, was the way she put what he'd done whenever she gave a rundown of her pre-Raleigh life. It sounded neutral, and she felt neutral about it all these years later. If only the same could be said for Anthony; it was a lot easier to be divorced than it was to be fatherless.

But if Santos had stuck around, she and Anthony might never have come to Raleigh. Her parents had chosen to move here when Ithaca's snow and cold became too much for them. Kim, being still single and an only child, had followed them to this warmer clime, thinking they'd have decades together to explore and appreciate the mountains a few hours to the west and the beaches a few hours to the east, the rich Piedmont culture, the warmer weather and (most years) absence of snow. She hated that her father had enjoyed only a handful of mild winters before pancreatic cancer stole him from them.

Losing her father had forced her to put things in perspective. She'd stood at his graveside taking stock: yes, she now had only one parent, and yes, she was still single, and yes, "a certain age" was encroaching on her youthful years. And it was true that her enthusiasm for dating, her willingness to endure the "meat market" environment of clubs, her tolerance for the well-meaning setups her married friends arranged, her ability to shrug off a failed romance, all these had diminished over the years. Still, she was healthy, employed, intelligent, attractive enough (thanks to yoga and moisturizer), and the parent of a bright boy with great potential. She had good friends and no shortage of interests. The right man might yet be in her future, if she'd keep herself open to the possibility.

Possibility: that was the gift that her father's death had brought her. Loss creates a hole, true, but it also opens space to be filled anew, a lesson she now imparted to her students with particular authority when they came to her with tales of their own heartaches. *Après la pluie, le beau temps.* After the rain, the good weather.

Kim had missed Ithaca, but Raleigh was her home now. She'd worked hard to fit in here, joining the PTSA when she'd taught in the public school system, the Parents' Association and Fine Arts

Guild at Ravenswood, joining her neighborhood's garden club, attending plays, going to festivals, getting Anthony into soccer—even buying a minivan. She'd made friends with coworkers, with the other soccer parents, with the parents of some of her students, with the employees and manager of her mother's store. Her best friend, Rose Ellen, said that she'd been here long enough and had assimilated the culture well enough to earn "honorary native" status—and coming from Rose Ellen, who'd been born and raised in nearby Southern Pines, that was an accomplishment. Kim supposed her migration to sweet tea and her love for biscuits and sausage gravy hadn't hurt her cause.

And then there was William. Despite fraternization rules and despite her reservations about indulging in personal relationships in the workplace, what she and William had between them had become more than a friendship.

Initially, though they'd connected nicely when she interviewed for the teaching job, there had been nothing improper between them. All last year, she'd focused on proving herself to the Ravenswood faculty, some of whom were skeptical that her public-school-honed style and abilities would be a good fit there. William was nothing more than her (attractive, congenial) boss.

Then, in late June she ran into him at the downtown Farmers' Market. Instead of his familiar uniform of a tailored button-down and tie, he'd been wearing a T-shirt, and a snuggish one at that. And shorts! He had nicely muscled legs that went quite well with his nicely revealed upper body, which all went very well with his warm, caring, intelligent personality. They'd had lunch there at the market. They'd gone for a long walk around Pullen Park. He'd mentioned a film she wanted to see, and they decided to go together on the following weekend. They'd seen the film, then gone to Lilly's for pizza afterward, and in the pleasurable glow of it all—the summer evening, the companionable conversation, the laughter, the ease—made plans to do it again. The attraction was unspoken, but it was mutual and it was real.

Now they had more than a friendship, but less than an outright romance. More than a flirtation, but less, far less, than a commitment. Really, she didn't know what to call it. Just yesterday she'd told Rose Ellen, who was a dean of students at the high school where Kim had taught before Ravenswood, "It's not fish, and it's not foul," and Rose Ellen said, "Which leaves mammals, amphibians, invertebrates. . . ."

Kim had laughed. "He's certainly a mammal, and a fine specimen at that."

"Then treat him like one," Rose Ellen advised. "Quit worrying about his position over you and start thinking about getting him in position over you."

That was one approach, certainly.

Whatever it was that she and William had going on, the fact of it going on at all gave Kim a thrill she wished she could express openly. As it was, besides Rose Ellen, only her mother had clued in to Kim being smitten. "There's a spring in your step that almost matches your hair," her mother had observed last night.

"And I have to keep both my hair and my step under control. It's only friendship, *comprenes?*"

"Too bad. But it's still early for the two of you. For all that your father and I were helplessly bound from the day we met, we didn't acknowledge it right away."

"You and Dad didn't have to worry about breaking any rules, though."

"You forget, I was a Jew marrying a goyim. According to my mother, we broke *God's* rules."

William had not yet made a move to kiss Kim, but she had the strongest feeling that he wanted to kiss her—and how funny was she, how perfectly juvenile, for wanting him to make the first move? Faculty meetings were the most delicious events, William looking at her like she was the rich desert he was dying to try. And passing him in the hallway, the glances, the smiles . . . They might as well be the teenagers they spent their days managing, that's what she'd told her mother. How they would take the relationship to its natural next step was a problem she had not yet been able to solve. But she was working on it, and she was pretty sure he was, too.

Kim ate her lunch seated on the windowsill, where she could watch with equal ease the finches and chickadees and titmice that gathered at the feeder outside, and the five students now working in the studio.

They were a varied bunch. Vanessa, Robert, and Channing: sociable, but not serious about art, here trying to catch up or improve mediocre work in hopes of improving mediocre grades. Cassandra Lynn and Richard: not very sociable, but very talented, ridiculously so in Cassandra Lynn's case, here to perfect work for their portfolios. All of them except Richard were what Kim thought of as "very Southern," meaning born to native families that had been sending their children to Ravenswood since the school's inception in 1855. Richard was like Amelia Wilkes, Southern, but the first in her family to attend private school. Such kids were considered a step above the carpetbaggers—Yankees who had come south for the opportunities to grow wealthy researching, designing, selling pharmaceuticals and electronics, who then put their children in Ravenswood in many cases simply because they could, and in other cases to help gentrify the family, making country club life so much more comfortable. And the carpetbaggers were a step above the flukes—the scholarship kids and the staff kids like Anthony, who, no matter where they'd been born, ostensibly did not belong in Ravenswood's hallowed halls, but who fate had put there anyway.

The studio door opened and Anthony appeared. He strolled in, nodding to the other students as he crossed the room toward the windows. Kim admired the ease with which her son moved through space, the liquidity of him. A young Antonio Banderas, that's who he reminded her of, his nose just hawkish enough to be interesting without overpowering his face, his long-fingered hands grown substantial and capable, well suited to the work he was doing for Habitat for Humanity. He was a sight on the soccer field, all boundless, gravity-defying energy. She wouldn't call him an egoless player—was there such a thing among teenage boys? But he was a responsible one, conscious of his teammates and the big picture.

Even so, Kim knew from long experience that every teen was, potentially, a hormonal catastrophe waiting to happen. She was forever counseling her female students who, because of her role in their lives—not simply as teacher, but teacher of creative and romantic arts, subjects they responded so well to—turned to her with their laments and confessions. Those teenaged girls, whose Ithaca counterparts she had happily hired to babysit for Anthony when he was younger, were now the sorts of girls she would be willing to pay to stay away from him. They had social networking pages and blogs that were plastered with provocative pictures—of themselves, of their friends—that looked like ads offering sexual services. They flirted with boys by texting photos of themselves in their bikinis or bras. Rose Ellen had been bringing snacks to her son Mark and his friends one day and had found the bunch of them—three girls, two boys—playing pool half-naked! Kim wondered whether some hidden additive in the juice boxes she and every mother she knew had supplied to their children could have diluted kids' sense of propriety, removed their inhibitions.

She'd had no such embarrassments with Anthony, though that might owe more to luck than to his innocence. He'd had plenty of girlfriends, and plenty of opportunities to fool around. You couldn't supervise a teenager the way you did a younger kid; they had friends with cars, they had latchkey friends, they had cars themselves. And even when they were home, even when you thought you knew what was going on, they might at any moment be peeling off their shirts and bras for a racy game of pool. Or worse.

At fourteen, Anthony had said he was going to "save himself for Miss Right," and no doubt he meant it—inasmuch as any fourteen-year-old could forecast his or her future. But Kim was not about to put any money on it. Before he began dating Amelia, whenever she'd observed a girl getting enough of his attention to raise the "Miss Right" question in her mind, he'd move on to someone else. The relief she felt each time was unsettling; her long-held attitudes about teens and sex—that sex was a healthy and necessary part of their development—should not defy her when it came to her own child.

Now that he'd fallen in love with beautiful, serene, steadfast Amelia, he was sunk as surely as if he had jumped into a river with a boulder tied to his leg. It hardly mattered whether or not they'd had sex yet; even Kim could see that sex was, if not beside the point, only one facet of a complex, surprisingly genuine love. She'd been infatuated with Santos for a time, but she had never loved a man with wholehearted abandon, with the rapturous blindness that seems possible only for the young. No one had ever adored her without reserve, planned his life so that it would braid with hers, not simply coexist. What must that feel like?

As a mother, Kim wanted to be skeptical of teen love, to warn Anthony not to put too much of himself into a romance that was unlikely to last into adulthood. As a woman with a heart that yearned for its match as strongly as anyone's did, who found beauty and solace and inspiration in the ways artists throughout the ages rendered love in words and paint and stone, she had to admit that if there was such a thing as true love, it wouldn't know boundaries. If there was such a thing as true love, these two epitomized it.

Kim watched Anthony and expected to see Amelia appear behind him; they always had lunch together. She would pass them, now and then, in the cafeteria with their friends, a gaggle of kids so bright with promise, William had joked, that the lunch ladies were demanding he supply them with protective sunglasses. He saw the kids as proof that his efforts to make Ravenswood a model for prep-school achievement were succeeding. Kim knew that when William watched them laughing and horsing around, they appeared to be

nothing more than eight or ten teens poised on the brink of adulthood, a precious few months away from springing themselves off
the edge of the nest and into the world to do him and Ravenswood
and their parents proud. As with the rest of the faculty, William
wasn't aware of Anthony and Amelia as a subset. Though Kim would
have enjoyed his knowing, enjoyed being able to talk about it all
with him, she kept their secret in order to protect the kids and
William both.

Anthony dropped his book bag on the windowsill. Kim said, "I
thought you said you were going out for lunch today."

"I was," he said, taking one of her carrot sticks.

"Where's Amelia?"

"She forgot her computer and had to go home to get it. Her
mom was supposed to bring it, but she got held up. In traffic," he
added, a joking reference to the way a few of their Ithaca friends
still warned them, quite soberly, that "Raleigh-Durham has some
rough areas. You need to watch yourselves." Judgment that was
based on rumor, on misinformation, yet dispensed authoritatively
as fact.

"I gathered," Kim said, smiling. She reached out to ruffle his hair,
and he let her. Not only that, he sat down beside her and draped his
arm over her shoulders, completely unconcerned about how the
other kids might see him. What teenager hugged his teacher-
mother in front of other teens? Kim was suffused with pleasure and
tenderness, and the thought, which would soon be tested, of how
incredibly lucky she was.

5

"Hey, Winter," Rob Calloway greeted Anthony in the Ravenswood hallway as the two of them arrived at their lockers before fourth period.

"Hey," Anthony said, tucking his phone into his pocket. He'd texted Amelia three times and tried calling her twice, and gotten no response. Probably her battery had gone dead, or she'd left her phone at home while getting her laptop, something along that line. Probably she would appear here in the hallway at any moment, wearing a sweet, apologetic smile above her gray cashmere cardigan and pleated navy skirt, ordinary clothes that on her may as well have been woven by fairies. To Anthony, the simple fact of Amelia, her very existence, was proof that there was magic in the world.

He might even say so out loud, except that they were keeping their relationship under wraps for now. But if he did rhapsodize on Amelia's magical qualities, no doubt his loser classmates would say he was a sucker, dweeb, homo (which wouldn't make sense, but they wouldn't worry about the incongruity). He'd forgive the soulless bastards, and, as if he were the praying kind, offer up a prayer for their improvement. The world needed less cynicism, more love. Love was the answer. Love made the world go 'round. Love was all you needed. Love, actually, was all around.

He opened his locker and pulled out his AP Calculus textbook; not much love there. As competent as he was in math, he hated it. How were imaginary numbers relevant to writing plays, which he was getting better at, or performing in them, which he did pretty well already, or to any aspect of a play's production: direction, interpretation, set design—all things he'd be studying while earning his degree at NYU? Imaginary *people,* though, he could get into that. He imagined a kind of calculus for drama, exercises that involved putting characters into all kinds of theoretical situations in order to solve, or at least explore, the complex problems of the world. As with solutions in higher math, successful drama resulted from a kind of alchemy—in this case of script, direction, and acting that, when it was done right, was transformational, for the actors and the audience both. He couldn't wait for the time when he and Amelia would be immersed in that kind of problem-solving.

"Ready for the quiz?" he asked Rob.

Rob shook his head and grinned. "Not really. Peyton's parents were gone this weekend, so, you know, we decided the time was right to do the deed. More than once," he added with a short laugh, as if this fact surprised him. His ears reddened and he gave his full attention to carefully working his combination lock. "Didn't really think about studying."

"O-kay," Anthony said. "Yeah, I can see that."

He liked Rob. Unlike some of their rich-kid classmates, Rob seemed pretty real, despite his new Mazda RX-8 and his family's season tickets to Carolina Panthers games, and the so-called Calloway Compound (thirty acres, with a twelve-thousand-foot house, a pool, hot tub, stables, riding ring, and dirt-bike track), and Rob's mother's constant presence in the Ravenswood student services office, where she was a dedicated volunteer. Rob and Peyton weren't just a weekend thing. They'd been dating since school started at the end of August. Peyton, he knew, was already browsing the jewelry store cases, eyeing diamond engagement rings, and thinking about china patterns. Amelia was trying to get Peyton's head out of the clouds, encourage her to expand her horizons wider than marriage and babies, do something with her Ravenswood college-prep education—at least until Rob knew for sure that he wanted to follow in his investment-broker father's footsteps. Peyton, though, was "very traditional," as she put it, happy to become the same sort of woman her mother was—and Amelia's was, for that matter.

Anthony knew that when it came to being a macho asshole, wealth wasn't really to blame. You could find the same kind of demeaning attitudes in guys who were growing up with next to nothing. Rednecks, which there'd been plenty of at his old high school. Gangstas. Religious fundamentalists of every kind. It was about culture. Values. His mother and her friends talked about this stuff all the time. For whatever reasons, too many guys sidelined females, sexualizing them or dismissing them or both, mistakes he would never make with Amelia.

Not only was she possibly the most beautiful woman yet created by the gods, but she spent her time and energy on things that mattered. His mom had pegged her when she said, "Amelia's the least frivolous girl I've ever met." Sure, she wore the popular labels and drove a new BMW and had a debit card that her dad kept stocked so that she never had to worry about being able to pay for lunch or put gas in her car. The thing was, she was ready—no, she was *eager*—to give all that up for what really mattered to her. To them.

Rob shut his locker. "Did you study? I'll just sit behind you and look over your shoulder."

"Actually, I worked all weekend," Anthony said, which was not a lie, but which also had not kept him from studying. Business at record stores like the one he worked in was growing ever-slower, now that most kids got their music online. Their customers tended to be middle-aged music lovers who either preferred old technologies or were avoiding new ones, and they tended to shop primarily on Saturday mornings and Sunday afternoons.

Not that he'd tell Rob (let him earn the grade he deserved), but Anthony had managed to both study and make a new playlist for Amelia, a compilation of songs from Coldplay, The National, Paramore, Owl City, and a couple from a band called The xx, who he'd discovered thanks to *Rolling Stone*. His manager said the band was "just another group of London punks," which only made Anthony like them better.

He told Rob, "Maybe Rickman will go easy on us."

"Not likely." Rob smirked and said, "He's the one who really needs to get laid."

Anthony shut his locker and looked down the hallway once more before heading for class. Still no Amelia. He said, "True that."

"What's *your* excuse, Winter? Is Amelia really saving it for marriage? Or wait, don't tell me—you're practicing to be a priest. Father Anthony," Rob said, laughing. "I can totally see it. You've got that whole cool, caring guy thing down."

"Actually," Anthony said with a sad shrug, "it's because Peyton's already got a man." Deferring questions about his sexual status with humor, as he usually did, kept the vultures from circling.

"You bet she does." Rob grinned at him. "Well, I'm sure you and your right hand—or is it your left?—will be very happy together until your luck changes."

Anthony held out his right hand as though to shake Rob's and said, "Honored to be in the company of an expert."

"Not anymore, man. I got it now. I got the real thing."

The real thing: this was supposed to mean "love." But no question, there was also the physical aspect to be considered.

All Anthony had known about Amelia before he met her was that her reputation was clean—too clean, as far as a lot of the guys were concerned, but that didn't mean she was what some of them claimed: frigid. Lesbian. Secretly engaged to an older, wealthy guy none of their classmates had ever seen but could easily imagine existed. It had to be one of these things, they said, because otherwise wouldn't she flirt, tease them, taunt them the way the other good-looking girls did? She wouldn't be so standoffish if she were normal. No, none of them had ever asked her out or tried to get a real answer to the mystery, because why put yourself out there like that, just to get shot down? There were so many easier fish to catch.

Before long, though, Anthony came to see Amelia as being in a class of her own. She represented the difference between *general* and *specific*. He'd always found girls generally appealing. He generally enjoyed girls' company. But Amelia had looked at him from across the stage, blue velvet curtains hanging behind her, stage lights illuminating her auburn hair, and a jolt of something—call it electricity, call it whatever you liked—went through him and he'd literally stopped breathing. What he'd wanted to do was drop to his knees. What he'd done instead was turn to Ms. Fitz and say, "There's my Rosalind."

Ms. Fitz looked to where he pointed, then back at Anthony. Her thin eyebrows rose and her painted lips parted, but they did so strangely, as if she weren't in charge of her expressions. "So it is," she said.

"But, Ms. Fitz," Chris Harrington had complained, "you said you were thinking of *me* for Orlando."

Ms. Fitz blinked at the boy. Once. Two times. "Yes, well, there's nothing to be done about that. You'll be a fine Oliver."

That was just the way the universe worked when Amelia was around.

Undeniable. This was the word Anthony felt best characterized his relationship with Amelia. It was that, and she was that.

The physical aspect: their first kisses had been tentative, almost chaste, him following her lead so that he wouldn't come on too strong and scare her off. Unlike other girls he'd known and encouraged, she didn't press herself against him, not flirtatiously, and not purposefully. She trembled the first time he moved his hand from her shoulder and ran it along the side of her breast to her waist.

The first time he kissed her deeply, with his hands wrapped in her hair and his hips grazing hers, making his desire for her obvious to both of them, she'd gasped. Actually *gasped*. He hadn't expected that.

"Sorry," he'd said, quickly pulling back.

"No, it's okay." Her face was red, her eyes wide—but she was smiling. Not frigid. Not gay. Not unavailable. Just inexperienced.

A few weeks later, after an *As You Like It* rehearsal, they'd stood together in the parking lot, sodium lights buzzing overhead, talking about how she wished she could date him openly. Her father wasn't a bad guy, she said. He worried about her, is all. She'd had some troubles when she was younger, and he was protective.

"Trouble?" he asked, his imagination answering the question with obsessive boyfriend, abusive boyfriend, secret drug abuse, bulimia—

"A problem. A . . . a defect, you could say." Avoiding his eyes, she told him that she'd had a stutter for years. There'd been therapies, she said, and lots of evaluations by various shrinks. When she looked at him again, she seemed to be wincing in anticipation of his response.

"You obviously beat it," he said. "That's impressive."

"Yeah?" She brightened. "Thanks. I used to think I was, I don't know, a freak. I don't talk about it. A few friends know."

"I won't mention it, if you—"

"No, I'd appreciate it if you don't. Keeping it hidden from everyone was good practice, I guess, for this." She smiled and gestured to indicate the two of them.

"And while I'm confessing things?" she added. "You should know . . . I wanted you to know that I'm still a virgin, so . . ." She shrugged, letting her words trail off.

"I figured. It's fine. It's *good*. What's the rush, right?"

"You don't mind?"

"Since confession seems to be a theme here . . . I'll confess that I really like the idea of maybe getting to be your first."

What followed over the next few months were stolen minutes spent making out behind her father's roadster garage, the "stables," on frosty nights; late-night text messages when they should have been asleep; emails she'd painstakingly composed between rehearsals or lessons—she wanted to be clear that her desire for him was so much more than lust. Other kids rutted for recreation, just one more bit of fun on a night filled with easily accessed booze and party drugs. That was not her wish at all, not her style, and she was adamant that he know it, that he not lump her in with the group of privileged kids who too often substituted cash for good judgment and good morals.

Anthony was more than ready to go further than the heated kissing and touching, but Amelia wanted to wait until the end of the school year, when their schedules eased up and the weather would be warm. Late June looked ideal, given their obligations, and her monthly cycle, and the fact of her leaving July second to spend eight weeks at her beach house. "Is it lame that I want it to be really special?" she'd asked.

Amelia did things to him, to his brain, to his heart, that no girl had ever done before. She could make him dizzy, literally, just by standing close enough for him to smell her. And his longing—well, suffice it to say he'd tested out how well the cold-shower theory worked. The worst of it was also the best of it: though the idea scared the shit out of him—how could it have happened so soon, and so fast?—he knew he'd met his soul mate and that his life was, from the moment he laid eyes on her, hers.

Their plan was to begin that *really special* night with a romantic dinner at a little French place her parents would never think to go. She'd fake a sleepover at Cameron's and he'd fake staying at Rob's, and they'd get a hotel room at the Marriott in Durham—a good distance away from any of her father's dealerships, so that there was no way she'd be recognized by an employee who might, say, be there with visiting family members or friends. They couldn't be too careful. He'd make a pitcher of strawberry margaritas—his mom never checked their liquor supply—and pack it in ice, for them to drink at the hotel. He was in charge of the music, Amelia would bring bubble bath, and they agreed that they'd brave a visit to Rite Aid together, to buy "protection."

It was a good plan, but as the poet Robert Burns put it in his ode to an unearthed field mouse, "The best-laid schemes o' mice an' men/ Gang aft agley." *Often go awry* was the translation. A good plan, but a plan that would be undone, altered by events outside of anyone's control. Even so, at the time Anthony would not recall the poem's next lines: "An' lea'e us nought but grief an' pain,/ For promis'd joy!" That recollection would come months later.

The day the plan got changed, they'd been backstage after the Raleigh Little Theatre's final performance of *Our Town* in mid-June, the weekend after Erica Gold, a freshman friend of theirs, was killed when her brother Barry lost control of his car and crashed into a stand of trees. Barry hadn't been drunk, he hadn't been speeding, the roads had been dry. . . . At the funeral on Thursday, Barry's parents kept saying, "It had to be a deer, or a dog. A possum, maybe. A fox." They didn't know, and Barry, still unconscious at WakeMed, hadn't been able to say. The randomness of the accident reverberated through the teens who knew them. Some dealt with it by partying, some by praying. Anthony and Amelia and the others in their circle had gotten together at Blue Jay Point on Friday afternoon and tried to write a song for Erica, but ended up tossing rocks into Falls Lake and counting the ripples until it had gotten too dark to see.

In *Our Town,* Anthony was George Gibbs to Amelia's Emily Webb, a casting coup that only reinforced what they were sure was true: Fate wanted them together. Amelia had reported that her father had a different view ("That Winter kid *again*? I don't like that boy sniffing after you this way. . . ."), but the audiences responded to them with such genuine care and enthusiasm that the director was going to pair them again next spring in *Kiss Me, Kate*. And who knew? Maybe New York directors would cue in to their tandem experience and keep putting them together—not as leads, okay, not right away; they'd need to pay their dues first. Still, to work together on a regular basis was their dream and their goal. If that also meant that when the other lotharios came sniffing around, he'd be there to warn them off, all the better. He knew that once Amelia was in the world—the real world, the New York City world—men would be drawn to her the way they were to Broadway star Idina Menzel. Amelia's face would be the jubilant one on the Times Square billboard, she would be the costumed woman whose image would decorate buses and bus stops, whose autograph on a playbill would one day become a talisman for any number of young hopefuls.

The Raleigh Little Theatre's audience was filing out, and behind the curtain, the actors made their ways to the dressing rooms to wash off stage makeup and transform back to their everyday selves. There was backslapping and merriment over a job well done. Amelia, however, had looked troubled.

Anthony pulled her aside. "You okay?"

She tugged at the high neckline of her white ruffled blouse, then undid the top button, and then the next, and the third. But there was nothing suggestive in her actions. In fact she seemed unaware of what she was doing as she watched the other actors go.

She turned toward Anthony and said, "We did this play, what, eleven times? And listen to everyone, laughing and happy. . . ." She shook her head. "It's like they haven't paid attention to the substance of it at all. Are any of them even *thinking* about act three?"

Act three was the somber, existential part of the play. Emily, after her death, witnesses her own funeral and muses about life: "It goes so fast. We don't have time to look at one another. . . . Oh, earth, you're too wonderful for anybody to realize you. . . . Do any human beings ever realize life while they live it—every, every minute?"

Anthony thought for a moment, then said, "Some are thinking about it, sure—maybe all of them. Could be that's why they're happy."

Amelia turned to him, her eyes wide. "Why are we waiting, Anthony? It could all be over any day, any minute."

"We don't have to wait," he said.

"If it was up to you—?"

"I want you any time, all the time. But I want you to be happy about it, so—"

"All our plans . . . that's not what's going to make it special. It being us is what makes it special. Anything might happen in the next two weeks."

She was right. Still, he said, "Nothing will happen."

"Probably not. I hope not. But you don't know. Nobody *knows*." She checked that they were unwatched, then put her arms around his waist, moving so close that he could feel her thighs, inside her skirt and petticoat, against his own. "Meet me in the clubhouse at eleven."

"You sure?" he asked, already feeling his blood rush at the prospect.

"Completely."

At ten minutes before the hour, he'd parked his car on the service road a half mile from Amelia's house so that there was no chance the sight or sound of a car—especially a sunbaked, dinged-up, decade-old beater like his—would draw attention. Then, with his heart thumping against his ribs even before he set off, he jogged the distance to the far side of the Wilkeses' property. He was experienced and knowledgeable enough to feel confident about the mechanics of what they were about to do, but he'd never been quite so anxious about getting things right.

Amelia's clubhouse was a small cottage set just beyond the patio and lawn, at the wood's edge. Modeled after her mother's favorite Thomas Kinkade cottage, it was built of stone and brick, a full one story in height, and with a real thatched roof. He'd seen it once in daylight, as one of probably thirty teenagers there at the Wilkes home last February to celebrate Amelia's seventeenth birthday. Harlan Wilkes had engaged him in conversation:

"So, you're the one whose mom's the teacher—you all came from New York, that right?"

"Yes, sir," he'd said, the way his mother taught him he needed to address Southern men if he didn't want to raise their hackles—and where Harlan Wilkes was concerned, he wanted to go as unnoticed as possible.

Wilkes watched Anthony watching Amelia and three of her girl-friends, who were playing Twister. Mary Beth Pernelli's low-rise jeans were threatening to show more of her backside than she intended. Wilkes seemed not to notice, saying, "Your mother, she teaches French."

"Art and French, yes, sir," Anthony said, casually turning his eyes away from the game (from Amelia) and to the kitchen, where Sheri Wilkes stood with several other women, mothers of partygoers, in the same manner he was sure they'd all done a dozen years earlier. The same way his mother had done with her Ithaca friends, while he and his playmates built LEGO towers or ran around in Batman capes.

Wilkes remained at his side. "You're a junior, like Amelia?" he asked, and Anthony nodded, wishing someone would come along and save him. "You do sports?" Wilkes asked.

Anthony said, "Soccer, yes, sir. We're just starting practice for spring rec league, and I played for the school this past fall, varsity."

"What're you planning to major in—assuming you're planning on college."

"I am. Fine arts—drama."

"That's a degree?" Wilkes snorted, then patted him on the back,

saying, "I wish you luck with that," before wandering off to grill another of the dozen boys there.

That day, the day of the party, had been too cold for them to be
outdoors. From inside the family room's towering windows,
Amelia's cottage had appeared austere, its surrounding rosebushes
and hydrangeas cut back in anticipation of spring. This June night,
with those same plants lush and blooming, their colors deepened almost to black in the moonlight, the cottage beckoned Anthony as if
it, or he, had been put under a spell.

He tapped on the door, then opened it. Amelia was there with a
quilt and a candle, wearing cotton pajama shorts and the thinnest of
lace-edged tank tops, a wisp of a garment. She took his hand, then
closed the door and wedged a heavy stone against it. Turning to him
again, she said, "It's not exactly a nice hotel room—"

"It's perfect." He leaned in to kiss her, adding, "Just like you."

When Anthony looked back on this night—and he would, often,
during the dark, empty days after the trouble began, he'd savor
what had, at the time, been a rush of sensation and emotion.
Amelia's smooth skin flushed and glowing in the candlelight. Her
hair loose and flowing over her shoulders like a stream of dark silk.
Her hands beneath his shirt, lifting it up and over his head—and
then lifting her own, and then the contact of her skin against his,
breasts to chest, pounding heart to pounding heart.

He would recall how they'd laughed when he stumbled, stepping
out of his pants, and then how she'd grown serious, reverent almost, when she knelt down and peeled off his boxers and ran her
hands over him. She drew him down onto the quilt, then sat back on
her heels. "Wow, look at you, you're amazing. Stay just like that."

He'd thought she was reaching for a condom when she grabbed
the little quilted bag that usually held her wallet and phone, but it
was her phone that emerged. This surprised him, but only for a moment, when he realized what she had in mind.

She said, "You look like a statue of some Greek god—Apollo,
the god of prophecy and truth."

"And of justice, and plagues, and poetry, don't forget." English class, asserting itself in the most unlikely of times.

She held the phone up in front of him, then took a picture. "Hmm . . ." she said, viewing it. "Bend your leg—no wait, lean back on one elbow, then bend your leg. Right. Like that." She took another picture, viewed the result, and said, "I need more light for this."

"But not for *this*," he'd said, reaching for her hand and bringing her down onto the quilt.

They kissed, they touched each other with slow deliberation, the crickets thrummed and the frogs sang from the trees and from the creek bed. Anthony reached for his jeans and took out one of the condoms he'd brought and Amelia rolled it onto him. She lay back then, blushing under his regard.

"Is this all right?" he asked as he pressed into her, watching her face, ready to stop if she flinched or frowned.

She whispered, "This is amazing." Her expression was so serious, as though he were not only making love to her but also tethering them, binding them, something like the way the choir sang of in *Our Town*. "*Blessed be the tie that binds our hearts. . . .*" He wasn't a religious person, but this, what he was feeling, it was spiritual. He wanted to say something significant, maybe quote something, maybe the song, but the sensations, the heat of her. . . . "I love you," he rasped, the best he could do.

"I love you," she said, gazing up at him. She pulled him closer and put her lips to his neck, in the sensitive spot beneath his ear.

Just that—the touch of her tongue—did him in. "Amelia . . ." he groaned, but there was no stopping it now. In a blinding moment unlike any in the past, he let go. When his vision returned, he was looking through tears at her own tearful, happy face.

"'Every, every minute,'" she said.

Driving home later, Anthony left his windows down. As he'd done on the night he'd first seen Amelia at auditions, he sang her name to the tune of *West Side Story*'s "Maria."

"A-mel-ia, I'll never stop saying A-mel-ia." Then he laughed aloud. "Ridiculous, dude. You've got it *bad*." Turning his car onto the highway, he said her name again, "Amelia." This time it was a sigh.

The chilly wind was bracing, and he felt he'd become a part of the universe in a way he'd never been before. It wasn't just the pleasure of sex—though it was that. And it wasn't just the pleasure of love—though it was that, too. It was, he thought, the combination of those two things, along with a sense of timelessness, and the feeling of being somehow miniscule and also tremendous at the same time. As though he, Anthony Winter, was a mere pinprick of energy, in the way the stars appeared to be when seen from Earth, while being, in fact, incredibly powerful and strong.

A little over two weeks later, Amelia and her parents were en route to Bald Head Island. Anthony pictured her sitting in the far backseat of the posh SUV for the four-hour drive, her dog, Buttercup, taking the middle seat, her parents up front talking ferry schedules or dinner plans they'd made with their island neighbors. This trip, she'd said when they talked earlier that morning, was the antithesis of getting to realize her life—or the life she wanted, at least. But she was going to try her best to appreciate the sand and sea. The turtles. The marsh birds. "I know that's life, too. I just want you to be in it."

"Trust me," he said, "I'd be there if there was any way. My mom just doesn't have the bucks." To rent even a townhouse there, the smallest of the island's accommodations, cost more for a week than the monthly mortgage payment for their house.

She said, "I know. My dad's yelling for me—I gotta go. I cannot *wait* to be eighteen. I'll text you when we're on the road."

He heard from her about an hour later, by text, as promised. The photos she'd taken of him were so dark, she wrote. She could see him in the photos, but only sort of. More or less. Mostly less. She'd uploaded them to her computer and tried to improve them, but it was hopeless. Would he use his camera and take a couple new ones of himself, and send them to her? To help her get through the eight interminable weeks they'd be apart?

Anthony, lying on his bed with a nighttime sky poster decorating the ceiling overhead, wrote, *It wont be quite the same if i do. Not a genuine souvenir of that night.*

It can be close. Pose the way you did for me, she wrote.

You want the exact same effect? he asked, thinking again of what she'd been doing right before he'd laid down. The thinking of it had almost as strong an effect on him as her doing it.

Is that possible right now?

If I can remember what we were doing . . . he teased.

See? Im gone one hour and ur already forgetting me.

Not even. If u could see me u would know.

I wish i could, she wrote.

Me too. More later . . .

He'd stood up and closed his bedroom door, then locked it. The sun streamed into his room and across his bed; plenty good lighting now, he thought, stripping off his T-shirt, then his shorts and boxers. His erection hung heavily, making him feel slightly ridiculous as he positioned his camera on his bookshelf—a feeling that, of course, reduced the weight, which made him feel less ridiculous, but which also diminished the effect he was going for in the photo.

He sat on the edge of his bed and thought for a moment about not bothering to get it exactly accurate—or do it at all. But he didn't want to disappoint Amelia. If it made her happy to have these pictures to go along with the others she'd taken of him at rehearsals or at school, or that had been taken by friends or by him and forwarded on to her, then he'd get it done. All it would take was a moment to get into character, so to speak.

A few seconds of concentrated recollection, eyes closed . . . Now it was a matter of quickly switching on the camera, setting the timer, jumping back on his bed—leaning back, knee up—and, done. He checked the results, took two more, checked those; seeing himself naked reminded him of pictures his mom had taken of him when he was a baby and toddler—he had not, she said every time the photo albums came out, been fond of clothing.

He got dressed again, trying not to stress about how to fill the fifty-six days ahead of him. It didn't matter that he'd been bracing himself for the separation for months. *Now* felt very different from *eventually*. Eight weeks was a damn long time to be apart. But, he could be patient, he could be generous and not begrudge her parents this last summer with her. He and Amelia would have their whole adult lives together, after all.

He did a quick upload of the photos to his computer, sent them by email to Amelia, then sent her a text that said, *Check ur email. I miss you already.*

I miss you.

Hope the pics help.

They might make me miss you more. . . .

Will you send me some of you?

Ok. When i can.

In the kitchen, he got out bread and peanut butter, Oreos, a tall bottle of Gatorade. He was slicing a banana for his sandwich when his mother came in from weeding her garden, smelling of greens and damp earth.

"Off to work, or Habitat?" she asked, turning on the faucet to wash her hands.

"Work," he said. "Habitat tomorrow morning."

"What's your schedule today?"

"Noon to close."

"Do you have plans for after?"

"Nope."

As if noticing his uncharacteristically terse replies, she'd turned around and leaned against the counter, studying him. "Ah—the Wilkeses left for the beach today, right?" He nodded. "You know the saying: 'Absence makes the heart grow fonder.'"

"I hope so."

"She won't forget you. With the technology you kids have at hand, you won't even have a chance to miss each other."

He thought of the photos he'd just sent, and the ones he hoped to get from her. "Maybe not," he said.

6

HARLAN'S CURIOSITY AS TO WHAT AMELIA'S LAPTOP HELD had led him, first, to her email account. He'd scanned the sender names and subject topics, clicked open a few, read with mild entertainment Amelia's friend Lori's outraged account of having her phone taken away by her parents—for what, the email didn't say. Harlan supposed it was excessive usage. Lori, when she was over to visit with Amelia, never shut up.

He read that Amelia's voice teacher was rescheduling next week's lesson, and she urged Amelia to think carefully about what she'd sing for "that New York audition," which he supposed had to do with the camp she'd mentioned to him and Sheri—some intensive, competitive theatre group thing up in the New York wilderness that he'd scoffed at as a waste of her summertime, when she ought to be spending it entirely at Bald Head like always.

He read that the French Club was organizing a ski and snowboard trip to the Swiss Alps during spring break, and felt a surge of pride that he could send Amelia, if it turned out that she wanted to go.

She *should* go, he decided. Using his all-purpose, does-everything smartphone, as they called the things, he pecked out the details on its tiny keyboard, then sent the info to Sheri so that she could follow up.

Harlan's next thought was to check Amelia's Internet browser's history. It appeared, he saw, that she'd been researching African elephants, presumably for school. She'd browsed leather satchels and striped wool sweaters on Banana Republic's site. She'd checked the weather forecast, looked up "1960s fashion," and visited the Tisch Department of Drama's stage productions schedule page. He thought he recalled a Tisch performance as being on the Ravenswood Drama Guild's itinerary, during their trip to New York in a few weeks. Tisch. If that wasn't a faggy name for a drama school, he didn't know what was.

This would be the first time Sheri hadn't accompanied Amelia on a school-sponsored trip. The thought of Amelia on her own with that bunch of kids, and the adults who, best he could tell, pretty much devoted their lives to costumes and makeup and talking about *American Idol,* didn't thrill him. Sheri had insisted, though, that the chaperones were responsible people, and reminded him that Amelia had been to the city several times before, so it was familiar to her— and, Sheri said, with Amelia being almost eighteen, it would do them all good to let her have an experience that was, if not parent-free altogether, at least free of her own parents. This was what was on his mind when he clicked on the computer's little camera-photo icon next. The icon bounced a few times, catching his attention, and then the program opened.

What he saw first were pictures of a bunch of teenage girls goofing off together, laughing and making faces in what looked like a Taco Bell restaurant. The date displayed beside the photos showed that these were the most recent. He scrolled down, and found images taken in the stands at last weekend's football game, then images from somebody's slumber party—some of those girls looked way older than their ages, he thought. He averted his eyes from a few that he would say were pretty suggestive; girls acted like *that* when they got together? But then he looked again, figuring it would be good to know which of Amelia's friends he ought to maybe caution her about.

He noticed, on the left, an index that included "flagged" photos, and clicked on that—then jerked back in surprise. He looked away and scanned the room around him (*cabinets . . . windows . . . bottles of olive oil lining the sill*) as if making sure he was still anchored to reality in spite of the twisting of his gut. Then he looked, again, at the screen.

There were six images in full view (and in *full view,* good God!), and at least three more peeking from the bottom of the screen below these. He stared. It was easy enough to identify the boy (the *man,* not really any question, physically). But how in God's good name had Amelia gotten these, and why did she have them? Did "flagged" mean she intended to report him, that son of a bitch Winter—maybe had done it already? He prayed that was the case.

Another possibility—that she had them *voluntarily*—flitted into his mind like a huge, dark moth, then flitted out again, no light to be found there.

Harlan sat back, his brain suddenly crowded with questions (*Why hadn't she told them? Was Winter some kind of porn actor? What damage had these done?*), and fears (*Would this give her unhealthy attitudes or, heaven help them, desires?*), and the creeping black veil of anger, of outrage. His baby girl had been attacked in a way he struggled to define. *Defiled,* he decided, by these lewd pictures—had doubtless had them forced on her by that wannabe-movie-star, thinks-he's-God's-gift, Anthony Winter.

Oh, Harlan understood guys like Winter—join the drama club, seduce as many girls as possible, get them to fall in love while, to Winter, they were nothing more than playthings, ego food. Thank

God Amelia was too smart to be fooled by his act. The question was, how was she handling this harassment? Probably she'd been embarrassed to bring it up to him and Sheri—Harlan could understand that. Or maybe . . . maybe she was afraid to. Maybe Winter had threatened her. But even if he had—especially if he had—this was exactly the sort of thing parents needed to know about, so that it didn't turn into something worse.

He heard the door behind him opening and he swiveled around, snapping the computer closed as he did. Expecting Sheri, his pulse jumped when he saw it was his daughter instead.

"Hey, Daddy," Amelia called as she closed the door behind her. "I didn't know you'd be home. Mom was supposed to—"

"That Winter boy," Harlan blurted, "do you hear from him a lot? Does he bother you at school?"

Amelia stopped still in the kitchen doorway. Harlan noted, almost despite himself, that her blouse was undone one button lower than he thought she used to wear it. She said, "What? Why? What's going on?"

"I just need to know."

Red blotches bloomed on Amelia's face and neck, and Harlan saw the muscles working in her jaw as she considered an answer. It was just as he suspected: she was reluctant to say anything. She'd been intimidated by the kid, he was sure.

"He . . . I mean, I see him sometimes. He's in my English class, and I see him a lot when we're in plays together. He doesn't bother me, no."

Harlan drew a deep breath, then let it out slowly. She looked scared. Still, he had to push for answers. "Your computer . . ."

"I came to get it."

"Honey," he moved over a little and rested his hand on the computer. "Ladybug, now, I'm gonna ask you something, and I apologize for invading your privacy, but, well, I am your father after all."

Amelia's face had reddened fully, but she said nothing.

"Those pictures, did he send them?"

Amelia continued to stand there, motionless.

"You can tell me," Harlan urged. "I know this kind of thing goes on. Some guys . . . well, they just aren't right about things, and they try to get young girls to—"

"How did you get into my computer?"

He paused, then said, "I know you're worried, him being a classmate and all, but I won't let him trouble you after this. I guess it was email, right? Did you report him already? 'Cause if not, I'll need to—"

"No. I mean . . . yes. Yes, I did report him, and you don't need to do anything else about it. It's, it's already done and . . . and I was going to get rid of the pictures. Now that I did it. Reported it."

"To school? To Mr. Braddock?"

She nodded.

"So I'll guess he was suspended, then." Expulsion would've been the better action—get the kid away from Amelia, and all the other girls, too. Though that wouldn't prevent his doing what he'd done, harassing them through email. Christ, he could do that from *anywhere,* and to as many girls as his sick mind desired. This, Harlan realized, was a bigger problem than he'd thought.

"Um, no," Amelia said. "He . . . I think . . . just detention." She nodded. "Really, it's n-not a big deal. I mean, kids are always sending pictures around." She paused, visibly took a breath, then said, "Lots of people do it."

"Filthy pictures like those? This, what he did, it isn't like your little friends vamping for the camera. And I *told* you, I said that kid was after you. No . . . I think we need to make sure this is put to a real stop." He took his phone from its holster and, thinking for a moment on who was best to handle the trouble, dialed.

"Who are you calling?"

Harlan held up his hand to silence her, and then when the 9-1-1 dispatcher answered, he gave his name and said he had an emergency he could not detail on the phone—no fire, not an injury, just send the police.

———————

Amelia felt the world upend. She grabbed the door frame to steady herself, to ground her so that she could think. As calmly as she could manage, she said, "What are you doing? W-why did you call the police? I *told* you, it's nothing. It's fine. He's not bothering me at all."

Her father looked at her with sympathy. The stutter——when had he last heard that? "Maybe not now, Ladybug, but who's to say what else he'll do if he's not set right? When the police get here, you tell 'em whatever you know about it, and they'll take care of the rest, don't you worry."

She crossed the room, trying to think of how to plug this leaking dyke before it broke open and flooded them all. Bad enough that he'd seen the pictures. Bad enough that he'd hacked her computer to do it! God knew what else he'd found . . . maybe nothing, though, since by all indications he was upset, not angry. Bad enough that this was for certain going to mean that she and Anthony would have to go completely underground until graduation next spring. But police involvement? She felt sick at the thought.

"Daddy, no," she said, speaking slowly, calmly. "There's no reason—I mean, he already got in trouble, and really, I don't want to have to tell some strangers that . . . that I saw . . . He won't do it again. It was, you know, it was just a joke."

Her father shook his head, mouth turned down in that stern head-of-the-household attitude he took whenever he was trying to teach her right from wrong. *Because you know, Ladybug, there are standards worth upholding,* she remembered him telling her some years back, when she'd faked being sick one Sunday so that she wouldn't have to go to church.

"I've done wrong myself," he said that day, hoisting her out of bed and pushing her toward her closet, to get dressed. "I know how bad it can rot you if you stick on that path." That was his thing: he'd lived a hard life, growing up, so he knew everything about what not to do. Amelia tried not to discount his upbringing, and the sad, hidden-from-the-public fact that his mother had been a stubborn alcoholic who died of cirrhosis still pining for Amelia's grandfather. As Amelia heard it told, the woman had adored him right up to her last breath, though he'd run out on her years before and was presumed dead. ("Wow, that's like a bad country song," Anthony once remarked, and Amelia replied, "I guess *someone* has to inspire them.") Amelia respected how much her father had accomplished, she truly did. His concern and protectiveness were sometimes like a noose, though, threatening to cut off her air supply.

Now he said, "Listen: I don't know what kids think these days, but sending smut like that to an innocent girl is no joke. I'm sure the police will tell you the same. I'd be surprised if there wasn't a law against it."

"Please," Amelia said, trying to beg without being so desperate that he'd cue in to the truth, "call them back and say don't come. Anyway, I *can't* stay. I have to get back to school." If she didn't leave now, Anthony would be left wondering what happened, why she wasn't meeting him in the hallway before class. She felt her pocket for her phone, intending to text him the minute she got free to say she was running late, then realized she'd left her phone in the car.

"We can talk about this later, okay?" She reached for her computer, but her father grabbed it first, and tucked it under his arm.

"I know this upsets you, and I'm sorry. But this is something you just can't go being nice and forgiving about. You're a lamb, honey, and I'm so glad you are, but you don't understand how men can be. Maybe . . . maybe I should'a been plainer about all that."

He paused as if considering what he should have done differently, then added, "He won't let you alone unless we make him— and what about other girls? You want him thinking he can harass them, too?"

"He won't," she insisted.

"That's what we're gonna make damn sure of. Now park your-self. I don't want to have to go looking for you when the police get here." He went to the refrigerator. "Want a Co-cola?"

"No." Amelia sat down at the table, back straight, eyes focused on her mother's new beaded place mats. Brown, orange, rust, red, gold, yellow . . . tiny beads, thousands of them . . . There had to be some way to fix this mess, some story that would satisfy the po-lice that there was nothing here worth their time or trouble. Some way to protect Anthony, to defer her father's doggedness—the trait that had led him to grow the largest automotive franchise in the South from what had begun as a single used-cars lot in nearby Zebulon, something he never let her forget. She had to make this go away, and fast.

"They're here," her father announced from the front hall. Buttercup sat up and gave a threatening bark. "Put her in the base-ment," he said. He waited until Amelia stood and grasped the dog's collar, then he opened the front door. As she led a growling, displeased Buttercup across the kitchen, Amelia saw her father step onto the columned front porch and push his hands into his pockets.

No solution came to Amelia's mind. Her father had seen the pic-tures, and now he'd show them to the police. Anthony was easily identifiable in most of them—no getting around that. . . .

She waited for Buttercup to start down the basement steps, then closed the door and went back toward the kitchen, stopping at the wide entry so that she could see into the front hall.

"I'm Harlan Wilkes. Come in," her father was saying.

Two male officers, both white, both young, the pair of them dis-tinguishable primarily by hair color, remained on the stoop outside the door, alert and with hands poised at their sides. Brilliant blue lights strobed the stone walls of the porte cochère behind them. The blond one asked, "Sir, what's the nature of your emergency?"

"I need to report a kind of sexual assault, I guess you'd call it—that happened to my daughter. Amelia."

"Is the suspect present?"

"Oh—no. No, that boy wouldn't dare come here—but I know how to find him. Come on in, we'll go into the kitchen, where my daughter's waiting."

The dark-haired officer stepped inside first. Amelia moved silently into the kitchen as he said, "When did this incident take place?"

Her father told him, "I—well, I just learned of it today."

"I'll go out to the car and call it in," the other officer told his partner. Amelia heard his hard-soled shoes on the marble, avoiding the rug, she supposed.

Her father called after him, "And could you kill those lights, too?"

Then there was the sound of the two men coming toward the kitchen. Amelia's heart thumped double time while her brain remained petrified, useless.

"Miss," the dark-haired officer said, nodding to her as he came to the table. He pulled out a chair and sat, then took out a notebook and pen. "Amelia . . . Wilkes, is it? W-I-L-K-E-S?" She nodded. "And what is your age?"

"Seventeen—I'll be eighteen in February," she added.

"And you live at this address?"

"Yeah. Yes, I do."

He said, "Okay then," and looked up at her, his expression as neutral as she'd ever seen on a man. She wondered whether he'd had to learn to do that, or if it came to him naturally. He said, "Can you describe the event?"

Her father, now standing behind her chair, put his hands on her shoulders and said, "It was pornographic emails."

The officer glanced up, then back at Amelia. She said, "Not really."

"Oh yes, really," her father said.

The officer pursed his lips and ran one hand over his close-cut hair. "I'll need you to be specific, and start from the beginning."

"It's nothing—"

"He's threatened her or something," her father said. "She won't say, but I'm sure of it. This kid—"

"Sir? If it's all right with you, I need to get your daughter's statement first, and then I'll hear yours. Miss?"

"I really can't see the point of this. I'm fine. No one is harassing me." *Except my father,* she added silently.

The officer nodded. "I'll just need my report to be clear. You received an email—or emails—containing what, exactly?"

"Just pictures."

"Of?"

When Amelia didn't answer immediately, her father set her computer on the table and opened it. "Go ahead, honey, show 'em."

Amelia shook her head.

"All right, I'll do it," her father said, as the blond officer came into the room. Amelia gripped the table as she watched her father type in her password, then she turned her head away, dreading what they were about to see. Poor Anthony! What her father had done was already a terrible invasion of her privacy—and Anthony's. But *this,* oh, she hated this for Anthony even more than for herself, and hated her father for forcing the issue, for exposing Anthony this way, and hated herself for leaving the laptop behind this morning. Stupid. Stupid, careless, *stupid* thing to do.

She waited, eyes averted, mind spinning now, in search of a trapdoor out of this bizarre scene. For a moment, no one spoke. Then her father cleared his throat and said, "You see what I mean." She heard the soft click of the computer being closed again.

"Miss," the officer said, "can you identify the person in those photos?" He was as businesslike as before, but whereas he'd sounded bored prior to seeing the photos, now his tone was purposeful. Almost eager. A cat who'd caught a mouse's scent.

"No, sorry," she said, wanting to save Anthony the indignity, knowing it was hopeless.

She could feel her father's frustrated glare, hear the edge in his voice as he answered for her. "Anthony Winter's his name. He goes to her school, Ravenswood, and his mom's a teacher there. Kim Winter, I think it is."

"Thank you. Is that information correct, miss?"

Amelia ignored the question and instead told him, "I have no idea who sent them. It could have been anyone."

Her father pulled out the chair beside her and sat facing her, challenge plain on his face. "Amelia. You said—"

"No. *You* said. You assumed. But, well, I never knew *for sure* who sent them." She avoided his eyes. "I think it was some random email address."

"Do you have the original email?" the officer asked.

Careful to sound sincere, she said, "No, sorry, I deleted it."

"I'm sure these came from him directly," her father said, sounding as if he wasn't sure whether to be angry or perplexed at this alteration to her story. "I know the guy, he's been trying to get at my daughter since the minute he started at her school."

The blond officer said, "Don't worry, there's ways to backtrack it. We have forensic technicians that can recover pretty much anything, even things that were deleted. People don't realize that everything they do on their computers lives forever, deep in the hard drive. Kiddie porn, poison, bombs, guns, whatever people spend their time on, it stays in there somewhere."

Amelia was suddenly nauseated. *Everything* lived on? If they dredged her computer's hard drive, they'd find so much more than these few pictures—flagged because she'd been tinkering with edits to this particular group, changing exposures and color tones and shadows, cropping, enlarging, applying effects. Anthony was so beautiful, his lean body as ideal as the sculptures she'd seen in museums, as perfect as the subjects of Michelangelo's paintings. She had these pictures, and pictures of herself, and a bunch more of the two of them together—not doing anything smutty, but not always dressed.

Suppose they found those? Not to mention that while browsing what her parents always referred to as "inappropriate content" (they believed her when she said she never looked at that stuff), she'd viewed and deleted things she'd be embarrassed to show Anthony, let alone have revealed by some über-geek and shown to God-knows-who.

Her father was saying, "So then, you just take the computer and have it checked, then you'll be able to charge him?"

She covered it with her hands. "You can't take my computer; I need it for school."

The seated officer said, "To be honest with you, I don't specifi-cally know what the charge for this might be—"

"But it is a crime," her father said, as if instructing the officer, or trying to persuade him. "You'll be arresting the guy."

Amelia's heart plummeted. "*Arresting?* Doesn't that seem, you know, like overkill? I mean, it's just pictures—there's no actual harm in it. After all, I've seen paintings of nude men, so what differ-ence?" She gave the officer her wide-eyed look, *sincerity,* moving a strand of hair behind her left ear for good measure.

The officer glanced at his notes. "The DA's office has to make that judgment. A couple more questions, miss. If you don't mind." He looked at her again, straight on this time, in a way that struck a low, clear note of fear in her heart. His words, innocent as they sounded, confirmed the feeling. He said, "You claim you deleted the email, okay, but you've got these pictures saved, and in a file marked 'flagged.' Why is that?"

Her mind scrambled like a rat in a maze. "I—"

"For proof," her father said. *Yes!* she thought, recalling the quick lie she'd used in her first attempt to stop this. He went on, "She said she already reported him to the school, but, I don't know—" He turned to Amelia. "Did they ask you to show 'em to them?"

"They . . . Well, no, they, they just took my word for it." *Please God,* she prayed, *don't let them ask the school for confirmation.*

The officer stood. "Excuse me just a minute while I make a call." Amelia's breath caught, then eased as he added, "This is something I haven't dealt with previously, so I'll need to get a read from the DA's office."

Powerless to do anything other than wait, Amelia crossed her arms in front of her on the table, then leaned over and rested her head the way all the kids used to do during quiet time at school. As a child, she'd let her mind wander, idly turning over pleasant thoughts as if they were stones in a stream. Now the stones were boulders and there was nothing to do but pray for help in lifting them. *Please God help me please God help me please God . . .*

"Sir?" The blond officer stood in the doorway, and her father motioned him into the kitchen. "What we're going to need to do is have Miss Wilkes surrender her computer, for further investigation."

Amelia's hands began to tremble, and she squeezed them into fists. "Wait," she said, knowing now that the only way to stop this about-to-topple boulder was to confess. "Wait, that won't be necessary. Okay, yes, Anthony did send them, but . . . but it's not what you think."

All three men's eyes were on her now, but that was all right. She was used to the spotlight. She knew what was required of her.

Straightening her back and squaring her shoulders, she lifted her chin and said, "The truth is, I asked him to send them. It's all my fault. It was my idea. He didn't do anything."

The police officers glanced at each other in a way that said, *This changes things.*

"She doesn't mean that," her father said. "He threatened her, intimidated her. Something. I know my daughter. She wouldn't do that, and she wouldn't lie about doing it unless he'd got her afraid of him."

"No," she said firmly, feeling an odd satisfaction in shattering— or at least trying to shatter—her father's blind faith in her innocence. "I swear. I . . . we . . . This is really embarrassing, okay, but,

I thought he was good-looking, and I wanted to see what he looked like . . . you know. Undressed. I was . . ." She shrugged. "I was curious. I'm sorry. I know it was wrong."

"Amelia." Her father's voice was careful and stern. "It's obvious you're scared."

"Daddy," she said, shaking her head, "I'm sorry. I know you're disappointed in me." She dared a look at his face. "But I *am* almost eighteen."

"So, just to confirm," the dark-haired officer said, "you're saying it was this man——"

"Boy," she said. "He's a senior, like me."

"This Anthony Winter is the person in the pictures, and they were sent by him, using email, at your request."

She nodded.

"What would you say is the nature of your relationship?"

"We . . . we're friends. Good friends is all," she said, hopeful that she might yet save them from complete exposure, put all this to rest without endangering the system that had worked so well for them up until now.

The officer shut his notebook and said, "All right, then. Looks like we're finished here."

Amelia looked from his face to the other officer's, afraid to be relieved, yet hopeful she had saved Anthony, even if she'd gotten herself into what would surely be boiling-hot water with her father. "That's it? We're done?"

"We are, yes."

"I can keep my computer?"

The officers, now both standing, both nodded. "If we have any other questions, we'll get in touch. What's the best number to contact you?"

Her father took the man's elbow and steered him toward the front hall, saying, "I'll give you one of my business cards, it has all the ways to find me."

The blond officer gave Amelia an appraising look, then followed the other two men to the front door, where Amelia could hear her father saying, "I have to tell you, boys, I'm not entirely satisfied here," and her interrogator replying, "The DA gets the final word, sir."

Meaning what? That Anthony might still get into trouble? That they might still check her computer?

Despite the laptop remaining in her possession, Amelia had a sinking feeling that the final word, the word that would come to characterize their situation, would be one a polite girl would never utter. She formed it letter by letter using sign language, F-U- . . . Then she leaned her forehead against the table and prayed— because praying couldn't hurt, though she wasn't sure it had helped so far—that she was wrong.

A minute later, Amelia's father returned to the kitchen rubbing his jaw thoughtfully as he walked. He stopped in front of her on the far side of the table, tucked his hands into his pockets, and said, "Seems like this is worse than I thought."

"I told you, I'm sorry."

He picked up her computer. "He's sunk his claws into you right good, that boy has. Where's your phone?"

"Outside. In my car."

"I'll get it. Go on up to your room."

"What?"

"I said get to your room. Go on."

"Daddy, I'm not a five-year-old. You can't just take my toys and send me to my room."

His raised eyebrows and tight jaw dared her to protest further. "I believe I can do exactly that, and you had better get. I'm in no mood to debate with you right now. I need some time to think."

"Oh, and you can only think when I'm locked up in my room, is that it?"

"Amelia." He appeared baffled by her sarcasm. "What in God's good name is going on with you?"

"You were trying to get an innocent person arrested!"

"He is *not* innocent, honey. Let's just stop right where we are and back up a minute."

"*I'm* the one who caused the problem."

"Which never would'a happened if he hadn't somehow got to you. He's a slimeball, trust me, I know the type."

They stood there, facing off, Amelia ready to dig in further, and then her mother came clattering into the mudroom from the back door with a cheerful, "Well, hey, I didn't expect to find both of y'all home." The cheerfulness vanished quickly, once she saw them. "What's wrong?"

Amelia let her father recount the tale of her secrecy and the photos, the excuses she'd tried to make to both him and to the police, and then he absolved her completely by the end of it. He said, "Somehow, Winter's got her covering for him, but we're goin' to make sure we've put an end to it so that Ladybug here can get back on track."

"Momma," Amelia said, getting up so she could take her mother's hands in her own, "it isn't like Daddy said at all. *I'm* the one who did the wrong thing—voluntarily, totally on my own. Anthony doesn't deserve to get in trouble."

"Harlan?"

"She said this before, too. Amelia, it's all right, you can tell us the truth."

"I'm *trying* to, but you won't listen!"

"The police," her mother said, looking at her with concern, "they're done with this?"

Her father said, "They'll have to question him, too."

"They do?" Amelia said, startled. "I thought they were finished." She'd thought—well, she'd hoped—that what trouble might yet come would be through her father raising it with Ms. Winter, maybe with the school, since she and Anthony had a class together.

"*Your* part is finished, but they have to go see what he has to say for himself, 'fore they take the information to the DA—waste of time if you ask me."

Her mother, face fixed in a reassuring expression that did not re-assure Amelia at all, said, "I'll suppose that if he's done nothing wrong, they'll find that out quick enough."

"What? Come on! You're siding with Daddy?"

"I'm saying, it can be hard to tell what feelings are real and what are . . . provoked, by situations." Her mother seemed far away for a moment, but then she focused on Amelia again, saying, "You're only seventeen. It's not like you really know your own mind when it comes to . . . to this kind of thing."

"Not to mention understanding that boy's motivation," her father said.

"Unbelievable," Amelia said, backing away from both of her parents. "You'd *do* this, subject an innocent person to who knows what kind of mess just because you don't want to believe I'm capable of this all on my own?"

Her father frowned at her. "You act like that boy did not provide you with pornography. The evidence speaks for itself, miss. Now go on like I said. We'll take this up with you later, after your momma and I've had a chance to talk."

Her mother watched her with eyes that seemed sympathetic and knowing at the same time. "Harlan," she said, then went to him and whispered something in his ear.

"I did, yes, and I thought of that, too."

When Amelia got upstairs, she stopped in the game room to call Anthony from the home phone, discovering from the absence of a dial tone just what it was that her parents had both foreseen; her father had unplugged the phone base so that none of the extensions worked.

So okay, they could predict that she'd try to use the phone, but that didn't mean they really knew her, or even truly wanted to, or ever would.

———————

Cameron had what Amelia wanted: a mother who was a girlfriend, who liked the things she liked, who supported Cameron's future goals 100 percent, who didn't use the time she spent with Cameron directing and managing and educating. Not that mothers shouldn't do those things, but did hers, Amelia's, have to do *only* those things? Mrs. McGuiness knew where to draw the line; she didn't let Cameron drink or swear or run wild. The difference between Cameron's mother-daughter relationship and her own was that when Amelia was hanging out with Cameron, and Mrs. McGuiness was around, Cameron talked and acted in exactly the same manner she did when her mother was not. Cameron's mother didn't only support and encourage her daughter, she *enjoyed* her, actively and obviously. Cam's mother *got* her—and the reverse appeared to be true, too.

Amelia was fifteen when she and her mother had driven together to Greensboro, where she was to perform solo in a singing competition. They'd left home midafternoon, with Amelia working on homework and her mother listening to an audiobook during the ninety-minute drive. At their hotel, they'd unpacked their clothes and toiletries, and argued about which of the two outfits her mother had packed for the competition was best, given that the next morning was forecasted to be rainy and cold. Amelia wanted to wear the burgundy pencil skirt they'd bought a week earlier at Saks, with a short-sleeved pearl-gray blouse they'd found at Uniquities. Her mother, who'd been fine with both items—she'd paid for them, after all—was now pushing for the black turtleneck and hunter-green plaid skirt, with black tights, an outfit that had seemed perfect six months earlier but now seemed desperately childish to Amelia.

They left that matter unresolved and shifted to debating the song Amelia had prepared, "What I Did for Love" from *A Chorus Line,* which her mother worried was a bit slow and serious, and which Amelia explained had been chosen for exactly that reason. They debated whether she should audition for Ravenswood's next production, for which she was almost sure to get the lead role, or try for a lesser part in the upcoming Raleigh Little Theatre play. Amelia argued for the latter, watching the lines between her mother's eyes deepen until her mother said, "Amelia, be sensible. You're the rising star at school, Ms. Fitz says so. I don't see why you want to take a step backward. Thrive where you're planted."

"But what does that add up to, if all I ever do are school plays and these competitions?"

"Why does it need to add up to anything? You're doing great and having a good time, isn't that what matters?"

"Yes, but Momma," Amelia insisted, "what if someday I could transplant myself—to Broadway, for instance—and thrive even better?"

"You know what Daddy says, and I agree: choose something practical."

"But you did what *you* wanted. Why shouldn't I?"

"I'm not sure you want that. Not really. Girls always have big dreams, but once you're grown? Well, let's just say we ought not always follow our first impulses. Now let's go find us some supper."

They'd gotten directions to a one-size-fits-all restaurant nearby, but then on the way, Amelia spotted a Japanese restaurant and begged her mother to go there instead. "Please? We never eat Japanese."

"Daddy doesn't like that kind of food."

"What about you, though?"

"Well, I don't really know, to tell you the truth."

"That's why now is a perfect time to go," Amelia said. Seeing a chance to make her point from earlier, she added, "It's good to try new things."

"Sometimes it is," her mother agreed. "But other times it causes nothing but trouble, trust me on that."

After they were seated in the restaurant, Amelia unwrapped her chopsticks, saying, "Let's get some sushi."

"Raw fish?" her mother said dubiously.

Amelia scanned her menu. "Look." She turned it so that her mother could read where she was pointing. "It's not only raw fish. This one doesn't have any fish in it at all. And did you know that sushi's good for you? Japanese women have the lowest breast cancer rates of any developed nation."

"Now, how do you know that?" Her mother unwrapped her own chopsticks and set them on the table, where they began to roll, slowly, toward the table's edge.

"We learned it in Health and Fitness," Amelia said, intercepting the chopsticks and resting them across her mother's plate.

In Health and Fitness they'd also learned that using birth control pills could lead to blood clots, heart attacks, and ovarian cancer, a lesson that she and her friends had all agreed was Miss Jones's attempt at a scare tactic. They'd looked up "oral contraceptives" online and gotten the facts—which were that those side effects were possible, yes, but extremely rare. Some of her friends were already in need of this information, while Amelia had wondered whether she would ever be. Still, all of them were glad to have access to the truth without having to go ask their parents, who were not, in many cases, any more reliable than Miss Jones. "Technology to the rescue," one of the more mature girls said, clicking a link that led her to the Planned Parenthood site.

Miss Jones had insisted, too, that although Ravenswood was not a parochial school, it was her personal duty to remind the students that hell was a real place, and she would be awfully sad to see any of them end up there. Which of course prompted a lot of after-class laughter about how, exactly, Miss Jones might know who went to hell, and the viewing, later that week at Robert Sorensen's house, of a very grainy, very dark online video of the classic porn film *The Devil in Miss Jones*.

What was it, Amelia wondered, that made adults so conservative about sexuality? Everyone who was presently an adult had been a teenager before, so surely they had the same curiosity, the same preoccupations, the same pressures that Amelia and her peers did. A person had only to read Jane Austen or the Brontës or Shakespeare to know that feelings of love and desire and passion were as prevalent among teenagers in those authors' times as they were today, and would have been when Miss Jones was young—which, based on the way she talked, may well have happened during Queen Victoria's reign, or, more fittingly, at the time the Puritans were settling New England, and she simply looked young for her age.

Love was not a force that could be legislated and prevented until after a person turned eighteen or twenty-one. Amelia, at fifteen, believed this quite firmly even though she had not yet experienced it for herself. She'd believed it even as she was sure nothing so amazing and wonderful would happen to her—at fifteen or any -teen, and possibly not for a very long time after that. Possibly not ever. For all of her advantages, and for all that she'd been petted and admired for—her pleasing looks, her quiet, polite demeanor, her well-written essays and high test scores—she'd felt she wasn't worthy. For some reason that no one had ever been able to pin down, something inside her brain had, at age five, gone wrong, causing her to stutter, making it so that she'd spent eight years of her life seeing psychologists and speech therapists, and hiding her defect from everyone. The boys seemed to sense that she was glitchy; they kept their distance, and why wouldn't they, when there were so many other smart, pretty, talented girls to choose from?

At fifteen, she believed in love but knew better than to look for it. Instead, she sang about it, read about it, lived it vicariously through movies, and waited to be considered old enough to act it out onstage.

"Watch me," she told her mother, chopsticks in hand. "I'll show you how to use them." Amelia used her chopsticks to lift the silverware, her napkin, the wrappers, and then helped her mother try to do the same, to comical effect. "Okay, okay, one thing at a time," her mother laughed, laying down the chopsticks. "It'll be enough of a challenge for me to eat sushi at all."

They studied their menus. Her mother asked, "Which kind are you having?"

"I like the tuna. *Maki*, which is the roll." Amelia set down her menu. "Did you know Juliet is only thirteen?"

"Juliet who?" her mother said. "Maybe I'll try this one, with the cucumber and crab. Did I tell you how we used to go crabbing, my brothers and me, when I was little?"

Amelia tilted her head, intrigued. Her mother rarely spoke of her life before this incarnation, mother of Amelia, wife of Harlan. "No, I don't think so," Amelia said. She waited for more, and when it didn't come, she said, "Juliet Capulet, from *Romeo and Juliet*."

"Was *thirteen*? My, it's hard to think that's right."

The waitress came to take their orders. When she'd gone, Amelia said, "You didn't meet Daddy until you were thirty, right?"

"Yes. He hired me to decorate his first house."

"And you fell in love with him right off."

"No, not right away," her mother said. "He was a client, and I took my job very seriously. But yes, after a time, we decided it might be nice to see each other."

"What about before Daddy?" Amelia asked.

"What do you mean?"

"Did you have a high-school boyfriend? And what about later, when you were in design school, and afterward?"

"Of course I dated some, but I'm sure your daddy wouldn't appreciate me talking about that." She waved her hand dismissively.

Grinning, Amelia leaned forward and whispered, "Was there someone special? It's okay, I won't tell him you told."

"I'll suppose this one is soy sauce," her mother said, shifting her gaze and reaching for the condiments caddy. She touched the lid of one bottle. "Same as at Chinese places, right? But what are the other sauces?"

"Momma, come on, tell. Was he from High Point, too, or was it after you moved to Raleigh?"

"I said I'd rather not discuss that. Drop it," she said sharply.

Amelia sat back, stung. "Why? It was a long time ago. What's the big deal?"

Her mother pushed the sauces back to their spot near the wall. "Come to think of it, the burgundy skirt and gray top is probably the better choice for tomorrow, what with the rain. Black will seem gloomy, don't you think so?"

Amelia fought back confused tears. "Whichever you want," she said. "I just want to sing."

7

AP ENGLISH WAS ORDINARILY ANTHONY'S FAVORITE CLASS. Yes, because Amelia was in it with him, but also because this was the one class he had where discussion got them into the meat of things. Mr. Edmunds, his teacher, was that right combination of cool and youthful, intellectual without being a geek; he regarded literature as relevant, and insisted his students do the same.

Today's discussion centered on *The Perks of Being a Wallflower*, a book Anthony thought got at the heart of being a teen, a book that, true enough to its billing, got into the issue of "passivity vs. passion." This interested him because he saw in himself elements of both—more passion than passivity, whereas with Amelia it was the other way around, and maybe that was what made them fit so well. He'd been eager to talk about the book. Now, though, he sat with his phone in hand, waiting—and waiting, and waiting—for Amelia to text her explanation for going missing. When he wasn't glancing at his phone, he was watching the door.

At the bell, he bolted from his seat. Mr. Edmunds snagged his arm as he passed. "Hold on."

"What's up?" Anthony asked, moving aside as his classmates streamed past, some of them wearing the same expression of curiosity that Mr. Edmunds showed.

"My question exactly. You were pretty tuned out today." The teacher's thick eyebrows were raised behind his black-framed glasses, but the unsaid question—was Amelia's absence part of this?—was not one that Anthony would answer. Maybe Edmunds knew, or thought he knew, about their relationship, but either way, Anthony wasn't going to confirm it with a careless display of concern.

"I know," he said. "I'm sorry. Distracted." He edged toward the door.

"Can I help?"

Anthony shook his head, already on the move. "Thanks."

Outside the classroom, he dialed Amelia as he walked, and ducked into the bathroom, where he'd be able to talk unseen by faculty. Again, he got her voice mail.

Next period and sixth, too, were a repeat of fourth, only with teachers who seemed unaware that he had little to contribute today. Nothing improved even after final bell; it wasn't as if he could go running to Amelia's house, looking for her.

He found his mother in the classroom where she taught sixth-period French. She was cleaning the whiteboard and singing along to an Édith Piaf CD that was playing on the portable stereo she toted with her from classroom to classroom.

"*Non! Je ne regrette rien. . . .*"

Anthony said, "*Ça va, Maman?*" and she turned to him and waved. He closed the door and leaned against it. "Was Amelia in class just now?"

"No—I figured on asking *you* why she wasn't here. Thought you had the inside track—or maybe something to do with it?"

"*Non, je ne sais pas où elle est,*" he said, trying to shake off his anxiety by indulging in this practice they had, of his working to become fluent. In his pre-Amelia days, he and his mother had made plans to spend his graduation summer in France. Lately, he'd been trying to talk her into including Amelia, whose French was far better than his. "Did I get that right?"

"You don't know where she is," his mother said, nodding.

"I haven't heard from her since she went home to get her computer."

"Maybe she had an appointment and forgot to tell you."

"Peut-être," he said, though he knew better.

"Do you work tonight?"

"Yeah—but not till five."

"I have yoga, so I guess I'll see you later. Oh—there's leftover tuna salad, if you want to take it with you for dinner."

"Maybe," he said again, this time in English. "So, okay, see you." At the doorway, he turned and added, "If you hear anything—you know, about Amelia—let me know."

"I'm sure there's a simple explanation, and you'll laugh about it later. I can't tell you how many times that's been true for me worrying about you."

He nodded, recalling some of those times—most of them when he'd been out riding dirt bikes or bridge-jumping into Falls Lake with friends a couple years older than himself, friends whose mothers were, then, at the stage his mother was now. Acceptance, or maybe resignation. Bad things rarely happened, and Anthony and his friends were old enough to manage them when they did.

"Yeah, I'm sure you're right." He waved. "See you."

"Je t'aime."

"Love you, too."

As he approached his old Mini sitting in the emptied student lot, he dialed Cameron, hoping she'd have heard something. She hadn't, and was worried, too. He dialed three more friends, and none knew anything. He tried Amelia's phone yet again, and this time the line didn't ring, it went straight to voice mail.

Anthony pounded the car's roof once, then got in and headed home. He drove with little conscious awareness of the drive itself; his mind kept turning over the ways he might go to Amelia's house before work, go see her, or see about her, without risking discovery. He could do as he usually did: park some distance away and then walk or jog through the woods, but the odds of him being seen by one of the neighbors whose property he'd be crossing were much higher in daylight, and he didn't want some freaked-out old lady calling the police about a prowler. Or . . . maybe he'd try driving directly to Amelia's house, telling the guard at the neighborhood's entrance that he was dropping off homework. That should work as a onetime deal. *Good, okay*, he thought. He'd do that. That would at least get him there . . . and he could pull the same act with her mom, if she happened to be home.

What he hoped was that for some yet-to-be-revealed good reason, Amelia had neglected to tell him she was going to stay home and take a nap. He hoped he'd ring the doorbell and after a minute she'd pad to the front door and greet him with a sleepy smile. He'd seen that smile once, when she'd slept over at Cameron's house and he'd come by first thing in the morning, to join them for breakfast. He wanted more than anything to see that smile every morning, and he mentally marked, again, that he would be able to beginning about two hundred and ten days from now.

On his street, he was nearly at his house before he noticed the Raleigh Police car stationed a hundred feet or so away. He pulled up to the curb and parked, thinking this was another case of a concerned neighbor requesting them to do some speed-limit enforcement. People tended to drive too fast on through-streets like theirs, endangering the kids who played outside on bikes and skateboards and scooters. He went inside and took the stairs two at a time, swung into his room, and booted up his computer to check his email. If for some reason Amelia's phone had stopped working, she might have contacted him this way. He pulled off his navy V-neck sweater and sat at the table that served as a desk, waiting, tapping a pen against his palm. "Where *are* you?" He knew that only some crazy sequence of truths would lead to her being away from any kind of phone but at the same time near a computer, hers or any, but at this point, even crazy sequences of truths were worth hoping for.

The hope didn't last long. *"Merde,"* he said, when he saw that none of his new messages had come from her.

When the doorbell rang a minute later, Anthony still had not connected the police presence to his own life. Expecting his grandmother, who often dropped in unannounced, he went downstairs and pulled open the door to find two blue-shirted cops waiting there. "Anthony Winter?"

As implausible as it was, Anthony's first thought was that they'd come to tell him Amelia had been hurt or killed. His breath caught and he choked out, "Yeah?"

"We'd like to ask you some questions. Can we come in?"

He stepped back and let them in. The three of them stood in the small foyer for a moment, and then one of the officers took out a notebook and said, "Would you confirm that you live at this address?"

Anthony nodded. "What's going on? Is this about Amelia? Is she okay?"

The two exchanged a glance, then one cleared his throat and said, "We've had a complaint. What do you know about Amelia Wilkes being in possession of a number of photographs that feature you without . . . that is, in an unclothed state?"

Anthony blinked, and blinked again. "Sorry?" He had not seen this coming, not at all, not in any way. Christ. How could the cops possibly—?

Then the pieces tumbled into place. The forgotten computer. And . . . maybe Amelia's mom hadn't gotten delayed at all. Maybe she'd tricked Amelia into coming back home, where she could then confront her. And, apparently, sic the cops on him.

The officer said, "Miss Wilkes has photos, and she has given us an account of their origin, but we'd like to get your side of the story."

Miss Wilkes has photos. His relief over knowing she wasn't sick or hurt was quickly giving way, replaced by dread over what she must have endured in order for this pair, these boys in blue whose smug expressions told him they'd seen everything he had to offer a woman, to now be at his door. No way had she given up the info voluntarily.

He said, "Even if it was me, how would this be, you know, something involving the police?"

The dark-haired officer said, "Right now, it's important that you answer the question. Do you know how Miss Wilkes came to have these photos?"

Though Anthony was wary of saying too much, he wanted to deflect any responsibility from Amelia, so he said, "I sent them to her just, you know, for fun. She didn't have anything to do with it. Why?"

"So she didn't invite you to take and send the photos?"

This made him pause. If she'd told them she asked him to send them, would it be better to back up her account, or contradict it? And either way, he didn't see why the police were getting involved—maybe as a favor to Harlan Wilkes? Had Wilkes set this up in order to scare him?

Anthony said, "She's seventeen, you know. Eighteen in February. The age of consent—not that *that* is what this is about, but, you know, where sexual stuff is concerned—is sixteen."

The blond officer said, "We're aware of the law—and it's good to know that you are, too. All we need to know is whether what Miss Wilkes said is accurate. You're not accused of anything related to sexual . . . er, relations."

"Okay. Because, you know, not that I'm saying we've had 'relations,' but if we had, she's old enough to decide to have them." He wiped his clammy palms on his pants.

"The photos?" the dark-haired officer prompted.

Anthony weighed the matter as best he could with the two cops staring at him, and decided he should back up Amelia's statement so she couldn't be accused of lying. And maybe there was a way to lessen the trouble, make her look innocent just the same.

He said, "Well, now that I think about it, maybe she did ask me. Yeah, I think that's how it went. I think she was intending to use them for an art project, something like that. Did she say?"

The officer made some notes. "Did you send the photos using email?"

What difference did that make? He thought of the various ways she'd gotten the photos. Her phone, his phone, his camera, hers, email, text message. Email seemed no better or worse than the others, so he said, "Um, yeah. I think so."

"All right. Your account is pretty much what we heard from Miss Wilkes. As of now, we're going to file our report, but we'll need you to remain available this afternoon, in case we have any further questions."

"I have to work." He told them where, and they took down his cellphone and work phone numbers. Then they put their hats on and left the house.

Anthony followed them onto the porch, watched them get into the cruiser without either of them saying a word, and watched them drive away. He could only imagine the conversation they must be having right now: rich girl who lives in a mansion surrounded by forest, a girl so lovely that none of them (himself included) could possibly rate a real chance with her, keeps provocative, show-all photographs of guy who lives in little row house with a single tree growing on its pitiful square of lawn. Rich, lovely girl gets busted by mother—who would without a doubt be extremely pissed, so complaint gets filed with the cops. What a joke it must be to them, doing the bidding of people like the Wilkeses. He could just see them placating Sheri Wilkes by agreeing to question him and file a report. Placating Harlan, too—she'd probably gotten him to come help with the crisis—with their questions and their notebooks and their serious yes-ma'am, yes-sir faces. And coming here, questioning him, the poor SOB in the photos, who was probably going to get a real ass-kicking from the girl's father . . . they had to be having a good laugh about that.

A warm breeze stirred the big maple tree, which was half shaded by the house. He looked up at it, and saw that the top leaves glowed as if set afire.

He was still there on the porch a half hour later when the cruiser reappeared, this time pulling into the driveway. "Mr. Winter," the blond officer said as he stepped out of the car, "We're going to need you to come with us."

"What the hell?" The handcuffs were icy, and far heavier than Anthony would have imagined, the weight and position pulling his shoulders back uncomfortably and straining the buttons of his white oxford shirt. Quickly, though, the officers escorted him outside and folded him into the backseat of the cruiser, and then his discomfort increased tenfold.

"The DA is issuing a warrant for your arrest."

"What's the charge?" Anthony said. The door thumped shut and the officers got into the front seats without answering. "This can't be legal," he told them through the vertical bars that separated the backseat from the front. No response. "And how about a seat belt?" he said as the car pulled away from the curb and a pair of curious neighbors watched them go.

There was nothing in the back of the patrol car except Anthony himself. No belts, no latches, no knobs, no handles, no mats on the floor. No way to brace himself, except awkwardly, with his elbows and feet. Bars on the door windows, bars dividing front from back. No way to get free or get out. "Can't you tell me anything?"

The blond officer didn't even turn around as he said, "The magistrate will spell it all out for you." Then he closed a plastic panel that separated the front and back compartments even farther, presumably to mute the arrestee's outraged, angry, or annoying outbursts, or to prevent being spat on.

"Magistrate?" Anthony said, raising his voice. What or who the hell was the magistrate? Wasn't that a British term? Right, he thought—British, for basically a judge. He was going to see a *judge*? "What do you mean by magistrate?" he tried again. No answer. "Yo! Officer! Why am I going to see a judge?"

They continued to ignore him, and he was tempted to kick the seat, not that it was likely to do any good. "Fuck all," he said, slumping down in the seat. A magistrate, okay, fine. Who would tell him what, exactly?

Arrested, shit. Arrested, and then what? If he was going to see a sort-of-judge, when was he supposed to get to talk to a lawyer? Did he even need a lawyer? This was all some kind of screwup in the first place, had to be, because how could sending some photos at the request of an over-sixteen-year-old girl be a crime?

The drive to wherever he was being taken seemed to last for hours as they moved through the stop-and-go flow of late afternoon Capital Boulevard traffic. His cellphone vibrated in his pocket. He twisted his arms around to his side, touched the edge of his pocket with his fingers, but couldn't reach into it. *Amelia.* He was sure, or he wanted to be sure, that it was Amelia trying to call him, somehow, finally. Did she know he was going to be hauled in? Was she calling, thinking there was time to warn him?

Anthony had no idea where the police station was located, and was surprised when they wound their way into downtown Raleigh and then pulled into a parking garage that, after the brightness of the afternoon, was suffocatingly dark.

The rear door was opened, and he scooted out. "Where are we?"

"Jail."

Anthony's stomach lurched. "Come on, seriously?"

"What, you thought we were going to McDonald's?" The dark-haired officer laughed at his own lousy joke, then left them, telling his partner, "Catch you after."

"What about a lawyer? Don't I get to talk to a lawyer?"

The blond officer nudged him toward a door. "We go that way," he said, then put his hand on Anthony's shoulder to show that Anthony should precede him. "The magistrate will instruct you," he said.

He heard the officer announce them, presumably using the radio device he'd noticed was strapped to the fronts of the officers' shirts, then the door opened with a resounding clatter. Anthony hesitated, then stepped inside; the door closed behind them with an even louder clank.

A short walk through the most featureless, colorless hallway he had ever seen led them to another secure door, which opened as if by magic and admitted them to a longer, more sickly looking version of the space they'd just been in. Jaundiced yellow-tan walls, floors, lights, and absolutely nothing on the walls, no pictures or posters or even windows to the outdoors, *nothing,* except for doorways now and then. And even the doors were yellow-tan, with small windows protected by yellow-tan crosshatched metal.

"Go left here," the officer said. Anthony turned left and walked through an open doorway, finding himself in a long box of a room that featured eight short metal benches bolted to a dirty, grayish tiled floor. At the front of the room were four crosshatched windows in a painted concrete wall, something like the teller windows in a seedy Roman arena he once visited with him mom and his uncle John, when he was fourteen. They'd been there to see some alt-rock band, but the band had failed to show. To make up for the disappointment, John had taken them to one of Trastevere's ancient, amazing squares and said Anthony could have as many *gelati* as he wanted. He'd had three scoops of *panna cotta,* then struck up a rudimentary but entertaining conversation with two giggly Italian girls who'd mistaken him for a local.

This was definitely not that.

Anthony was directed to wait on a bench while the officer went to the one occupied window at the far left and handed some paperwork over to a clerk, a long-faced fat man with droopy eyelids. He listened for clues on what, exactly, he was being charged with, but the officer and the clerk talked football scores. Football! Who the hell cared whether East Carolina was having a better season than last year, or if the team's starting quarterback had a shot at next year's NFL draft?

Anthony let his head hang and felt the stretch in his neck. It was The System. He'd been swallowed up by The System and had become, in the time it took to crank the cuffs onto his wrists and put him in that cruiser, a nonentity. He, an actual person with an actual life, no longer existed. No one but these two football-obsessed men and the dark-haired cop had any idea where he was. Amelia, his mother, his grandmother, his friends, they were all in The World, totally ignorant of his sitting here being digested—slowly, so that the resulting agony was sure to leave an impression that he'd carry with him into the next world, whatever it might be.

"Now you," the officer finally said, nodding to him as if the room was filled with prospective arrestees. "Approach the window and stand on the line."

Anthony got up. The handcuffs were cutting into his wrists, and he needed to use the bathroom. "How long before I—"

"Stand on the line," the officer repeated.

Anthony walked to the line, a three-foot-long battered strip of what appeared to be duct tape. "When do I get my phone call?"

The officer rolled his eyes and said nothing.

The fat man, wearing a grungy, grayish dress shirt—was this the magistrate?—sat behind the window at a gray metal desk, his eyes on the paper in front of him. "Verify your name, date of birth, and address."

Anthony recited all. The man, still not looking at him, said, "Any distinguishing marks? Tattoos, piercings, scars, gold teeth?"

"No, not unless you count the—"

"Remain on the line and look into the camera until after the flash," the man said, leaving Anthony to finish his statement silently, *The birthmark on my hip*. Anthony did as directed, looking up at the camera mounted just above the window. *Mug shot,* he realized, as the camera flashed. Then the police officer told him, "We're going to exit the room," and waited for Anthony to precede him again.

"Now go left," the officer said, and they were back in the bland hallway. It smelled, oddly, of ozone and popcorn, and, now, of his own nervous sweat.

Next, they entered a much smaller room occupied by one wide desk, behind which was a man who looked to Anthony like Ichabod Crane reincarnate. There were two short benches in front of the desk, one of which was occupied by a wiry black man whose neck and forearms were tattooed with elaborate scrollwork. A black-shirted guard with bulging biceps and pecs, and chains dangling from his belt, stood by while the arrestee was told to empty his pockets and surrender any and all accessories.

"This is where I leave you," the blond officer told Anthony while he fitted a key into the handcuffs, releasing Anthony's wrists at last.

Anthony let his arms relax to his sides, then slowly pulled them forward and upward, stretching his shoulder blades, one eye on the muscled guard in case the guy mistook his stretching as a grab for his holstered gun. He rubbed one wrist with his thumb and then did the other, trying to smooth out the red indentations as if doing so would erase the whole surreal experience. No such luck.

He sighed and looked around while he waited for his turn to cough everything up. The walls here were papered with fliers advising that certain dangerous items were sometimes easily concealed, or that innocuous-looking things could be used as weapons. *Be on Your Guard!* one sign warned, in towering mimeographed letters, circa 1980. Was this sign supposed to be for Anthony's safety?—suppose the tattooed guy was in for violent assault, or murder, and might lash out if he got the chance. That was more comforting than thinking the sign was for the guy whose job it was to pat down the newly arrested, as the guard was now doing to the tattooed man. Pretty scary to think the guards needed reminders. Wasn't knowing what to look for the thing they were trained to do? The thing they did multiple times every single day?

Ichabod Crane turned his attention to Anthony, repeating verbatim the directions he'd given the tattooed man, never once looking Anthony in the eye. Anthony emptied his pockets of what little he carried with him: phone, wallet, and the half-dollar-sized pewter charm Amelia had given him last Valentine's Day. The center of the disc had been punched out in the shape of a heart. She wore that heart on a long leather string around her neck.

Amelia. What was she going through at home?

He emptied his wallet: license, student ID, condom—how incriminating was that?—ticket stub from the Rialto theatre, fourteen dollars cash, a receipt from Taco Bell. Feeling exposed and absurd, he unbuckled his belt and yanked it from his waist, then leaned down to untie and unlace his shoes. What, did they think that he, a guy who had done nothing except snap a few naked pictures and share them with his steady girlfriend, was going to suddenly become murderous and try to strangle the other inmates with shoestrings? Or maybe it was that the other prisoners would attack him for the laces, then use them on the guards. Actually, he thought, they probably worried about people—what was the term from the cop shows? Perps?—they probably worried about perps becoming suicidal after extended exposure to the pervasive yellow-tan, fluorescent-lighted environment, and hanging themselves with their belts. How did these people stand this environment all day, every day?

His belongings were inventoried onto a typed list, then zipped into a canvas bag.

"Review this," Crane said, handing him the list.

Anthony looked it over. "Fine," he said. He slid it back to the man.

The guard barked, "Stand facing the wall." Anthony stood. "Arms up, spread your legs."

Anthony closed his eyes while the guard patted him down, armpits to ankles, crotch to ankles, waist, thighs, ass to ankles. He wanted to say, *You forgot my ears, nose, and throat*, but kept it to himself in case the guard took him seriously.

"Now here." He was led to a machine for fingerprinting. The guard told him to relax his arm, then put his hand and fingers through a series of ink-free, computerized scans—probably sending out all his info to every state and to the Feds, probably Interpol too, because he was, after all, an accused criminal and you couldn't be too careful in these post–9/11 days.

They left that room and continued down the hallway, Anthony shuffling so that he wouldn't walk out of his shoes. Now he could hear men's voices, some screaming in anger, others loud with laughter. Then, the closed-in smell of the hallways and rooms he'd been in gave way to the rank odors of locked-up unwashed humans and stale food. They reached an intersection, where Anthony could now see where the sounds and smells were coming from; here, to his right, his left, and along the hall where it widened and continued ahead of him, were the cells.

He'd expected bars. Instead, there were rooms: some cubicle-sized, others larger—the larger ones holding groups of men, he saw as he passed. Each had a door with a barred window, and then a large barred window beside the door. He kept shuffling forward, waiting for the guard to direct him to whichever of these was going to be his temporary home. There had to be toilets in these rooms, though he wondered if, under these conditions, he'd be capable of using one.

"Hey!"

Anthony jumped at the sound of a short, hairy man pounding the glass of a cell window at his immediate left. "Gringo! Hey! Take his keys, get me out of here, take his keys!"

"Keep walking," the guard said tonelessly.

As Anthony neared the end of the hall with still no direction to stop, he slowed and looked over his shoulder. The guard pointed to a door just ahead, on the wall in front of him. Anthony went that way.

Inside the doorway was a smaller version of the first room. There was only one Plexiglas teller window here, in which there was a single, golf-ball-sized hole. "Stand on the line," the guard said.

Anthony took his spot on another battered tape line, and the man behind the glass began speaking. Anthony caught the word "magistrate," and "serious sexual offense," and ". . . corrupting young girls?" but couldn't hear clearly. He stepped closer to the glass and leaned toward it.

The presumed magistrate jerked backward and shouted, "Get the fuck away from that window!"

"Stay on the line!" the guard said, yanking Anthony's shoulder.

"Jesus!" Anthony nearly toppled backward. He was horrified to feel tears threatening. "Sorry! I'm sorry, I couldn't hear him." His heart pounded his ribs as if it, like he, wanted out, wanted to run fast and far and never look back.

The magistrate scowled and continued, louder this time, "As you have no priors, I'm going to waive your bail, on your promise to stay away from Ms. Wilkes and report to the court as directed." He didn't wait for Anthony to promise before passing some rolled sheets of paper through the hole and nodding his dismissal to the guard.

"Let's go," the guard said, handing the papers to Anthony.

They left the room and entered a short hallway, then went to a door that clattered open the way the first had done. Anthony shuffled forward, the guard stepped into the chamber beside him, then the door closed behind them with a bang. The guard handed him the bag with his belongings. "You can have these back," he said, and as soon as Anthony had fished out the contents and put his phone and wallet back into his pockets, the door in front of him opened onto a small stoop and an empty parking lot.

The guard said, *"Sayonara,"* and motioned Anthony forward, outside into the harsh circle of a glaring sodium light, and then the door clanked closed behind him.

Anthony stood there stunned, shoelaces and belt dangling from his hands, his bladder now painfully full. That was it? A mug shot, fingerprinting, a lecture from a crazed man, and now out on the street? He was free to go?

It took a minute for his comprehension to catch up to his experience. The magistrate had said no bail, okay, right, good. The papers—he squinted at the top one, scanned it; it appeared to be his arrest warrant—maybe the papers would help him get straight with this. His offense was listed as something called DISSEM MTRL/PERFORM HARMFL MIN. What the hell was that supposed to mean? He read it again but the jumble of abbreviations remained unclear. In the box below this was THE STATE OF NORTH CAROLINA VS. and then his name and address and phone number, his race, his sex, his birth date, his driver's license number. He read this several times and thought, *Seriously?* The State versus him? Despite the document in his hands and despite the experience he'd just endured, he was having trouble believing that after the police had taken Amelia's statement and his own, after they knew she'd invited him to send her the photos, they'd decided that he'd committed a crime against her. Her name was listed below his info, at the bottom in a box that asked for the "*Names & Addresses Of Witnesses (Including Counties & Telephone Nos.)*." Only her name appeared.

The rest of the form consisted primarily of a large white box in which his "offense(s)" was described in embarrassing detail—and in a box at the left, he saw he was said to be "*In Violation Of* G.S. 14-190.15."

Maybe all this was just a technicality, something along the lines of a convenience store selling cigarettes to someone under eighteen. At the far left bottom of the page, a box was marked, showing that his was a *Misdemeanor Offense Which Requires Fingerprinting Per Fingerprint Plan*—and what was up with the capitalizing-every-word thing, anyway? Could a friggin' form sound more self-important?

A misdemeanor—that was good. Still, the whole thing was bogus. What he'd done—whatever the abbreviations meant, exactly—was "HARMFL," right. Then teachers ought to get arrested for taking students to art museums where they'd see sculptures of naked adults. His mother should be arrested for letting him page through her coffee-table books on Renaissance art—and imprisoned for life for taking him to the Louvre when he was only fifteen. He folded the warrant, and the other form—a CONDITIONS OF RELEASE AND RELEASE ORDER—into a tight square and pushed it into his pocket.

The night air was damp, cold on his bare arms, and he shivered as he slipped his belt back into its loops and then stepped farther into the shadows to relieve himself. This, he thought as he stood close to the building feeling shameful and desperate, must be how the homeless felt. Through volunteering for Habitat, he knew guys who'd suffered a lot more than one aberrant evening out in the cold, peeing furtively against a fence or wall or tree; he tried to consider himself lucky.

He finished and moved away from the wall, then crouched down to lace his shoes. There was so little light that the black laces were almost indistinguishable from the black eyelets. His fingers trembled, making the task stupidly difficult, but he kept at it, pushing the lace through every eyelet, making sure to get the ends even, then pulling the lace snug and tying the two ends before doing the other shoe.

There. Done. He stood, drew a deep breath, let it out. Taking his phone from his pocket, he started walking toward the sound of passing cars. At the corner of the building, he stopped to see who had called. His boss, Eric. Eric again. Two of his other friends. His mother, three times—she'd left a message, too, which he expected had to do with wondering how he'd gotten to work without his car.

And that was it. Nothing from Amelia, damn. Obviously her parents had taken away her phone—gotta keep her away from the criminal, after all. The sex offender.

He walked a block, then another, then stopped a portly, fiftyish man in a suit to ask which direction was north.

"North?" the man said, as if the word was unfamiliar.

"Yeah, like, toward Wake Forest."

The man paused, assessing what he saw: presumably a shell-shocked but decent-looking young man in a dress shirt, gray pants, black shoes. "Are you lost? Can I call someone for you, or—"

"No. No, I'm just . . . I have a phone." He took it out and held it up to prove it. "But thanks."

"Okay, well. Hmm. I think it's that way." The man pointed and Anthony nodded his thanks, crossing the street in the indicated direction before the man ID'd him as someone who'd obviously just left jail. Or maybe it was too late. Maybe the stench of the holding cells clung to him. Maybe the man could smell the annoyance, disbelief, fear, and anger that Anthony imagined oozed from his pores right now, recognized it as being common to criminals. Maybe the guy thought he'd just escaped.

He broke into a jog, then a run, moving along the darkened sidewalks, seeing few pedestrians and ignoring the ones who swiveled as he passed them, running until he felt clearer, less contaminated. When he finally stopped, he leaned over, hands on knees, to catch his breath, and then when he thought he'd sound normal again, he called his mother.

"Hey, it's me. I'm in downtown Raleigh and I need a ride. Can you come pick me up? I'll explain everything when you get here."

8

KIM WINTER HAD COME TO PARENTHOOD LATER THAN A LOT of women she knew, and with more ambivalence than most of her friends would have guessed. Every sane person was ambivalent about parenthood, but Kim's fear and uncertainty were of a different nature because, to begin with, she'd persuaded her then-husband to do it based on little more than a whim.

At thirty, she'd been going about her life happily enough, married five years but childless by choice, and when the younger teachers around her talked in the faculty lounge about ticking biological clocks, Kim talked about summers spent trekking through Wyoming, Spain, Costa Rica, Nepal; her lazy Sunday mornings with nothing more pressing than brewing tea and reading *The New York Times;* the luxury of uninterrupted sex—of uninterrupted sleep, for that matter. She'd gotten to this age without having any urge to gestate, birth, feed, diaper, or dress another living being. There'd been no ticking for her yet, and, imagining that at thirty she was mature and wise, she didn't expect that there would be.

Her life was full and satisfying. She'd been in love with art and books and culture—French culture in particular—since she was a teenager, and had turned that love into a teaching career so that she could both continue to be surrounded by her passions, and pass them on to others. She had a different, indulgent sort of love for Santos, who'd been born in Spain and had such captivating looks and personality that she'd willingly disregarded the downside of having such a man as a spouse. His joie de vivre was a pleasure, yes, and an asset, especially when they socialized; everyone loved him. However, that *joie* also led him to charm his way out of doing house-work, led him to spend most of their extra money in coffee shops and trendy bars where he and his friends congregated most nights—but *that* led him to make up for his weaknesses with cham-pagne and favors she blushed to mention to her friends later. They spent their free time traveling, or in museums and galleries and parks, or driving her rust-dappled Saab convertible around the countryside, finding cheap antiques or just letting the wind infuse them with the scents of flowering honeysuckle and pine.

As far as she could tell—and her instincts and experiences had proved reliable so far—the so-called biological clock was a myth, something women claimed they heard when they needed a way to get their husbands off the fence about having kids. Santos was child enough for her, she didn't need actual children. Her life was perfect just the way it was. Yes, she had a lonely moment every now and then, an empty hour when, after viewing Mary Cassatt's winsome mother-and-child paintings, say, she allowed herself to ponder questions of purpose and mortality and leaving at least a small mark behind, even if just to say "I was here." Those times were limited, though, and she didn't think they should outweigh all the benefits she took from living her life for herself. She was a teacher, after all; she was making a contribution.

Then, on the evening of her thirty-first birthday, after several bottles of wine shared with their best friends, Kim and Santos were walking along Ithaca's Commons. The sun was nearly gone, the western sky glowing a deep orange-pink that saturated the brick storefronts. They came to a furniture shop, where a washstand caught Kim's eye. She stopped, taking a closer look. An antique; walnut; 1940s, she guessed. It had a short spindle rail running along its front: a changing table, she realized suddenly.

"Someone had to have retrofitted that," she said, pointing.

"Mm. I like the poker table. And look—that little one's got a chessboard carved into it. Can you see a price tag?"

She was still looking at the washstand. The walnut gleamed, and she yearned to stroke it. Those drawers, with their pewter half-moon pulls, they'd be ideal for storing diapers and those omnipresent tubs of wipes she saw at friends' homes and in diaper bags. She imagined a little chubby buddha of a baby, a gummy grin, hands and feet waving in the air, a gurgle, a coo.

"I want one," she said.

"Yeah? And we could get one of those hand-carved wood sets. Or glass? Crystal? Would that be too expensive?"

"What?"

"Chess pieces. Or did you mean you want the poker table?"

Kim started laughing then, so hard that she had to lean over and brace her hands on her knees to catch her breath.

"I should have cut you off sooner," Santos said, shaking his head and laughing, too, as if whatever she had was contagious.

She chuckled all the way back to their late-eighteen-hundreds Tudor, a quirky little house they'd bought for a song and had spent the last few years renovating and furnishing with inexpensive original art and antiques she'd restored herself. A house, she often said, for grown-ups.

When they got inside, she set her purse and gift bags on the foyer table and then headed up the stairs, Santos trailing behind her. At the top, she turned toward the smallest of their three bedrooms, the one that went mostly unused.

"Where you going? Come on," Santos said, pulling her by the hand toward the master bedroom.

"Just a minute," she told him, freeing her hand and turning again toward the spare room. "I want to look at something."

He stood behind her and, with his mouth against her neck and his hands sliding up her waist to her breasts, said, "I've got something for you to look at."

"Hold on." She pulled away and went into the room. "I just want to . . ."

The bedroom held three chairs she'd been meaning to refinish, some artwork made by past students of hers that, while not to her taste or really worthy of display, she'd had trouble parting with, and several boxes of Spanish tiles hand-painted by Santos's cousins and shipped from Spain by his mother, who was unconcerned when Kim explained that the tiles, though lovely, and such a thoughtful gift, really didn't suit their décor. "So we re-*décor*-ate when I come to see *bebé*," his mother replied, also unconcerned that no *bebé* was on the way, nor even planned.

But that washstand . . . Wouldn't it look perfect there to the left of the windows? And those tiles, with their vibrant blues and reds and golds, wouldn't they delight a baby's eyes? Shaking her head at her foolishness, Kim went to join Santos, who then distracted her completely.

For three days, Kim did her best to put the matter out of her mind, and she mentioned it to no one, not even Santos. So she'd imagined she wanted a baby. It was meaningless. It was the wine. On the fourth day, at dusk, she went into the spare bedroom and stood there again, wondering, did anyone build cribs from walnut? She wanted the crib to be walnut, with spindle rails to match the washstand.

On the fifth day after her birthday, she made detailed lists of pros and cons (the cons being far more numerous) that did nothing to diminish her desire, then returned to the Commons, found the furniture shop, and bought the washstand. So *this*, this illogical, unreasonable craving, was what other women felt, what motivated so many of them to "forget" to take their pills or use other birth control, to browse the infant-clothing sections and baby food aisles long before there was any need, to sit in the teachers' lounge talking about ovulation the way men talked sports. Now she understood.

A day later, noting that she was, in fact, smack in the middle of her menstrual cycle, she made Santos's favorite dinner and poured him some wine, and told him she thought it was time they bring a "new little Santos" into the world. She'd expected an argument, or at least a little hesitancy, but he'd said, "Yeah? That's what you want?"

"That's what I want."

He'd shrugged and smiled as if to say he was powerless to resist the woman he loved. "Sounds like fun. Let's get started."

Getting pregnant had taken three months; plenty of time for them to rethink their decision—if you could call it a decision. It felt to her rather like the universe had shifted slightly, so slightly that the only evidences of it were things like the magnetic pull of polished walnut gleaming in the setting sunlight, things you might not even notice if you hadn't had several glasses of wine and your first over-thirty birthday. Three months, during which they had a lot of what she called procreational sex that she and Santos partnered with a wine-tasting endeavor. She was sorry to see that end when she found out she was, finally, with child.

With child. Those two words had come to define her life from the moment of confirmation until *this* moment, the one in downtown Raleigh almost nineteen years later, when Anthony sat next to her in her car and said, "So here's the thing: I'm in some trouble."

During her pregnancy, she'd been outwardly confident, wearing a calm, serene mask for the benefit of her fellow teachers and her friends, while with each passing, expanding month her confidence in Santos's readiness decreased proportionally. He was living his life as if nothing had changed or would change, as if her swelling middle would never become more than a novelty. Still, she wasn't panicking; other women's husbands behaved similarly and ultimately "came around" when they had to. So would Santos.

And then he bailed. How would she face the world now, abandoned at the worst possible time as if she, in her cranky whale-state, had driven her husband away? How would she raise a son on her own? Each day throughout the next week she intended to buck up and tell her friends, her parents, her brother. Each day, she couldn't bring herself to eat or get dressed or pick up the phone—suppose Santos changed his mind? But when mild contractions began and she was sure he wasn't coming back, she went to her mother for confession and comfort, and was assured, perhaps falsely, that no two people could offer a child more than Kim would provide herself.

Bless her mother; she'd come to Kim's emotional rescue so many times. In the car now, hearing Anthony's startling words, Kim thought she might need her mother's calming influence again very soon.

"Who's pregnant?" Kim said, as if the answer wasn't obvious. Then again, she didn't want to presume.

Anthony shook his head. "It isn't that."

"What, then?" She'd picked him up at a gas station at the far end of Capital Boulevard, a part of town she wouldn't ordinarily feel safe stopping in. What had he gotten involved with? Drugs? Gangs? Neither seemed likely. She'd know if he was into any of that—but then wasn't that what most parents said?

He braced his hands on the dashboard and hung his head for a moment, then said, "I got arrested. Earlier. They let me go without bail."

"What?" she said, her voice shriller than she expected. "Arrested?" The possibility had not occurred to her, not this night, and not ever. She'd raised him to question authority, yes, but not by breaking the law. She said, "What happened? Why—"

"Okay, it's really lame, but Amelia . . ." He sighed heavily. "That is . . . This is stupid, okay, but, what happened was, I took some pictures of myself, and I sent them to her, and her parents must have found them and freaked."

"Pictures? How would that get you arrested?"

When he didn't answer immediately, when she saw the tight line of his mouth, lips compressed, eyes wide and nervous, the answer dawned on her. She said, "Pictures that aren't . . . appropriate. That's what you're saying."

He nodded.

"Oh Jesus." She pressed her fist to her mouth for a moment, then said, "Anthony, what were you *thinking*?"

"That they would be just between her and me. It's none of her parents' business."

"None of their business?" she said, her voice rising. "You can't really think that."

"She's almost eighteen."

"She's their *daughter*—and not exactly a girl you'd expect would have pictures of—" She stopped herself, not wanting to imagine the details. "Of *course* they're upset."

"Oh, nice," Anthony said, crossing his arms over his chest. "*Now* you want to defend them? Now that they've screwed me over, you're suddenly all parental?"

"What?"

"Where was all this . . . all this *sympathy* for them when you were going along with keeping our secret?"

Kim stared. Oh God, he was right. Where was her sympathy? Where were her priorities? But she knew: they'd been tied up with her son, and her own heart, which was now twisting into a confused knot.

Anthony seemed smaller, sitting here next to her, his limbs drawn in, his shoulders hunched, his lower lip protruding a little, the way it used to whenever he was on the verge of tears. She couldn't remember when she'd last seen him cry, seen him even on the verge. He was no longer her little boy, no longer a boy at all. He was a young man who could, and had, shared who knew how many kinds of intimacies with a young woman who was no longer her parents' little girl. How natural this progress was, and yet how cruel it seemed. Why couldn't they stay young and innocent always?

"Are you okay?"

"The magistrate made it out like I'm a *rapist*," he spat. "A 'serious sexual offense,'" he said mockingly. "Like it doesn't even matter that Amelia asked me to send the pictures—she told the cops she asked for them, before they even talked to me."

"When did all this happen—the questioning, I mean. Was this why she didn't come back to school?" Anthony nodded. Kim went on, "She *asked* you to, really?" About this, Kim was surprised. Amelia? If ever there'd been a teenaged girl who wasn't ruled entirely by her hormones, who appeared to be infused with all the good sense most of her peers lacked, Amelia was the one.

"Yes, really, and I have pictures of her, too, okay? God, everyone's acting like we made a porn flick and screened it in the gym."

"Can I see that?" Kim asked, pointing at his release order. He handed it to her, and she switched on the dome light and put her glasses on to read it. It was a confusing fill-in-the-blanks form that revealed little beyond the charge and a hearing date that was only nine days away. She looked up at her son, who was biting a hangnail. "What are you supposed to do to prepare? Do you need a lawyer? What did they tell you?"

"They didn't tell me anything."

"They must have," she said, reading the document again, front and back, and coming up with nothing more than she had the first time. "What does this mean? What happens in court?"

"Mom, I don't know. It was . . ." He turned toward the window. She could see his face, a ghostly reflection on the window glass. "They handcuffed me and pushed me around, and nobody would answer my questions—like I was some kind of lowlife. It was bullshit."

She took his hand and squeezed it, though whether she was giving or receiving reassurance she wouldn't have been able to say. "Okay, well, look: we'll figure it out. We'll make some calls, get some answers. . . ."

Anthony rubbed his face, then reached for the dome light's switch and turned it off. "Okay, but right now, let's just go home."

"Are you hungry? We could stop, or—"

"Home," he repeated, a hairline crack in his voice that made Kim wish he could have stayed in Neverland just a little while longer—or why not forever? It wasn't about the innocence so much as the safety of youth, protection from adult urges and adult consequences. Gone now.

Kim spent the twenty-minute drive considering ways to handle the situation, while Anthony spent it staring out the window, saying nothing. If Kim had to guess, she'd say it was likely that Amelia's parents had pulled every plug where communicating with Anthony was concerned, and she couldn't blame them if they had. Bringing in the police, though? Having Anthony arrested? How could they possibly think that had been the best response? Granted, she hadn't raised a daughter, and granted, girls came with added complications, such as possible pregnancies and the problems that then followed. Even with all of that, though, and even considering Amelia's particular potential and her parents' expectations, Kim could not see how they could respond to the discovery of photos of someone they knew—even if those photos were indecent—by calling the police first.

At home, Anthony headed straight upstairs. "I gotta change clothes . . . and I need to call Eric," he said.

"Sure, but listen—"

He paused on the stairs and leaned over the banister to look at her. "Yeah?"

"It might be wise to hedge a little on why you weren't at work. Food poisoning would be a good excuse for being unable to call."

"I don't see what the big deal is—I didn't do anything wrong, so why not talk about it?"

"Honey, I know you see it that way . . . and I'm sure Eric and a lot of other people would, too. But—"

"But I'm supposed to worry about what closed-minded, uptight people will think of me if they hear? You're the one who's always saying we have to fight ignorance."

"And we do. We do. This, though—you have a lot at stake right now. You need recommendations and references for scholarship applications, so why give people a reason to decline?"

"Anybody who knows me—"

"Why take the chance?" she insisted, feeling like a hypocrite. How different her ideology had become now that her own son's future was on the line. She said, "We have to weigh cost and benefit."

"Fine," he said. "I get it. But it's complete bullshit."

"I'm going to call Amelia's parents. Maybe . . . I don't know, they probably reacted without thinking. Maybe we can undo this and, well, handle the whole situation like grown-ups. I mean, if you two are truly serious about your plans—"

"We are. You know we are."

"Then the Wilkeses deserve the opportunity to get on board, don't you think?" As she said the words, she couldn't fail to note the irony that only *now* was she spouting this high-minded ideal, when it would have been far better for all of them if she'd taken this position in the first place. She should have insisted that they not go behind the Wilkeses backs. How ironic that only now, when her one and only son, her only child, was facing trouble, was she questioning whether keeping the kids' secret had been the right choice. Thinking this, she felt small.

Anthony came back down a few stairs. "If we thought they would get on board, we'd have told them right away. You see how they are."

"They had a shock, honey—and I'm not taking sides, saying this. It's a fact. Finding pictures like that isn't an ideal way to learn about some boy's relationship with their daughter. Give them a chance. I'm sure they'll be more rational now that some time has passed."

"Oh really? Then why isn't she answering her phone? I know why, and so do you."

"Be patient. Parents can be slow about these kinds of things."

"Hers are glacial about everything." He took the jail paperwork from his pocket and said, "I'm gonna go see how screwed I am," then went off to his room, presumably to research the offense online.

Kim put up water for chamomile tea and sat down at the kitchen table, where she'd been grading French assignments before Anthony's call. What to say to Amelia's parents? They'd met—twice now—which should make things a little easier. Though maybe not, since they clearly elected not to contact her when the storm blew in. And, she supposed, it wasn't as though the kids were six-year-olds who, during a playdate, had broken a lamp or something and then hidden the evidence. Amelia, their baby, had photographs of a naked young man—had them on purpose, had asked to have them. If Amelia's parents were as conservative and protective as they appeared to be, and as uninformed as the kids (and she, Kim) had intended to keep them, she could hardly expect their reaction to have been any different than it was.

There, good. She'd reasoned her way into their point of view, which would make talking with them easier. Thank God she'd had a lot of practice at this kind of thing—dealing with unhappy parents—over the years.

With her mug of tea at hand, Kim looked up Amelia's parents' contact info and dialed their home number. As prepared as she thought she was, her heart was behaving otherwise. There was a difference in making such a call as this one in the role of mother, rather than teacher, whether her brain wanted to think so or not.

A man's gruff voice said, "Wilkes residence."

"Hello. I'm calling for Mr. or Mrs. Wilkes. This is Kim Winter."

She heard a snort, then, "Guess you know about the trouble your boy's got into."

His tone rankled her. "That's why I'm calling, yes. Is this a good time to talk?"

"Not unless you're calling to say he's been locked up or you've had him castrated."

"Mr. Wilkes, I know you're angry," she said, struggling to maintain her "teacher voice" despite his hostility, "but really, that's not called for."

"I'll tell you what's not called for: your son putting perverted ideas into my daughter's head the way he's done. I don't know what sorts of standards you single-mom types have, but good families teach their sons to respect a young lady, not corrupt her—*prey* on her like . . . like she's some common little whore who'd welcome that kind of thing." His voice cracked as he spoke. He cleared his throat, then added, "Don't think William Braddock isn't goin' to hear about this. 'Fact, I'm fixin' to call him right now."

Kim opened her mouth to reply and heard the dial tone buzzing in her ear. She dialed him back and got his voice mail. He really was calling William. She tried William's phone, and that call went straight to voice mail as well.

"Shit," she said, imagining what Harlan Wilkes must be telling him. The man was *crazy*. He hadn't even given her a chance to speak. She tried his number again. Again, she got no answer.

Without giving in to the anger and self-doubt she knew would swamp her if she thought too much about what had just happened, she looked up Sheri Wilkes's cell number, and dialed it.

"Hello?" a woman said, in the soft, Southern tones Kim recognized as Amelia's mother's.

"Mrs. Wilkes, this is Kim Winter. Maybe you heard, I just tried speaking with your husband—"

"Would you mind holding just one minute?"

"Oh, all right, sure."

Kim waited, counting backwards from ten and breathing deeply as she did it. Sheri Wilkes returned at three, saying, "Thank you so much. I'm sorry to keep you waiting. I needed to find a quiet place to talk."

"I understand. So then, did you hear the conversation?"

"As a matter of fact, yes, I did, and let me apologize for my husband. He isn't really himself just now."

"I understand," Kim said again, an overstatement. His anger and dismay, yes. His behavior, no. She continued, "As I told Anthony, this must be very surprising and stressful for you and Mr. Wilkes. But I'd hoped we could have a conversation about it, all of us, maybe, and . . . and I hope set things right."

There was a short pause, and then Sheri Wilkes said, "Ms. Winter, if there was a way . . . I came home after Harlan had already contacted the authorities. To be plain with you, I thought he might have jumped the gun—though let me stress that I'm not happy about this either, not a bit."

"Of course not. When our children keep secrets—"

"But he has his reasons, which I support."

Kim bit back the reply she'd have liked to give, a remark about thinking for oneself, and said instead, "Why don't we all sit down tomorrow sometime and talk about all of this. The kids can explain their plans, and—"

"Plans?"

"Well, what they intend, for after graduation—"

"Ms. Winter, even if I was inclined, you don't know my husband. As far as he's concerned, your son is . . . well, let me just say it would be best"—and she stressed *best* in a way that Kim knew meant *required*—"for your son not to have any contact with our daughter in the future."

"Have you talked to Amelia about any of this? You do know that she and Anthony are, well, they're in love." Her embarrassed laugh came out sounding more like a hiccup. "I know they're young, but when you see them together—"

"How long have you known about this?" Sheri Wilkes said.

Oh hell, Kim thought, bringing her hand to her mouth. "Mrs. Wilkes, my son and I, we're very close. I raised him on my own; my ex-husband has never been involved. We talk about everything that affects him. And I'm sorry I didn't . . . I'm sorry you didn't know about them before now. But the fact of the matter is that regardless of how you or I or your husband feels about it all, they're a pair of very mature, very determined young adults who are planning a future together. I think we should try to respect that."

Sheri Wilkes sighed. "That may all be as you say. My husband, though, is of the view that your son has had . . . undue influence over Amelia. She hasn't had much experience with boys."

So far as you know, Kim thought, not ungenerously. She said, "With due respect, he's mistaken. Anthony is not that kind of person."

"I'm sorry, Ms. Winter. I'm sure it will be hard for him but, really, it'd be best if you tell him to stay away from Amelia. Her father has already made it clear to her that she won't be seeing him again. Thank you so much for your call."

So that was it? Kim dropped her phone onto the table, stunned at how these people had shut her down so quickly, with almost no consideration at all.

She'd hardly had time to breathe the deep, calming breath she'd learned in yoga, when her phone rang. William. Kim picked up the phone, her thumb moving automatically to the TALK button, while her brain protested the spinning ride she'd been thrown onto. *Stop now, I want to get off.* But it was only just beginning.

Tuesday morning, Kim modified Sheri Wilkes's message before passing it on to Anthony. "Amelia won't be able to see you for a while," she told him, standing in his bedroom doorway at ten after six.

Anthony rolled over and looked up from his bed. His dark expression said what she knew he wouldn't articulate, at least to her (*Fuck that*), so she tacked on a warning. "You'll earn a lot more respect by being cooperative, you know. Her father's a little hot-headed. Let him cool down." Then she broke the worst of the news. "I spoke to Mr. Braddock last night—Harlan Wilkes called him—and Amelia's going to be out of school for a while."

Anthony sat up, alarmed. "What?"

"I don't know the details."

"They can't take her out of school," he said. "That'll screw up everything!"

"Anthony. Let it be for now. Let's focus on you and this court business. I'll be calling some lawyers today to see what you're supposed to do."

"I'm supposed to meet Amelia in the parking lot before class. And then I'm supposed to eat lunch with her. We're supposed to sit together in English, and talk about a book that illuminates the bullshit teens have to deal with." He was nearly spitting the words.

"Get dressed," Kim said. "You'll be late."

He grabbed a T-shirt from a chair-back and pulled it on. Calming down, he said, "Just so you know, I looked up the charge. It's a misdemeanor, which is good, but apparently it's the worst kind."

"Meaning?"

"Probably not jail time, since this is my first arrest."

Kim considered the words *jail* and *arrest* and how out of context they were, coming from him. She really hadn't had enough caffeine for any of this. She said, "Well, that's something, I guess. But we won't let it come to that anyway, if we can help it. We'll get it all straightened out."

Anthony, though he looked at her skeptically, didn't reply.

9

Amelia's alarm, a gentle Eastern chime, began rousing her at five-fifteen. In the predawn darkness, before wakeful recollection took hold, she lay beneath her smooth sheets and the lightweight, down-filled comforter the housekeeper laid on her bed spring and fall, smiling at the remnants of a dream. She'd been onstage with Anthony, footlights shining upon them, warming them the way sunshine would. . . . He was holding her against him, telling her something important about flowers, and snow. She tried to keep hold of the dream . . . it faded, though, as the alarm sang on and her memory of last night's troubles filled the space the dream had occupied.

She pushed her feet out the side of the covers, letting the room's cool air in, then swung her legs over the bedside and got up. In the bathroom, she pulled her hair into a thick ponytail and put her contacts in. Then she began the other part of her morning routine, the part she had begun originally at age five and been officially excused from three years ago, but which she continued on her own, as insur-

ance against the stutter's returning like a cancer that chemotherapy
had missed.

She began with a low, breathy sort of warm-up song, choosing,
today, a C scale. She heard her speech pathologist's voice coaching
her, *Long A sound,* and she sang, "aaayyyy," *long O,* "ohhhhhh," *long E,*
"eeeeee," *long I,* "ahyhe," *long U sound,* "you-u-u-u." *Again.* She went
through her litany twice more, then began the consonants exercise:
"Bat, pat, dot, tot, kit, git. Bit, pit, dock, talk, kale, gale." Though it
all came easily now, the shadow of the affliction cast a pall that, so
far, refused to leave her for long.

Usually she'd go online to check the weather before heading out
for her run; usually, she had a smartphone. Today, she opened the
window to gauge the temperature, then got dressed in running
pants, sports bra, tank top, and a long-sleeved shirt. She tucked her
pewter charm on its leather string into her tank top and then, shoes
in hand, left her room, heading for the main stairway, and was surprised to see lights burning in the wide front hall and then, as she
went down the broad, winding staircase, lights on in the living
room and conservatory, too—where her parents were seated, already showered and dressed, and with a platter of ham biscuits waiting on the coffee table in front of them.

They looked up as Amelia came into the doorway. Their faces
were calm, placid even. Her mother held a mug in both hands and
was blowing into it to cool its contents. Steam leapt up and around
her mother's properly made-up face, done with the most flattering
foundation color, the softest pale powder, the finest eyeliner, mas-
cara, and the most modest touch of blush in the slight caverns of her
cheeks. Rosy lipstick complemented her silk sweater, and her man-
icured nails matched both. She was so pretty, so pulled-together, so
perfect. So careful.

Her mother's family, the Kerrs, were furniture makers who'd
opened a factory in High Point shortly after the Civil War. They
weren't wealthy in the way that so many people were these days;
furniture-building made a man a living, not a fortune, her grand-

father was known to say. They lived well, which was to say that the kids were always dressed right for the weather, always had hot suppers, didn't have to work in the factory, and mostly didn't die from the diseases that used to be prevalent: polio, measles, diphtheria. The Kerrs were as sturdy, upright, and high quality as the ladder-back chairs they made. Her grandfather prided himself on his broad-mindedness: if you worked hard and did right, it didn't matter who your people were or where you'd gotten your start. To him, Amelia's father was a hero, one who had apparently rescued her mother from the lonely single life she'd been leading. "She's lucky you'd have her," her grandfather sometimes said, patting her father on the back.

That lucky woman was the one sitting here now. Amelia preferred the mother she sometimes found on Saturday mornings lounging in the sunroom with the *News & Observer* spread about on the floor around her green toile-covered chaise. The robed, tousled, relaxed-looking woman who knew she had no immediate task ahead of her, no audience, no impending appearance at a Women's Club function or Ravenswood fund-raiser or Helping Hand Mission activity or church coffee-service. Somewhere behind the perfect makeup and silk sweater and camel-colored wool slacks that Amelia saw before her was that Saturday mother, the woman Amelia wished to know better. Because even on Saturdays, her mother was careful with her words, measured, as if she, too, had once fought off a stutter—though Amelia knew that wasn't the case.

Her father clapped his hands once and stood up.

" 'Mornin', Ladybug."

"What's going on?" Amelia asked, holding her running shoes to her chest as if they were a shield.

"Momma made us some breakfast, wasn't that good of her? We thought we'd have a bite to eat together and talk some. Last night . . . well, I was upset, plain and simple. Thought maybe we'd try this again."

"Let me get you some juice," her mother said, standing.

"No thanks. I really need to get going so I'm not late for school."

"Couldn't you skip the run this morning?" her father asked. He looked so hopeful and apologetic that she softened toward him. Maybe he'd reconsidered his actions and was going to clear Anthony after all.

"I'll shorten it," she said.

Her mother walked past her and paused for the slightest beat, laying her hand on Amelia's shoulder as she passed. "I'll get your juice," she said.

Amelia set her shoes on the rug and sat down in the upholstered chair nearest the piano, a Steinway Parlor Grand that their house-keeper kept polished as though her life depended on guests being able to see their reflection in the glossy black surface. Her father sat with his elbows on his knees and his hands clasped in front of him, the way he often did while watching football. She waited for him to say something, but he was apparently waiting for her mother's return.

"Here we go," her mother said, handing her a glass of orange juice. Then she took a small china plate and set a biscuit on it, and passed it to Amelia's father.

"Thanks, hon," he said. "These sure do look good."

"Amelia?"

"No, Momma, I'm not hungry, thanks."

Her mother's smile was pained. Amelia's throat tightened. They did so much for her, and she'd let them down, disrespected them by going behind their backs. Even now, they didn't know how bad it was, how she'd hidden so much more from them than photographs.

Amelia pulled her feet up and tucked them beneath her. "Maybe I will have a biscuit," she said.

"Harlan, pass this to her."

The house was silent save for the ticking of the grandfather clock in the front hall. The faint sound of geese honking in flight grew loud, then louder, and then receded, and still no one spoke.

"What your momma and I want to know first," her father finally said, "is the straight story about the Winter boy."

"The straight story?"

"You told me one thing, then told the police another, and what we need to know is the truth. Why are you covering for him? Neither of us believes that you're the kind to go asking a boy for naked pictures just for sport."

"Why not? Because I get good grades? Because I'm always in by curfew?" She spoke the questions softly, gently. "I'm practically an adult, you know."

"Every kid your age thinks so," her father said. "But no, it's not your grades or your good behavior—"

"And it *is* good, and we appreciate that so much," her mother added.

"It's that we know the kind of person you are," her father finished. Despite Amelia's thoughts to the contrary last night, they did know her, at least well enough to know she wasn't the kind to ask for such pictures from any friend—let alone from a new acquaintance, which she knew other girls at school had done.

Her father continued, "So I have to think you never asked him to send them at all. Which means you're hiding the truth—and we need to know why."

Amelia pulled off one sock and began picking at a toenail. She said, "You're right; I have been hiding the truth. But," she added, looking up at her parents, "I've also been telling it. I did ask him for the pictures. Just not for the reasons I said."

Her father put his plate down. "Now, come on—"

"I'll explain," she said, drawing a breath. Here, finally, was her chance to tell all. "He's . . . Okay, so, we met last year at school, when we did *As You Like It*. Remember, he was Orlando? And I thought he was so talented and good-looking, and he thought the same about me, and, well, we started going out."

"'Going out,'" her father said, mimicking her tone. "You started 'going out' with a boy, without telling us."

Amelia gave a small shrug that said, *What else could I do?* "You're always talking about the right kind of guy for me—but what you want's not what I want. I knew you'd reject Anthony without even knowing him—and this, the way you've reacted, the way you're accusing him and ignoring what I keep telling you? This proves it."

Neither of her parents responded right away. They peered at her, they looked at each other, her mother picked invisible lint from the front of her sweater. Amelia wondered if they hadn't drugged themselves with tranquilizers.

"What else?" her father asked.

"Well, that's pretty much the whole story."

"Those pictures, though . . . He did send 'em to you. And what you said, about asking him to, that's just you being nice, trying to protect him."

Amelia felt a flush rising from her collar. "No . . . That is, it's complicated. I took some, he took some—I'm not a child, Daddy. In seven more months I'll be on my own."

"Is that how he's put it? Because being at college, that's not like being on your own. Not when it's your daddy's checkbook that's making it happen."

"Which is why you're not going to pay for my college," Amelia said. "And I'm not going to Duke, I'm going to NYU—that is, if I get in."

Her father's forehead wrinkled and he said, "Come again?"

"New York University, in New York City. Anthony's applied there, too."

Her mother's eyes grew very round as she said, "You applied to New York University?" Amelia looked away. She and her mother had worked together on her college applications, to Duke, and to UNC and Wake Forest and Davidson, her "back-up plan." They'd all visited the campuses together last spring.

Her father no longer looked relaxed. "And who do you imagine *is* gonna pay—not him, that's for damn sure, unless he's got a daddy somewhere with deep pockets."

"We're going to get financial aid, and apply for scholarships, and we'll work, too—maybe not on Broadway at first, but there're lots of other paying theatre jobs, and, you know, regular kinds of jobs too."

"And live where?" her mother asked.

"In an apartment, off-campus—the school has a housing office just for off-campus, and we probably would share a place with some other students, to make it more affordable."

Her father said, "So this is what the two of you have cooked up, is it?"

Amelia nodded.

"And what was wrong with Duke—or, let me guess, he couldn't get in."

Her father's sarcastic tone put Amelia on guard. "He didn't apply," she said, trying not to take the bait. "Duke is fine, I'm sure . . . but they don't have drama, and, you know, it's not in New York. I'm sure Anthony could get in to Duke if he applied. His grades are as good as mine. But he's always known that NYU was where he'd go," she continued steadily, as if by staying calm she would calm her parents. "He wants to be a playwright and director, and he's an amazing actor—but then, you've seen him; I don't have to tell you."

"Oh, yes, without question, he is definitely a good actor."

"Harlan," her mother said, "is that tone really necessary?"

He frowned at her. "I'm trying here, but this is, well, this is . . ." He stood up, set his plate on the coffee table, ran his hands through his hair, and told Amelia, "Your momma and I talked a lot last night, because it's our jobs as responsible parents to make sure you don't turn left when you need to turn right. We've been around that whole block, so we know—I know especially—where you should and shouldn't go."

"Is this about me majoring in business?" Amelia said, praying it would all come back to their old argument, rather than to Anthony. "Because it doesn't matter where I end up going—I'm not doing it. I love *theatre*. I love *music* and dance and performing. You pursued your passions, both of you did; how can you say that I shouldn't?"

"Nobody's saying don't," he told her, beginning to pace. "But it's no *life,* Amelia, that starving-artist bit. Sure, it looks all pretty and shiny when you sit there in New York watching the plays, but all the rest of 'em, the ones who aren't stars, how do you suppose they live?"

"Like regular people—in apartments. And okay, so they don't live like this," she indicated the room and the house with the sweep of her arm, "but so what? Most people don't."

Her father stopped pacing and faced her. "You aren't 'most people,' Amelia. You think I've done what I've done for *me?* It's for you, and your mother. You do not want to live like 'most people.' Believe me—I grew up in a trailer that was already old when my *parents* were born. You want to sing and dance and act? Fine, wonderful. Do it as a hobby. Get yourself a real profession, like your mother did—and I guarantee you'll meet a terrific man who you can trust and admire, and who'll give you everything you and your children need when that time comes."

"I don't want a man to take care of me, and I don't want children, and I trust and admire Anthony," she said carefully. "He understands me. He loves what I love. He *is* what I love."

"That's not love," her father said, waving his hand dismissively. "Somebody who fills your ears with what you want to hear is a con man. We're doing you a favor by keeping you away from him."

"Keeping me away from him? Meaning what?" she challenged.

Her father held out his hand to her mother, but her mother shook her head and said, "This is not on me. You tell her."

"All right, fine, I'll be the bad guy: we're taking you out of school for now, and all the rest—computer stuff, phone, social stuff, all that will be limited and/or supervised. And no more theatre, no dance or voice lessons. That's done for the time being. You need to focus, and all that is just a distraction."

Amelia knew her mouth was hanging open, yet she was powerless to close it. They could not be serious. This had to be a joke, or some kind of perverse scare tactic.

"It might be good for you to have a break from all the . . . pressures," her mother said, her voice sounding small in the high-ceilinged room.

"Momma, I can't leave school."

"You'll have a tutor—we'll do the same as if you were injured or sick or had to work, like Elise." Amelia's classmate, Elise Vawter, was a high-fashion model who often jetted to Paris or Milan or Buenas Aires to be draped and photographed. Most of the girls hated her. There were so many ways to not fit in.

"You'd still graduate from Ravenswood," her mother added.

"My New York trip coming up—"

"Forget it," her father said.

"I *have* to go, I have an appointment at NYU. To get in, y-you have to audition."

He said, "No need. It's out, Amelia."

"You can't tell me w-where I'm going to college," Amelia said, losing her struggle to keep calm.

"I can prevent you from making a gigantic error, and that's what that school would be. We're goin' to have you see someone," her father said, "to talk about all this."

"See someone?"

"A doctor."

Amelia stood up. "No sir, I'm n-not seeing any doctor. I'm not sick, in any way—and I wasn't even upset or anxious or anything, until now." She paused, upset by her stutter and fighting the pressure in her chest that was stealing her breath. "I guess the only thing I'll have t-to tell this doctor is how upset I am about what you're doing to me, and to Anthony."

"We didn't expect you to agree with us, Ladybug. You're not thinking clearly, that's the point."

Amelia closed her eyes for a second, summoning calm, then opened them again. "Anthony Winter is an amazing human being. I have not been coerced, not by him or anybody else. You just want to think so, but guess what? I'm not the perfect, innocent little girl you want to force me to be."

"The subject is closed."

Amelia, fuming, started to put on her shoes, but her father said, "Hold up. You're not going running this morning, not unless you use the treadmill downstairs. For now, you need to be where your mother or I can keep an eye on you."

"You aren't serious," she said, tears springing to her eyes. She had a regular route through the quiet, hilly roads surrounding their neighborhood. Her pleasure in running came as much from the landscape as it did the exercise. "You don't trust me to go *running?*"

"Obviously you've been hiding things from us, so it's best we limit your opportunities for trouble."

"Harlan, let's not be—"

"I n-need to run," Amelia said, unable to stop the tears, her fortitude crumbling under this additional insult. "I *need* to. If I don't, I'll . . ."

"Honey," her mother said, putting an arm around her. "Let's all just calm down. It's going to be fine—"

"It isn't," Amelia said, pulling away and backing out of the room, into the front hall. "Anthony is my best friend. Everything I want to do with my life includes him. Why do you want to ruin it this way?"

"Ruin?" her father said indignantly, following her. "My job—our job—is to protect you, which right now means from yourself *and* him, until you get right about things again. Everything was fine and on track until you met this boy. Before you met him, we knew who you were."

"My life started when I met him," she said, before she turned and crossed the hall to the wide, winding stairway of this ridiculous home that had now become her prison.

If you were to poll Amelia's close friends with this fill-in-the-blank statement, "Amelia Wilkes is many things, but she is mostly _____," answers would vary, but all would be synonyms for *de-*

termined. Amelia was the toddler who, with the towering bars of her oak crib keeping her from her beloved stuffed giraffe, piled her pillows and comforter and less-loved animals and climbed them so that she could get a leg over the rail. She was the first-grader who circulated a petition to get the school to add a second playground water fountain (the boys often bullied the girls to the back of the line, little silent Amelia in particular). In response to her dance teacher's warning that she'd better find a way to keep her blossoming curves at bay, she began running and, at age thirteen, set a new all-school record for the mile, then went on to place third in state competition. Amelia, at sixteen, raised more money than any other North Carolina high-school student in a Change for Change campaign, winning a trip to Washington, D.C., and write-ups in all the metro North Carolina newspapers. She worked hard at her studies, each high mark a defense against low self-esteem.

That her parents saw great potential in her was no surprise, and, if Amelia thought about it objectively, she appreciated their confidence. She valued their support. But their involvement came with a price: her father felt that because he'd produced her life, he was entitled to direct her entire life story.

Given the way he'd reacted to the photos, Amelia was trying, now, not to hate him outright. He wasn't ordinarily controlling. Not an ogre. Not harsh. His strict views on her dating had been easy enough to get around—he hadn't done before what he now insisted he had to do. She would not hate him for reacting this way, and she would not hate her mother for going along with him. She would simply find a way to get around this new, high, heavily guarded wall until the time came when they couldn't hold her inside it any longer.

In her room, she changed from her running clothes into jeans and a fitted tee and a black hoodie, then stood in front of the cheval mirror that had been her mother's mother's, its frame made from hand-cut polished hickory, and brushed out her hair, trying to see herself the way her parents saw her. Did she look obedient?

Innocent? Sensible? Naïve? Did they still see her as the barefooted six-year-old running in the surf, as in the portrait of her that hung above the conservatory's sofa? She frowned at her reflection. Was she supposed to still be that girl? What if she became, instead, The Girl Who Ran Away?

As appealing as the idea was, it wasn't really a temptation. She had to finish high school or there would be no NYU education. No valuable mentors. No New York connections to Broadway work, or none that would come as naturally and easily as they would if she and Anthony immersed themselves in the school's theatre culture. For all that she dreamt of starring, of headlining, on Broadway, she knew it was going to take a lot of effort and no small amount of good luck—but, Thomas Jefferson said that hard work made good luck, and she believed this wholeheartedly. The hard work was just going to have to include whatever her parents heaped on her these next seven months. But that didn't mean she had to like it.

She backed away from the mirror and draped herself across her bed, facedown, feeling empty and wronged. This, she thought, was not so different from the way young queen-to-be Victoria must have felt, severely overprotected in order to make sure she would live to take the throne when her uncle died. Lying there, Amelia let her imagination drift, thinking of silk taffeta and velvet gowns, of corsets and lace, and of playing Victoria one day onstage, or playing Elizabeth—or Medea, who wouldn't hesitate to punish those who'd wronged her. Amelia let vengefulness fill her, but without a vengeful character's role to hold it, the feeling poured out as quickly as it had come. She simply wasn't the type.

The phone rang at eight o'clock, and a few seconds later her mother yelled up to her, "Amelia, Cameron is on the phone. Do you want to talk to her?"

Amelia opened her door and walked to the landing that overlooked the living room. "Am I allowed?" she asked with deliberate sarcasm. That, she could manage.

"Come to the kitchen," her mother told her, and then told Cameron, "she'll be just a second."

When Amelia took the phone, she said, "Hey Cameron, sorry, I had to come all the way downstairs."

"Are you okay? Anthony told me what's going on. He's really pissed, as you might guess."

Amelia wanted to ask for details, but her mother was hovering. "I would've called you yesterday if I could."

Her mother said, sotto voce, "Tell her you have mono. That's what the school will be telling everyone."

"I'm supposed to tell you I have mono," she said, turning her back to her mother. "But really, I'm under house arrest."

"Amelia!" Her mother took the phone and told Cameron, "She's kidding, Cameron—and I'm so sorry, but right now she needs to get back into bed and get some rest. Call later, won't you?"

"Come see me," Amelia said into the phone over her mother's shoulder.

"Have a good day, Cameron," her mother said, then hung up the phone. She glared at Amelia.

"She already knows—and anyway, what do you expect?" Amelia said, answering the glare with her own. "You want me to just lie down and take it, but that's not how you raised me, and that's not how I am."

"I expect you to cooperate with us," her mother said, sounding hurt. "It'll go so much easier if you do."

"Easier for you, sure, but it'd be wrong. Momma, tell me, how is it you can think I'm smart and capable about every other thing in my life, and think that when it comes to Anthony, I'm suddenly an imbecile?"

"I don't think that. What I know is, emotions can be poisonous to good judgment. Falling for the wrong person can ruin your life."

"Having a certain kind of parents can ruin your life."

"Being duplicitous can ruin your life," her mother said pointedly.

"Sure, if what a person's hiding is dangerous." Amelia's gaze challenged her mother to argue the point. When that didn't happen, Amelia softened, saying, "Falling for the right guy can make life amazing and wonderful, right? How is it that you and Daddy imagine you can know which it is for me? You've never spent time with Anthony. You don't know anything about him."

Her mother shook her head. "We don't know him, that's so. But it's plain enough that he's the sort who'll lead you where you ought not to go, wouldn't you say?"

"I would say that you and Daddy are overreacting," she said. "Please, Momma. I know you don't agree with Daddy about all this. Call whoever it is you need to call so that they'll let Anthony be."

Her mother averted her eyes. "What?" Amelia asked. "What's going on?"

"Even if I wanted to go against his wishes, there's nothing I can do. Anthony was arrested yesterday."

Amelia stared. "He was not. Cameron would have told me."

"I imagine she would have if you'd talked longer. Look, I couldn't do anything even at the time; it was too late. The best thing is to accept that it's over and done. He's not the one for you, I promise."

What insubstantial things, dreams. Amelia watched the one she'd conjured and nurtured and kept before her for twelve brilliant months dissolve like a sand castle in the onrush of a rising tide.

10

HARLAN'S CAMPAIGN TO PUT HIS WORLD BACK IN ORDER began with a list, which he wrote out in small, neatly printed letters on *Wilkes, Inc.* letterhead. He did this from his desk at Wilkes Honda, his flagship store, while outside his office windows the sales consultants, as they were called nowadays, stood with customers and talked up the superior features and benefits of Honda automobiles, the finest vehicles in their class. It didn't bother Harlan a bit that he had employees two miles away doing the same thing but with Toyotas, and five miles away with Volkswagens. You told your buyer what he or she wanted to hear—that's what sold cars.

He wished positive persuasion was as easy with teenage daughters. That Amelia imagined herself in love in the first place was ludicrous to Harlan. He'd been seventeen once—granted, forty years earlier—and knew very well that the feelings she was having for that slick piece of work, Winter, were no different than sweet little Tanya Hill's had been for him at that age. Tanya had been quite willing to give him her heart, and whatever else he wanted, but that supposed love had turned out to be no more real than a three-dollar bill.

He wanted to give Amelia more credit than what he ascribed to Tanya. Amelia was in every way a superior young woman, thanks to the care he and Sheri had taken with her all along. He was reasonably certain that when it came to getting physical with Anthony Winter, she'd had far more sense than Tanya'd had. The trouble was that no girl of that age could be trusted to know her own mind or heart—especially heart. And if you didn't stop them in time, the way he'd cut himself loose from Tanya back then, they might never get wise. They might, at seventeen, marry the sweet-talking devil whose souped-up 1940 Dodge D-17 Special had been won in a bar's backroom poker game, making him appear to be a hot high-roller, rather than the reckless good-timer he really was. From there they might have a kid who, cute as he'd be, wouldn't rate high enough on the list of after-work attractions (parties, bars, beer, joyrides, parties, beer, joyrides, bars) to get much notice. Such a woman might stay blind to good sense her entire life and die of a ruined liver with a no-good man's name on her lips.

No. You had to stop the train before it even left the station.

Harlan's train-stopping list began with William Braddock's name. After Braddock were the four local television news stations, and then the N&O and Wake Weekly. With the same diligence that had ultimately won him business dominance and the respect of not only his peers but of the community at large, he looked up the names and phone numbers of every Raleigh, Wake Forest, Cary, and Garner public high-school principal. It was only right, he thought, to make educators aware of the Winter kid and the danger he posed. Harlan's grandfather had liked to say, "It's not until you shine a light on a snake can you really tell what kind you're dealing with." Harlan would be the light for the whole community. That way, not only would he stop Winter in mid-slither, but he'd likely force some of the other snakes out there back into their holes, for good, he hoped.

"William Braddock, please," Harlan said, reaching over to close his office's interior blinds. "It's Harlan Wilkes." When Braddock came on the line, he said, "Thanks for taking my call. I wanted to just touch base with you this morning."

"It's no trouble," Braddock said. "I'm hoping that having a chance to sleep on things has changed your mind. As I said last night, given the nature of the trouble, keeping Amelia in her regular routine is really the best thing for her."

"Mm. Well, I'm sure your intentions are good and you are, of course, an expert, of a kind, where kids are concerned. But—and this is no dig—you're not a parent, and especially not Amelia's parent. You'll have to leave 'what's best' up to my wife and me."

"Ah," Braddock said, and there was a short silence on the line. He coughed, then said, "So if you haven't changed course, what can I do for you this morning?"

"Given that the DA saw fit to arrest Winter, I'd like to suggest that you expel the boy, as protection for the other girls. I know his mother's a teacher there, but that shouldn't matter—plus, it's not as if you'll lose any revenue with him gone. And while I'm on it: you need to find out how this happened under her watch. Winter is her kid, and Amelia was her student—which, to my thinking, means she's doubly responsible."

"Mr. Wilkes, your concern is admirable, and I appreciate it. I've already begun looking into the matter, and I assure you, appropriate action will be taken just as soon as the situation is fully known."

"Why wait? Every minute he's there, you're endangering every girl in your charge."

"Kim Winter is a good teacher and a valued asset here," Braddock said, "but Ms. Winter notwithstanding, due process demands that I give the matter a full, fair hearing. I'll be talking to both Ms. Winter and Anthony in detail, as well as consulting with the advisory board, and appropriate action will be taken."

Harlan sighed. Men like William Braddock were too caught up in "consulting" and "process." The man needed to have some balls and just make an executive decision and move on with things.

"Keep me posted," Harlan said, then moved on to phoning the next principal without taking a break. These calls were announce-ments, warnings. Not everyone on his list was available to take his call. In the cases when the principal wasn't, he requested one of the assistant principals. He spoke anonymously, a "concerned father" who, to protect his daughter's identity, declined to reveal his own. "But I promise, this is no prank. The arrest is public record," he said, and provided all the details that would let them find the Wake County arrest log themselves, assuming they, like Braddock, would have to weigh and measure and discuss before taking action to pro-tect their students.

His approach with the news stations was similar. But here, all he needed to do was point the dogs in the direction of the arrest log and mention that the kid involved attended "one of the prominent private schools," and he knew they'd go running for the story like Buttercup used to go after the neighbor's cat when it came around taunting her.

He was about to contact the newspapers when his wife called. "Have you decided whether you're golfing today?" she asked, sound-ing tired.

Neither of them had slept much last night, and they'd gotten up for good at four-fifteen. Sheri went to shower and Harlan, seeing her there, slim and firm as a lot of women half her forty-nine years, took off the clothes he'd just put on and stepped into the shower with her. It'd taken some persuasion to get her to go along with his interest, but he'd prevailed. Fifty-eight years old, and he was still more than able to make love standing up in the shower—not as easy as it looked in the movies. The very fact of this accomplishment gave him a little surge of manly pride, and why not? He knew men a decade younger who were popping Viagra and griping about need-ing knee or hip replacements.

Afterward, Sheri grabbed her robe and wrapped it around her-self without toweling off.

"Cold?" Harlan asked, still standing in the wide, tiled expanse of shower that was—he'd measured it—bigger than the entire kitchen of the trailer he'd grown up in. There were two shower heads and a dozen spray nozzles placed along the walls so that, if you wanted it, you could have a shower that felt like you were standing outside during a September hurricane.

"Mm," she said, noncommittal, and began pressing her hair with a hand towel.

"'Cause it's a little late for modesty." He laughed. She didn't. He didn't pursue it. Women were too damn complicated.

Now he said, "You know, I think I'm gonna stay here and finish up some business. I'm not really up for golf, anyway. Think I used up my sports energy this morning."

"I found a tutor," Sheri said. "She'll work with Amelia's teachers, and come in for three hours a day, Monday through Thursday until school's out for winter break. I don't know what we'll do then."

Harlan leaned back in his chair. "She won't need a tutor during break."

"I mean about her being home for near three weeks with nothing to do. Honestly, Harlan, that's the least of it. I truly do not know what we'll do with her being home all afternoon and evening *every day,* and all weekend."

"What'd you do when she was little? Just do that."

"Tea parties and playgroup and grocery shopping?" Sheri said. "I can't think that's going to work very well at her age."

"I didn't mean literally. You're great at the mom thing, is what I mean. The togetherness will be good for you, don't you think? And I'll fill in what blanks I can," he added, envisioning himself and Amelia taking the new GranCabrio out—he'd let Amelia get behind the wheel, give her a taste for what a truly fine car was like for the driver—and she could join him on the golf course, too. He couldn't remember the last time she'd golfed with him. "And how about this?" he added as another idea came to him. "We'll go away for the holidays—take your parents with us and head to Mexico for a week or so."

"Maybe." Her voice thickened as she said, "You can't imagine how she's been today. I told her the Winter boy got arrested, and she looked at me like I said I'd just run over the dog."

Harlan shook his head. That Amelia could be reduced to this state over anyone, and especially over someone with so little actual worth, made him wonder where he'd gone wrong—and, more to the point, what Winter had said, what he'd done to trap her. Some poetic bullshit, probably. Amelia, sweet as she was, was probably vulnerable to that. He should've seen it coming. Amelia wouldn't fall for the bad-boy type that had entranced his mother. For her it'd be the artsy guy with the high IQ, who could easily identify a doe like Amelia, draw her in, and hypnotize her with his spotlight eyes.

He said, "I'm sure it must be rough for you both. Maybe take her out for lunch. Go to that nail place you like and get your toes done. I want to thank you, by the way, for putting all your things on hold while we straighten this out. I'd do the same if I could."

"Would you?" she said flatly. "See you at dinner."

As soon as he ended that call, he was on the phone again. The woman he spoke with at the newspaper listened politely, asked him three different times to identify himself, then told him she'd let the appropriate reporter know, but made no promises about running a story. She said, "Frankly, I'm not sure I can see how this is newsworthy."

"You want someone like him preying on *your* daughter?"

"If I had a daughter, I would not want her preyed upon, no. But honestly, Mr. Whoever You Are, I can't say that the behavior you've described is predatory."

"The DA thinks so."

"The DA thinks prayer should be made mandatory in public schools."

"Well, what's wrong with that?"

"Thank you so much for your call," she said.

11

For Anthony, school on Tuesday was still school and not the rumor circus it would soon become. Except for the occasional question from a friend either verifying Amelia's having mono, or asking whether he'd heard that she did, no one behaved out of the ordinary. Word hadn't gotten out. No one looked at him, yet, as if he'd grown a third eye on his forehead. No one avoided him in the halls. The teachers did not view him as an object of pity, nor an object of scorn, and Mr. Rickman did not yet treat him as if he were a scourge and the school in desperate need of disinfectant.

Amelia's absence, though, was a stain on the day.

Third period was four minutes from ending when Anthony heard the crackle of the room's intercom, then the secretary's voice saying, "Mr. Rickman, please dismiss Anthony Winter to Mr. Braddock's office."

"Whoa, Winter," his classmates hooted, while Rickman raised an eyebrow and waved him off.

Though his anxiety made him want to run—not to Braddock's

office, necessarily, but somewhere, anywhere—Anthony made himself move at a normal pace down the hall to the stairs, and then to the administrative offices.

Braddock's secretary avoided looking at him as she said, "Go on in, he's waiting for you."

He grasped the handle and turned it, expecting nothing good as he pushed open the door. A lecture probably. Advice, if he was luckier.

"You rang?" he said, as if this visit was another request to script some jokes for morning announcements, or act as ambassador to a prospective student from upstate New York.

"Hi, Anthony," Braddock said. He was sitting on the corner of his desk, one pant leg hitched up high enough that Anthony could see the top of a brown-on-brown argyle sock. "Tough week, huh?"

"I've had better."

"Take a seat. Let's talk for a minute about you and Amelia Wilkes."

Anthony sat in the proffered seat, one of four padded leather captain's chairs. He said, "What do you want to know?"

"You've been accused of providing her with . . . inappropriate materials. I spoke to your mother; she says you sent the pictures at Amelia's request. I'm curious as to why Amelia would do that."

"Did my mom tell you that I've been going out with Amelia for the past year?"

Braddock's mouth tightened before he said, "She just mentioned that you'd been dating, in secret, yes."

Anthony rubbed the chair's polished arms. "Well."

"Well?"

"What goes on between Amelia and me is private, okay? It would be . . . ungentlemanly to say more."

"While I admire your sense of honor, the fact is I can't make informed decisions unless I have information." He clasped his hands in front of him.

Anthony considered what he might say that would satisfy

Braddock. "It's like this: she likes the way I look, and I didn't mind her having pictures of me. Pretty simple. Older generations are too hung up on nudity."

"I think maybe honesty is as much the problem here."

"You think that if her parents had known we were dating they wouldn't have called the cops? I doubt that. If Amelia thought they'd be rational about it, she'd have told them right from the start."

Braddock took off his glasses and rubbed his eyes. He looked younger without them, Anthony thought. Less like a headmaster and more like a guy who might show up in Anthony's kitchen some Sunday morning in a T-shirt and pajama pants, sitting across the table from his mother—something that in all of Anthony's eighteen years had never occurred. Not that he thought about it much, but he figured his mother must have been intimate with a few guys over the years and must have kept it from him. Maybe she and Braddock were keeping that kind of secret right now. Not every secret was harmful or shameful; sometimes secrets were practical. Necessary.

After replacing his glasses, Braddock said, "I wanted to discuss this with you personally because I think it's only fair to give you a heads-up. The fact is, I've got a parent who's out for blood right now and who will, I expect, become vindictive if he doesn't find satisfaction anywhere."

Anthony said, "Mr. Wilkes."

"Yes. He's convinced that you're a danger—"

"Come on," Anthony protested. "A *danger*? I didn't rape someone. I didn't beat someone up."

"I know, okay, but for your sake, it might be best for us to take action that respects Mr. Wilkes's concern, and keeps you out of harm's way. I have a meeting Thursday evening with my advisory team—"

"What action?"

"Most likely it would be suspension from school and extracurriculars, until after your court appearance."

Anthony said, "I don't see how suspending me makes sense. My situation has nothing to do with school—and Amelia's not even here, so it isn't like you'd be preventing us from having contact."

"Mr. Wilkes believes you're a danger to young ladies in general. And despite my personal feelings," Braddock said, with enough emphasis on "personal" that Anthony could hear the subtext, "it's possible that I'll be compelled to take action so that—"

"So that your ass is covered," Anthony spat. "There—I'll give you a real reason to suspend me."

Braddock looked at him evenly. "I'll know more on Thursday, and I'll give you and your mom a call afterward, to let you know how things went. Now go on, get some lunch," he said, "and hang in there."

"Oh, gosh, thank you so *much,* Mr. Braddock, sir. I feel immensely better."

"Anthony—"

"Save it," he said. He wiped his palms on his pants legs, stood up calmly, then left the office and headed for the student parking lot.

When he got to his car, he climbed onto the hood and lay there, reclined against the windshield, eyes closed, soaking up the sun. He was not really angry at Braddock, just angry in general. He recalled a line from the play *Henry VI,* a summer stock production he'd done two years earlier, and recited it aloud: "What fates impose, that men must needs abide; It boots not to resist both wind and tide."

As if that helped in the least.

While Anthony might have been said to be a decent actor when on-stage, playing a role all day—a role he hadn't wanted, hadn't tried out for—wore him down until, at three o'clock, he hardly cared that the rest of his afternoon and a portion of his evening were going to be taken up by legal consultations. They had to choose a lawyer, and fast, or he'd be at the courthouse next Wednesday morning with little idea about what was going to happen or how he was supposed to handle it. The court had a website, and he'd found an FAQ page on what to expect, but that was geared to people who'd been arrested for DWI or speeding or other misdemeanors that, if you pled guilty, could result in fines, and maybe license points lost, but not jail time.

The site presumed that most defendants would appear without counsel. He didn't have the first clue on how to represent himself, or whether he'd get a chance to explain to the judge what was really going on, or whether if he did, the judge would give a damn. Probably Amelia's father played poker with all the judges. He almost certainly sold them their cars, and likely had contributed money to a lot of political campaigns. Without a lawyer looking after his interests, Anthony would be as vulnerable as an orchid in a blizzard, to use one of his grandfather's sayings. He was sorry his grandfather wasn't around to lend his wisdom directly.

Anthony's mother met him at home. He'd changed clothes, not into shorts and a T-shirt, which he'd usually choose after ditching his school uniform, but into the pressed khakis and golf shirt she'd bought last night and left on his bed. The combination of the outfit and the reason for wearing it made him a prep and a perp at the same time. Shakespeare, he thought, could have had a lot of fun with that wordplay setup.

"You look great," his mother said, trying to smile; the furrows between her eyes were more truthful than her words or tone.

"So do you," he said honestly. She was in a conservative black-and-white outfit: tailored pants, white blouse, black ribbed cardigan, simple silver hoops in her ears. A confident woman, not at all the type whose son could need a criminal attorney.

The white-knuckled way she clutched the notebook, though, in which she'd jotted the names, addresses, phone numbers, and appointment times, told a different story. He wanted to tell her to relax, and would have, if he'd had less guilt working on him. As it was, that she'd tried talking to the Wilkeses, that she'd made the appointments with the lawyers, that she'd bought him the new clothes he was wearing, that she'd run interference with Braddock, all on his behalf, made him feel that he was, to say the least, a disappointing and unworthy son.

She said, "We'll have to take advantage of our appearance and get dinner someplace nice when we're done." This statement, so reasonable-sounding when she made it, would become more of a rueful joke once they were through.

The first of the lawyers they saw was a partner in a law firm comprised of four names so ordinary that the firm's name could have been a joke. Misters Jones, Johnson, Peterson, and Brown had offices as nondescript as their names, and Brady Johnson, when he came into the conference room wearing a dark gray suit with a light gray shirt and a tie with a background of blue so pale that it was almost white, was bland as well. His face was round and smooth and, though he didn't seem that large overall, his chin merged into his neck without even a line of separation. His voice, when he spoke, was monotone.

"You're Andy?" he said, extending his hand across the faux-mahogany table.

"Anthony."

"Right." They shook hands, then Johnson tugged his jacket straight, undid its button, and sat down at the head of the table.

"This is my mom, Kim Winter."

Johnson nodded at her. "Unfortunate situation," he said, glancing at the legal pad he'd carried in. "Tell me what happened."

Anthony gave a short summary, saying that Amelia was his girlfriend, that she'd asked for the photos—though not when, or why, and he didn't describe them except to say he'd been undressed.

The attorney made notes as he listened, then said, "Do you have your arrest warrant?"

Anthony looked at his mother; she shook her head. "Nobody said to bring it. I gave all the details to the woman who answered my call and made the appointment."

Johnson skimmed the legal pad again, then lifted its top page, to find nothing written beneath. He folded his hands atop the pad. "What's the statute they pegged you with?"

"I—do you mean, what's the charge?" Anthony asked.

"The charge, yes."

"It's like, 'harmful dissemination to a minor,' something like that."

Johnson raised his eyebrows as if to say, What sort of imbecile doesn't know what he's charged with? He said, with exaggerated patience, "The trouble with these kinds of charges is, some are felonies and some are misdemeanors. Without knowing exactly which one yours is, the advice I give you today won't be very specific."

"It's a misdemeanor," Anthony said.

"You're sure?"

"Yeah—that is, that's what it said on the warrant, and I looked it up, so . . ."

"All right, then, we'll work with that. To represent you on a misdemeanor, the fee begins at twenty-five hundred. When are you supposed to appear?"

Anthony was startled by the amount Johnson had just quoted. Two thousand five hundred dollars. Two *thousand*. Plus *five* hundred more. It took him a moment before he caught up with the question and said, "In court?"

"Yes," Johnson said with a slight smile, or maybe it was a smirk.

Anthony said, "Next Wednesday, at nine A.M."

His mother added, "Is that normal, for it to be so soon? Doesn't it take time to, well, design a defense, prepare—whatever it is you'd need to prepare?"

"Mrs."—he consulted the pad, stifling a yawn—"Winter, this is a misdemeanor, and regardless, it's not as if there will be a trial."

"I'm not saying there would. But . . . what will there be?" she asked.

"A conversation with the prosecutor. We meet that morning in court, we decide what makes sense, agree on terms—my job being to see that Anthony gets the minimum punishment possible. It's a few minutes, and then you're out."

Anthony bristled. "*Minimum punishment?* Why should I be punished at all? The charge is crap."

"Listen, what I said, that's just an outline. If you retained me," he said, sounding as if watching paint dry would be more interesting to him, "I'd need to review the charge, get a statement from you, see what case law there is, and go from there." He rolled his chair away from the table, stood, and offered his hand again. "I have another appointment, so, thank you for coming by. Let us know what you decide. We can't wait to get to work for you," he said as Anthony grasped his hand reluctantly. "Angie will show you out."

Neither Anthony nor his mother spoke until they were in her car.

"What did you think?"

"I wanted to kick him."

"He didn't inspire confidence, did he?" his mother said.

Anthony shook his head. "And that's a lot of money to ask for just talking to the prosecutor for five minutes."

"It is. But we don't really have a choice, do we? Anyway, I have a few dollars put aside. We'll manage."

"I'm not letting you pay."

She said, "Keep your money for school."

"School, right," he said, staring out the window. "NYU's gonna want to put my application at the top of the pile."

Their appointment with the second attorney was a rerun of the first, except that this man, Stevenson Hadley, was half again as old, twice as fat, and about ten times wealthier (if his shiny suit, silk tie, and four rings he wore were to be believed) than Brady Johnson. His fee was four thousand, he told them, glancing up from his notes as if to see whether he'd dissuaded them, possibly freeing himself up for something more interesting. When neither Anthony nor his mother protested, the attorney added that he was reasonably certain that he himself would be able to make Anthony's hearing date, though it was possible that something would come up and he'd have to send an associate. "Let Stacy know what you decide," he said, rising. "Now I have an appointment, so I'll have to leave you."

"What were *we*, then?" Anthony said as Hadley disappeared into another conference room.

"Filler," his mother replied. "Let's go."

Across downtown, they parked in an empty public lot as the sun dropped behind the buildings around them. They crossed a street empty of its earlier traffic and entered the offices of the third attorney, Mariana Davis, with low hopes.

Inside the glass door was a desk, behind which sat a woman with the darkest skin Anthony had ever seen. Her eyes and her teeth stood out vividly as she smiled in greeting. "You're the Winters?" she asked. An enormous striped cat sat at the edge of her desk, its tail hanging over the side and thumping against the wood. Anthony petted it as his mother answered, "Yes. We're a little early."

"That's fine. Have a seat. Mariana will be free shortly."

The waiting area was pleasant and well lighted, oriented as it was next to a window with a view of the street. A trio of wide-leafed potted plants were centered in the window, above which were tall white letters, backward to Anthony's view, reading *Davis & Associates, Attorneys at Law. Integrity, Commitment, Results.*

Right, he thought, sitting down in a simple but new chair. Great slogan, but was he really supposed to buy it? More accurate would be, *Indifference, Condescension, Reluctance,* if what they'd seen so far today was representative of criminal attorneys—and they'd all be happy to lighten your wallet while you decided which was the truth.

His mother sat beside him. "Not bad," she said. "The plants are a nice touch."

They each chose a magazine from among the dozen or so that had been fanned across a corner table. Five minutes passed, then ten, and when they'd waited twenty minutes, Anthony dropped his *Newsweek* back onto the table and said, "What if I just save us a few grand and represent myself?"

"Oh no, son, you don't want to do that."

Anthony looked up. A tall black woman in a pin-striped brown skirt and crisp blue blouse stood in the waiting room's doorway. Her dark hair was long and pulled back into a neat, girlish ponytail, but her eyes were all business. She said, "The prosecutor would eat you for breakfast. I'm Mariana Davis." She offered her hand and Anthony stood up to shake it. "Come on with me and we'll see if we can't get you out of the fix you're in."

The Davis & Associates conference room looked largely the same as the other two had. Anthony wondered how many people had sat in this room sweating figuratively and literally, as he was doing now.

"Did you bring your arrest warrant?" the attorney asked.

"No, but it's a misdemeanor, and my court date is Wednesday, and the charge is, I think, 'disseminating harmful materials to a minor.'"

"Well," Ms. Davis said, sitting back. "What makes me think you've run through this a time or two before now?"

Anthony said, "Everyone asks the same questions. I'm just trying to save time."

"Good. All right, then, here's what I know: the charge, North Carolina Statute 14-190.15, Disseminating harmful material to minors, is a Class 1 misdemeanor, which under certain circumstances is punishable by jail time. The DA really had to go digging to find this one," she said. "Who, pardon my language, did you piss off?"

Anthony smiled slightly. "Do you know Harlan Wilkes?"

"Wilkes, of Wilkes BMW, etcetera?"

"He's the one."

"Hmm. So maybe that explains it," she said. At his questioning look, she elaborated. "Why the local five o'clock news led with the story, just a few minutes before you got here. You look older in your mug shot."

"Bad lighting," he muttered, fighting the sinking feeling in his gut.

"His picture was on the *news?*" his mother said. "How in the world—?"

"It's all public record, Ms. Winter, and the charge is . . . unusual and provocative, so even if Wilkes isn't engineering coverage, the charge would stand out amongst the usual list of speeding tickets and DWIs and minor assaults and failures to appear in court. It being the lead story, though—"

"What did they say?" his mother said, asking the question he wasn't sure he wanted answered. The fewer details you knew, the less real a thing seemed.

"They said that he'd been arrested for allegedly providing pornographic materials, featuring himself, to an underage girl at a prominent private high school. Basically," she said, assessing Anthony with a gaze that he thought didn't miss much, "they made you out as a sleazeball."

"How can that be fair?" he said, and as he spoke, his phone buzzed. The display showed an unfamiliar number. He let the call go unanswered.

"It's not fair," Ms. Davis said. "But our media gets a lot more mileage out of convicting the accused right off, haven't you noticed? The Duke lacrosse situation, for example."

"What can we do to fight back?" his mother asked. Anthony's phone buzzed again, this time with a text message. *Channel 11 news: Want ur side of story,* it read. *How well do u know the girl?*

"How did they get my number?" he said, dropping his phone onto the conference table. "The news is *texting* me."

Ms. Davis said, "You start by saying nothing, and I mean absolutely *nothing,* to anyone—the cops, the news, your neighbors, your coworkers. And you hire me."

Anthony hated the distress that was being etched, bit by bit, into his mother's face with each encounter today, each little smoke bomb of discouraging people and words and events exploding around them. He told the attorney, "From what the others said, I guess your job is to get me a minimal punishment, but what's the full penalty? You know, if I'm convicted?"

"You've never been arrested before, for anything?"

He shook his head. She said, "Then some type of probation, community service for sure—and this is a worst-case scenario, but since this is considered a sex crime, you could be required to register as a sex offender."

"A *sex offender?*" His mother was half out of her chair. "You cannot be serious!"

Ms. Davis held up one hand. "I am, but your reaction is exactly correct. Which is why my aim would be to get the charges dropped."

Anthony said, "All right: you're hired."

"I'm not cheap," Ms. Davis added. "My fee is five thousand dollars for serious misdemeanors like this one."

"Which I presume you then earn," his mother said hotly, "based on that scenario you just described."

"I can't guarantee any particular outcome—no attorney can, so if you've heard otherwise, don't believe it. The county's prosecutor is what we refer to as a 'victim's DA,' and procedural rules make it doubly hard for defense attorneys. I won't even be able to see the police report before the hearing. But I care deeply about justice and about providing effective counsel, and I'm happy to show you past clients' testimonials on that account."

Anthony watched her face carefully. This was no spiel—or if it was, she was so convincing that it really didn't matter. If any attorney they'd met today could restore normalcy to his life, Mariana Davis was the one. "You're hired," he said again. There might be others like her, and they might charge less—but they might charge more, and how many of these consultations would he and his mother have to endure before they knew they'd found the right lawyer?

"Just tell me what I need to do."

"Well, to start, your mom sketched out the situation when she set the appointment, and I have some notes on that, but why don't you take it from the top for me. How did you get to be on Harlan Wilkes's bad side?"

Anthony pushed his hands through his hair and imagined, despite himself, the news broadcast and his mug shot, now the evening's sensational story for all those parents prepping dinner for their families, all the retired people who liked getting their news early, people who kept their radios tuned to 101.5 and heard the local news broadcast live. Undoing this mess was going to be even more of an ordeal than he'd imagined.

He said, "I got on his bad side by falling in love with his daughter."

"That," the attorney said, "is going to be a tough one to fix."

12

WILDFIRE STARTS SMALL—FROM A DROPPED CIGARETTE, someone burning leaves or trash, a single lick of lightning to a vulnerable tree—and then spreads in every opportune direction, eventually becoming so hot that nothing short of a torrent, man-made or otherwise, can put it out. To travel, it needs little more than favorable conditions and available fuel to feed on, and will grow without conscience, disregarding wildlife, structures, prayer.

Kim, having spilled coffee on herself just before she'd been about to leave the house, was running late on Thursday morning. The faculty parking lot was full and quiet when she arrived, but she could see students still outside the building, savoring their final few minutes of free time before being tasked with schoolwork. Her mind was already on that work, on the assignments she'd failed to grade the night before, on her plans for what she'd be doing in each of the classes she taught—all things that had been planned out previously but which, given Anthony's arrest, were refusing to stick with her very well. Fortunately, her day began with Art Studio, more supervisory than instructional. She'd get her act together once she finished taking attendance and had the students on task.

She passed a group of whispering teens and went inside, heading directly to her first-period classroom. The fire that would in time threaten to consume everything she'd ever valued in her life was still small, still for the most part contained, and its spread was at first invisible to her. She rushed through the hallways, her mind on the clock, not feeling any of the fire's heat, not yet aware that news of Anthony's arrest was already moving from student to student to teacher to secretary to maintenance worker to friend, relative, neighbor, parent at the speed of a whispered aside, a forwarded news website link, a text message, a chuckle or sneer or concerned *"Did you hear . . . ?"* over a four-dollar latte at a coffee shop up the road.

Jim Rickman was the first of the faculty to engage Kim directly. He stopped her outside her classroom on his way to his own. He was an imposing man. Tall, with a linebacker's build and deep-set, hawk-sharp eyes under thin, dark brows. Kim didn't like him. The students didn't like him. No one liked him, William had told her, but he was incredibly good at teaching higher math to the small-but-important group of students who intended to get into fiercely competitive engineering programs. Kim understood the politics behind keeping teachers like Rickman on staff. They were assurances of quality and value to parents who, if their child attended Ravenswood from k through 12, would have invested more than two hundred thousand dollars in their child's education (and would be preparing to repeat the expense for college).

Rickman nodded to her and said, "Kim. I see our young Anthony's gotten into a scrape."

She thought of Mariana Davis's direction to say nothing to anyone, and so far, the only people she'd discussed the trouble with were her mother and her friend Rose Ellen, both trustworthy without question. Rickman was very much the opposite.

The trouble was, saying nothing wasn't so easily done when you were put on the spot. He, and others, would expect a real response. Her impulse was to say she couldn't speak about it—but that might make the situation sound more serious than it was. What she wanted to do was defend her son.

She said, "It's a misunderstanding."

Rickman looked at her straight-faced, but said drolly, "Of course it is. You have my sympathies."

Then it was Audrey Evans, a tall, square-figured former Olympic swimmer who taught civics and was often allied with Kim when conversation in the teachers' lounge turned into debate, as was sometimes the case. Audrey waved to Kim and came into the classroom. "Saw the news," she said, as Kim was laying her sweater over the back of her chair. "Is it true?"

Kim opened a desk drawer and dropped her purse inside. She said, "It's not what you think," but her shaky words lacked the conviction they'd need to slow the fire's spread.

"Then what is it?" Audrey asked.

Kim wanted to tell her. What harm could it do? Audrey would surely be an ally. There was no time now, though. "A misunderstanding. I'll have to fill you in later."

Her first-period Art Studio class wanted to talk of nothing else as they worked, despite her telling them that she couldn't speak about the issue, which was true, and that there was nothing to tell, which was less so, which the students seemed able to sense as if smelling smoke in the air. Art History, second period, was much the same—limited, though, because unlike studio, there was little time for indulging in conversation. In third-period French I, she insisted that if anyone was going to ask about the matter, they had to do so en français. For the few who managed it, she answered in kind, and while these beginning students didn't have the vocabulary to understand what she was saying, they surely understood the tone in every ambivalent word. Kim worried that they'd all leave her class with their curiosity piqued rather than quelled.

Kim was exiting the classroom when she saw Anthony and a few of his friends as they were leaving for lunch. He looked wrung out, as if he, too, had spent the morning stamping and swatting at the flames. She wanted to take him home, fix him a bowl of alphabet soup, then read him a happy story and tuck him into bed for a nap, a routine that had worked beautifully when he was three.

He told his friends to hold up, and crossed the hall to where she stood. "Has Rickman said anything to you?" he asked.

"I saw him earlier, and all he said was he saw you'd had some trouble. Why?"

"He's such an asshole. He kept calling on me in class, even after I told him I didn't do last night's homework."

"None of it?"

A boy's voice from down the hallway: "Winter, hey, when are you doing *Playgirl?*" followed by another, calling, "Yeah, and when's the calendar coming out? My sister wants a copy."

Anthony paused, collecting himself, then turned their way and called, "Nice. Why don't you ask my *mom?*" And as he pointed at Kim, she saw the boys who'd been harassing him, neither of them her students. They avoided her gaze and hurried past, shoving each other and laughing as they went down the stairs.

"Who were those kids?"

"Idiots," Anthony said, turning back to her. "Anyway, no, I didn't get any of it done. I was too busy ignoring calls and texts from pretty much everyone in Raleigh. So just a warning: you'll probably hear reports from Rickman and Edmunds."

She said, "Okay," her voice sounding weary even to her ears. "I guess . . . I thought maybe you'd find homework diverting."

He was already moving away from her, signaling to his friends that he was coming. "Right, I wish it was as easy as that."

Anthony had learned to read at his grandfather's knee. On slow days at the bookshop, his grandfather, Phil, would pull a book from the piles of advance copies publishers sent him and sit in an armchair to read, and Anthony, adoring his grandfather, would take one of the books Kim packed for his day with Grandma and Grandpa and sit on the floor in front of him, apparently as engrossed as Phil. Kim often discovered them this way when she returned from her day, teaching at Ithaca High. Anthony would sit facing the store's front, as her father did, and he would pore over the pages—initially of his board books—wearing the same look of concentration her father wore, with the curls she couldn't yet bear to cut hanging in front of his eyes. Periodically he would hold up the book, which Kim would have read to him scores of times, and point at a word or picture.

"The hippopotamuses are int'resting," he'd say in his squeaky four-year-old voice. "You know, they live underwater a lot."

"That so?" his grandfather would remark, leaning his own book against his chest and gazing at Anthony over his reading glasses.

"Oh yes. And they are herbisaurs."

"Herbivores," Kim would correct, fighting a smile.

"Herbivores," Anthony would repeat. "Like Mommy." Or more accurately, like she had tried to be; the vegetarianism experiment, well intentioned as it was, collapsed the next time she'd come into proximity of bacon cooking. From then on, she'd struck a balance of omnivoriety—another of Anthony's terms—that led to one of her favorite Southern meals: the Carolina Classic, a hamburger topped with chili and coleslaw, a real offense to human herbivores, no doubt.

At fifteen, Anthony and his conversations had grown a bit more sophisticated than in his preschool days. Before going to yoga one chilly Saturday, Kim dropped off Anthony at her parents' Raleigh shop, an expanded version of their Ithaca shop, pairing bookstore with a small adjacent art gallery. Anthony enjoyed spending his weekends there—he would bring his homework and camp out on one of the sofas, taking time to talk with the regulars, and hanging out with his friends when they came in. Soon he would be old enough to drive himself, and soon her father would begin feeling poorly, and soon, too soon, the Winterses' world would destabilize, shake, and split. But this particular Saturday lived in Kim's memory as a sort of perfect example of how, and who, her father and her son had been.

When she'd returned from yoga, her mother motioned her into the gallery, a long, narrow, partitioned room filled with spotlit original art of all kinds. The best of Kim's own work—small oil paintings of still lifes, Impressionist-style—were offered for sale alongside photos, collages, watercolors, and sculptures done by local artists and friends of hers. Painting, for her, was an occupation akin to other women knitting sweaters or arranging flowers, a small passion that soothed and pleased her, a tangible record of her existence.

She was not an amazing talent. Her skills wouldn't transfer well to larger canvases. She knew this, and heeded it, which she thought made the difference between contentment and discontent. Her identity by this time was fixed in being a teacher of teens and a single parent. She would not be a professional artist, and that was fine by her.

The trick to "fine," of course, was in getting enough experience in and exposure to things to be able to identify one's outer limits. With Anthony, whose interests had been, at first, so varied and boundless, she'd been on the go endlessly during their summers off—to zoos and museums and parks and galleries, to beaches and mountains, fields of cotton and corn, to the workshops of potters and blacksmiths and jewelers, to archeological digs, to farmers' markets, to skate parks and bike tracks and concerts of every kind. To soccer practices and games and tournaments. And to the bookshop and library. There had not been a day when his nightstand wasn't cluttered with books. Everything from superhero comics to H. G. Wells to Michael Crichton to "the Bards," as he referred to Shakespeare and Marlowe and Wordsworth. He had exhausted Kim at times, frustrated her with his mercurial interests and the expenses that sometimes went with them. She knew, though, that the stress of keeping up with him wasn't really his fault. The fact was, she had trouble saying no because a two-parent family could have handled this one child easily, and she'd be damned if she'd let him suffer for his parents' errors.

The fact was, she was proud of him. If Anthony had outer limits, he certainly hadn't reached them yet.

"I want you to hear this," her mother said that chilly day, nodding in the direction of deep voices coming from the bookshop side of the building. "Your father's got him talking about literary philosophy, of all things."

Kim unwound her scarf and unbuttoned her coat, listening.

"Aristotle says it's a flaw of judgment, not a character flaw, that defines the tragic hero." This was Anthony.

"Judgment, yes," her father said, "but arising from the character flaw. Think of Oedipus, or Shylock."

"Think of Juliet—"

"She's not a *hero*—"

"Heroine, same deal," Anthony told him. "Point is, she shouldn't have agreed to Romeo's plan, right? It was too risky. She used bad judgment. Her love for Romeo made her reckless."

Kim moved to the wide doorway that led into the bookshop as her father said, "Recklessness: character flaw."

She saw them, her dear father and his eager protégé, seated across from each other at one of the chess tables in the shop's center. Anthony looked so much like a man in almost every way. How, she wondered, could this have happened to the warm, milk-scented infant she'd nuzzled and rocked and fed? An odd mix of happiness and regret had welled in her chest, along with a wish to freeze that precise moment in time. The things he was discussing were only loosely familiar to her, but her pleasure in his ability to discuss them in the first place was that of every mother who witnesses her child's accomplishments, no different than if the child had made a great pass in a soccer game, or earned an A on a tough math test, or conquered a phobia, or dissected, with grace and precision, a fetal pig in Biology class, aiming one day to be a surgeon.

"But Juliet wasn't a reckless person," Anthony argued. "It's just that the plan was the only way she could see for them to be together. That's devotion, which is no flaw."

"Lady Macbeth was devoted, too, you'll recall—and no question it was her fatal flaw. Your man Shakespeare seemed unable to decide if Aristotle was right."

Anthony laughed. "Whatever. Either way, Shakespeare was friggin' brilliant. He made his own rules."

"Yes, he did—and look what happened," her father said with a smile.

"Right," Kim agreed, going over to them. "Imagine, being able to make such a difference in people's lives," and in saying this, she was thinking of her son's future and the wonderful things it must surely hold for him. Why else would he be so talented and have such intelligence and heart, if not because he would become someone who mattered in the world? In what way, though, she could never have guessed.

13

THE RINGING DOORBELL WOKE ANTHONY AT 10:18 FRIDAY morning. Orienting himself (*Friday, suspended, Mom gone to school*), he got up, grabbed a shirt, straightened his boxers, and went to the window. He could see only the bumper and right taillight of a white car that had pulled all the way into the driveway.

He wasn't expecting anyone. His friends were all at school, where, thanks to William Braddock's suspending him out of "concern for you, Anthony, until this all gets resolved," he was no longer allowed to be. In one sense that was fine with him. By the end of Wednesday he'd been more than ready to leave and not come back. Then he'd suffered through Thursday, too, because how cowardly would it have been to stay home? All day, he'd gotten looks, and questions—which he couldn't answer except to say, "It's bullshit, trust me," but not everyone trusted him. He was the guy who'd been secretly sending out porn to underage girls, a real creeper. Except for Cameron and the few other girls in his circle, the girls at school had avoided him and the teachers had acted as if he'd been skulking around the local preschool looking for victims to flash or abduct. Except for the black mark it was going to be on his school record, Braddock's decision to suspend him was a favor.

The car outside obviously wasn't UPS or FedEx. It was possible that the mail carrier drove a white car, and was delivering a package that wouldn't fit in the mailbox. If so, the ringing bell would be a courtesy only, and at any moment he'd hear the carrier return to the car and he'd see the car back out and leave.

The bell rang again. Something that needed to be signed for, then. This was what he hoped as he made his way down the short hallway and down the stairs, and as he pulled open the door. What he found instead was a somber-looking pair of middle-aged men, one in a button-down white shirt and gray pants, the other in a khaki uniform shirt and black tie, black pants. The first was holding up a sheet of paper. "Are you Mr. Anthony Winter?"

"Why?" Anthony challenged, then, thinking better of his attitude, he said, "Yes. Why?"

"I'm Investigator Ronald Winship, with the Wake County Sheriff's Office. This is Deputy Morales. I have here a search warrant to find and remove from these premises any and all of the listed items."

He handed Anthony the warrant. It was similar to his arrest warrant, a fill-in-the-blanks official form that in this case gave permission to search for and take into custody a list of things that made Anthony's eyes widen as he read: laptop personal computer, desktop personal computer, all portable data storage devices, portable media storage devices, any personal or business-use cellphone that had a camera device and/or the ability to display images, any and all cellphone portable data storage devices, and any kind of camera, digital or other, and applicable portable data storage devices that he or his mother might own, along with the necessary cords for powering the devices.

"Hang on. What's this for?" he asked, though he had a good idea of the answer. The thing was, he hadn't anticipated the police coming for his computer, let alone anything else. He'd worried only that his mom would want to check it, so he'd moved certain things from the computer to a flash drive, and password-protected others. Which was fine subterfuge under normal circumstances. "Normal," however, no longer applied.

"For search and seizure of the items as stated. Please stand aside and allow us to enter."

Anthony remained in the doorway while he tried to think of a way to stop them. "I'm, what, supposed to just give you all my stuff?"

Winship nodded, and made a note on the warrant. "That's correct. We prefer that you surrender it willingly, but we're authorized to get it by whatever means necessary."

Anthony saw the deputy move his hand to his waistband, where a simple dark holster held a pistol and the too-familiar handcuffs. Whatever means necessary. He couldn't imagine they'd actually shoot him, but hell, maybe they would. Or maybe they'd haul him back to jail for another talk with the magistrate. He said, "Look, I didn't mean I *wouldn't* . . . So, yeah, okay, I guess you should just, er, come in." He backed up from the door so they could step inside.

Winship said, "I'll start down here."

"Maybe I should call my lawyer first?" Anthony said.

"Sure, call," the deputy told him, "but it's a *warrant*. Your consent is not a factor here. We will detain you during the search if required."

He recalled the press of cold metal against his wristbones. "No need. I'll just—my stuff, it's upstairs, so I'll just get it—"

"Deputy Morales will accompany you," Winship said.

"Oh. Right, okay."

Anthony led the deputy upstairs to his room, wishing he'd gotten dressed before coming to the door. A quick glance confirmed that his phone was not in sight, as he'd thought. It would be tucked under his sheet or pillow, still waiting for Amelia to get access to some telephone and give him a call. What little he'd heard about her since Monday had come solely from Cameron, who'd told him about the Wilkeses' spin story claiming she was out with mono. Now, of course, thanks to the vultures who'd reported his arrest, everyone knew that he'd gotten busted on porn charges, and while most would not connect his legal troubles with Amelia's absence, their close friends already had. Cameron's job now was to keep the lid on things so that Amelia would remain safe from the wolves that had been snapping at his heels all week. And to keep him apprised of how Amelia was doing, and to let Amelia know that he was all right.

"Why was the warrant issued?" he asked, grabbing his jeans from where he'd left them on the floor, and stepping into them. Not that wearing pants made any actual difference; the violation was going to take place regardless.

"Additional information is required, pertaining to your arrest earlier this week."

"Like what?"

"Like, additional information."

"When will I get my stuff back?" Anthony said, as he reached for his desk's top drawer.

"Slowly!" the deputy barked, startling Anthony. He glanced over his shoulder to see the guy standing with his hand on his gun.

Anthony moved aside so that the deputy could clearly see his hands opening the drawer. Opening it s-l-o-w-l-y. His hands shook. "I don't—that is, don't worry, I don't even own a gun. Not even a BB gun. I used to play paintball, but I sold the marker on eBay a while back." The camera waited right on top where it had sat, unused, for months; Amelia's was the one they used. He took his from the drawer and handed it over. "The memory stick is in it."

Morales opened the access door to the camera's battery and, yes, memory stick, then snapped it shut. "The iPod too," he said, indicating it with a nod.

"Why do you need that?" Anthony asked, dread creeping over him, filling him, cinching his stomach and gut. They would not find pictures of him on there; they'd find pictures of Amelia. Amazing, beautiful pictures from late summer taken inside an abandoned barn, images never meant for anyone else to see. His password would be no barrier for the techies whose job it was to recover or remove data.

"*All* electronic media storage devices. Do not attempt to alter the data," Morales said, hand extended.

Anthony took it from his bedside table and gave it to the deputy. Morales unplugged the headphones. "You can keep these. Where's the power cord?"

"Here, hooked to my computer," Anthony said, going to his desk and unplugging the iPod's cord. "This is a desktop, obviously, so—"

"I just need the tower," the deputy said. "Do not attempt to power it up. Disconnect the power and peripherals and flash drive—which I'll need, and carry it downstairs."

"When will I get my stuff back?" Anthony asked again, as he worked to disconnect all the cords from the back of the computer. His hands were sweaty, and he could not stop them from shaking. If they found everything that was stored in his computer and on his iPod and in his phone, his troubles might be only just beginning. They'd pinned him with a charge he never knew existed, so there was no telling what else he might face. Worse, if Amelia's father got the report, he would lock her up or move her out of the country. He'd file a restraining order. He'd come after Anthony with pruning shears and rope.

Anthony continued, "Because, you know, everything I do— homework, email, check the news, the weather—I mean, my life is pretty much all in here." As well as more photos, and emails, and things he'd written about her that were intensely private. Suppose Wilkes got hold of the sonnet where he'd described the sea-brine taste of her, or the soft slope of her inner thighs? Suppose he read the journal entry about the day they cut their afternoon classes and made love three times in the woods near Falls Lake? The details— positions, explorations of acts they hadn't tried before—weren't fit for any father's eyes, let alone a father whose daughter was thought to be not only inexperienced but chaste.

"When the investigation has been completed and the case resolved, you'll get it back," the deputy told him.

Anthony finished with the cords and turned the tower back around. "How long does that usually take?"

Morales paused, then asked, "Are you employed?"

"Yeah. I work part-time—I'm still in high school."

The deputy didn't ask why he wasn't at school this morning; maybe that answer was apparent. What he did say was, "You might want to think about investing in new stuff."

"Are you serious? That long? How can that be legal?" Anthony stared at the deputy, whose round, smooth face betrayed no opinion. "Anyway," he said, "I already told the police what happened. She already told them, too, and our statements match, the police told me they do. I don't see how any of this is necessary." He should never have let them in. But what choice was there? Sour dread rose in his throat, and he thought he might be sick.

"Lift that, and precede me downstairs," Morales said, in a tone that reminded Anthony which of them was in possession of both a weapon and the authority to use it. He swallowed hard, and complied.

In the living room, Winship waited with several empty bags in hand, in varying sizes. The deputy handed him the camera and Winship selected one of the bags, each of which was clearly marked with the word *Evidence* in bold letters, and dropped the camera into it. He used a Sharpie to write on the bag, then he set it on the end table and picked up a roll of tape. "Set that here," he told Anthony, then quickly taped the disc drives shut before pulling an evidence bag over the top of the tower and then upending the bag, which he wrote on as before. They went through the routine again with the flash drive.

Winship said, "Your phone, son, where is it?"

"Lost."

"Is that right?"

Anthony said, "I've looked for it everywhere. I don't know what happened to it."

"Have a seat, then, and Deputy Morales will keep you company while I try to resolve that problem."

"It's not here," Anthony said. "I'm pretty sure I lost it at the mall. And I called them, but nobody turned it in yet. Probably got stolen."

Winship nodded to Morales, who put a hand on Anthony's shoulder and pushed him slightly, a suggestion, an encouragement, to take a seat.

He sat, and listened miserably while the investigator moved about his bedroom right overhead. His pulse pounded, making his head throb. Morales stood with feet splayed, hands clasped behind his back, watching Anthony, saying nothing, waiting for what Anthony suspected he knew was about to happen.

"Eureka," Winship called.

Morales smirked at Anthony. "Good try," he said.

When they were finally gone, Anthony paced from the front door to the back, living room to kitchen, his feet traversing a straight line because his thoughts were anything but straight. He'd been raped and robbed, that's how it felt, and it was a travesty—and it wasn't as though he could call the police and report the crimes. He knew he should tell his mother, but he didn't want to call right now and disrupt her day. He couldn't call Amelia. He should, he supposed, call Mariana Davis, so that at least she would know how he'd been screwed in yet another way. And to ask what he could do to protect Amelia. Maybe Davis would be able to get an injunction or something, whatever it was that could prevent the police from investigating further. Didn't they need *just cause* to do this? He had certain rights, didn't he? If he had a goddamn computer, he could look it up.

The attorney's business card was tacked to the refrigerator door. Anthony got the house phone and dialed her number. When her assistant put his call through, he said, "The cops just came with a search warrant and took pretty much every electronic device except the TV, and I need to know if you can stop them, and if you can't, I need to know whether whatever they find in my stuff is going to get back to Harlan Wilkes."

"Okay, first, take a breath. Are you breathing, nice and deep?"

He did as directed, feeling some of his anxiety escape as he exhaled. "Yeah, I'm breathing."

"All right. Now, if they already got a warrant, it isn't likely I can stop them. Tell me what they're going to find," Davis said, and when he told her, she replied, "Hm. That's unfortunate. You'd better strap yourself in. Wilkes may become the least of your troubles."

Anthony said, "If you mean statutory rape, then A) everything was consensual, and B) I thought that only applied to people under sixteen."

"Oh, no, it's completely legal for you two to have sex. I don't want to be alarmist, all right, so I'm not going to predict anything specifically. But if the DA takes a shovel and flashlight to the statutes, he might dig up some ugly charges for you. I've worked in Wake County for six years now, and I can tell you, Gibson Liles— he's the DA—has a moral streak that would make a preacher want to adopt him."

Anthony cringed, thinking of such a man at his desk with the photos and emails and journal details spread before him like a feast. He cringed at the thought of Liles phoning Harlan Wilkes—they were probably already pals—to describe for him the road his daughter was traveling. "I'm worried for Amelia. It's already martial law over there."

"Your loyalty and concern are honorable, but not practical. We have to focus on you right now."

"It's not me versus her."

"It will be."

ACT II

What is this thing that builds our dreams,
then slips away from us?

—QUEEN

14

KIM WINTER STOOD INSIDE HER CLOSET, A SMALL WALK-IN that the home's previous owner had outfitted with cedar paneling, and breathed deeply. The pungent scent always reminded her of her Ithaca house and, tonight, a simpler time. In Ithaca, she'd never had such anxiety when preparing for a date—because in Ithaca, she'd never dated a man who wasn't supposed to date her, and who really should not, now, be seeing her romantically when her son, a student under his charge, was having a run-in with the parent of another of his students, and with the law.

Lunacy, that's what this was. She knew it. William knew it, too. And yet, he'd stood there in the art studio earlier today after it had emptied of students, watching her while she made what was her third pass at a 4x4 canvas on which she was painting a wren, and said, "I'd love to see you, later."

She'd pushed her unruly hair from her face using the back of her hand and looked at him critically. "Not really."

"Yes, really. Are you still angry with me?"

She had been. For a week she'd avoided him at school, avoided everyone but her students, cursed, silently, the uptight attitudes of the Ravenswood advisory board members who'd unanimously recommended that Anthony be suspended until he was cleared—*if* he got cleared—and cursed William for caving in to them. She'd asked him, "And if he's not?" He had answered, "One thing at a time, all right?"

One thing at a time. Who ever had that luxury?

By the time she stood there in the school's studio working on the wren, however, her anger was gone. She'd had time to think it over, to talk to her mother, to talk to Rose Ellen, who'd said, "And I thought Mark's girlfriend's pregnancy scare was stressful. But listen, Anthony's mess isn't William's fault, right? If our kids would just keep their pants on, they wouldn't *have* these problems."

Kim had to agree. And, given the situation, he had been right to suspend Anthony. She set her paintbrush down and told William, "No, I'm not angry. I understand, and really, he's better off at home."

"So, I'll pick you up?" he said, his eyes so compassionate, so *blue* behind his wire-rimmed glasses. Kim felt a flutter low in her belly. What caused that butterfly sensation—*physically* caused it? And why did William have to provoke it so easily? She really ought to be sensible, to resist.

"I'll meet you there," she said.

"I haven't named a place."

She'd smiled. "Name it."

Now Kim stood in the closet in her panties and bra, unable to decide between wearing a skirt, or a dress, or pants. They were going to an intimate little bistro, where they'd hear the jazz trio that played there on Friday nights. If this night had been taking place two weeks earlier, she'd have been excited, anxious in an entirely different way. As it was, the hollowness in her gut and the way she kept catching herself clenching her teeth were akin to anticipating a lousy performance review (which she'd never had but always, always feared). She wanted to see William, was, truly, eager to see him, and yet there was no denying that the timing was incredibly bad.

That lousy performance review was sure to come, though it would be about mothering and not work, and would probably not come from William. It would come from other women whose sons had managed to either avoid or evade run-ins with the Moral Authority. William would be mostly concerned with maintaining order at Ravenswood while being subject to judgment himself. How, the Authority was sure to ask—had begun asking already, if rumors were to be believed—could he have permitted such an environment as had bred behavior like Anthony's? That behavior was expected at *public* school; what was their tuition money being spent on, if not an educational experience that was in every way superior?

If she chose the dress she'd ideally wear to this kind of restaurant—say, this sleeveless plum sheath in embroidered silk that she'd bought in Italy for next to nothing, would William be more likely to set aside his own anxieties regarding Anthony's situation, or would he think she was trying to distract or influence him? And, well, wasn't she? And in asking her out tonight (regardless of what she might wear), wasn't he in essence saying he wanted her to distract and influence him?

She groaned. Why did this have to be so damned complicated? Eyeing her cellphone where it sat atop a pile of folded T-shirts, she reached for it. How much easier she would make things by simply canceling the date. No dress, no tension. She could stay home, build herself a chocolate-chip macadamia nut sundae. Start that new Elizabeth Berg novel her mother just finished. She could iron . . . something.

"Oh, just deal with it," she said, laying the phone down again. She chose the plum dress, and a delicate black cardigan, and the engraved silver bracelet her parents had given her when Anthony was born. "To remind you that you are still you," her mother had said, fastening it around her wrist. Over the years, Kim had found that she often chose the bracelet when she needed that reminder. It was so easy, far easier than she'd imagined when she set out on the journey, to lose yourself in the job of motherhood and not realize you'd gone missing. Tonight, she wanted to be Kim Winter, amateur artist, lover of French culture, lover of the ocean, of the forests, of the lingering scent of rain on fallen leaves. She wanted to reclaim Kim Winter, lover.

She left her room and stopped in Anthony's bedroom doorway to say she was leaving. She found him lying on his bed with his feet propped on his headboard, reading a slim paperback that he held in one hand with the cover folded behind it. In his other hand was the charm Amelia had given him. He turned it end on end and passed it from finger to finger like a magician keeping limber.

"What's that you're reading?" she asked.

"Shakespeare's poems. 'The Rape of Lucrece,' 'A Lover's Complaint,' like that." He laid the book on his chest.

"I thought you were scheduled to work tonight."

"Eric gave me the night off."

"Why?" This seemed unlike the man who owned and managed Anthony's workplace, a fastidious, terse, single man whose entire existence centered on music and its production and reproduction, and the running of his store. She could not recall one time in the year that Anthony had been working there when Eric had altered the schedule in an apparent fit of generosity.

"He felt like it," Anthony said, too casually.

"Try again."

"Okay, fine." He stilled the charm and closed his hand around it. "He asked me to stay away, for the moment. He thinks maybe I've been bad for business. Anyway," he said, not giving her a chance to protest what surely could not be true, "you look great. Have a good time—which means, don't talk about me," he said wryly. "Take the night off."

Kim dredged up a smile. "Thanks. I'll try. You should, too. Maybe find something more upbeat to read."

"Upbeat. What a novel concept." He pulled his feet down and turned onto his side, propping his head on his hand. "But hey, I wouldn't want to spoil my righteous anger."

"Maybe you should get out, too. Do you have any plans?"

He raised and lowered one shoulder. "Maybe."

Eleven days of separation, during which Cameron McGuiness was his only connection to Amelia, had been a strain and a test of his endurance unlike anything soccer had ever demanded of him. To his credit, he'd spent a lot of the time working on the play he was writing for his senior project, starting over, writing it out in long-hand in a notebook. He wouldn't tell her much about it. She was sure, though, that it wasn't a comedy.

"Have you heard from Amelia?"

"Like that could happen," he said.

"From Cameron, I mean."

"Nothing new," he told her, but he averted his eyes.

She went to him and kissed him on the temple. "Be good."

"How could you imagine I wouldn't?" he said.

She wished she had some way to comfort him. As long as she was wishing, she wished she had done a better job of whichever parenting aspect applied to teen love and sex and the exploding capabilities of electronics. Or that he had done a better job of policing himself and Amelia. She wished he had chosen a girl who didn't feel her parents needed to be deceived.

"I won't be out late. But if you go anywhere, leave me a note—and lock up."

"Don't I always?" he said, resuming the position she'd found him in.

"Yes, you do. You do," she said, an apology and acknowledgment, both. "Don't mind me. I'm just a little scattered, you know?"

"Tell me about 'scattered,'" he said, waving his good-night.

Outside, Kim pulled her sweater closed and buttoned the top

button, then left the house, stepping out into the twilit world. She
stood on the porch long enough to catch the minty scent of bee
balm in her flower beds, to admire the deepening blue of the sky
and the sweep of two bats crossing paths beneath the streetlight,
where bugs still swarmed in November. Anthony had been delighted by this their first year in North Carolina. Kim had been delighted by the reason for it: warm days that in most years continued
into December. A twentysomething woman jogged past with a large
dog at her side, its collar jingling, and then the evening was quiet
again, interrupted only by the noise of Kim's not-so-sensible heels
tapping the sidewalk as she walked to her car.

Driving out of the neighborhood, Kim tried to shake off her
stress—not an easy task, despite the dress and the bracelet and the
shoes. There was a lot to shake off. She'd plodded through the days
that followed their descent into the world of criminal defense angry
with the Wilkeses, furious with the television news stations and the
way they'd framed the situation, sickened by the story that had run
on the front page of Thursday morning's *Wake Weekly,* and ready to
shoot every reporter who'd called the house or the school or had
called or texted Anthony. Even if Harlan Wilkes was the impetus, as
Mariana Davis had suggested, why was so much being made of so
little?

The worst, though, had been the cheerful TV reporter who had
come to their house looking for Anthony on Monday afternoon
while the vividly marked news truck sat provocatively at the curb. A
skinny young man with gel-combed dark hair had come to the door
and asked, "Hi, is Anthony home?" as if inviting him to come out and
play.

He was home. Because of his suspension he was home and
brooding. He texted Kim several times each day, venting, causing
her to be, at turns, upset *for* him and upset *with* him. He needed to
settle down and keep a positive outlook, not complain about
William, or about Harlan Wilkes, or about the ravenous media and
the salacious tale they were building from the slight information

they had. The newspaper's headline had read, RALEIGH MAN AR-
RESTED FOR PREYING ON PREP-SCHOOL GIRL.

Kim told the reporter, "Nope, he's not here."

"I'd like to talk to him about—"

"He's not home, I said."

The man eyed Anthony's car, which was parked at the curb in
front of the house, then said, "Are you his mother? Can I ask you a
few questions?"

If Kim had possessed claws, she'd have slashed the reporter's
face. She forced herself to keep her voice calm and even. "No, you
can't."

"No statement? People would like to know Anthony's side of the
story."

"*His* side? They don't even know—" She'd almost said Amelia's
name before remembering that her identity was protected because
of her age. Not that this practice had to be observed by the accused's
mother, but Kim had no desire to complicate the situation by giving
the Wilkeses another reason to despise Anthony. "They don't even
really know *the girl's* side," she said, "so it won't matter much if they
don't know his, either."

If she set an example of levelheadedness, there might yet be a
chance (granted, a slim one) for the Wilkeses to relax their stance
and for the kids to resume their relationship. They might all be able
to one day look back on this week and if not laugh about it, at least
smile ruefully and shake their heads. That, they might all say, was
such a crazy situation, but all's well that ends well!

Kim, with this in mind, told the reporter, "It's really a misunderstanding. A mistake."

"Is it?" the reporter asked eagerly, making Kim sorry she'd said
anything. "Why is that? What happened?"

"Mariana Davis will be happy to answer your questions," Kim
had said. She closed the door and turned to find Anthony watching
her from where he sat atop the stairs, his arms wrapped around
himself, mouth clamped shut, angry wariness in his eyes.

Now she parked her car in a lot across from the restaurant, wishing she could relax, wishing Anthony's appearance in court two days earlier had been the end of things. Instead, they'd shown up at nine, along with a great many other unfortunate citizens (some of whom were badly in need of a shower), and waited anxiously to see Mariana Davis. When she came in forty minutes later, one of a dozen lawyers milling about the room, having whispered consultations with clients and with one another, they'd watched her meet up with a dark-suited man near the judge's bench, speak to him quietly while other defendants stood before the judge and were processed, and then she'd waved them to the exit. Outside the heavy double doors of courtroom 3-C, Ms. Davis said, "We've pushed the hearing back. He claims they don't have their paperwork in order, but I think they're buying time to wait for the results of the search and seizure."

Search and seizure. Never, never would Kim have imagined that this term would attach itself to her life. And the words *criminal defense*—that *this* was the term for the service Mariana Davis was providing Anthony made Kim's stomach turn far more than it did over parting with money that was intended to take them to France next summer, and to help Anthony pay for college. The term seemed wrong for a service that existed in support of another term, "presumed innocence."

Though Anthony was not, in fact, innocent, not when it came to the letter of the law. As the attorney had explained, Anthony had provided the police with all the information the DA needed in order to convict him of the charge. When Kim had asked her if his statement was admissible, given that they hadn't first read him his rights, Mariana Davis said, "The police can ask any question they like when investigating a complaint." She'd looked at Anthony and said, "Never, ever say anything to the police unless you're the one who called them."

Their defense, then, was not to prove his innocence, but rather to persuade the assistant district attorney who'd been assigned to the case that the charge itself was, in this situation, misapplied and absurd.

Arriving at the restaurant, Kim went inside and spotted William sitting at the bar, laughing and talking to the bartender. She slipped off her sweater and hung it over her arm, and watched him for a moment. He had the ageless good looks of a man who'd once been a boy growing up at the beach. His short, blond hair, mussed a little, held the golden highlights of summer (he was, he'd told her, still a surfer). He wore a suede sport coat over a white open-necked dress shirt, and stylish new glasses that made him look smarter and sexier than the simple wire-framed pair he wore at school. He was her age, forty-nine, divorced five years earlier, no kids. He was good-hearted and clever and resourceful. Standing there in her plum silk dress, one hand twisting her bracelet, she wanted as much as anything she'd ever wanted before to *have* him, to *be* his.

He saw her then and waved her over, standing up and pushing his hands into his pockets as he watched her cross the room. The smart thing would be to run the other way, she thought, walking toward him anyway, as if her sense and sensibility were completely disconnected. She wanted no complications and no hesitations. But the course of love did never run smooth. It was sometimes catastrophic, in fact. He was, she confirmed to herself, worth the risk.

"Hey," he said, putting his hand on her shoulder. "You look fantastic."

What warmth infused her entire body with his touch! *Ludicrous,* she thought, then she said, "You're looking pretty good yourself."

They ordered drinks and talked, first, about the easy topics. The good weather the area had been having, the jazz trio, and the great charm of the bass as an instrument. Crab dip with artichokes, crab dip without. Not until they were each into their second glass of wine did William ask about Anthony.

He said, "Is he doing all right? The lawyer you hired, what's her strategy?" Kim felt a thorn's prick of irritation, of impatience. Not with William, whose concern she valued, but with Anthony, for the mess that had spilled over onto her life, and William's. Anthony knew what sort of man Harlan Wilkes was; *why* hadn't he thought about the potential consequences before sending Amelia the photos?

Kim said, "She's aiming for complete dismissal. She asked Anthony to write up a detailed narrative for her, which he did, and she's set him up with a psychologist who'll assess his capacity for sexual deviancy—deviancy! As if half the teens in the world aren't doing this kind of thing! I'm sorry"—she interrupted herself—"I told myself tonight wasn't going to be about Anthony. *He* told me to make sure it wasn't."

"My fault. But look, if we don't talk about it, it'll just hover around us as 'the thing we're not talking about,' don't you think?"

Holding her wineglass up to the light, Kim swirled its contents, watching the garnet-red liquid slide along the sides of the glass. "I do, yes. So . . . we'll go back to the courthouse a week from Tuesday for his rescheduled 'appearance,' and the attorney will iron things out with the prosecutor then. We hope. I thought it was called a hearing, but I guess not. It's funny, you think you know a lot about the court system—all those TV shows and books, right? But now that we have to navigate it, I feel like I'm swimming underwater in the dark."

"I've done that," William said. "It's damn scary."

Kim set her glass on the bar and turned toward him. "Thank you," she said sincerely. Then, feeling the moment drawing out in a way that, if they'd been alone, might have led to a more personal expression of her appreciation, she fingered her bracelet and said, "The law, the statute they've charged him with, it's intended for creepy, predatory old men and the like. Nasty guys who are trying to entice— though God knows how they could be enticing—or corrupt young girls. It's not supposed to apply to kids like Anthony."

"I agree—which is why it pains me to have anything to do with the anti-Anthony camp. The board's viewpoint is that Ravenswood has an accused sexual predator among its ranks. I didn't have any choice except to suspend him; parents expect me to protect their daughters."

"Then you'd better suspend Cy D'Angelo and Mike Hartsfield— I think those two were born with leers on their faces. And I have no doubt that they're in active pursuit of any girl who seems even remotely willing to entertain them."

"Yes, well, those two have managed to not be caught doing anything against school policy, let alone against the law."

Kim said, "He's miserable, William. They took his computer, his camera, his iPod, his phone. . . . And he didn't call me afterward. He sat at home, sulking."

"So would I. What are they looking for?"

"The attorney thinks they want to see whether there are more girls involved—which is ridiculous."

"So they won't find anything, and that will help prove his case."

"Maybe. But in the meantime, he's almost entirely cut off from Amelia, he's been publicly embarrassed, the other kids are having a field day trashing him, his boss doesn't want him around. How can he deserve all that? The worst of it is that his arrest and the suspension will make NYU think twice about his admission, and if he can't go there . . . William, that's all he's ever wanted."

"I'll give them a call on Monday and explain the situation, all right?"

"Will you? That would be great, thank you. Thank you," she repeated, reaching for his hand.

He pressed her hand between his palms, then turned her hand palm-up and traced a line with his index finger. "Hard times, leading to renewal—it's all right there."

"Details, please."

"For that I'm afraid I'll need my crystal ball," he said, releasing her hand with a squeeze. "I can say, though, that it's good that the charge is relatively minor, and whatever the outcome, it'll all be re-solved soon."

"I'll drink to that."

William raised his glass and touched it to hers. "And then . . ."

"Then?"

He smiled, a sultry sort of half smile that made her feel half her age and entirely female. "I don't know," he said, leaning close to her, then closer, and then brushing her lips lightly with his. "But by God, we're going to figure it out."

Anthony paced his room. They'd gone eleven days with no direct contact.

Eleven.

Miserable.

Days.

Eleven days that felt more like years, without hearing Amelia's voice or seeing her or touching her or reading a text or an email from her. He was surprised he'd survived it.

Anxiety. Agitation. Mood swings. Insomnia. Depression. Nightmares. All explainable by his run-in with the law, true, but also symptoms of withdrawal—he'd done a report on addiction and withdrawal for Chemistry class. He was addicted to Amelia the way he was addicted to air. The only antidote was exposure.

The question was, did she still feel the same way about him? Suppose her parents had convinced her that the media version of him was his real self? Suppose she'd used these eleven days to reevaluate what she wanted in her life, to change her mind? He didn't want to believe she would, or even could, stop loving him just because they were cut off from each other. God knew he was as crazy for her as ever. It was the separation, the blackout, that made his fears grow like mushrooms after a heavy rain. They defied logic, but then so did love. He tried to take comfort from that.

When the phone finally rang, he snatched it off his bed and answered, "Well?"

"I got it," Cameron said.

"Eight o'clock?"

"Be there."

15

FRIDAY EVENING IN THE WILKES HOUSEHOLD MEANT MEATLOAF. Amelia had pushed her slice around her plate while giving better attention to the green beans, knowing that if she didn't eat something, her parents would add that to the list of things she needed to do better, or differently, or to quit doing—like being argumentative with the tutor, a sour, demanding woman who had taught in public school before a car accident left her face partially disfigured. Apparently, the woman had tried to go back to work, but the students were so cruel that she'd filed for disability and began taking selective tutoring jobs instead. She'd told Amelia all of this in an accusatory tone, as if Amelia were to blame for all of it. Amelia didn't deny the woman's right to have a bad attitude, she simply wanted the woman to acknowledge that she, Amelia, had the right to one as well.

This was what Amelia had said to the counselor, in their second meeting on Wednesday afternoon. She'd said her attitude ranged from sad to disgusted to angry to despondent, which had sent the counselor into a long interrogation to determine whether Amelia was clinically depressed. Did she have thoughts of cutting herself, perhaps? Of vengeful suicide? Did she harbor any violent thoughts toward herself or her parents? "No," Amelia had answered again and again. "No. I want my life back is all."

After eating two bites of the meatloaf, she picked up her plate and carried it from the dining room to the kitchen, just as the phone rang. She grabbed it before either of her parents had time to react.

"Hello?"

From the dining room her father called, "That better not be Winter."

"Hey, jailbird." It was Cameron. "So they're finally letting you answer the phone?"

"Not exactly, *Cam*," Amelia said for her father's benefit, and was surprised that hearing Cameron's voice made her teary. She cleared her throat and sniffed. "I got lucky is all."

"*Bad* lucky is what you got, but that is all about to change—at least a little bit. You're not going anywhere, are you? Because I'm coming over, and I'm bringing . . . a surprise."

"Well, we were talking about going to see a movie." Her mother thought she needed to get out on a Friday night, to have some sense of normalcy—as if going to the movies with her parents was normal. "But I don't have to go," she said, "if you need me to, um, help. What is it?"

"They're listening, aren't they?"

"Uh-huh. We just finished dinner." She could hear her mother collecting plates and silverware to carry into the kitchen.

"Okay, well, I've arranged for the delivery of some contraband," Cameron said dramatically. "And I mean *seriously* forbidden stuff."

Amelia's heart leapt. The most forbidden thing she knew of was Anthony. She said, "What time?"

"I'll be there in like twenty minutes, and then I'll fill you in on the rest of the plan, okay?"

"Okay."

"But listen, he's had it pretty rough this past week," Cameron said. "I don't know what you've heard——"

"Nothing. Zilch. I have a tutor come for half the day, then we run errands and eat out and come home and I read a lot."

It was, Amelia thought, a strange limbo. She spent a lot of her time—when had she ever had so much free time?—unintentionally doing nothing. She'd catch herself at it when she was supposed to be doing schoolwork or when she'd been sitting in a sunny alcove with a book in her lap. Her mind would wander, often to thoughts of Anthony, but to other things as well. Memories from her childhood. Questions about the future that she knew were pointless to ask, since her parents, too, seemed to be waylaid with her in this netherworld, as if they'd all been on a trail through ten-foot-high grass and had come to a clearing, only to turn and find that the grass had closed in all around them. There was no way of telling where the forward path lay, and they couldn't go back the way they'd come, and so they were waiting for some sign, some event, to show them where to go next.

Cameron said, "Well, to begin with, his arrest made the news. TV and newspapers and online. Then Braddock suspended him because your dad called and had a total fit—said Anthony's dangerous to all us innocent girls—as if anyone in the Upper School is innocent, right? Amber Hartfield, maybe, with her violin and all that acne. Anyhow, your dad told the news that, too. They quoted him as 'the victim's father' without naming names. And oh, man, at school——"

"Oh my God," Amelia said, horrified at her father's actions. It was all she could do not to glare at him as he followed her mother into the kitchen. She turned away from them, going into the pantry as if she'd planned to get a Milk-Bone for Buttercup. "At school?" she prompted, needing to not think about her father just now, or what might she say to him in her anger? And then he'd send her to her room again and forbid Cameron's visit. No Cameron equaled no Anthony.

"A lot of the kids are talking shit about Anthony, like they always knew he was a perv and they're glad he's in trouble, and some of the girls are saying he propositioned *them,* or they're claiming to be the unnamed victim so they can get all the attention."

"Who's doing that?" Amelia said. Buttercup trailed her into the pantry and sat down expectantly. Amelia found the Milk-Bone box and took out two biscuits.

"Camilla Duffy, for one. That's no surprise, right? Our gang knows what's really up—and nobody's telling, I made them all swear on their lives. Officially you still have mono, but you're getting better and hope to be back after Thanksgiving. Anthony is supposed to be able to come back after his case is settled, but . . ."

"But?" Amelia set the biscuit on Buttercup's nose, then gave her the signal to toss and catch it. Buttercup was her single comfort these days.

"But, some other stuff has happened, and his first court date got delayed—did I tell you that already?—and he's just really pissed. But—a better 'but'—he's really, really happy about coming to see you tonight, so I have a plan and all you have to do is say I'm coming over for help with my English paper—and make sure we can be in your room. Okay?"

"Okay," she said, already feeling the heat of nerves and anticipation rising from her collar and coloring her neck. "See you soon." She stayed in the pantry and fed Buttercup a second biscuit, hoping a few deep breaths would relieve the flush.

When she left the pantry, her parents were still hovering in the kitchen, something they never did when they weren't suspicious of her every move and word. She squatted down to pet Buttercup, telling them, "Cameron's on her way over."

Her father frowned. "I'm thinking you might've asked us first."

"It's *Cameron.* You don't believe me? Check the caller ID. She needs help with her English paper, and I told her she can sleep over."

"Oh, *you* told her, did you, without—" her father began, before her mother put her hand on his chest and said, "I'm sure it'll be fine, it *is* fine for Cameron to come and sleep over."

Amelia stood and faced them with arms crossed protectively. "She said Anthony's arrest was all over the news."

The guilty looks on her parents' faces confirmed Cameron's story and their own deceit. Of course they'd deceived her. They were her captors, and she was at the mercy of their whims. They would feed her only the information they wanted her to have. After all, why upset poor, misguided little Amelia with the information that the man she thinks she loves is now infamous—thanks very much to her father? Why tell her that the whole population of central North Carolina likely now believes he is, as Cameron put it, a perv? An informed prisoner is a difficult prisoner.

If this was how it was going to be, they'd be better off giving her a lobotomy.

"Thanks again," she said, softly, "for screwing up both our lives."

"Amelia—"

She ignored their responses and walked off for added effect. It was, in part, an act. She knew she couldn't lay all the blame on them. She'd been stupid to forget her computer last Monday, stupid not to do a better job of hiding the things she didn't want found. Or maybe she shouldn't have tried to keep her love for Anthony secret until she turned eighteen. If she had been straight with her parents right from the start, and brought Anthony around so that they could get to know him, maybe none of this would have happened.

Yeah, right. Wishful thinking. She was getting really good at that.

From upstairs, Amelia heard the doorbell signaling Cameron's arrival, but couldn't make out the conversation when her father answered the door, only the sounds of his voice, deep and curt, and Cameron's, brassy and unremittingly cheerful.

Cameron was a pixie of a girl, barely five feet tall, with long, untamable copper hair and a spray of freckles across her cheeks and nose. She was so energetic and whimsical that if she'd sprouted wings and begun to fly like a fairy, it would not have surprised

Amelia in the least. In fact, she wished Cameron would do exactly that, and grant her another wish or two while she was at it.

"Thanks, Mr. Wilkes, but I know the way," Amelia heard, followed by the sound of tennis shoes bounding up the wooden stairs.

Amelia waited at the top of the stairs, and when Cameron appeared in her usual jeans and hoodie and black-sequined high-tops as if nothing in the world had changed, Amelia felt tears threaten again. Tears, when it used to be that the main emotion Cameron evoked was mirth. *Okay God,* she thought, *it's enough already. I get it.*

Cameron slung an arm around Amelia and pulled her along to Amelia's room. "Your dad's in a mood. He asked me—politely, but I could tell there was only one possible answer—to leave my phone with him until I go."

"He did not," Amelia said. "He wanted your phone, really?"

"Mm. So I gave it to him, hoping to heaven he wouldn't ask to search the *bag,*" she said dramatically. "Which he didn't. He got the phone, so he's happy—*ish.*"

Cameron dropped her book bag onto Amelia's bed, a four-poster with pale green brocaded curtains gathered at each post and a canopy overhead. "Jesus, you look terrible. Your hair's a mess. Ever hear of a shower?"

"I showered yesterday," Amelia said, going over to shut the door. "I'm pretty sure, anyway. Do I really look that bad? Do I have time, before—?"

"He won't care, and no, you really only look tired and stressed out." Cameron squinted, assessing her. "Okay, you could brush your hair."

Amelia went to her mirror. She did look bad. Bloodshot, bruised-looking eyes, hair that was as listless as she'd been lately. Without the routine of school and dance and voice lessons, without the regular interaction of her friends and their dramas and their joys, without Anthony's regular presence, she was adrift. She missed his humor and affection. She missed the companionship she'd grown so comfortable with. Before, she might not see him alone for more than a few minutes in a given day, but they were in touch end-lessly, perpetually. He was always at the other end of an email, a text message, a phone call, a glance across a classroom, across a stage. Having him, his steadiness, his certainty that life was a glittering gem and every facet hers to explore, had been like water and sun-shine to a wilting plant. His absence was a drought, and her parents, she thought, indulging another metaphor, were like blazing-hot dual summer suns that refused to set.

"I'm not sleeping much," she said, turning to Cameron. "They act like everything is completely fine. They haven't told me any-thing."

Cameron stood up and climbed onto the bed's footboard, bal-ancing by holding on to the canopy rail overhead. "Here's what I know," she said. "He goes to court again a week from Tuesday. Since it's a misdemeanor and he's never been in trouble before, *probably* the worst that'll happen is he'll get, like, probation and community service."

"And a record."

"So? Lots of people have them. It'll just make him seem danger-ous and more exciting," Cameron said, waggling her eyebrows.

Amelia sat down on the floor, her back against the wall and her legs extended, bare feet turned outward in ballet's first position. She pulled a section of hair in front of her face and held it up to the light, examining it for split ends. "But what if it means NYU won't let him in? And if they won't, no other place worth going will, ei-ther. There has to be some way to fix this mess. Wait—did you say a week from Tuesday?"

"Yeah. Why?"

"Nothing." She let go of the hair and pulled up another section to examine. "We were supposed to be in New York doing evalua-tions that day, is all. Do you know if he rescheduled?" She desper-ately hoped so, and hoped she'd be able to as well, if she ever got a chance to contact the program. Maybe Cameron could do that for her.

Cameron said, "I don't know if he has or not."

"When will he be here?"

"God, it's all Anthony, Anthony, Anthony," Cameron complained, tossing her hair dramatically. "You sure know how to make a girl feel welcome."

"I'm sorry, Cam."

"And I'm kidding, okay? Lighten up. Eight o'clock, and I brought this," she said, hopping down and unzipping her book bag's main compartment, then tilting it so that Amelia could see inside.

"What is it?" Amelia asked, unable to make sense of what appeared to be a coil of gray cable.

"Fire escape ladder. My dad just put one of these in all our second-floor bedrooms. 'For an emergency only,' of which this is clearly one."

Amelia heard a noise outside her door. She jumped up and hurried over, ready to throw it open and catch her parents spying—but when she opened it, there was Buttercup standing at the door with hopeful eyes and a low, wagging tail. Amelia leaned down and kissed the dog's muzzle, then checked the hallway and peered into the nearby rooms with Buttercup following her. When she was satisfied that the noise had come from the dog only, she and Buttercup returned to her room.

"No one there but the dog," she said, then pointed at Cameron's bag. "That ladder? I can't leave, they check on me too often."

"No *problemo*. It's for him to come up."

"Suppose he doesn't show?"

"He will."

"Is he on his way?" she asked, taking her spot on the floor again. "Did you check before giving up your phone?"

Cameron pursed her lips, then said, "I didn't want to tell you before, in case you freaked and your parents heard, but he's phone-less himself. The thing is, the cops came and confiscated it, and all his electronics, probably to try to catch him on other charges."

Amelia thought of what the police were going to find if they searched his things. "Oh God," she groaned. "If my Dad finds out . . ." She shook her head. "This just gets worse and worse."

"What, don't tell me you guys made a sex tape."

"No," Amelia said. "Give me *some* credit."

"Credit," Cameron squeaked.

"Anyway, never mind. It's done now. Maybe they'll just see that it's all him and me, and that will prove his story, and they'll leave it at that."

Cameron frowned sympathetically. "I hope. So, I talked to him a little while ago, before he left his house, and he was definitely planning to be here. I can't think much of anything would stop him."

"After what my father's done to him, I wouldn't blame him if he decided to cut me loose, go find some girl who won't get him arrested. Go find some other girl, period."

Cameron squatted down and put her hands on Amelia's face, then pressed her nose to Amelia's. "Hel-lo? This is Anthony Winter we're talking about. The guy who's insanely crazy about you, remember? He'd die first."

Amelia pushed her away. "I don't deserve him."

"Whatever," Cameron said, sighing. "Shape up, or he's not going to feel very welcome when he gets here."

Amelia's first sight of Anthony was his hopeful face looking up at her as he climbed the rungs of the narrow, slight ladder. Cold air rushed in through the bathroom's window, cooling her cheeks, slowing her heart rate. He'd shown up. He wanted to be with her. He loved her, still.

The relief on his face before he wrapped her in his arms was her undoing; she started to cry. "I'm so sorry," she said, her tears wetting his collar. "How awful—"

"Shh." He leaned back to look at her face, then gently wiped her cheeks with his thumbs. "It'll be okay."

"I tried to stop my dad," she said, forcing herself to speak slowly, to think each word and then say it. "I did everything I could."

"You don't think I blamed you?"

She shrugged. "I hoped you didn't," she said, and looked up at him.

"We'll get through it. Where's Cam?"

"Keeping watch."

"Ah." He tilted her chin upward and kissed her, softly at first, and then, as she pulled him closer, the kiss became more than a comfort. When they eased apart, she nodded toward the wide, sea-green cotton rug that covered the middle of the tiled floor.

"Right now?" he said.

There was plenty of room, and if they were quiet, not even Cameron would hear them. "Do you want to?"

"Of course I want to, but—"

"'Every, every minute,'" she whispered, starting on her shirt's buttons.

"I need to warn you about something." She stopped and looked up. He said, "Did Cameron tell you about the search warrant?" and paused as she nodded. "My lawyer says the DA is probably looking to see whether I've been messing with other girls. Amelia, they're going to find *everything*. Your dad . . ." He shook his head. "I keep thinking, you're seventeen, almost eighteen . . . you could come stay with me and, I don't know, petition for emancipation or something." He took her hands in his and kissed each palm, then folded his fingers over hers.

Amelia said, "I doubt your mom would go for that."

"She might."

"And then she'd lose her job after my dad gave Braddock unbelievable grief for getting involved."

"He wouldn't fire her; he likes her too much."

"Whatever, it doesn't matter," Amelia said, " 'cause I'm not going anywhere. This will all blow over. My dad's going to have to face reality, and when he does, we'll get everything back on track."

"What if it doesn't blow over? You want to stay here like this?" He gestured to themselves, to the fact of their meeting in her bathroom, to needing a coordinator and a lookout even for this. "It's going to get worse when he hears what's in my—"

"Maybe he'll never find out."

Anthony said, "And maybe pigs will all sprout angel wings and take to the skies."

The image made her smile. "That would be pretty cool, wouldn't it? But okay. Fine, then. I'll just tell him. I'll tell him before the police do, and I'll keep working on him, and he'll give in and accept it. He's not evil. He thinks he has to protect me in some certain way, but when he sees that I'm still me even after having been defiled by you," she said, smiling and tugging on his shirt's hem, "he'll realize it's all going to be fine. He'll put me back in school, and we'll reschedule evaluations—did you call them already?"

"No dice," he said, his expression darkening. "There's no more openings. They're booked solid, so—"

"Hey," Cameron said, knocking softly on the bathroom door. "Someone's coming upstairs."

"Damn it." Amelia shut her eyes and drew a deep breath. Why couldn't they catch a break? She kissed Anthony quickly and said, "Stay here, okay? Stand in the corner of the shower; I'll shut off the lights, they'll never look."

"I want to. You know I want to, but it's too risky," he said, opening the window wide. Then he pulled her into his arms and buried his face in her hair.

Cameron knocked again. "Amelia," she hissed.

Anthony released her. "Throw the ladder down as soon as I'm off it, and I'll take it with me."

Amelia blinked back tears. "If I don't see you, good luck in court."

He kissed her hard, then carefully climbed onto the windowsill and out onto the ladder. "*Adieu,*" he said, smiling sadly. Amelia watched him descend the tiny ladder while, in the bedroom, Cameron was saying, "She has a stomachache. This stuff about Anthony upsets her, Mrs. Wilkes, I won't lie."

Anthony jumped from the ladder and waited while Amelia carefully unhooked it from the sill and let it fall.

"Amelia?" her mother said, knocking. "Are you all right in there?"

Amelia turned toward the door. "Would you bring the Pepto?" she called. "I'm not feeling so good." She leaned out the window once more and saw Anthony winding up the ladder. He was barely visible in the moonless night. He waved to her, then disappeared into the woods.

"Okay, I'll get it," her mother said. "Is there anything else I can get you?"

Amelia leaned her forehead against the window frame and thought of Anthony's arms wrapped around her just a minute before, and of his gentle hands, and of his soft, generous mouth. She imagined walking up Manhattan's Seventh Avenue hand in hand with Anthony on a chilly night with the city's lights glowing on their smiling faces. She envisioned her father in a dark gray tux, toasting her and Anthony at their wedding reception, saying how glad he was that he'd given them a chance to prove him wrong.

"Oh, Momma," she said, "I'm not sure there's a medicine that'll do what I need."

Anthony got into his car and sat there in the dark, cooling down, hating that his time with Amelia had been so brief, loving that he'd been able to see her at all, hoping that she hadn't gotten caught. The sight and feel and taste of her were to him like blood to a starving vampire. He was restored, slightly. Enough to take the edge off. But she was his drug of choice, and if their communication didn't become more frequent and more satisfying, he didn't know what he'd do. Warring impulses (*Stage a protest sit-in on her front porch? Have her father and the DA knocked off?*) took his mind off the immediate questions of when and how he was going to be able to see her again— for about as long as it took him to put on his seat belt, start the car, and put it in gear.

When? How? He sat there, the engine idling, his heart rate slowing to a heavy thump of indignation. What right did the magistrate have to forbid him to be in touch with Amelia? What right did her parents have to isolate her? How could what they'd done together, the private souvenirs they'd made, be criminal? So many things in the world made no sense at all, but he and Amelia? He and Amelia were as right, as sensible, as the sun's rising in the eastern sky and falling in the western. All these people who were acting like it was otherwise needed to lighten up, open up, and recognize that while maybe they hadn't ever been as fortunate or had anything as genuine or as right, some people did. Love was real, and it wasn't only for the over-twenty-one crowd, damn it.

Disseminating harmful materials to a minor. If these words, this charge, hadn't fucked up his life, he'd laugh at them.

But okay, he thought, taking his foot off the brake. Moving on. Friday night. Can't sit here waiting for the world to turn, as if by sunrise the laws would have changed and his life would be put back in order.

There were plenty of things he could do tonight—catch a movie with Rob and some of the other guys, drop in to a party at Brittany Mangum's, go to Frankie's Fun Park and waste a few dollars playing old-school video games the way he and his friends sometimes had in his pre-Amelia days. Nothing much appealed, though. Frankie's was neither cool nor fun to do alone, and any social appearance would mean he'd spend all night fending off questions, some well meaning, some not.

Fine, then. He'd go back home. Read something. Write something. Whatever.

16

WHEN THE DOORBELL RANG EARLY SATURDAY MORNING, Amelia barely heard it over the treadmill's humming motor and the rhythmic thumping of her feet as they pounded the track. She'd logged six miles and was considering a seventh when the sound of Buttercup barking made her slow down, and then, when the barking continued, made her stop.

Using the towel she'd draped over a rail, she wiped her face, still listening, then grabbed her water bottle and headed upstairs from the basement fitness room. Buttercup continued to bark her frightened warning bark. Amelia started up the steps cautiously, calling, "Momma?" as she went. As she neared the top, she heard her mother saying, "I'm sorry, hang on," and then the sound of the dog's nails scrambling on the tile floor as her mother shut Buttercup away, presumably in the conservatory.

From the top of the steps, Amelia saw a woman in a Wake Forest Police uniform holding a canvas bag and standing to the right and slightly behind a tall man in a blue dress shirt and tan slacks. Both faced away from Amelia, watching her mother latch the conservatory's wide French doors.

"I'm so sorry," her mother was saying as she turned back toward them. "She's not usually like this, I don't know what's got into her." The words could have applied equally to Buttercup or to Amelia. The dog sat with her nose against one of the glass panels, snuffing and whining and pawing the floor at the door's base.

"Yes, ma'am," the man said. "It's quite understandable." His deference, genuine as it sounded, unnerved Amelia. What were these people doing here? She backed up a little, her hand gripping the polished rail, and waited.

The man handed her mother a piece of paper. "Here's the warrant. We'll be searching each room and whatever we collect will be bagged and inventoried. If you'd like to just have a seat, we'll let you know when we're finished." Amelia went cold, gooseflesh rising on her arms and neck.

Her mother looked down at the warrant for a moment, then said, "I don't—"

"I think you'll see that everything is in order," the man said reassuringly. "We won't bother anything that isn't specified." As he spoke, the woman gazed around the front hall, taking in all the things that were so familiar to Amelia that she never noticed them anymore. The antique chest of drawers that stood outside the conservatory, a piece her mother said had come from an Irish castle and dated back to the eighteenth century; the wide Aubusson rug, in the thickest wool of the creamiest ivory, with a delicate ring of blush roses and greenery in its center, wisps of blush ribbon curling about the ring and stretching into the corners, all bordered by roses and greenery. It was, to Amelia, the Spring Wedding rug, on which she and Cameron had once played Make-believe Bride. The elaborate hickory grandfather clock, hand-carved by her grandfather and her uncle Alan as a wedding gift to her parents twenty years earlier, would seem impressive to new eyes. The conservatory, where Buttercup still whined, and where, in the morning's accommodating sunshine, the gleaming piano threw light onto that good-little-girl portrait, was an impressive, unusual room.

"I don't understand," her mother said, cupping her elbow with one hand while the other went to her collarbone. "Why on earth are you here for her things? My daughter told the other officers everything there was to tell."

"You'll want to contact an attorney for all the details, ma'am. Our job is to collect the items, and then we'll be out of your hair."

Her mother's mouth and brows tightened. "I'm not sure about this. . . . Won't you come in and have a seat while I check with my husband? He's just gone outside to the, to the garage."

The pair glanced at each other, then the woman said, "Ms. Wilkes, you're free to call him in if you like, but this is a *search warrant*." She enunciated the two words carefully. "It's authorized by the court. We're going to get started now." With this, the officer walked across the hall and out of Amelia's sight. The man followed with a brief glance back at her mother, who remained standing near the door.

Amelia went to her then. "Momma, I heard the police come in."

"Oh! Amelia. Yes. They have a search warrant. . . . Now, where did I leave my phone? I'll call Daddy."

Amelia followed her mother into the parlor, where her mother's antique maple secretary sat among the plush upholstered furniture and velvet curtains. Although there was, in the mudroom, some sort of electronic panel called a Smart Box, which had the circuits for controlling the lights and home audio and security system, the real domestic control took place here at the maple desk.

"There it is," her mother said, going to the desk.

"Wait." Amelia rushed to put herself between her mother and the desk. "Don't. Leave him out there in the stable."

"What? Why?"

"He'll m-make it worse. Please."

"He'll have a fit if this goes on and I don't tell him."

"Momma"—Amelia grabbed her mother's hands—"for my sake,

please, just let them take the things and go. There's n-nothing he can do anyway."

"What are they looking for, Amelia? What did that boy tell them?"

"I don't know," she said, letting go and edging away. "You won't let me talk to him."

Her mother grabbed her shoulder. "The two of you—what else have you done?"

If not for her mother's accusatory tone, and the sound of footsteps in the hallway, and the long tradition of saying everything except what was revealing and meaningful, Amelia might have answered her mother's question candidly. She might have expressed the dread that came from knowing what the investigation would soon uncover. If she'd felt she could truly talk to her mother, she might have suggested that she take cover because soon, and possibly without any further warning, the sky was going to fall.

17

When Harlan Wilkes was asked, later, to describe how he felt that Monday night when the navy and gold Wake Forest Police cruiser arrived unexpectedly, he would struggle to comply. What words could do justice to the feeling that he'd been thrust onto one of those centrifugal motion rides and the bottom had just dropped out? How could he confess to feeling struck—literally slammed, wind knocked out of him—by the thought that Sheri and Amelia had been right, that he had overreacted from the start, and that his doing so had led to this, the arrival of the police to take his daughter to jail? No way could he say that aloud, he could hardly admit the possibility to himself. "I guess I just couldn't believe it," he would say. "I guess I hoped that whatever it was about, it was going be in her favor. My daughter is innocent. There was no reason to think they'd arrest her."

Before the police's Saturday visit—a travesty itself, he would say, without mentioning how he'd only learned of it afterward—

he'd begun his day by sending off Amelia's girlfriend, Cameron, and was thinking about whether he should limit Amelia's access to her, given that Cameron's phone log showed recent calls to a number that he'd found was Kim Winter's home listing. He was pretty sure Cameron hadn't been talking to the teacher. He'd gone out to the garage where he kept his collectibles, thinking about the possibility that the Winter kid had something going on with Cameron separate from Amelia, and if so, he wanted to break the news to Amelia gently.

He'd been tinkering under the hood of his 1939 Bugatti Type 57C, his "gangster car," he called it, when the police came to the house with the search warrant. He'd never heard a thing. Not until they'd been and gone and he'd come inside for lunch did he know that his daughter had come under investigation. Sheri sat him down after he'd passed Amelia, brooding as she headed for her cottage, and told him what had gone on while he was in the garage. He had been outraged—"Outraged!" he would later say—that no one had come for him or called him in to deal with the detective. If they had? Well, if they had, things might have gone differently—no, no, he couldn't say how, exactly, but surely he was deserving of a chance to do something. Sheri's reasoning—that she'd decided his presence would have made it even worse than it was—was no comfort. His own wife acting against his interests, and didn't that just figure. It amazed him how you could admire and trust and marry a woman, live with her for twenty years, and not know her in the least.

Sunday had been no picnic either, he'd say. Amelia stayed shut in her room, she would not go to church, she wouldn't answer his questions, she wouldn't talk to her mother. Only Buttercup was welcomed. Harlan had felt helpless and confused. He'd gotten in touch with his attorney, who'd promised to get some information, but as best anyone knew, something that was found in Winter's electronics led to the DA wanting to see what was stored in Amelia's.

He'd worked on Monday, as usual, making the rounds, having

meetings with his GMs (general managers—no way did he mean GM the brand, wouldn't touch those cars, that company was a disaster), and then returned home at his usual time, about six thirty. He and Sheri ate dinner, all like usual, though he would admit there was plenty of tension, what with her betrayal on Saturday and the question of the investigation hanging over all of their heads.

On Monday, he saw the cruiser from the window of his den, right around eight o'clock. Its lights were not flashing. No siren blared. He hadn't even noticed the car until he saw the headlights swing across the front of the house as it made the first curve of the driveway. And even then, he didn't expect what they were there for, didn't suspect it, would not have imagined if he'd lived to be a hundred years old that their mission was to come to his house unannounced—that son of a bitch DA hadn't even given him a warning—and with a warrant for Amelia's arrest.

"Mr. Wilkes," the officer had said, stepping out of the car. Harlan recognized him as the dark-haired cop from Monday afternoon.

"Well this is a surprise," Harlan said, reaching to shake the man's hand. The handshake was awkward, Harlan noticed, but he'd figured the awkwardness was deference. "I guess you've got some new information for me. Liles, he come up with anything more on Winter? I'll assume that whatever he's got now just confirmed my girl's account."

The officer cleared his throat. "Sir, is your daughter on the premises?"

"She is, but my understanding is that she's not feeling too good. Nothing serious."

"Sir," the officer said, producing a white sheet of paper, "I have here a warrant for her arrest."

Harlan took a step backward. "What is this, some sort of joke?"

"No, sir. Would you like to inform Miss Wilkes that I'll be taking her downtown?"

"I would not," Harlan said. "Explain yourself!"

"The district attorney's office has received information implicating Miss Wilkes in a crime. He convened the grand jury earlier today, and they have returned an indictment. Sir," he said, gesturing toward the house.

Harlan moved to block the door and pulled his cellphone from its holster. "The chief might have something to say about this," he growled.

The officer looked at him passively. "He might, but meantime, I have an arrest warrant which I am required to act on, and I am requesting that you step aside."

While Harlan held his phone to his ear and listened as the police chief's personal line rang and rang and then went to voice mail, his mind raced and his heart did, too, and his breath seemed to hitch up in his chest. He left a brief message, "Harlan Wilkes here. Call me as soon as possible on my personal line," and then tried a different tactic. He told the officer, "I do not understand what's going on. My daughter has been home, here, for two weeks. She couldn't have been involved in any crime."

"'G.S. 14-190.17, Second degree sexual exploitation of a minor,'" the officer read. "'G.S. 14-190.1, Obscene literature and exhibitions. G.S. 14-190.5, Preparation of obscene photographs.' These are some of the charges. I suggest you contact an attorney."

Harlan's mind spun with the impossibility of Amelia's involvement in such things. Sexual exploitation of a *minor*? Of who? Obscene *exhibitions*? Something, he was sure, had gotten mixed up. "There's been a mistake," he said, still blocking the door. "She was the *victim*. *She's* the minor. Anthony Winter, he's your perpetrator. You call in and check, you'll see."

"Mr. Winter's situation is being handled accordingly." The officer paused, then said, "As I hear it he'll be facing similar charges, in fact. Now, Mr. Wilkes, I will ask you once more to allow my entry and produce your daughter, or I will call for backup and proceed that way."

"God damn it," Harlan said, almost dizzy with confusion, sickened by his inability to stop the man in front of him from taking his daughter away. "God damn it all." He pushed the door open, growling, "I'll get her. Wait here."

Kim Winter parked her car in her driveway Monday night, having spent the evening at school working at the annual holiday-gifts fundraising bazaar. It had been an awkward evening for her, manning the popular student-art booth alone. Parents and grandparents couldn't avoid her, because that would mean not buying any of the paintings or drawings, the handmade mugs and bowls and plates, the sculptures, the willow baskets, the semiprecious jewelry, all the things their children had spent the fall semester creating with the bazaar in mind. The families were not, however, friendly in their transactions. They were silent, or terse, or in one case blatantly rude. She could see the distaste in their eyes, the realization that, *Oh,* you're *the one whose son is the sex offender,* despite the efforts she'd made to look as professional and upstanding as anyone there.

The worst of them were the well-preserved grandmothers, with their smooth, salon-quality makeup and long, polished nails and dyed, set, teased hair and brightly colored, perfectly matched tailored outfits, women who appeared to have been airbrushed to perfection before leaving their grand old estate homes. These were the women who, on the arms of smooth-haired, smooth-faced daughters or daughters-in-law looked her way and drawled their "Oh my word!" remarks loudly enough for her to hear them, before approaching her booth and glancing down their noses at her as they shopped. *Oh my word!,* Kim thought as they milled about the booth, *It's obvious* you *never had a chance at being foolish in love,* and, *Oh my word, I'm sure* your *children were all shining beacons of exemplary behav-*

ior. When she knew that, in fact, some of their children—the parents of her students—were in fact far less than exemplary in the ways they cheated on their spouses or their taxes or their business partners, paid tuition months late, served alcohol to minors in their homes, jetted off for vacations (or rehab), leaving teenagers home alone, unsupervised except by dear Grandmama, who called them at least once a day to make sure everything was truly fine.

Being home, finally, was a relief. She was opening her car door, looking forward to a long hot bath and a glass of Bordeaux with some Petrucciani jazz playing, when a car pulled in behind her. She glanced in her rearview mirror and was startled to see a light bar atop the car. Her side mirror confirmed it: a police car. She hoped she had been speeding, or that her vehicle registration was expired, or, even better, that a taillight was out and the officer was simply going to let her know about it. *Please,* she thought, *let it be something as simple as that.*

She got out of the car and pulled her jacket closed; the night had cooled quickly and there was a damp bite to the air. Inside the cruiser, the police officer looked up, saw her waiting, and nodded an acknowledgment. He typed something into the laptop computer mounted to the dashboard, then put on his hat and got out of the car. "Ma'am," he said.

"Good evening. Is it a taillight?" she asked, walking toward both him and the back of her car. Her heels, the same pair she'd worn on her date with William, clicked on the concrete, a jarring noise she still was not accustomed to making. William had commented on her shoes, or rather the visual effect of them, as they were leaving the restaurant Friday, saying, "You always look feminine and pulled together, but if you don't mind my noticing this aloud . . . well, you've got great legs."

Possibly the officer was noticing, too. He was slow to respond to her question, saying, "Taillight? Oh. No ma'am, I'm here to see Anthony Winter."

The hair on her neck rose. "See Anthony? At nine o'clock? What's going on?"

"You are . . . ?"

"I'm his mother. He's my son," she added, stupidly stating the obvious. "Haven't you already—that is, he's been through a lot lately, and—"

"I'm afraid it isn't over yet," the officer said, not unkindly. "I have a warrant for his arrest."

"His arrest," Kim parroted. "His *arrest*? That can't be. I mean, there must be some error. He was already brought in for that, two weeks ago. He was released. He's got a court date next week."

"No mistake." He showed her a sheet of paper that was marked clearly: WARRANT. She took it and turned so that the streetlight shined on its surface. Even without her reading glasses it was easy enough to make out today's date and the letters of her son's name. The officer said, "Is he at home?"

"I . . ." Kim paused, surprised at how tempted she was to lie and say he'd gone somewhere, anywhere, for the week. To what end, though? Supposing the police officer believed her and left, what would that accomplish? They'd go looking for him elsewhere, sure, but then she'd have to keep him hidden at home, imprisoned and waiting to be found. And that would mean, what, that she'd be guilty of harboring a fugitive? There should be laws, she thought, protecting mothers who protected their children. She handed him the warrant, then looked toward the house and said, "Probably. His light is on. But can I please ask you what's going on?"

"You might have seen, the warrant specifies"—he held it up to read it—"G.S. 14-190.1, Obscene literature and exhibitions, eight counts, and 14.190.16, First degree sexual exploitation of a minor, four counts, .17A, Third degree child pornography possession, five counts. Also 190.5, Preparation of obscene photographs, twelve counts."

The numbers—so many of them, so many counts!—rattled her.

"But, based on what?" she asked. "Is this from things on his computer?"

"Ma'am, my suggestion is that you contact an attorney. They'll be able to tell you whatever you need to know. Now, would you like to go ahead of me and have your son come out?"

Kim stood as if frozen in place, blinking at him. No, she would not like to do that. She could not see how to make her feet move from where they, in their silly high heels, had rooted to the driveway. Go inside and tell Anthony that he was being arrested again? Go inside and allow him to try to soothe her jangled nerves with the assurances he was certain to give even if frightened himself, and then watch him be taken away as if he'd done anything criminal? *Had* he done something criminal? Sexual exploitation, the officer had said. Of a minor. Amelia—or others? No, there couldn't be others. She knew her son. She was sure of it. Almost sure.

"Ma'am?"

She looked into the officer's face. He seemed kind. "Do you have children?"

"Ma'am, I'll need to be getting on with things. Would you like to go ahead of me?"

"He hasn't actually done anything wrong," she said, certainty returning. "Can't you . . . I mean, isn't there some way for me to talk to someone and straighten this out?"

"An attorney is the person for that." He stepped closer to her and put his hand on her elbow. "The sooner we get on with this, the sooner you can get your answers."

Kim said, "Obscene literature and exhibitions? What is that? How is that different from what he was charged with already? Isn't there some law against, what's it called, double indemnity?"

"Double jeopardy," the officer said patiently. "And no, his previous charge is different, and the legislature will have seen to it that there's no overlap. It's what they do."

The pressure on her elbow had the effect of persuading her feet to move, though she could not have said she wanted them to, or was making them go. No, that force came from somewhere outside her, and outside of the officer, too, despite his hand being the tool for it. That force impelled them without regard to their personal wills, and would be what Kim blamed for everything that was to come, when it was beyond her to do anything else.

18

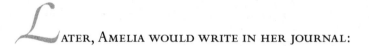

*L*ATER, AMELIA WOULD WRITE IN HER JOURNAL:

Biting circles of steel hold my wrists behind my back. Officer avoids looking at me or talking to me—feels like everyone I come in contact with while in custody has seen me naked, exposed. I spend the whole time with my neck and ears and face burning with embarrassment. But not shame. How many times will I hear that I "should be ashamed," before I'm brave enough to open my mouth and say, "I will never be ashamed of loving him!"

I stand against a wall and get patted down. Anthony must have stood in the same place when he was arrested, and gotten the same rough treatment from the guard. My fingerprints are copied and documented. Now I am trackable everywhere, forever. I notice the bland lifelessness of the hallways and the intake rooms and even the cells, with their stink of stale cleansers and dismay. How long can a person work in such a place before they become bland and lifeless, too? Everyone I have contact with has obviously been here at least that long.

The three women lounging in the cell I get assigned to all look sickly in the fluorescent light, and I figure I do, too. I feel sickly. I feel sick. The man who gave me life and raised me with so much generosity and love is the one I hold responsible for my being here. I blame myself, too, but differently. He willfully caused trouble for Anthony. He had an opportunity to be reasonable and fair, to believe what I told him—I was not misled by Anthony. I know, maybe better than Daddy does or ever will, what true love feels like—and he refused to consider it. In jail, I am embarrassed, and scared, and spend the time that I wait in the cell trying to think of how Anthony and I are going to get out of this mess, how we can still have the future we spent so much time planning. More than anything, I am livid with my dad for dialing 9-1-1. The only emergency, back then, was the one in his mind.

Nothing happens for thirteen hours. I spend them biting every one of my fingernails as far down as my teeth can make them go, and getting no sleep. Then I'm led to another depressing room where, from behind a glass partition, a magistrate tells me I am accused of "seriously troubling behaviors." He says that there is a real concern that a rule-breaker like me will try to avoid facing the consequences, and he is bound to set my bail accordingly. I don't understand the bail business, I only know that my dad will handle the $75,000 easily, and I am perversely happy that it could cost him so much.

My dad keeps insisting that I was victimized. I told him if I was, he's the one who did it, by overreacting. Maybe parents don't mean to mess up their kids' lives, but why can't they see that they're as prone to bad judgment as we are? How can they possibly think we should trust and believe them?

Sitting in her father's den late Tuesday evening, Amelia waited silently for her father to excuse her. She had not spoken a word since she'd stood before a magistrate in the Wake County Detention Center on Monday night and said that yes, she understood the terms under which she was being held. She had not spoken to the three women with whom she'd waited in the putrid-colored jail cell

until her father bailed her out this morning. She had not answered
her mother's questions about her welfare, once she was released,
and she was not, now, saying anything to her father or Mr. Acton
Hubbard, Esq.—"the best criminal defense money can buy," in her
father's words—as she sat in a heavy leather chair while he and
Hubbard discussed how best to approach her "situation."

Amelia disliked Hubbard by sight: he was a short, square-bodied
man whose head looked slightly too small for his body, possibly due
to the combination of his being bald and wearing a suit jacket with
boxy, broad shoulders. And by sound: his voice was nasal and he
brayed like a Southerner affecting a Bostonian or maybe a British in-
flection. Hubbard was Old South in that way her father admired so
much, even more Southern than her mother's family, and he had
come highly recommended by the man her father trusted with
his business's legal affairs. He was pasty and affected, and seemed
unable to stop sneaking looks at her as he listened to her father detail her innocence and his theory of how Anthony had unduly influenced her.

"Mr. Wilkes," Hubbard replied, "I expect you're exactly right
about how Miss Amelia got herself into this situation. It's a situation
that many an innocent young woman can become ensnared in."

"It is! These girls, they don't know how easily men can persuade
them. They don't know how men think."

Watching Hubbard watch her, Amelia had a good idea of how
certain kinds of men thought.

"So in addition to making the charges go away," her father went
on, "I want you to see to it that word does not get out to the media."

"I wish I could," Hubbard said. "Especially given that our fine
state chooses to treat seventeen-year-olds as adults in felony cases."
He sighed and rubbed the knuckles of his left hand with the fingers
of his right. "But unfortunately, the indictment was publicized. The
arrest is public record. Every detail, Miss Amelia's name included,
was put out to the press, and no doubt we will see a local wildfire
once somebody realizes Winter is the same person they were talk-

ing about recently. A wildfire that, of course, must be put out, yes sir, but they *will* make the connection, it's what they're trained to do. It is . . . a misfortune that our district attorney felt Miss Amelia should be in any way seen as a perpetrator of a crime. I and my associates will do every single thing within our power to alleviate the troubles."

"I appreciate that," her father said. "That's why I hired you. I'm expecting that you will go beyond the call of duty."

"The fact of an arrest most certainly does not indicate guilt," Hubbard said. "That's what we will need to get across to the reporters. We will be forthcoming that Miss Amelia is the victim here. We will," he said, tenting his fingers over his stomach, "let the court of public opinion help our cause by sharing the specific and correct elements of this story. Gibson Liles is very cognizant of public opinion. I expect he feeds on it the way you or I enjoy sausage gravy on a biscuit."

Her father shook his head. "To think I once supported the son of a bitch—sorry, Ladybug."

Amelia looked away. He was sorry for swearing in front of her. For *swearing*?

If Amelia had been able to avoid this meeting, she would have done so. That her father insisted she be present seemed less a matter of needing her there than of wanting to keep her from leaving his sight.

She knew he was hugely embarrassed by what she had done— eight counts on the harmful materials charge, seventeen for "preparation" of photos, three for possession of child porn, and twelve for exploitation, which, if she understood it, applied to all the photos she'd taken of herself with her phone and texted to Anthony, or took with her camera and emailed to Anthony. On the surface of things, she looked like a true ho, as the boys at school called girls who volunteered themselves in any sexual manner. There'd been no mention in the arrest warrant, no distinction made, that some of those twelve were her attempts at artful photography: a curve of her breast, close-up; the plane of her pelvis between her hip bones, leading to her thighs. Anthony admired her body the way an artist would. *She* admired it. Given her glitchy interior, that she had what could be considered an ideal exterior suggested, she felt, the possibility of grace. Or, it *had* suggested it, before. God was not doing her, or Anthony, any favors now.

For all that she'd been arrested and exposed in this way, her parents hadn't actually seen the evidence. They didn't know the full extent of what she'd done, and for that she supposed she should be grateful. All she had been able to tell them before the police officer handcuffed her and folded her into the cruiser was that no, there were not other people involved, so "sexual exploitation of a minor" must, logically, apply to herself. "Pictures of *me,* Daddy," she'd said, to be clear. "Pictures that I took on purpose, willingly, my own idea, and sent to him."

He'd been pale already, but grew paler at her onslaught. "When this is all over," he'd replied, "when I get it straightened out, there's one thing you can be sure of, and that's that you will not see that boy again. I don't mean to be harsh with you, Amelia, but by God, I will not let him ruin your life."

"He wouldn't—but it doesn't matter. You've done it already," she said. She had tried to hold back her tears, to keep some dignity in front of the police officers. The tears pooled anyway, and spilled over as the handcuffs were positioned and locked.

Her father had looked as if he would cry, too. "You don't know it, but I'm saving it. I'm *saving* your life, Ladybug." And her mother, who was standing in the front hall beside him, had put a hand on his forearm, briefly. Amelia got the sense that her mother was choosing sides—not Harlan versus Amelia, though. Rather, one side of herself versus the other. Amelia turned away from them then, and said to the police officer, in a voice that shook with barely suppressed anger, "Get me out of here."

Now Hubbard was saying, "What we'll need to do first is reconstruct a timeline of the relationship between Miss Wilkes and the boy. When they met, how he pursued her, what means he used to influence and persuade her. We'll get some statements from teachers and other students there at Ravenswood, look into his work life, find out about his people—"

Her father said, "His mother teaches there, at the school. There's something to that, don't you think? She must've known what was going on—she as much as said so to Sheri."

Hubbard was nodding heavily and rubbing his chin. "Yes, yes, I think so. I expect there's culpability there, civil if not criminal, but I'm thinking criminal, too. Willful endangerment maybe, or failure to report a crime, perhaps. . . ."

Amelia stood up. This had gone too far. "Stop it," she said forcefully. The men both turned to her with open mouths, as though they'd forgotten she was there. "Leave Ms. Winter out of this. I'm just going to tell the judge the truth, and whatever happens, I'll deal with it."

"'Whatever happens.'" Hubbard cleared his throat. "Potentially— and that would be if you did what you've just suggested you'd do, which, I should add, being your counsel, I could not permit, and won't"—he glanced at her father—"potentially, the judge would thank you very much for saving him the trouble of hearing my arguments in your favor, and send you away to the women's penitentiary for some ten or twelve years."

Amelia's breathing hitched, and she swallowed a hiccup. Surely he was bluffing. She said, "T-ten to twelve years? For letting my boyfriend see in photos what he can legally see in real life— something that shouldn't be a crime to start with? Y-you can't be serious. You're just trying to scare me."

Her father said, "Anthony Winter is *not* your boyfriend."

Hubbard nodded to acknowledge the interruption, then told her, "Oh yes. It's possible. Hasn't been done yet, but that doesn't mean it won't be. This country, the sentiment is swinging very conservative—people want a return to the old standards. Soft porn on family TV, crudeness everywhere, blatant sexuality—" He stopped and cleared his throat. "And we might, if our luck is poor, anticipate a *federal* charge as well, which could dictate fifteen years in prison. You *need* my representation, Miss Amelia."

Her father said, "Sit down, Amelia, and quit being so bullheaded. Mr. Hubbard is trying to help you. Now, I assume," he said to Hubbard, "that your first line of argument will be that charging 'child pornography' against the person who's the *subject* of the materials involved is a travesty of justice."

"I will be taking that line, yes, in addition to showing that Miss Amelia was in fact acting against her wishes—"

"But I wasn't," she said, still standing.

Hubbard eyed her and continued, "And, because of the boy's influence, threats, what have you—"

"I'll deny it all."

"—she was led to act in such a way that put her in serious jeopardy. Also, the very fact of these charges against her constitutes another layer of victimization, of consequence. We'll have a thorough examination by the best psychologist in the region, stating various things to this effect."

Amelia grabbed Hubbard's arm. "Then it will all be lies."

Her father pointed at her and said, "You are excused."

She let go and turned to face her father. "That's my defense? *Lies?* I see: any m-means to getting the end you want. How c-c-convenient," she managed finally. *Slow down,* she told herself, drawing a deep breath. *Think it through, then speak.* "What happened," she said, much more slowly, "to the 'honesty and integrity' you always spout in your commercials? Tell me that, would you?"

"You say things like that," her father said, taking her by the arm and leading her to the doorway, "and somehow you think we can rely on your judgment?"

She shook her arm loose. "What are you *talking* about?"

"Poison, Amelia. I'm talking about poison that warps your sense of reality. Do you want to go to prison?"

"Of course not. But w-why," she said, drawing another deep

breath and releasing it, "why aren't we figuring out a way to show the judge that what happened isn't actually exploitation or pornography?"

"Because it *is*," her father said. "It is exactly those things. That boy was trying to take advantage of you in every possible way, and God knows what he might have done with those pictures. Did you think of that, Amelia? Did you think of how he could be making some kind of website or selling 'em off—or even just passing them around to the other lowlifes he knows?"

"He would never do any of those things," she said evenly.

"Please. This is what I mean about you being blind and naïve. That's what these guys *do*. So all we have to do is show that you are not responsible."

"I am, though. I'm not going to lie in court."

He looked up as if in supplication at the sweep of the staircase where it met the second-floor landing. Or maybe he was looking beyond the landing, looking heavenward, though he had never been a truly religious man. She wanted to tell him not to bother; no one up there was paying attention anyway.

He dropped his gaze and looked at her again, his expression the same one he'd used with her when she was little and wanting to know why her Wilkes grandparents never came to visit them: gentle, measured patience.

He said, "Nobody's asking you to lie, Ladybug. You just tell it how it is, and the psychologist and Mr. Hubbard will see to it that the rest—the things you can't understand right now—are made clear. I know this is hard for you. I know you don't see what we all can see. But, baby, you need to trust your daddy on this."

He spoke with such conviction and such assurance that for a long, stressful, exhausted moment, despite her faith and her experience, she questioned her own mind. Could he be right? Could Anthony be such a good actor that she'd been thoroughly fooled? She didn't want to doubt Anthony, or herself. Neither, though, did

she want to doubt her father. This was no mere difference of opinion. This was a difference of belief.

She thought of Anthony, their meeting onstage at auditions, and
of the first weeks of their relationship, when he'd seemed as amazed
and as eager as she had been. He could not have faked his enthusiasm during hours and hours of conversation, scores of lunch dates.
He could not have faked the nervous, tentative passion of their first
secret nighttime meetings. He could not have faked the tenderness
she saw in every note and poem he'd written, or in his concern for
her, his support, when she'd laid out her father's expectations
against her own dreams. He wouldn't do all that just to get sex. He
didn't have to. Girls were waiting for him with their mouths and
legs open, to put it the way Cameron once had. But that wasn't
what he wanted. Anthony wanted her.

She said, "He loves me, Daddy. Why can't you believe that? Am
I . . . are you saying I'm not worth being loved?"

He stared at her, surprised. "No. No, of course that's not what
I'm saying. I'm saying he's fooled you."

"So, in your view, I'm that gullible."

"Yes," he said, gently. "I wouldn't have thought it—and don't go
and blame yourself, now. Girls are just gullible, I guess. Maybe it's
built into your DNA, and when you get the wrong guy in the mix,
it comes out. You know, like some disease that needs a trigger in
order to happen. You got fooled," he said, reaching out to brush her
hair back from her face, "but that doesn't mean you're a bad person,
or unlovable, none of that."

She could not be so gentle. She backed away from him and, voice
rising, said, "Well, I can see I was wrong to believe in *you* all these
years, so I guess you're right: in some ways, I've been gullible. What
I know is, Anthony loves me, the person I *actually am,* and the person I'm going to be—if you haven't already made that impossible."
Her hands shook and she clasped them together to stop the
trembling.

Her father's face hardened. "They *teach* you how to be so dramatic?" he said, his gentleness gone. She'd wounded him, and she was glad of it. "If that's what you've been learning in theatre class then I guess it's a good thing I've got you out of that, too."

"No," she said, unwilling to back down under his sarcasm. "No, Daddy, that was genuine. If I wanted to be dramatic right now, I'd stomp my foot and say, 'I hate you,' and run off to my room and slam the door."

"I'm surprised you're not."

"You would be," she snapped, making no effort to mask her disappointment in him.

His eyes narrowed. "That's enough from you. Go on," he pointed toward the stairs. "Go be ungrateful someplace else."

She was already moving. "You bet I will," she said.

In her room, Amelia, still dressed, retainer in, teeth unbrushed, turned off the lights and got up onto her bed. She unhooked each tieback and pulled the drapes closed, then, without untucking the sheet or blanket, slid underneath the covers, turned onto her side, and pulled her knees up close to her chest.

She'd done this often when she was younger, times when her heart was bruised by some injustice or some slight—after a school social, say, or a slumber party, when it seemed to her that every girl she knew was being pursued by a boy while she continued to be passed over, passed by. The other kids didn't know that she stuttered when she was upset or anxious. She'd hidden it masterfully behind a thoughtful, bookish demeanor. She was the girl to whom the others turned for homework help or a sounding board—but not for a "moonlight dance" in the festooned gym at the Holly Hop. Amelia was, in her girlfriends' views, a kind of angel, a supremely knowledgeable girl whom they admired greatly for staying coolheaded no matter which boy or boys were around. They were sure that she could choose any boy she wanted and was simply holding out for one who was the best match. In that sense, they'd been right: she had waited for her match. But for a long time, so long that, while she was enduring it, she thought she would end up growing white-haired alone and untouched, or at least unloved, she consoled herself by dreaming up a different life and time, one where men would find her demeanor and looks irresistible.

Back then, at age twelve, at thirteen, she'd imagined herself a lonely princess—Elizabeth I, say—living in a grand castle atop a mountain in a place she thought of as Faraway Land, the name a carryover from earlier childhood games. Outside her windows would be massive stone parapets and beyond those, the roiling sea. While she slept, tucked snugly into her curtained bed, a ship would be sailing toward the kingdom, its sails unfurled and billowing as it heaved and dipped. On board the ship would be a young prince (a *lad,* she thought, borrowing vocabulary from *Little Women*) who was a few years older than she, who would stand windward in his heeled black boots with his pants tucked into them, his fine white shirt billowing like the sails, his black hair, long and blown back by the wind, escaping its ribbon. He would have an earring, the result of a journey that found him living, for a time, with a pirate band. He would be sailing toward her father's kingdom to find the girl he'd heard of, a girl of refinement but of passion too, a legend of a girl he didn't know for certain existed. A girl reputed to be as fair-skinned as he was weathered, as gentle as he was wild—but (and he wouldn't know this, but he'd hope for it), her heart would be as wild as his, and he'd be glad to learn it.

He'd be coming for the girl—she decided in a new story twist—whose voice had been stolen by a curse. He would arrive offshore under a moonless sky, and, after rowing a dingy silently through the becalmed sea, somehow make his way up the cliffside and into her room while she slept. She would hear him and wake, and know, somehow, not to be afraid; she would feign sleep, though, and wait for discovery. He would light a candle on her bedside table and part the curtains and see her there, her hair fanned on her pillow, her dark eyelashes resting on her cheeks, and then he'd lean down and kiss her lips, so gently that a sleeping girl might mistake the kiss for a draft that found its way through the curtains.

He would love her instantly, love her completely. He would take her with him. This is what she dreamed.

19

ANTHONY SAT HUNCHED AT HIS ATTORNEY'S CONFERENCE table Thursday afternoon, listening carefully to her explanation of his second arrest.

"The preparation charge is self-explanatory, and a misdemeanor. 'Obscene literature and exhibitions' means, in this case, distribution of pornography, generally. The photos of Miss Wilkes—who is under age eighteen—constitute child porn, hence the 'Second degree exploitation of a minor' charge and possession of child porn. Those are felonies," the attorney explained, "as you are now all too aware."

It was four P.M., and he'd just been released from his pen at the jail, thanks to his mother promising away the equity in her house in order to post his bond, an arduous process of gathering paperwork, lining up an appraiser, getting the appraisal done, making sure the home's value exceeded the bond debt by twenty thousand dollars, minimum, and then filing more forms with various offices and waiting for approval—she'd told him all the details on their way here. It wasn't a happy story, but he preferred it to what he'd *been* hearing. For the better part of three days he'd been locked up, alone, in a small cell, listening to the trash talk of the inmates around him who, like him, claimed to have landed there on all completely bogus charges. He hadn't slept much on the understuffed bunk mattress, and now fought exhaustion and anger and a gnawing in his gut that had begun in the middle of his first night in jail, shortly after the man in the cell across from his informed him that if he didn't plead out and be done with it, it could take a year for his case to be tried. A year, maybe longer, and judges got cranky with self-righteous perps who wouldn't plead—he'd get the maximum sentence, that's how it worked.

A *year*. He was supposed to be well into his freshman year at college by then, waking up every day to see Amelia's long lashes resting against her cheeks, being greeted by her sleepy smile, cooking her eggs—over *gently,* that's how she liked them, for breakfast, and at the end of the day, tucking into bed and pulling her into his arms and breathing in the *Amelia* scent of her, rose petals and jasmine and her warm, smooth skin. He was not supposed to be hanging around Raleigh in limbo, waiting to see whether twelve of his fellow citizens would decide that he was, in fact, a reprobate, a perverted sex offender, a danger to society who ought to be punished accordingly.

Three days without a shower—he'd heard too many stories about what went on in jail to take the guards up on that offer. Three days wearing a demeaning Day-Glo orange and white striped jumpsuit. Three days without music, without a decent book. Another three goddamn days without Amelia.

"Felony," his mother repeated, as if learning a new word. He watched her face fall with the import of it, and fall further when Ms. Davis said, "Yes. The possession charge is class 1, which *could* mean a year's prison time."

"You're not serious," his mother said. "Prison?"

"I'm *not* going to prison," he said.

"But it wouldn't be a year, in this case," the attorney assured them. "Anthony has no priors, and it's not a violent crime." Anthony watched his mother rub her mouth as she processed this, while Ms. Davis continued, "The other charge, First degree exploitation of a minor, is class C, twelve years, max—though there's no judge in his right mind who'd impose the maximum. I have to doubt prison would be in the picture at all . . . but honestly, I don't know. We're on uncharted ground here."

His mother's hand stopped and her eyes grew as wide as he'd ever seen them. His had widened, too—he could feel his eyebrows practically at his hairline. Twelve? *Twelve?* The words that had followed could not compete with the impact of *twelve years*.

His mother said, "You say that, but no *prosecutor* in his right mind would consider what Anthony's done an actual crime, either. I'm not terribly reassured."

"Twelve *years?*" Anthony said, still stunned, while his mother wrapped her arms around her middle and closed her eyes for a moment. When she opened them, he saw something unfamiliar to him: fear. Seeing this in a woman who had never, to his knowledge, panicked about anything, made him flush with fear himself.

Ms. Davis said, "Only for repeat offenders, and particularly egregious situations. Don't worry."

Anthony snapped, "Oh, okay, right, 'don't worry'—for me it'd only be, what, ten years?"

"Anthony," his mother said, putting her hand on his. "Stop."

He pushed his chair back from the conference table and stood up. "I just want to know exactly, specifically, how fucked up this is getting. And don't ask me to apologize for the language," he added, going to the window, which overlooked most of Raleigh's pale, ordinary office buildings, all of them grayish under an overcast, pewter sky. "I think I'm entitled."

"Six," Ms. Davis told him. "No more than that—assuming the Feds don't bring charges, and I have to say, it's hard to think they would."

"Oh, only *six*." He turned to face them again. "Six years ago I was a twelve-year-old. I barely *remember* six years ago. That's a third of my life. Six *years*," he said in disgust. "Six years—from whenever I actually get sentenced—is when I'm planning to be writing and act-ing in plays, and taking the subway to the Met, and listening to Amelia sing, I don't know, 'Thank You for the Music,' maybe, eight shows a week." With his words came a memory of her singing this while they walked along the street from Cameron's house to the park and playground nearby. She had the perfect balance of sweet-ness and soulfulness in her voice, and hearing her sing opened his heart, splayed it so that he was helpless to resist her. He could not spend six years away from that, from her.

His mother said, "Am I completely dense? Because I just don't understand how his having pictures of a seventeen-year-old who is his girlfriend can be considered 'child pornography.' She's not a twelve-year-old, for God's sake, and he's not exploiting her. No one else ever saw the photos."

Ms. Davis said, "The law requires that a person be eighteen or older to view or be represented in images considered to be overtly sexual. Period."

"Eighteen," his mother said, "when they can legally be having sex at *sixteen*. They can get *married* at that age, if a parent allows it, and at *fourteen* if they have a court's consent, isn't that right?" She rubbed her mouth again, then went on, "'Sexual exploitation'? Come on. I'm not saying that what they did was the smartest thing, but please," she urged, "tell me how this makes any sense at all."

"Ms. Winter, if I let those kinds of questions bind me up, I'd never be able to do my job. For our purposes, we need to stay fo-cused on what to do about the charges so that your son gets the best deal possible."

"Deal?" his mother said. "Do you mean as in plea bargain? What happened to dismissal?"

"Felony charges resulting from irrefutable evidence, that's what happened. I spoke with the prosecutor on the case several times this week, and there's no question that Liles, the DA, is gunning for incarceration—so unless a judge is inclined to cut Liles off at the knees, which we shouldn't hope for, the realistic scenario is that Anthony pleads to the most minimal charge I can get away with."

"How do you know it's 'irrefutable'? What if there's been, I don't know, evidence tampering, or . . . or there's some loophole or technicality—"

"Ms. Winter, look, I realize that kind of thing happens a lot on TV. I enjoy a ninth-inning save as much as the next person. And I'll be seeking out every possible route to that result. My job, though, is to help Anthony, and you, get real about the situation we're facing. Given that he admitted to some of it already—"

"But wait," his mother said, sitting up eagerly, "he said those things before they read him his rights, so doesn't that make it inadmissible?"

Ms. Davis shook her head. "He wasn't being arrested at that point. They asked him questions, and he chose to answer them. He didn't have to." She tapped her pen on the table and looked at Anthony. "Never tell the police anything."

"You've said. I was trying to be cooperative."

"Well, stop it," she said, smiling slightly.

"I didn't know what we did was a crime."

"It shouldn't be. But, strictly speaking, it is, so we have to react accordingly. The question, however, is why the DA got his shorts in a twist about two teenagers who are in a consensual relationship. It's got to be a political ploy. . . ." Her voice trailed off for a moment, then she added, "And while you also won't want to hear this, I need to tell you that defending you against the new charges means an increase in my fees. We have a great deal more work to do than if this had remained . . . contained, let's call it."

"I understand," his mother said, in a voice strangled by the tightening grip of his stupidity. "We'll manage."

Anthony leaned against the wall and said, "How much?"

"Honey," his mother said, that awful expression of fear still in her eyes, "it doesn't matter."

"Ms. Davis?" he demanded. It did matter. He was already the cause of a burden his mother shouldn't be shouldering—though if he understood the bond process, she wouldn't actually lose any of her equity in the house as long as he remained in town and showed up for any and all court dates. She'd written the lawyer a check for five thousand dollars already; he was not going to let her carry the rest of the expenses, too. It mattered because he needed to figure out how much, beyond his college savings, he'd need to raise—and how to do it.

"Double the misdemeanor fee," Ms. Davis said, "so ten thousand to start, but there will be other costs, too, especially if we end up in front of a jury. The psychologist can run two to three thousand—unless your health insurance covers it?"

His mother said, "Not likely, but I'll check."

"And I strongly suggest you retain my private investigator—he's a pro, I've worked with him for more than five years. We'll need to talk to her teachers, neighbors, friends—"

"Whose?" his mother said.

"The girl's. Miss Wilkes's."

Anthony pushed away from the wall, newly alert. "Why would we need to do that?"

"For this to not be your fault, we'll need to show that it's all her doing. You were coerced. She enticed you with, what might we say, promises of access? Young men are too easily influenced by aggressive young women. You had no idea that what you were being led to do was illegal."

He shook his head. "That last part is right, but I'm not going to lie about Amelia to save my own skin. Find some other strategy."

"I can make peripheral arguments in hopes of reducing the charges, but if we have to go to trial—and we need to be prepared for that possibility—that's *the* strategy. I told you it'd come to this. If the jury sees you as a victim, they won't convict you as a perpetrator. And trust me, she'll be using the same strategy in her own defense."

Anthony heard the words *in her own defense,* but couldn't make sense of them. "What do you mean? Defense against what?"

His mother looked at the attorney first, then at him, then back at her and said, "I didn't tell him yet."

He said, "Tell me what?"

"Listen, Anthony, sweetheart . . . I didn't want to trouble you with this until . . . Well, I don't know," she said, "I didn't want to tell you at all. Not that I wouldn't have. Amelia . . . Amelia was arrested Monday night, too."

"What are you talking about? Who told you that?"

"The news is everywhere. The DA has charged you both."

"Same charges, more or less," Ms. Davis added.

Anthony gaped at her. "Same charges? How?"

"She took and sent photos of herself, right? Thus, she was preparing and distributing pornography. Child pornography, because she's a minor."

"That's insane—and 'exploitation'? A person can exploit *herself*?"

"The law doesn't differentiate. The only reason they didn't peg *you* with this the first time around is because you're eighteen."

"When I called you, why didn't you tell me this could happen?"

"It wouldn't have changed anything. Given the DA's actions, it appears that whatever they found in your computer and such got Liles thinking he had something more to work with. He must've had a sense that he would to begin with, or he'd never have bothered with the search warrant."

"So I guess Wilkes didn't sic them on me." This was what he'd imagined had been the case, until hearing this, about Amelia.

"Mr. Wilkes is, I expect, tying himself in knots right now, given his original involvement—and, I'm sure, writing out a very large check to counsel whose fees make me look cheap. And speaking of which," she said, closing the notebook in which she'd made her notes, "I'm going to need another check from you, and then I'll get started trying to untangle yours."

20

RALEIGH, NORTH CAROLINA, AND ITS METRO NEIGHBORS OF
Durham and Chapel Hill, known together as "The Triangle," was
home to nearly two million people on that mid-November
Thursday evening, the evening of Anthony Winter's release, when
one of the leading television news stations made Amelia and
Anthony the subject of a community-interest series. One of the station's producers had, perhaps without thinking, titled it "The
Terrible Teens," not intending to label the couple who'd inspired it
as "terrible," but referring instead to the teenage years and the dangerous behaviors of teens. "The Terrible Teens" series would span
three evenings and feature a different "expert" each time.

Harlan Wilkes, who knew very well the demographics of the
area, who'd studied them carefully and had written out a long-term
plan for additional business growth based on demographic trends,
was not a news-watcher by habit, but since Amelia's arrest on
Monday night he'd found himself tuned in to all the news sources
obsessively. TV, radio, newspaper, websites . . . as with witnesses to

a plane crash, he was unable to tear himself away from the spectacle. At work, he kept his smartphone in his hand and checked the Web every spare moment, hoping to find nothing, dreading everything.

His day started with an examination of the Raleigh newspaper. A small, tucked-away article had run in the Wednesday edition, a recitation of facts: Amelia Wilkes had been indicted, arrested, and charged with multiple counts; she was the daughter of Harlan Wilkes, head of the Wilkes Automotive empire ("empire," he liked that, at least they got that right); she'd been released Tuesday morning on $75,000 bail—which Hubbard had tried to get reduced, but here, Harlan being head of an "empire" worked against him, because the magistrate reasoned that any less of a penalty might not motivate Harlan to keep his daughter close to him and ready to appear in court when the time came. As if he might send the girl out of the country to live at his Swiss chalet, or some such. As if the Wilkeses were the Vanderbilts, or royalty. Harlan had spit nails about her having to stay in jail overnight and about the bail, but there was no arguing it, not unless he wanted his little girl to spend two more nights there, because she couldn't see a judge for a bail review before Thursday. He absolutely would not allow them to keep her locked up like some common criminal, so he'd cussed the magistrate (to Hubbard), then called his banker and had him deliver a check to the courthouse personally.

On Wednesday, the news websites and TV news had no mention of her arrest, and Harlan thought, for a brief, pleasing little while, that they'd escaped negative publicity with only a scratch. He didn't bring up the newspaper article to Sheri, or to Amelia, who had not left her room since Tuesday night, though what she could be doing in there was beyond him. Buttercup stayed in the hall outside her door full-time, moving only when Harlan called her to go out. Sheri'd brought meals upstairs for both daughter and dog, which Harlan didn't approve of. If they didn't bring Amelia any food, she'd get hungry and be forced to come out, wouldn't she? But as touchy as Sheri had gotten, he kept his mouth shut on that one.

Harlan went into work on Thursday with every intention of getting himself re-engaged with the business of running his "empire." He'd driven the Maserati and surfed the local radio channels, hearing nothing mentioning the Wilkes name, save for three of his commercials. With Thanksgiving coming up and one of the slowest car-buying times of the year to follow, the ad agency was saturating the market with enticements designed to get folks into the showrooms—because from there, it was easy to make the sale. Who didn't want to buy a glossy new car to drive to the in-laws' house for Thanksgiving or Christmas? What better way to show the family that you weren't one of those unlucky SOBs who'd been hit with layoffs? Or, conversely, why not, if you could swing it, commit the charitable act of keeping the car salespeople and the factory linesmen and loan processors from getting pink-slipped? His agency was covering every angle.

Thoughts of this nature kept his mind occupied as he finished the drive and parked in his reserved spot at Wilkes Honda. It was early, a few minutes ahead of eight A.M., so the place was quiet. Only two detailers, a pair of twenty-year-olds who'd transferred over from the Zebulon location, were there, having a smoke and drinking those mega-caffeine, mega-sugar drinks while waiting for either Harlan or Les Greer, his general manager, to arrive and open shop. The newspaper had been delivered and was waiting, still wrapped in its clear plastic bag, on the ground beside the door.

Inside, Harlan had gotten the first pot of coffee going, bought his usual day-starting can of the soda he'd been raised to call Co-cola, and gone to his office. He ignored the files waiting on his desk and, still standing, took the paper from the plastic bag, unrolling it gingerly across his desk. There, just above the fold, began the headline: WILKES HEIRESS CHARGED and then, below the fold, IN SEXTING SCANDAL.

He pressed his hands against the paper. *Those bastards*. He couldn't get them to care at all when the story was what Winter had done to an anonymous daughter, but now, now that they knew it was *his* daughter, oh, now they were interested all right. So interested that they made it a front-page story, big news, with as misleading a headline as they come.

Sexting. This was a word that wasn't in his vocabulary. And *scandal*? Amelia's situation wasn't a scandal! What was scandalous was the way the paper was using his name and his baby's misfortune to sell more copies. "Damn it all," he said through clenched teeth. What gave them the right? "I ought to sue the sons'a bitches," he said. *Wilkes Heiress*. Like she was some spoiled rich girl who'd gone wild.

He got out his phone and dialed Hubbard, left him a strongly worded voice mail, and then dropped into his chair and picked up the paper again to read the entire article, if only to see how many ways he was going to put the screws to whoever had written it and whoever had authorized it to run. He spent a hundred thousand goddamn dollars a year running ads in that paper, and they gave him *this*.

The story went simply enough at the start. It began with an introduction to what was called "sexting," a catchall term for sending explicit photos by email or text message. And apparently there'd been some bad seeds who'd previously gotten caught engaging in similar behavior in other areas throughout the country, which the article blamed on the proliferation of cellphones that had built-in cameras. Harlan blamed it on the proliferation of kids whose parents, like Kim Winter, did a piss-poor job of raising their children right. The fact was, in the same way that one molding slice of bread spoiled the whole loaf, one charismatic, sly teen could get a bunch more acting out in ways they'd never dream of otherwise. "Bad influence, bad influence," Harlan muttered, talking back to the article, "not the phones. That's like blaming drunk-driving on the car."

He was halfway through the article when his phone rang. He checked the display: not Hubbard, Sheri. He answered, and she said, "The paper—"

"I'm reading it."

"How can they do this?" Her voice was hoarse.

"I told you, it's public record."

"No, I mean, how can they make her out that way? Where is the decency?"

"I haven't read the whole thing. Let me finish and call you back."

The reporter, having established what sexting was, went on to say,

Amelia Wilkes, 17, heiress to the Wilkes Automotive empire, is a senior at the prestigious Ravenswood Academy who has demonstrated her appeal in a number of local theatre productions. She allegedly demonstrated it far more explicitly to one of her fellow students and costars, Anthony Winter, eighteen, a senior and free-ride student at the school, where his mother, Kim Winter, is an Upper School teacher. Winter was arrested earlier in the week for allegedly sending explicit photos of himself to a female, in a related charge. Both now face felony charges that could put them in prison. It is unclear whether other individuals may have been involved. Further investigation continues. Wilkes posted $75,000 bail and was released under stipulation that she not have contact with Winter, who at this writing remains jailed on $30,000 bail. The disparity in the amounts reflects the differences in the defendants' charges, and the families' differing financial circumstances. Amounts this high are unusual for nonviolent crimes. A source in the DA's office says the pair are considered a strong flight risk.

Harlan sat very still. He read the article once more. When his phone rang again, the caller was Hubbard, who said, "Mr. Wilkes, I'm very sorry that your morning started this way. I've seen the article—"

"It's obscene!" Harlan interrupted, or more accurately *erupted*— that was his sensation as the words pushed up from his gut. "They've made it out like she's the one to blame, the one who got Winter in trouble. She's, Jesus Christ, she looks like she's a porn actress, or wants to be."

"The wording could be seen as . . . let us say *salacious,* yes. Unfortunately, it is also, strictly speaking, truthful."

"It's not! How can they say that, about 'other individuals'? They're making it seem like they got a sex ring going."

"Do you have a copy of the warrant nearby?"

"No, I'm at my office."

"All right, well, I'll tell you, then. The warrant, you'll recall, details the actions behind the charges, and it's a long list, and someone not privy to all the particulars could hypothesize or speculate as to there being others involved."

"Then you get on the phone to the newspaper and you tell 'em there aren't. And tell 'em that it was Winter who started all this trouble, who corrupted her, and tell them, by God, they better watch themselves, because I will not see my good name and my daughter's dragged into the mud this way!"

It was, he knew, already too late. Still, he could not keep from venting. His anger was lava—not spewing, but bubbling up and boiling over, the deepest well supplying it and no discernible end in sight. He felt the burn of it on his face and neck, and hoped he would not burst into flames.

After a walk around the lot, he managed to cool down slightly by the time the sales and finance and administrative staff arrived. While he would have liked little better than to remain shut away in his office and never have to face any of them, he knew that was the surest way to get them thinking that he or his family had reason to hide. So, at nine forty-five, when he knew everyone had come in, but before they opened the doors to customers, he got on the PA and requested that they all gather in the showroom for an announcement.

"Good morning," he said from atop the reception desk, once his employees had fitted themselves in among the four vehicles on display. His staff answered in kind. Then he said, "First of all, I want to thank all y'all for the hard work you've been putting in so far this month. Our numbers are slightly above what they were this time last year and, given the sorry state of things, that is saying quite a lot—so I commend you, and I encourage you to keep up the good work.

"Second, well, I'll suppose that a good many of you have heard the news by now. My little girl was arrested on Monday evening and, yes, I know it looks pretty bad, but I want to say it isn't at all like it seems. Not at all. A lot of you know her. She's a sweet, quiet, good girl, real devoted to Sheri and me, a great student—pretty sure she'll get into Duke on early decision, that's how hardworking she is. And anyway, what happened was she got taken in by this sleazeball guy—good-looking, real smooth-talking, an actor. She never knew what hit her."

No one spoke right away, and then the buzz of a few people who hadn't heard asking for details prompted him to add, "It has to do with him sending indecent photographs using cellphones and whatnot."

"Oh my God, Harlan," said Joyce Potts, his bookkeeper since the Honda store opened in '97. Her wrinkled face with its wide-eyed expression of surprise and dismay was almost as dear to him as his own mother's would have been, if she'd been much of a mother. "How is she? Poor thing!"

"Thank you for asking, Joyce. She's hanging in there. I'd appreciate it—as would Sheri and Amelia—if you, all of you, would help spread the word and ask folks not to believe what all they hear or read. Her being charged this way is a travesty of justice, and you know me, I'm not gonna sit still and take it."

"That's right," one of his better salesman shouted. "You go get 'em."

Harlan gave a thumbs-up, then got down from the desk, but not before noticing that a few of the guys hanging at the back of the group—those two detailers, plus a parts guy and a couple of the mechanics—appeared to be snickering and nudging one another. That feeling of lava rising again made Harlan itch to go storming back and knock some heads together—something he'd never done, but which sounded like what you'd do with these sort—and he stood there for a few seconds, watching them, until the parts guy noticed him. Harlan turned his attention to the group of people surrounding him, wanting to extend wishes for good luck and a speedy resolution. "Prob'ly be a good idea," he overheard one of the salesmen say to another as the pair walked toward the offices, "if I delete some of the stuff I've got on my phone." The other laughed and said, "Yeah, you don't want your wife catching up with that."

And then came Thursday evening's television news. Harlan had come home early in order to catch the broadcasts, turning on the living room TV so that Sheri, who was chopping celery and garlic for a chickpea dish Amelia loved, could watch it from the adjoining kitchen. He set up the picture-in-a-picture feature that, in the past, had been useful for watching multiple bowl games or sports matches. He enjoyed not having to choose. With the news, though, he'd be able to hear only one station at a time.

Each station began with the day's headlines, which he listened to bits of by flipping from one to the next. Sheri said, "Maybe there won't be anything. Maybe now they'll all have moved on to other stories." Harlan, seated on the leather sofa—a sofa that had cost eight times as much as his first car, truly—turned and told her, "I put Hubbard on this. He's supposed to have contacted each news outlet and asked for some consideration."

"Then why are you sitting here, watching?"

"You don't think they're all going to cooperate, do you?"

She stopped chopping and said, "Don't you think you might have made a mistake, getting the police involved?"

Harlan had an answer on his lips, a denial that he would have spoken with assurance, but it died away when the mug shots of both Amelia and Anthony appeared on-screen together with the accompanying words, "Area teens face prison time on sex crime charges."

He heard Sheri make a soft "Oh" sound, while pain like a blade of fire sliced through his stomach.

Amelia's photo was the least flattering he'd ever seen of her. It appeared as if it had been scissors-cut from its original background, whatever that may have been, and superimposed on the news channel's vivid blue background, then framed in silver. Her hair clung to the sides of her face; a blemish on her chin stood out like a bright pockmark against her white, flash-lit skin. The tops of her cheeks were rosy—meaning they must have been bright red in person—and she looked indignant. Winter's photo, similarly displayed, was also raw, and he looked frightened. Harlan scowled. Didn't it just figure that Winter would put on an act even while being booked? If all a person had to go by was this display, they'd label Amelia as the troublemaker for sure. Amelia.

He said, "Where's Amelia?"

"Upstairs. She was watching a movie, but I heard it end a little bit ago. She's in her room, I'm sure."

"Maybe go check? I don't want her seeing this." But Sheri remained where she was, as unable to tear herself away as Harlan was himself.

The mug shots remained while news anchor Mark Hoffman summarized the story, not failing to mention that Amelia was Harlan's daughter. Then he turned toward a pale, plain-faced woman in a gray suit jacket and white blouse—a child psychologist, he said—who was seated at the corner of the news desk.

Hoffman, who had bought his last three cars from Wilkes Lexus, was beloved by his viewers. His Rock Hudson face grinned at drivers from billboards all around the viewing area. *News and Views You Can Trust!* the signs insisted, and Harlan understood people well enough to know that most of them believed what they were told. The pain in his stomach flared again.

"Dr. Patrice Shriver, thank you for joining us this evening.

Can you give us some insight into the troubling story of these teens?"

"Thank you, Mark. Yes. What we have here are two people who, perhaps because of her privileged upbringing and his exposure to that lifestyle there at school, have elected to disregard the parameters of common decency that keep most of us from wanting to expose ourselves to others so explicitly. One can only speculate as to what problems there are in the home—I'm given to understand that the young man was raised without a father? And this can lead to a lack of effective discipline or lack of transfer of desirable values— and so they act out in oversexualized ways. Our culture, with its depictions of skin and sex, and the objectification of women in general, just adds to the trouble."

"I see. Well, and isn't the easy availability of phones and cameras and computers a part of the problem?"

"Absolutely. Children do *not* need cellphones," she said vehemently. "When we put them in the hands of children who don't have the self-regulators they need to have, whether due to young age or, as with these two, perhaps a sense of entitlement or being above the law—"

"But do kids even know they're breaking any laws when they're doing what this pair has allegedly done?"

"Even if they haven't heard of other cases of sexting, I think they know they're breaking *rules,* certainly, and an eighteen-year-old male is going to be well aware that his age is the threshold for legal access to pornography, so producing photos for or encouraging or accepting lewd photos from an underage female would of course be a criminal act."

"What can viewers do to prevent their children from ending up like Miss Wilkes and Mr. Winter, who theoretically could be facing *years* of *prison time* for their misbehavior?"

"Excellent question. Build in them a strong sense of self-esteem and good moral judgment. Let them know that their body belongs *only* to them, and that it's not to be shared casually in any manner with anyone. Also, limit or deny access to all these unnecessary gadgets, and *never* give a teenager unsupervised, unregulated access to a computer. If you must give your child a cellphone, get a model that doesn't have a camera. Girls of this age, especially the ones like Miss Wilkes, who are both attractive and have advantages that young men desire, often recognize that they have a lot of power over those young men and, without a carefully laid foundation of right and wrong, they'll make use of that power."

"What do you think they're getting from using it?"

"Oh, all kinds of things, but worshipful attention seems to be the primary attraction, in my experience. Their parents are often very busy and neglectful. It's a sad, but not irreversible, state of being. Counseling, along with education, usually helps build a healthy self-worth."

"We're out of time, but thanks very much, Dr. Shriver. Good food for thought. Join us tomorrow at six for the second part of this series, with our guest Olivia Sanchez, who's with the district attorney's office. We'll be talking in detail about the laws affecting teens who sext, and the life-altering consequences of breaking those laws."

"Neglectful?" Sheri challenged. "I do not neglect my daughter."

Harlan felt his mouth hanging open, and closed it. His throat was tight, and his face and neck and ears were burning. Sheri rushed over to him, asking, "Are you all right?"

He couldn't speak. The protest that had been ignited by Shriver's bullshit, uninformed, sensationalized "expert opinion" of his daughter and his home and his life stayed lodged like a boulder in his chest, threatening to suffocate him. He put his hands on his knees and leaned over, hanging his head, trying to catch his breath. He felt Sheri's hand on his back. "Harlan," she said. "What is it? What's wrong?"

He coughed hard, caught his breath, and, looking up at her, said, "What's *wrong*? Did you not hear that woman?"

She moved her hand and sat back. "Yes, of course I did. I just thought that you were . . ."

"What I am," he said, sitting up again, "is sick to my stomach over the lies these people are telling about Amelia. And she made us out as failures—practically said we're the ones to blame!"

Sheri sat down next to him. "Maybe we are to blame—not for all of it, but—"

"This is Winter's fault, and if any parent's to blame, it's *his* mother, not you. I swear to God, if it's the last thing I do, I'm going to set the record straight."

Amelia heard her father's declaration from where she was sitting in the game room on a luxurious velour sectional, her knees drawn protectively to her chest. The TV, a sixty-five-inch plasma screen on which she'd been watching *A Chorus Line* to pass the time, was now tuned to the same local news broadcast that had provoked her father.

Seeing her mug shot, and Anthony's, had horrified her. Hearing the psychologist's disparaging judgments of Anthony and their parents and herself had horrified her, too. But it was her father's vengeful words that cut like a newly sharpened blade.

Unbidden came the rhyme, *Sticks and stones may break my bones, but words will never hurt me.* Words, oh, they could hurt all right. They could trip you up. They could pull you down. They could cut your heart right out of your chest and make you wish you had never been born—or that you were born to someone else.

21

"Explain this bond business," Marta Winter said to her daughter, Kim, in Marta's sunroom early Friday morning. "The arrest, all right, I see how that all works, but this I'm not sure I understand."

Kim took the cup of coffee her mother offered and sat down in a chair upholstered in a raucous print of orchids and colorful long-tailed birds. The room, a small add-on to the back of the '60s split-level that was located in an area called Five Points, had the feel of an exotic aviary. One of her father's last projects before his illness had been to build what he'd called "your mother's bird box," a floor-to-ceiling cage, three feet in depth, eight in length, for finches. Inside the wire enclosure were mounted various branches and baskets and ropes, seed trays, and water bins. The inhabitants were six pairs of finches, two each of zebra, society, and the color-blocked gouldians. They chattered and hopped about cheerfully, which Kim usually enjoyed. Today, their beauty and music and the fact that they paired faithfully, for life, was depressing. Why should it come so easily for them while humans, purportedly the highest of Earth's life-forms, had so much trouble finding mates—and when they did, their fellow humans so often worked against them? What did people like Harlan Wilkes and Gibson Liles—Liles especially—have against love?

She'd looked up Liles, and what she'd found had chilled her. He was forty-one years old, a handsome enough man (though his ears stuck out a bit far), father of three girls, married to his Kinston, North Carolina, high-school sweetheart. He had the kinds of church affiliations she'd come to expect from politically ambitious men everywhere. None of that troubled her. His agenda, though, the one that had boosted him up from being just one more eager prosecutor for the State, was that he was unapologetically, overtly, rabidly conservative. Now, Kim certainly wanted criminals off the streets and punished appropriately. She believed there were moral "oughts" and "musts." As an educator of teens, she knew as well as anyone that precocious sexuality was unhealthy, and that young women were especially susceptible to pressures from boys, from the entertainment media, from advertising, from popular music. She was glad that there were laws protecting children of all ages from perverse and predatory activities. It was obvious, though, that in the case of Anthony and Amelia, Liles was using a definition of *criminal* that happily twisted the intent of the law to suit his moral outlook—or, perhaps, the moral outlook that he knew would propel him further up the prominence ladder. When asked, in an interview Kim watched as an archived video clip, whether he might like to run the state, he had said, "If the good people of North Carolina and the good Lord in His wisdom see fit for me to do it, it would be my profound honor to be governor one day." Asked on Thursday for a comment on "the Ravenswood sexting scandal," he'd said, "We cannot have young people behaving in ways that will damage them so profoundly as taking and sending sexually explicit photographs is bound to do. I want to send a message to all the teenagers, my own daughters included, that such behavior is in every way wrong. In *every way*," he'd repeated. "We need a lesson here. Actions bring consequences." Yes, Kim thought, especially when the state's prosecutor found it expedient to make it so.

Kim shifted so that her back was to the birds and told her mother, "The court sets a bail amount—a ridiculous amount, in both kids' cases—and then you either pay the entire amount, which they hold until after the case resolves, or, if you don't have enough, you get a bondsman to pay it for you for a ten percent fee, or you get a property bond—a promise to pay that's secured by your home's equity, which is what I did."

Her recollection of the past few days was a blur. The arrest, a panicked call to the lawyer, a first night with no sleep at all when she'd sat up staring into the darkness wondering if Anthony was doing the same, feeling as if she'd been jettisoned into a nightmare from which she would one day emerge battered and bleeding but, until then, she would remain its helpless captive.

The next morning, Tuesday, could not come fast enough. She'd gotten right to work on Anthony's release, getting her home-purchase paperwork from her bank safety deposit box, scheduling an emergency appraisal (for five hundred dollars!), then expending her nervous energy cleaning the house from corner to corner and top to bottom in anticipation of the appraiser's Wednesday morning visit. Throughout it all, she'd watched the clock. Every minute she had to wait was a minute that Anthony was passing locked up unfairly. Caged. Frustrated. Cursing his bad luck, bad karma, the random vindictiveness of the universe. Stunned that his love for Amelia, and Amelia's for him, could get him into this mess.

Love: it had the power of flowing water to find even the most miniscule crack and to seep through it, then widen it, and then, in the case of a dyke or a dam, to burst the structure entirely. Love was a pleasure and a danger at the same time, a force of nature that humans naïvely imagined could be controlled.

Kim said now, "I could have gotten him out sooner if I'd used the bondsman, but I can't afford to just give away three thousand dollars—that would've been the fee, ten percent of thirty grand."

"I wish you had called me first. Maybe I could have liquidated something and paid the whole thing."

"Mom, thank you, but I wouldn't think of compromising you that way. If the accused person doesn't show when he's supposed to, the court keeps all the money—which isn't to say that I don't trust Anthony, but . . ."

"But?"

"But, there are a lot of pressures on him, and he's very angry, and I *think* he'll handle the next weeks, or possibly months, all right, but what if he doesn't?"

Her mother looked aghast. "If the accused person doesn't show up, the court gets to *keep* the money, really?"

"Yes—to pay for pursuit efforts, I suppose. It's . . ." Kim clenched her fists, then opened them. "It's insane, this whole thing, it's just ludicrous. Both kids are being treated like criminals, and for what?"

"So the DA can look like a hero to his supporters, I'd imagine." Her mother wrote out a check, then carefully folded it back and tore it from its pad. "Here. Please let me know if I can do more."

Kim took the check gratefully and said, "Everything I'd put aside for his school is gone to the lawyer. Our trip to France next summer: gone. My house is tied up until everything gets resolved, so I can't even touch the equity if I need to. I can't buy groceries unless I use a credit card—or couldn't, without your help. Thank you. I'm paying you back as soon as I get paid."

"It's all right, there's no rush."

"Look at me. A professional woman, a homeowner, and thanks to one uptight, reactionary father and an all-too-eager DA, I can no longer help my son afford college—assuming there will still be a college that will let him in when this is done—and I'm scraping the barrel just to get by until payday. My son is being painted as a sexual predator and pervert, and I'm being made out as neglectful. He *loves* Amelia. It's ludicrous." She put her hand to her forehead and said, "And listen to me, I'm a broken record. *Ludicrous,* that's my new favorite word."

"It's apt," her mother said.

Kim slumped back in the chair. "Thank you for not judging him, Mom."

"He's not the first, you know. *They're* not the first, none of the kids out there who are doing this are—and I'm sure there are plenty. A lot of people did the same thing with those early instant cameras. You won't remember, probably, but we had that Polaroid, the Swinger—and so did a whole lot of teenagers, who took a whole lot of what everyone called 'dirty pictures' when, of course, plenty of adults were doing it, too. The difference between using those instant cameras and using cellphones and such was there was no way of tracing where the picture had come from."

"The real difference is that sending pictures of a minor by text or email, or even viewing them electronically, is a *federal crime,* Mom. It's already ludicrous—Christ, there I go again—it's already ridiculous, crazy, insane, unbelievable, absurd that they were charged with possession and production crimes, but we're also waiting to see whether the Feds get involved."

"Oh, honey." Her mother reached for her hand and held it between her own. "What would happen then?"

"I'd have to find about a hundred thousand dollars somewhere, for one, just to pay the lawyer. Buy a lottery ticket or two, will you?" She laughed ruefully. "And Anthony . . . God, I can't imagine." She could, though, and what she imagined struck terror in her heart. He was not a person who could be imprisoned—especially for such a noncrime, not without losing every meaningful part of himself, not without his soul withering and leaving him an empty, angry pessimist. The world certainly didn't need more of those. And she knew she would not be able to stand having him locked away, knowing what he was going through. She would fight for him, do everything she could to right the wrong. But you didn't get to almost-fifty without seeing, again and again, travesties of justice that took years to work their way through the appeals system—and no guarantee of a good outcome. Even if his sentence were short, he'd spend the decades afterward as a registered sex offender. How would he ever get a job, or credit? How would he be able to rent a place to live—and supposing he managed that, would his neighbors fear him, harass him, assume the worst without ever asking for his side of the story? And if they asked, would they believe him?

Ludicrous.

She thought of what he'd said in the lawyer's office yesterday afternoon, the questions he'd asked about Amelia, the objections he'd raised to Mariana Davis's defense strategy. She told her mother, "He's more concerned about Amelia than about himself."

"You raised him well."

"I have a feeling you're in the minority with that opinion," she said, standing up.

Her mother stood too, and followed her to the front door, saying, "I'm sure that's true. We have to admit, there's no question that the kids would have avoided all of this if they had just been more judicious and stayed clothed—"

Kim turned. "Of course they would have! But for God's sake, when was the last time you saw a pregnant teenager and her teenaged boyfriend arrested for what *they'd* done? When were the musicians and filmmakers and advertising agencies and, and, and magazine publishers hauled in for subjecting children to explicit language and soft porn? I mean, yes, I wish they *had* kept their clothes on, and I'm pissed that they didn't, because wouldn't we all be a lot better off right now if they had? But can we *please* get some common sense here?"

Her mother's eyes were sympathetic as she said, "I doubt it, but I hope so." She hugged Kim, then kissed her on the forehead the same way she'd done when Kim was a fourteen-year-old raging at the world's injustices.

"Thanks for letting me vent. I better get going. I've missed three days already. It won't look good if I'm late this morning."

"If there's anything I can do for you, you'll let me know, right?"

The lump in Kim's throat grew. "I feel so powerless," she whispered. "I'm his mother; I'm supposed to be able to fix things for him. It's all so wrong, and this time I can't undo it."

Her mother drew back and looked into her eyes. "Believe me, I know just how you feel."

At Ravenswood, Kim walked into the faculty lounge, a square room arranged with chairs and sofas and resembling, more than anything, a Starbucks, and conversation stopped. Then, following an awkward pause in which she simply stood and returned the stares, it resumed in such a way that Kim could tell everyone in the room had abruptly changed their subjects.

Astonishingly, not a single one of her fellow teachers greeted her. No one offered support, or asked for information. These people who had welcomed her, commiserated with her, laughed with her over coffee or cocktails, were now apparently reconsidering their fondness for the mother of an accused sex offender. She was the elephant in the room. She pulled her shoulders back, gritted her teeth to keep her lips from trembling as her colleagues resumed their exclusive conversations. So be it, then.

She was pouring coffee into her mug when William came in. The room quieted again as he came up to her. In his black pants and pinstriped dress shirt, cuffs rolled to his elbows, wire-rimmed glasses giving him a studious look that disappeared when she saw him in sunglasses, tennis shoes, and shorts, he was every bit *Mr. Braddock*. He kept his hands at his sides and said, "Can I have a word? In my office?"

"Of course. Sure. I'll be right there."

"Great, thanks."

She watched him pivot and leave without engaging anyone else in the room, rare for him. At work he was, under ordinary circumstances, that lovely combination of sociable and authoritative, resulting in respect given freely rather than grudgingly—which was more often the case with administrators, if respect was accorded them at all. As a headmaster and as a friend, he got invited to and welcomed at cocktail parties and dinners and birthday celebrations and nights on the town. Which explained in large part how he had managed to see her publicly without raising suspicions. That he had been so brief just now did not bode well.

Kim took her time getting the pint of half-and-half from the refrigerator, opened it slowly, poured it slowly, closed the carton, and returned it to its spot on the top shelf. If she didn't appear stressed or hurried, her son would look less guilty, wasn't that how it worked? As conversation resumed once more, she took a teaspoon from the sink, rinsed it off, stirred the cream into her coffee, rinsed the spoon again, and set it in the drainer. On her way to the door, she stopped to speak to Shirlene Marshall, a fellow art teacher whose specialties were pottery and papier-mâché.

"You did a wonderful job with the new display near the office," Kim said.

Shirlene looked at her archly and replied, "I'm surprised you noticed."

Bryce Edwards, next to Shirlene, said, "Give her a break, Shirl."

Kim touched his shoulder and moved on.

The passage leading from the lounge to William's office went through the main office, where Sue Pender and Andrea Barnett, who habitually stopped what they were doing in order to chat with passersby, remained occupied as Kim passed them, knocked once on William's door, then let herself inside.

He was standing near the windows, with their view of rolling lawn and pin oaks that had stood since Civil War days. As she entered, he turned toward her.

"So, that was awkward and unpleasant," she said. Getting the words out eased the constriction in her chest, slightly.

"I'm sorry. I tried to get you on your cellphone—"

"You did?" she said, taking it from her pocket. The display was black, and remained black even when she pressed the power button. "The battery's dead; I forgot to charge it, no real surprise. On my way in, I saw that my gas gauge is on E, and twice this week I wrote the wrong year on a check."

William looked sympathetic, but he remained standing where he was. "How's Anthony?"

"At loose ends, as you might expect."

"I had a seven o'clock meeting this morning," William told her, tugging at his ear. "With the advisory board. This kind of situation is unprecedented here. The calls we've been getting, the emails . . . I've gotten everything from demands that we confiscate cellphones and disable our Internet connectivity—as if kids only use these things inappropriately at school—to detailed proposals from counseling agencies who'd like to do programs here, to diatribes—really vitriolic stuff—over how I could be so blind to the obvious pornography ring operating here, right beneath my nose. Three parents— so far only three—have threatened to withdraw their kids."

She moved toward him. "William, I am so sorry—"

"The worst, though," he said, looking defeated but holding a hand up to keep her at a distance, "is that I am required"—he sighed heavily—"to put you on leave without pay, indefinitely, effective immediately, while I conduct an internal investigation—which I will do as quickly as I can, I promise you. And I need to warn you, the State Bureau of Investigation is likely to show up at your door to question you, soon."

Kim stared at him. "Me?"

"There could be charges, if they determine that you knew what was going on and didn't take any action, inform me, inform the Wilkeses, that sort of thing."

She sank into a chair. "Jesus God, that's just what I need," she said. "Who told you that?"

"One of the school's lawyers."

She thought of all the time she and William had spent together, the conversations they'd had about their childhoods, their aspirations, the goals they still had, and the way they both sort of circled around the unspoken possibility that they'd pursue those goals together, somehow. They'd talked a lot about Anthony, too, and his plans, and she'd let William speculate on Amelia's uncommon talent and love for theatre and her post-high-school plans, wanting to share what she knew, forcing herself to keep quiet. They weren't close enough for her to share secrets. And now, with this new layer of complications . . . now it looked as if they might never be.

Hadn't she earned some happiness of her own, some companionship, a shot at something lasting—especially now, when she was about to have the time to give it her best? How was this fair? Right, sure, *life's not fair,* and hadn't she tried to calm Anthony with assurances that *things could be worse*? How easy it was to speak in platitudes.

She said, "I didn't know the specifics of what was going on, the things they've been charged with."

"I believe you."

"Even if I *had* known, it wouldn't have occurred to me that they could be charged with felonies for it. I . . . I wouldn't have reported it," she said, turning her palms upward. "That's the plain truth. Maybe that does make me culpable."

"You're not saying you'd have condoned it?"

"*No, I—*"

He paced in front of the windows. "We *tell* them—it's in the Health curriculum—'respect yourself, make good choices regarding sexuality, recognize the dangers out there.'"

"We don't tell them to avoid taking and sharing private photos."

"They should know this," he said, turning toward her. "It should go without saying."

"Well you'd better tell them anyway, because clearly they *don't* know. Smart kids don't know."

"Or they do it anyway. They do it anyway," he repeated, shaking his head. Then, as if catching up again with the reason for this meeting, he said, "You really wouldn't have told the Wilkeses that Amelia was involved in this kind of thing?"

Kim stood up, preparing to leave. Indefinite suspension without pay—how was she going to manage that?

"Don't judge me, all right? You don't *know*—you *can't* know what it's like, how different things feel when it's your own kid who's involved in some situation."

"These kids are just as important to me as my own would be—"

"That's head," Kim said, pointing at his. "I'm talking about heart." She touched her chest. "Now, if you'll excuse me . . ."

William stepped in front of her and said, "Kim. I wish I had a choice, here. All of this is getting out of hand."

"I'm sorry," she said stiffly, "and I'm sure I speak for Anthony, too."

"Don't be like that." He took her hand and studied it, then looked up at her and said, "Don't think I blame you. It's just an unfortunate situation."

"Yes," she said, pulling her hand back.

He let it go, emitting a small sound that Kim heard as resignation, an acknowledgment that what *was* no longer could *be*. The sound was a rending of the delicate fabric they'd been weaving these past several months.

He said, "I wonder if we shouldn't try to get everyone who's involved together in one place—the kids, you, the Wilkeses, your attorneys—and see if there's a way to put this to rest. It would be hard for Liles to press on against a united front."

"You think the Wilkeses would unite with us, do you?"

"Now that Amelia's been charged, yes, I think they might. And at any rate, what can it hurt to try? I'll talk it over with some people—strategize a bit—and then get up with the Wilkeses next week."

They stood there awkwardly for a long beat. Anything Kim might have liked to say refused to travel from thought to speech. There was as little chance of his welcoming the words as there was of the Wilkeses—Harlan Wilkes—agreeing to side with Anthony. The only action she seemed able to take now was to hold her head up as she left William's office and walked through the Ravenswood hallways to the exit, to the sidewalk, to her car.

22

On Friday morning, Anthony left his newly adrift mother working on a new oil painting, and arrived at the Habitat building site hoping to paint, too, if in a less artful way. Their strange situation—both of them free on a weekday at the height of fall, both of them suspended from school, neither of them earning any money at the moment—made him feel guilty and angry, and not good company to be around. She wasn't such good company either, and he was getting tired of hearing her say things about him and Amelia like, *Maybe it's for the best,* meaning maybe they should split for real, which was not going to happen. Getting back to work here would be a useful distraction, and gave him an excuse to be out of the house.

This house, his second construction project since signing on as a volunteer with Habitat for Humanity, was about four weeks away from completion. Though it was not yet nine o'clock, two cars were parked out front. He recognized them as belonging to Marcus, the project supervisor and owner of a contracting business, and Sam, who had worked for Marcus before his alcoholism got out of hand

and cost him his wife, his job, his driver's license, and his self-respect, until he dried out and got involved with Marcus again through Habitat. They were like brothers, and both had been quick to give Anthony a warm welcome and put him to work when a lot of the others on the crew kept their distance. He was a little different from their usual volunteers, he knew. No ties to a church, no real knowledge of Raleigh or the South before moving here, a kid who spent his breaks reading Voltaire or studying his lines for a play. That was okay with Marcus and Sam. As Marcus had once said, "If we all take the same road, we all end up in the same place."

The exterior of the house looked finished, though the property on which it sat remained a barren quarter-acre of reddish clay littered with nails and scraps of shingles. In four weeks or so, everything would be done: painting completed, cabinetry and fixtures and appliances installed, carpet and vinyl laid, and a selection of starter plants tucked into little berms of soil and mulch that would improve their chances of survival. And then, in a ceremony attended by all the volunteers who had worked on the project, the house would be officially presented to the new homeowner or homeowners.

At the ceremony for the first house Anthony had helped to build (a miserable project for most of the six months thanks to rain, and more rain, and then a fire, and then the theft of the kitchen cabinetry, for which every volunteer had been questioned), the new homeowner was a young widowed mother who had three children under age six. Michelle was her name. Michelle had cried and hugged every single one of them. Anthony, fifth in line, felt her grateful arms around him and started crying, too—just a few tears, which he laughed about and quickly wiped away on his T-shirt's sleeve. But he was hooked. All the aggravation they'd endured to build the little three-bedroom house, a home that was not very different from the one he and his mother shared, had been worth it to get that hug. Though his original commitment to the organization had been meant to make his application to NYU more competitive, he'd signed on for another house, no question.

This one sat up from the street and had a steep driveway that was going to delight the little boy who'd be living there. Seven-year-old Eric, skinny and gap-toothed with crazy blond curls, was a real skater kid. His father brought him around to the site regularly in the late afternoons when school was out, and he and Anthony had become fast friends. Recalling the schedule, Anthony intended, today, to assign himself to painting Eric's room if it hadn't already been done.

He walked up the driveway and entered the house through the side door. Marcus looked up from where he stood reviewing a list at the makeshift table—two sawhorses supporting a white six-panel interior door—and said, "Well, Winter, my boy. This is a surprise. I thought we might not see you anymore. Glad to have a couple extra hands today, thanks for coming."

Sam said, "Hey, Winter, didn't think you'd show up here. Thought they'd have reassigned you to ReStore." He laughed and slapped him on the back. ReStore was the donation-and-resale arm of Habitat in Raleigh, and the place where a lot of men who'd gotten in trouble with the law went to serve their community service hours. Sam added, "Figures, *white* boy makes bail and is out in minutes, no ReStore for him."

"Three days," Anthony said. "Not ten minutes." He glanced at Sam, then away. No gain in discussing how he'd managed to make bail at all, while Sam's brother remained in jail four months after arrest, awaiting trial for aggravated assault. "And no ReStore *yet*. Guess I don't need to ask whether you heard."

Marcus tucked his pencil behind his ear. "They're talking about you on the radio, my friend. You are the morning's entertainment for that bunch on G105."

"Nice," he replied, his voice flat. The bagel he'd had for breakfast sat in his stomach like a rock.

Marcus put his hand on Anthony's back. "You got a good lawyer, I hope?"

"I think so—Mariana Davis? I can't say much about the case. It's all crap, though. I'll say that."

Sam grinned. "So it's not you and the Wilkes girl running a child porn ring?"

"Tell me they didn't actually say that."

"Both y'all get arrested for possessing child porn and stuff, and you, with the giving porn to minors—see how many ways that can sound," Sam said.

Marcus asked, "But it's just the two of you, isn't it?"

Anthony nodded.

"Thought so. Somebody called in, said they knew you both, and that it was the two of you swapping pictures, and that kids are doing it all the time, 'sexting,' she said, and it's just that you got caught."

Sam snorted. "And Daddy Wilkes, bet he'd like to take a buck knife and raise your voice some octaves. Lucky you're not black. He'd a been waiting for you outside the jail with one of them knives, you know, like they use to gut deer."

"Wilkes is no racist," Anthony said. "Not that I ever heard of. But yeah, he's not happy with me."

Sam said, "You *defend* the guy?"

"He loves his daughter, same as me. I get that." Which was true. The rest of his opinion about Wilkes was best left unspoken, in case Marcus or Sam ended up being questioned. No sense digging himself a deeper hole—but *reticent* really was not his style. Speech was not exactly free when you were at risk of spending the better part of your life on the sex-offender registry.

"Bet Wilkes don't love either one of you too much right now," Sam chuckled. "What was your bail, anyway?"

"Thirty thousand."

Sam whistled long and low. "Your mom, she's a teacher, right? How'd you pull it off?"

"Property bond. Can we get to work now?"

"Touchy."

"We're painting today, gentlemen," Marcus said, drawing their attention to the business at hand. "Sam, you and I will work on the master bedroom and bathroom. Anthony, why don't you do the boy's room?"

"I was hoping you'd say that. Sounds good."

"He was asking after you, the boy was. Said you're almost as good as Tony Hawk."

Anthony shook his head. "Nah. I got a couple good tricks is all."

Sam said, "Hope you got one 'will get that DA off your back." He feinted a skateboard kick and twist, then hooked his arm around Anthony's neck and said, "'Else you ain't coming *near* my girls." Then, laughing, he released him to his work.

Anthony carried the paint up the stairs and into Eric's bedroom, glowering. Sam could joke; it wasn't his life being screwed with. Sure, Sam had been down, but never so far that he couldn't see a way back up. Never to a place so low in the public's esteem that even drunk-driving, philandering alcoholics like Sam had once been looked good in comparison. Sam had never lost his future.

Anthony went back downstairs for a stepladder, then down once more for the paint tray and roller and brushes. The color Eric had chosen was a bright green, sure to take two coats. Anthony put on headphones he'd borrowed from Cameron and set her iPod to play Train's "Counting Airplanes," looking for the lift that music never failed to provide—an even higher lift when Amelia's voice was the music he heard.

He was pouring the paint into the tray when he noticed feet in the doorway, running shoes, women's white-silver-pink. He looked up to see Caryn Pierce. A six-year Habitat veteran, her reputation was that she'd made volunteering there her career. Though she dressed in the same styles the teenage girls were wearing and had a youthful face, she had four sons, ages thirteen to seventeen, and a twelve-year-old daughter who, as best Anthony had been able to tell, did little other than beg for UGG boots and ride horses in her free time. The boys were all hockey players for the middle and high schools Anthony used to attend. Caryn had quizzed him about his transfer to Ravenswood, and he'd gotten the sense that she was jealous on her children's behalf. For all that she could afford to give her time away, Ravenswood was apparently out of reach for her family of seven.

"Hey," he said, moving the headphones to his neck.

"Marcus wants me to do the edging." He heard the grudge in her tone—because of the assignment?

"Oh, well, that'd be great—we'll get it done faster that way. I'm sure Eric will come by this afternoon, so it'd be cool if we had it done." She didn't reply. He tried again. "This color's gonna be a challenge. Marcus was a real softie to go along with it."

She continued to stand there and watch him, lips pressed into a firm line, one hand coiling her thick blond ponytail around and around. When she hadn't moved after he'd loaded his roller with paint and was preparing to start, he said, "Would you rather roll? I know edging's a pain in the butt."

"I can't do this," she said, backing out and leaving.

"Can't do what?" he heard Marcus say from down the hallway.

"Work with *him*," Caryn said, not bothering to lower her voice. "I tried, and I just won't do it. You know what he did."

"I know what he's been *accused* of doing, and it's not all that bad. And either way, he didn't do anything to you."

"As if that should matter. He shouldn't be here—you shouldn't let him be here. We are decent, God-fearing people. We can't have nasty sex-addicts sliming up the place, ruining it for the new owners. Get rid of him or I'm out of here."

Anthony let his arm drop. He didn't like Caryn that well to begin with, and wouldn't have said her opinions mattered to him one way or the other. The venom in her words and tone, though, might as well have been injected straight into his veins. He set the roller down carefully in the paint tray and left the room, finding them still standing in the drywalled, plywood-floored hall. Marcus was saying, "Can we be reasonable here?" and Caryn had her index finger pointing at Marcus. Anthony put his hand on her shoulder and said, "No trouble, Caryn, I'll clear out."

She flinched and jerked away from him, then he moved past her and squeezed by Marcus, who said, "Anthony, hold on——"

"Tell Eric and his family that I wish them the best here. I'll see you."

He left then, hurrying down the still-bare plywood stairs and out into the chilly morning, hardly feeling the cold.

Kim, dressed in her paint-stained sweats with a cornflower-blue bandanna holding her hair back, sat in her living room doing her best to stay focused on what the man from the SBI was saying. Why they couldn't have set up an appointment for her to come to them was beyond her, as was the reasoning for why the agent had to park his clearly marked SBI sedan right in front of her house so that all her neighbors would know she was sequestered in here with him.

It was good that Anthony had gone to work on the Habitat house this morning. He needed some outlet for, or at least distraction from, his frustration. With him out of the house, she could stop peppering him with suggestions that he and Amelia might be better off using this situation, their separation, as an opportunity to *be independent, get some space—reconsider their couple-ness,* she'd said once, and he'd looked at her like she'd sprouted horns.

The SBI didn't care whether Anthony and Amelia's romance would or should persist. She wanted to be cooperative, to allay their suspicions in order to, she hoped, avoid arrest, while at the same time give them nothing to go on that wasn't common knowledge or knowledge easily gained by talking to people who knew her. William, for example (who had yet to return her call or answer her emailed question about the possibility of appealing her suspension— he was avoiding her). To satisfy the SBI while also protecting herself and her son was a challenge not so different, she thought, from walking a tightrope while wearing a blindfold.

"Ms. Winter, just a few more questions. Did you know your son was in possession of devices which could be used for the production of pornography?"

Kim pointed at his phone where he had it holstered on his belt. "Does that take pictures and video?"

"Ma'am."

"Next question," she said.

He pressed his tongue against his upper lip, then said, "Did Amelia Wilkes ever come to you with information about her relationship with your son?"

"I told you, I knew they were seeing each other because my *son* told me. That's the whole story."

"But students do often talk to you."

"I see a hundred of them in my classrooms every day."

He smiled in the way people do when they aren't really amused. "Did you share this information about the relationship with Miss Wilkes's parents?"

"My son is eighteen. I no longer get in touch with his friends' moms."

"Even when that friend is potentially a threat, someone who'd cause trouble for him?"

Kim kept her face a mask of cooperative concern, but she knew what he was doing, where he was trying to lead her. "I have always regarded Amelia Wilkes as a thoughtful, responsible person whose welfare I care about very much."

"All the more interesting, then, that you didn't share those thoughts with her parents."

"I did, each time they came for conference."

"When you could easily have tossed in a 'Hey, how about our kids as a couple,' right? But you didn't. You encouraged this girl, who you say you care about, to lie to her parents continually. Nice."

Kim wanted to ask if he'd learned this hot-and-cold act by

watching *Perry Mason,* but not only was sarcasm unlikely to produce any positive effect, he was probably too young to know who she meant. She said instead, "My. Will you look at the time? Unfortunately, I have an appointment at ten-thirty and I'm obviously not dressed for it, so we're going to have to wrap this up."

He nodded, and his expression shifted from accusatory to sympathetic. "Ms. Winter, you know I'm just trying to get a clear picture, here, of how well these kids were able to fool you—we want to make sure that you missed *all* the signs, even when it was happening right under your nose, maybe in your own house, so that we all understand that you aren't culpable."

"I did miss them," she said easily, noting with satisfaction the way his eyebrow flared. He'd expected her to be defensive, to want to deny being so easy to fool. "I had no idea they were doing anything illegal. None."

He stacked his note cards together and tucked them into his binder. "All right, then, it looks like we're done, for now."

"For now?"

"There may be further questions."

"Well, okay," she said, walking behind him toward the door, "but there won't be further answers—not because I don't want to give them, but because there aren't any to give."

"Thank you for your time."

"My pleasure."

She shut the door, then pressed her hands and forehead against it and closed her eyes. *Deep cleansing breath, in, out . . .* Then she went to the kitchen, put the kettle on for tea, and dialed Rose Ellen, who surely would help her to make sense of a world in which teenagers could face felony charges for being in love and a parent could be charged for permitting it. She would like to have said this to the detective and asked him, "What the hell is wrong with you all? *Who* was being harmed before the police got involved?"

She said this to Rose Ellen. "Who? Tell me."

"William hasn't called you back, has he?"

"No, damn it." And although she sensed that the SBI wasn't through with her, the rest of their conversation was about Kim's ambivalence about the kids' relationship, her anxiety, and her bruised ego—no, really her bruised heart. William had no choice but to suspend her, she understood that, but did that mean he truly had to let her go?

23

*I*N HER DREAM, AMELIA IS ONSTAGE, FIXED IN THE BEAMS OF TWO *spotlights, naked. The audience, barely visible to her because of the lights shining in her eyes, mutters ominously and points at her. She wants to move, to run. She gives herself the directive. Move! Run! She hears Ms. Winter's voice calling out, "Quittez-vous!" Her body, however, seems disconnected from her brain. "You're thinking too much," her father says from the wings. "Less thinking, more doing, that's how things get done." She turns her head to look for Anthony——isn't he supposed to be here to support her on this, her opening night? Then, without warning, the lights shut off, and she feels a pain low in her abdomen, and the lights flash on again. She blinks, and sees sunlight cutting through the slit in her bed's curtains.* Morning.

Amelia rose and padded to the bathroom, the pain she'd felt in her dream hanging on as a shadow of itself, a cramp, probably premenstrual. Well, that gave her something different to think about, at least. Without her usual schedule to track the passage of time, every day felt the same as the one before it, and the same as she expected the next to feel. It was purgatory passed in a luxurious holding cell,

a holding pattern, like circling an airport while in a 747's upstairs
lounge the way they'd done once on a trip to Honolulu.

Her period wasn't due yet, but maybe the anxiety was skewing her
cycle, so she tended to that possibility while thinking how her parents
would have behaved if, instead of discovering the photos, she'd turned
up accidentally pregnant. There would be no police in that scenario, no
arrest, no immediate and forced disconnection from everything that
mattered in her life. Her parents might be angry. They'd surely be upset.
They might even try to keep her from seeing Anthony—but because
the baby would be his, too, they'd have trouble justifying that. In that
scenario, which was in every way a bigger problem than her having "indecent" photos, there would be no sex-offender business, no possibility
of prison time. Amelia gazed out her window as she bound up her hair.
She had never wished she would get pregnant, and she didn't wish it
now, not really; she wished there were something, though, to end the
waking nightmare she and Anthony were snagged in. This limbo, this
void, all the wasted time, the too-infrequent and always unsatisfying up-
dates Cameron gave about Anthony (and gave Anthony about her, and
thank God for Cameron), it was all so pointless and tiring and wrong.

A broad, orb-shaped spider's web stretched between a pair of au-
tumn cherry trees thick with brilliant, pink-tinged white blooms.
Amelia propped each foot on the windowsill to lace up each shoe,
desperate for the freedom to go running outside. She longed for the
scents of the fall morning and the puddles of sunlight that marked her
usual route with peace, assurance, and optimism as if gifts given from
Mother Nature herself. The treadmill, tucked away in the basement's
windowless room, had none of that. The treadmill was exactly perfect, though, for her current place in life.

When she'd finished her run and gone upstairs to the kitchen, her
mother was waiting, a strange look on her face. "Ms. McGuiness
just called; she and Cameron are bringing breakfast."

"Today? What about school?" Amelia said, before recalling that this was a staff training day, a day she'd have missed anyway because of the Drama Guild's trip to New York. The group had left yesterday, without her and without Anthony, and would right now be milling about in the lobby of a Manhattan Holiday Inn Express, eating cinnamon rolls and plotting the day's activities. If not for her father (if not for her mistake, if not for bad luck, if not for the fickle gods who loved to toy with mortals), she would be there, too, dressed in her black leotard, her gypsy skirt and purple ruffled ballet flats, her flowers-and-stars-embroidered black flannel coat, with a tatted, multicolored scarf tied around her neck and her hair hanging loose for the moment. Anthony would be waiting at the hotel's door in his charcoal wool peacoat with his blue scarf brightening his hazel eyes, instead of sitting on a bench in the Wake County courthouse and awaiting his turn to face a judge on the misdemeanor charge, as he must be doing right now.

She would be taking Anthony's gloved hand in her own and going out into the frosty morning, their breath rising from their noses as they kissed on the sidewalk, then they'd set off for the subway and Tisch. She would be happy and confident, and those traits would come through when she stood before the evaluation team and showed them why she deserved a spot in next fall's freshman class. And then she would wait for Anthony to do the same, as anxious for him as she'd be for herself, but believing firmly in their chances for success. Believing firmly in what should have been, but might not, now, ever be.

"Never mind, I forgot it was a staff day," she told her mother, forcing herself to put aside the resentment that wanted to replace her blood in her veins. The counselor she'd seen last week said she should remain focused on the positives, and the woman had been right about that, if about little else. The negative feelings would come—of course they would—but she could choose not to let them define her. No, she couldn't reschedule her evaluation, but there would be another chance to get into Tisch next year, assuming

Acton Hubbard did his job, assuming common sense prevailed. Her father might try to crush her dream, but she could not allow him to kill it.

She said, "What about the tutor? Isn't she coming?"

"Yes, she'll be here. Ms. McGuiness said they can't stay long, but she's got some pumpkin-zucchini bread and pumpkin-raisin bread for us, and homemade butter. Doesn't that sound delicious?"

If Amelia could muster an appetite, then yes, she supposed she would find it delicious. Why, though, was Cameron's mother coming over at all? If it was just to deliver bread, Cameron could do that on her own. Liz McGuiness was not part of her mother's circle; the two women knew each other only through their daughters, in a kind of casual pick-up, drop-off way that had ended when the girls got cars. For her to call and then come by to visit was surprising.

Amelia said, "Sure," and kept those questions to herself. "When will they be here?" she asked instead, checking the time on the microwave. Five minutes before ten. Anthony might be in front of the judge right now. According to Hubbard, the outcome of Anthony's appearance today would help them know what to expect when her turn came. Granted, he was only facing the misdemeanor charge at this appearance, but if the prosecutor agreed to dismiss the case, or the judge agreed with the lawyer's argument for dismissal, they could hope for similar results for her charges. Maybe the DA would be satisfied with having scared them and gotten a lot of publicity doing it. Maybe he'd intended only that all along.

Her mother looked her over and, frowning, said, "What a state you're in. I wish you had time to shower."

"They won't care."

"No one wants to see you—or smell you—in your sweaty, clingy clothes."

"Fine," Amelia said, though her tone said the opposite. "Everything has to be *your* way; I should know better than to even *think* I can decide anything for myself."

Her mother's tone was similarly sharp when she said, "And don't dawdle, they're due any minute."

Amelia pounded up the stairs. Thank God Cameron was coming over and something real was happening for a change. That she'd imagined her life was slow before all the trouble began was laughable now. Her life had run itself into a muddy ditch like the one that ran along the road her father grew up on, and had stalled, no jumper cables available, no mechanic in sight.

Cameron and her mother arrived at the house at ten past ten. Liz McGuiness, as enthusiastically blond as Cameron was redheaded, was dressed in black jeans and a green cashmere cardigan Amelia knew was Cameron's. Her heart-shaped face was youthful in spite of the deepening lines at the corners of her eyes, which Amelia saw as proof that she smiled a lot—a real contrast from her own smooth-faced mother. Liz McGuiness carried a picnic basket, which she set on the kitchen counter before reaching for Amelia and pulling her into a hug. "Oh my, look at you—I'm not a minute too soon with the bread. If you get any skinnier . . ."

"She insists on running every morning," Amelia's mother said. "And she only picks at her food."

Cameron, her back to Amelia's mother, rolled her eyes and said, "Who can blame her?"

Liz gave Amelia one more squeeze, then let go and opened the basket. She took out two towel-wrapped loaves, unleashing the scents of nutmeg and cinnamon and making Amelia's mouth water. Amelia wanted to cry with the pleasure of it all—the sight of Cameron, the feel of Liz McGuiness's arms around her, the scent of thoughtfulness, of concern, of support that wafted from the still-warm bread. In all the days that she'd spent here with her own mother, both of them trying to fill the long hours between wake and sleep that were not taken up by the tutor or by her father, not once had they baked something—together or separately. It was as though even the idea of baking, with its promise of comfort and pleasure, had become too hazardous for either of them to approach.

Cameron hooked her arm through Amelia's and squeezed. This made Amelia want to cry, too. Really, there was little that didn't— which she hated, because until three weeks ago she had not been the crying type.

"We should eat on the patio, don't you think?" Cameron said. "We'll go outside and clean the leaves off the table."

Amelia, hearing the cue in Cameron's voice, said, "Good idea. It's so nice out."

As the girls went out the back door, Amelia heard Liz McGuiness saying, "Sheri, if you'll get some butter knives, and let me just pop this tub in your microwave . . ."

Outside, Cameron began pushing the fallen leaves from the wide teak table's surface. Amelia stood with her face upturned to the sunshine and breathed in the earthiness of the morning. The slight chill in the air was offset by the sun, encouraging them all to pretend that the seasons weren't changing. Amelia tried to hold on to the moment, to the feeling of safety, the sense of benevolence, false though she knew it was.

She turned her attention to the chairs, pulling one out and brushing it off as Cameron said, "So here's what's really going on. Mom wanted to see you in person and see how things are going. She thinks you're getting a raw deal, and she wants to help you out." Cameron stopped her work and took her iPhone from the pocket of her jeans, checked it, texted a reply to someone while Amelia looked on enviously, then put it away. "Did you know that adding a line to a phone plan is only ten dollars a month?"

"No, I didn't," Amelia said, puzzled at the change of subject. "In fact, I've just about forgotten what it's like to have a phone. Why?"

Cameron started wiping down the table's surface. "My mom, she gives like two hundred dollars to charity every month. Food bank. Women's shelter. Red Cross."

"How much bread does she give?" Amelia joked, setting out the plates and waiting for Cameron to reveal whatever it was she was hinting at. Buttercup followed her as she circled the table, as if in a game of follow the leader.

Cameron reached down to pet the dog. "My dad says if Mom takes on one more cause or takes in one more stray he's going to have to get a second job." She took her phone from her pocket again.

"Anything from Anthony?" Amelia asked, watching Cameron read a message and then type one out.

Cameron finished and said, "Not since last night. So anyway, Mom thinks spending another twenty dollars a month for a really worthy cause would make her feel a lot better, and my dad doesn't need to know about it."

"Okay . . ." Amelia said. "But what does that have to do with anything?"

"*I* had to buy the *phones,* of course, but . . ."

"Buy what phones?" She looked at Cameron, whose eyes were twinkling with the fun of keeping her guessing. Then the door opened, and Cameron's face became a mask of innocence.

Amelia thought back: ten dollars to add a new phone to a cell account, Cameron had said. Twenty-dollar expense for a good deed. Cameron bought phones. "Oh!" Amelia said, getting it.

Her mother looked alarmed. "What's wrong?"

"Nothing. I . . . I just thought of something." She glanced at Cameron knowingly. *Phones,* for her and Anthony, so that they could stop using Cameron as their go-between. So that they could talk to each other again, directly. Such a common thing, and yet now it felt like a miracle, like God acting through Cameron and her mother. Cameron wasn't a fairy, she was an angel.

Liz McGuiness set a platter of sliced bread in the center of the table. "So, Amelia, how goes it with the tutor? It must be awfully difficult to be away from school and all your friends."

Her mother sat down, saying, "She's really better off away—other kids can be so cruel."

Cameron pulled out a chair and climbed onto it, tucking her knees beneath her the same way she'd done when Amelia met her in preschool. "Yeah, there are some real bee-otches out there talking trash, but there's also a Facebook page up supporting *both* of them," she said pointedly, then added, "Amelia *and* Anthony," in case Amelia's mother missed the point.

"Cameron," Liz McGuiness chided as she took her seat, "do you have to be so subtle?"

Amelia sat, too. "What are they saying?"

"Who?"

"At school."

Cameron shrugged. "What you'd expect. Jealous, snotty stuff. That you must be a slut—sorry, Ms. Wilkes—and that Anthony's your pimp. Intelligent stuff like that." Cameron pushed her wild hair behind her shoulders and said, "I told them all to screw off—"

"All of this must be difficult for you, too," Liz McGuiness interrupted, reaching for Amelia's mother's hand. "Are you doing all right? Can I help?"

"I . . . No, we're fine. That is, thank you. You're kind to offer." She could hardly sound stiffer.

"I'm sure you've found a great lawyer. What's the plan for—"

"We can't talk about it. I'm sorry, I don't mean to be rude. But my husband says the lawyer was quite clear that we shouldn't discuss it with anyone."

They were all quiet then, while they took thick slices of the warm bread and slathered them with the honey butter Liz McGuiness had made from scratch. When Amelia's mother remarked on the butter, Liz said, "There's a lot less to making it than you'd think. I buy the cream from a dairy out in Orange County, whip it into butter in about five minutes, add the honey, some cinnamon, some vanilla, and voilà!"

"Voilà!" Cameron echoed, pronouncing it with a *v* instead of a *w* the way her mother had just done. "Ms. Winter would be so impressed with your pronunciation, Mom."

"What are you all doing for Thanksgiving next week?" Amelia's mother asked, a clear subject change that couldn't have been lost on any of them.

Liz McGuiness said, "We'll be in town, doing our usual 'widows and orphans' dinner."

"We invited the Winters; maybe you guys could come, too," Cameron said, looking directly at Amelia's mother, "and, you know, think about burying the hatchet."

Amelia watched her mother's mouth tighten with the effort of determining how she ought to respond, and then Liz McGuiness rescued her, saying, "I'm sure you have plans already?"

"We do, yes. My family, in High Point." The Kerrs, who had made no secret of their feelings regarding Amelia's predicament, as they called it. Though her mother tried to keep these phone conversations out of Amelia's earshot, some of them had taken place without warning—while the two of them were at the flower shop, for example, ordering a bereavement arrangement for a friend of her mother's who'd been in the Women's Club. In the tiny, quiet space of the shop, Amelia had been able to hear her aunt Lou saying how shocked they'd all been to see Amelia on the news. "That's just the kind of predicament Daddy warned you about," Lou had said. "He hasn't forgot. You ought to hear him." Amelia had listened keenly, wondering how her grandfather—who was a distant man, and not close to her at all—could have imagined her troubles ahead of time and warned her mother about them. But then it occurred to her, as the brief exchange played out, that Lou might not mean this literally. It occurred to her that her grandfather's warning might have been about some other troubles, and a long time back. She listened for more clues or for confirmation, but her mother cut Lou off with a promise to call her back when she got home.

"But how about this," Liz McGuiness was saying now, "we'd love to have Amelia come to the beach with us this weekend. Cam's got it in her head to bake a Black Forest cake, and I was thinking we could pick up Amelia on Friday, unless you'll be going out of town early—"

"I think she'd better not, but thank you so much for the offer."

"Momma, why not? Daddy will be in San Francisco, so—"

"Another time," her mother said, politely but firmly. "I'm not even sure it's allowed."

"Allowed by who? The court, or you and Daddy? For God's sake," Amelia said, tossing her napkin on the table and standing up, "why do we have to live like cowards?" She started to walk away, then turned, grabbed her half-eaten bread, and headed inside.

The dog jumped up and followed, and Cameron did, too. "Good move," Cameron said after shutting the door behind Buttercup. "While she's out there apologizing to my mom for you being so troublesome, like you know she'll do, I can give you what's in my purse. Come on," she said, "let's go have your fit in your room."

Amelia's anger drained and her anticipation returned. She smiled at Cameron. "I am so grateful for you."

They hurried upstairs, Cameron leading, as if they were twelve-year-olds again in a rush to watch Miley Cyrus as Hannah Montana. For Amelia, the teen superstar had been a brief preadolescent interest, a look at what Amelia might be able to do with her own emerging good looks and appealing voice. She'd known pretty quickly, though, that the pop music, pop stardom route would never be for her, supposing she even had a chance at it. Hannah Montana was as much Miley Cyrus as the other way around; Amelia would never be able to put herself out there that way. She needed a character to inhabit who was not a glorified version of herself. She needed to be the vessel for the playwright and the composer, and in that way she could safely express, safely release all the things she kept inside.

Cameron climbed onto Amelia's bed, moving aside the journal, magazines, and pillows, and dumped out her purse. Among the hairbrush and wallet, lip gloss, keys, folded notes, and half-finished bags of M&M's that spilled out were two basic slider-style cellphones. "They aren't much, features-wise," Cameron said. "No

Internet service or anything, no picture-sending enabled. But they do have keyboards—I'm looking out for you, kiddo. You can call and text as much as you want." She pushed one toward Amelia. "I'll give Anthony his after he gets home from court, when we drop some bread off for them."

Amelia examined the phone, a rectangular silver and black device with the front display reading out the time, 10:37 A.M., as though it were a precious and rare artifact from another era. "You know that if I use this to get in touch with him, I'm violating my bail terms."

"Then you better not get caught this time; I'd hate for Mom to get in trouble." She winked.

"Your mom did this, really?"

"I coughed up one-fifty for the phones, but yeah, she was thrilled to go along with the idea. All right, maybe not 'thrilled.' But she kept saying how she had to do *something*, so I gave her a good idea of what the something should be. I said I was tired of being Ms. Ambassador Go-Between. Do I *look* like Switzerland?"

"Well, since you asked . . ." Amelia said, "you are kind of bumpy and angular."

Shoveling the spilled contents back into her purse, Cameron added, "If your mom had let you come with us this weekend, you'd have gotten the story behind Mom's *yes*."

"Tell," Amelia said, as she climbed up onto the bed next to Cameron.

"It's about my uncle, really, Mom's brother Boyd. And this girl he met in Ireland, when he was doing the exchange-student thing his senior year in high school—Rosaleen was her name. She was a year younger and *way* Catholic, and my mom's family were—are— 'holiday Christians,' right, and worse, Protestant. You can see where this is going."

Amelia slid open the phone and pressed some of the keyboard's letters, testing them out. In another few hours, Anthony would be at the end of her fingertips once again. The thought made her stomach flutter. She would have to be very careful about how and when she used the phone—not that her parents, if they caught her, would turn her in. But they would definitely lock her down themselves.

She said, "The girl's family didn't think he was the right kind of guy for her. Sound familiar? So Boyd, he came home broken-hearted. But Rosaleen wrote to him, and he wrote to her, and then her parents got wind of that and sent her to live at a convent, I shit you not. So, no more letters."

"A convent. Why didn't my parents think of that?" Amelia said. "What happened to Boyd? What did he do?"

"Not much he *could* do. He went to college and met lots of other girls, but he never got Rosaleen out of his mind. He was even engaged once, but his heart just wasn't in it, and he broke it off a couple weeks before the wedding."

"That must have been awful for everybody," Amelia said, imagining the jilted bride-to-be and the lovelorn Boyd with equal compassion.

"I guess it was. I barely remember any of this—I was in first grade when it happened."

"I wonder what happened to the Irish girl, to Rosaleen."

"Boyd wondered, too. For, like, ten years he buried himself in work—he's a software guru—and he didn't date, or not much anyway, and then when he got a chance to go back to Ireland, he thought, what the hell, why not look her up."

"Did he find her?"

"She's coming over for Thanksgiving," Cameron said, grinning. "Isn't that cool? They're both, like, forty years old, but I guess age doesn't matter. But Mom would tell you she doesn't want you and Anthony to have to waste half *your* lives trying to get back to where you are right now."

"Except, I don't want to be where we are right now."

"Where you *ought* to be right now," Cameron amended. "Where you'll be, soon, we all hope."

"Not 'all.' If it was 'all,' you'd still have the hundred and fifty. I'll pay you back, by the way." Amelia looked at the time display again.

She was about to say she wished Anthony would call Cameron, when Cameron's phone rang.

"Here," Cameron said, holding it out to Amelia. "You answer."

"It says 'Kim Winter.'"

"It's him. Answer."

Amelia took the phone. "Hey, it's me."

"Amelia?" he said, and she heard pleasure, exhaustion, and gratitude in that single word. "How——?"

"Cameron's here. Are you doing okay? How did everything go?"

What he told her made her want to cry and cheer, both. Everything was getting so very, very complicated.

24

$\mathcal{H}$ARLAN, WAITING TO HEAR FROM HUBBARD, DID HIS BEST TO not come across as impatient while Clem toured him around the gutted warehouse that was to become the country-and-western nightclub. Clem wanted him to see every detail, from the condition of the surrounding paved parking lot to the wiring to the plumbing to the steel girders that supported the twenty-foot ceiling. He wanted to tell Harlan every thought he had on insulation, HVAC systems, lighting, toilets, carpet—or tile, maybe, behind each of the three bars he'd have in the main club?—and the ideal dimensions of a dance floor if they got a lot of two-steppers, not just line dancers, which he was pretty sure they would. He wondered whether Harlan wanted to handle the liquor license and distribution matters, since liquor was where the profit lay and connections were everything.

This was all fine with Harlan; he liked to follow his money and make sure it was being well spent. Had he not been anticipating the outcome of the Winter kid's court appearance, he'd have been able to give Clem his full attention. As it was, Harlan did a lot of nodding, said, "Uh-huh, sure," repeatedly, and failed to retain any of the finer details.

His mind was occupied first with the question of how dogged Gibson Liles was going to be, a matter about which Harlan was ambivalent. He wanted Winter to be the example Liles wanted to make of him, and at the same time he wanted Liles to back off the issue so that Amelia didn't have to pay for Winter's crimes. It was a conundrum of his own making, he knew. Instead of calling the cops, what he should have done was taken the kid out and beat him until he bled, the way he himself had been a few times, when he deserved it. The old Harlan would have done that, the one who'd made the deal with Clem all those years back. The pre-Sheri version of Harlan. His wife had raised him up a few notches, which he'd wanted, yes, but that elevation meant you called the cops rather than making your own justice, and now look how things were going.

When Clem finally took a breath and suggested they go over to Snoopy's for a classic hot dog lunch, Harlan checked the time, then said, "Sure, just give me ten minutes to catch up on a few things first. I'll meet you there, all right? And then I'll need to run. I'm on a five-fifteen flight to San Francisco for that international car show."

"Would you listen to you," Clem said with clear admiration. Then he tipped his head back and looked around them, saying, "I'm getting a late start at the big time, but I'm gonna get there, too."

Harlan patted him on the back. "You will. I'm gonna see to it."

He went out to his truck, a new silver Tundra he'd taken delivery of the day before, and checked his phone. There it was, a call from Hubbard; Harlan listened to the message: *I happened to be in court myself this morning, and saw the Winter boy's appearance. It's not good news. Call me at your convenience and I'll fill in the details.*

Harlan scowled as he waited for the next message to play. The scowl deepened when he heard, *"Good morning, Mr. Wilkes, this is William Braddock. Given how the situation with your daughter has evolved so quickly, and not in ways you may have expected, I'm proposing we set up*

*a meeting that'd let us all put our heads together and find a solution that's
fair to both your daughter and to the Winters. Something we could take to
the DA that would satisfy him as well. Please call me when you get this.*"

"Not happening," Harlan said, deleting the message. No way was
he going to let Braddock use Amelia to help Winter or Winter's irresponsible mother—where were the man's priorities, anyway? If
Harlan had wanted to play pat-a-cake with them, he'd have taken
Kim Winter's offer back when she'd called him.

He placed a call to Hubbard's office. When the receptionist put
him through to Hubbard, Harlan said, "Don't tell me he walked."

There was a pause, then Hubbard replied, "We *were* hoping for
leniency, if you'll recall."

"But not for the prosecution to roll over like a whore before a
C-note. That boy deserves to be punished."

"Yes. So, happily—in that sense—his attorney did not prevail in
her attempt to get a dismissal. But apparently the prosecution's
terms weren't too palatable—though no one was giving me any
particulars, knowing I'm working for you. That hardly matters.
What matters is that no deal was made, and I regret to report that
they're bound over for trial."

"He didn't plead out? That's just hard to believe," Harlan said.
"Wouldn't his lawyer advise him he's got no defense? I mean, who'd
go to trial when they've already confessed *and* there's, what do you
call it, physical proof?"

"Ms. Davis—his attorney—gave a statement afterward. You can
see the video clip online if it suits you. Suffice it to say they are taking a very high road here, insisting the DA is misapplying the
statute. I doubt that'll hold any legal water, but it does make for
good theatre."

"Speak English. You're saying we're in trouble, right?"

"Liles appears to want to run with the ball as far as he can get,
yes, and I'm sure Ms. Davis's statement will provoke him further."

"Then I guess we're gonna have to knock him out of bounds,
aren't we? That's what I'm paying you for," Harlan said, starting the

truck's engine. "My little girl's fate is in your hands, Hubbard, so make sure you play this game right."

"Of course, Mr. Wilkes. And you can be sure we will all be doing our best work on her behalf. I do need to remind you, though, that it's possible Liles will be as rough with us when the time comes. I will press hard for dropped charges using a more diplomatic approach than Ms. Davis took today. But if Liles remains firm, we may want to plead, since a trial would be our only recourse."

"She's completely innocent, so she's *not* pleading, and you can't let this get to trial," Harlan said, trying to ignore the sharp stomach pain that followed his mental image of Amelia on the witness stand being badgered by Gibson Liles. Everybody watching her, judging her—*her,* not a performance in some recital or play. He could not allow that to happen. Suppose they got a jury full of bitter, judgmental old biddies or preacher-man types and Hubbard couldn't make them see the light? Southerners were funny about their morals—wasn't Liles proof of that?—so there was no telling what her chances would be with only twelve people to judge her.

He wasn't a fool, though. He understood that Hubbard, for all his connections and his relationships and his arguments, might not be able to make it go away any better than Winter's lawyer had. That being the case, the only right way out of this was to get the public on Amelia's side from the outset. *Create the reality,* same as he told his sales team when they all gathered for the Wilkes Auto quarterly huddle. He would come out publicly and in every possible venue with the message that his girl was being victimized by not only Anthony Winter but Gibson Liles, too. He would humbly ask for support and prayers and he'd mean every word. His daughter was no bit of merchandise to be moved. She was his heart, his pride.

"As soon as I get back in town from the car show Sunday morning," he told Hubbard, "I'm getting moving on some of those publicity ideas we talked about. When we get the word out on what really happened, won't anybody be willing to let Liles do my girl wrong."

25

THE SATURDAY MORNING BEFORE THANKSGIVING COULD HAVE been mistaken for a day in June if not for the palette of fall colors gracing the trees. Sunshine, a sky so clear and blue that Kim's Ithaca friends would cry with envy, the scents of roasting corn and grill-cooked beef coming from vendors' metal huts—it all added up to a perfect morning at the Raleigh Flea Market, where she strolled alongside her mother wearing shorts and sandals and sunglasses, wishing she could be strolling along with William at her side, holding her hand. How long had it been since she'd had that comfort from a man, that ease? Not that it would solve any of her troubles, no, but having a partner, someone whose interests were vested in yours, made the difficult bearable. Her mother was wonderful— Kim was grateful for her company and support. A mother, though, filled a different role. An important, even crucial role, but different. She supposed Anthony, steadfast in his devotion to Amelia, must be feeling the same way.

Kim wished, too, that it truly was June and that none of the issues that were keeping her and William and Anthony and Amelia apart this morning had ever happened—or that it was next June, and the issues were long resolved. She loved the sunshine, the warmth, but it felt artificial, like a July visit to an open-all-year Christmas decoration store.

Anthony trailed the women, more involved in a text conversation taking place on the cellphone Cameron had given him than with Kim and his grandmother. This gift of phones, which she had resisted at first but then, after arguing with Anthony, given in to, made her anxious—for all the kids. And for Liz McGuiness as well—wasn't she worried about the consequences she might face for getting involved this way? Maybe she was, and had done it anyway—in which case Kim admired her, truth be told, and felt ashamed of her own hesitancy to do anything that went against the court's instruction or the lawyer's advice. She should call Mrs. McGuiness, she knew she should. . . . Call and tell her to cut off the service before more trouble came along (and weren't they all trouble magnets these days?). She knew she should call, and yet she put it off because she was too softhearted, reluctant to deny the kids this one small joy. Maybe this afternoon she would talk to Anthony about it, reiterate to him the risk that Cameron's mother was taking, and then make the call.

Her mother said, "You're obsessing, aren't you?"

"What? Oh, sorry, Mom."

"I know that look. I remember when Dad gave you that big glossy Monet book when you were, what, ten?"

Kim recalled the birthday. They'd gotten dressed up—Kim in her first bra, making her feel so grown-up—and gone out to dinner. "Twelve, I think."

"Twelve, then. You studied every page, every painting, as if you had to memorize the entire book before you went blind or something."

"Do you know he lived to be eighty-six? And his birthday just passed."

Her mother smiled. "He's a lot like you, you know."

"Monet?"

"Anthony. I can only imagine how you would have been if cellphones and texting existed when you were his age."

Anthony caught up to them and said, "Sorry. Cameron wants me to look for knock-off Coach bags. Think they have any here?"

Before Kim could answer, she heard the phone buzzing again.

Kim had long grown accustomed to his frequent texting, though it had been so odd at first. He'd be texting while listening to music and doing his homework and recording songs onto a CD. How did he keep his mind on so many things at once?

When he'd gotten his first cellphone, she'd had strict rules about its use. No calls or texts during meals. No phone use at all when visiting with her friends or her parents. No texting at the movies—not that she and Anthony went to movies together terribly often even then, when he was fifteen. She had not, in the early days of his having his own phone, allowed him to keep it in his room overnight. Most of those rules remained in place as he got older, but keeping the phone overnight was one that fell away once he'd gotten his driver's license, and a job. He swore he was getting enough sleep, and his grades didn't suffer—in fact his grades at Ravenswood were better than they'd been before.

Even after he'd come home from auditions all starry-eyed about Amelia that night a year ago, she'd trusted him to make good choices. And he had, mostly. He didn't use drugs. He was an exemplary student. He did athletics, he read, he wrote, he didn't spend all his time in front of the TV or computer, he did theatre, he volunteered at Habitat, he worked part-time. He didn't smoke. He didn't drink, as far as she'd been able to discern. He might have been sexually active before his arrest, but Amelia wasn't pregnant by him, and neither was anyone else. No, he wasn't perfect. He left his dishes around the house, he had to be forced to clean his bathroom, he was sometimes stubborn and liked to debate her about rules now and then. He insisted that when he was in college he was going to track down Santos and show him how far he'd come, show how little the abandonment mattered (when, of course, he'd be showing just the opposite)—but she couldn't blame him for that. She didn't really blame him for giving in to his natural, built-in urges, either; if only he hadn't done it so *modernly*.

There were few remaining dictated rules in their house these days. Rather, they lived with a cooperative understanding of what was expected and appropriate. He was eighteen now. By law, a full adult. He could vote, he could be *drafted,* if things came to that, he could sign his own contracts if he made any, he could marry without her consent. Until his arrest—arrests, rather—she'd felt good about the job she'd done raising him on her own. Had she done it all wrong, all these years? Was she doing it all wrong now?

Her mother pointed ahead of them, at a table stacked with boxes of record albums. "I'm going to see if I can't find some of the big bands in there."

"Grandma, I told you, I can get you anything on CD—or we could move you up to an iPod. You already have a computer, so it'd be easy for you to get any music you want."

"I know, and you're right. It just isn't the same, though. There's more to music than the music."

They let her walk ahead to the table, Anthony responding to another text. Despite what he'd said, Kim was sure he was texting Amelia. That was the purpose of his having the phone. She knew this, and knew that if he was caught, it would be considered a violation of his bail terms—and Amelia's. His bail would be revoked, and he'd go to jail until the felony case was resolved. She knew she should intervene for so many reasons, and *still* she couldn't bring herself to do it. Who else but the Wilkeses would catch Amelia?—and they wouldn't be able to report Anthony without also compromising her. She was worrying too much. Obsessing, as her mother had said. She needed to relax.

"So how is she?" Kim asked him, trying to sound casual.

He looked up. "You just saw her yesterday."

"Come on."

Anthony held the phone out and said, "This? I told you, I'm talking to Cameron."

"It's okay, I'm not going to report you."

He offered her the phone. "See for yourself."

Her first instinct was to decline, to believe him. Then she reached for it, watching his face for any tic, any change, a sign that he'd been bluffing. There was nothing. He let go of the phone and said, "B-R-B," then walked off to join his grandmother.

Kim watched him go. Clearly, he'd known she was testing him, and now, standing here beneath the broad arms of one of the biggest live oak trees she'd ever seen, she was embarrassed and a little ashamed. Hadn't he always been honest with her? Maybe he wasn't blatantly forthcoming about what went on between him and Amelia, but what son *would* volunteer all that information to his mother? And besides, relationships were supposed to be private matters, not escapades lived out in front of others. He was in almost every way an adult; she tried hard to respect his privacy.

She hadn't asked for intimate details, but if she had, he very likely would have answered judiciously but honestly. As if to prove this to herself, she pressed a button on the cellphone to light its display, then another to look at the text message log. Cameron's name filled the display.

"Kim, come see this," her mother called, waving her over to the table.

She held up an album and, as Kim joined them, handed it over, saying, "Barry Manilow's *Greatest Hits,* 1978. I told Anthony how you wore out your copy. She was sixteen," her mother told Anthony. "You know how it is."

Kim held out the cellphone and he accepted it. "Yep," he said, "I do."

Anthony didn't enjoy deceiving his mother, and wouldn't be doing it if he had a real choice. As resigned as she was about his getting the phone from Cameron, and as reluctantly tolerant as she would probably be if she had seen Amelia's name on the phone's display just now, he couldn't afford to take any chances.

He, his mother, and his grandmother went from the record albums to an assortment of antique furniture vendors to, now, a big booth displaying Indian dresses and tunics and tapestries. When he was sure both of the women were well occupied, his mother trying on ponchos and his grandmother sorting through scarves, he said, "You know, this stuff's nice, but it isn't really my style. I'm going to go grab a Coke or something, okay?"

"Oh, all right, honey. I . . . I guess I'll call you, when we're done."

He left the booth, forcing himself not to hurry. What was about to happen had to look accidental to anyone who might observe it, an absolute fluke. Happenstance. Fate. Lots of people came out to the flea market on weekend mornings. There were great bargains to be had, and pens of energetic puppies awaiting adoption, and roasted corn on a stick. No gun-and-knife show today, but then, that only made the meeting more plausible. Few women turned out on their own when the place was crowded with hunters and collectors and macho types who wanted to lay their hands on semiautomatic weapons. You never knew when you were going to need to overthrow the government.

He passed families towing preschoolers in red wagons, parents pushing strollers loaded down with bags and babies. Ahead of him, a young couple walked hand in hand as if doing so was the most ordinary thing in the world. He watched them enviously. Why them and not him? Had they been smarter or purer than he and Amelia? Or were they just luckier? Had they done the same things he and Amelia had done, but not been caught at it? Had they done it but nobody cared? Were they lucky enough to fall in love *after* high school, when their parents' opinions, even if negative, were toothless? Or maybe they were lucky enough to have parents who approved. He could imagine such a thing; his mother was one. For what little good it did.

He passed a display of iron tools, rust-coated and strewn about on tables and on the pavement inside the vendor's square of display space. He passed a booth stocked with "designer" sunglasses, two pair for fifteen dollars. He passed an ATM machine, and a patch of wide lawn where a group of young Latina mothers sat together while their children raced around them, yelling in Spanish and laughing and tumbling on the grass. And then he saw her.

She sat on a bench in front of the Dorton Arena, facing the towering concrete waterfall feature, a huge rectangular block with water pouring down both sides into a round fountain pool. The spray coming off the waterfall made her appear as if she sat beneath a rainbow like a girl in an Irish tale. He saw her from the side in perfect profile, hair pulled back, smooth neck and arms and legs exposed to his hungry gaze. Famished gaze, more like. He stopped so he could simply look at her for a minute. She was an oasis, a gem, a haven, a salve for his wounds. She was every metaphor for beauty and desire and comfort that he might think of, and even then he wouldn't be able to adequately describe what seeing her did for his heart. Did to his heart. Amelia.

She turned then, as if she'd heard him. Her pensive expression disappeared and a grateful smile replaced it. Anthony could hear the thump of his heart as he closed the distance between them. He could hear the rushing of the waterfall, children yelling, a deep man's voice with a heavy drawl instructing a large, tattooed woman to get him some boiled peanuts and a beer, if she could find one. And then he heard music, Amelia's voice saying, "Well, imagine seeing you here."

He wanted to pull her up from the bench and wrap her in his arms, hold her against his chest, let her hear how his heart pounded and feel if hers did, too. What he did was sit down beside her and laugh, though the sound came out with an odd sort of gulp, as if what it really wanted to be was a sob.

He said, "Yeah, wow. What a weird coincidence."

"I had to escape into the bathroom *twice* to text. My mom acts like I'm a preschooler who's going to wander off if I'm not within a foot of her. Of course now she's worried that I'm not feeling well."

"God, I'm glad to see you."

She beamed at him, and he beamed at her, and for the two of them, the world stopped for a moment in recognition of a rare and wonderful thing. "'No sooner knew the reason,'" he quoted, "'but they sought the remedy.'"

She reached for his hands and grasped them in her cool fingers, which he then surrounded with his own warmer ones. Her hands seemed more delicate than before. *She* seemed more delicate. Paler and less substantial, except for her eyes—they were larger than ever, and as filled with longing and regret as his must be. He should have made sure she protected the photos more securely, buried them someplace deep in her computer files where no one could happen across them. Where they'd be tough to find even for someone who was looking purposefully. He'd been so certain of their rightness that he hadn't been thinking about the risk. He and Amelia belonged together. They had their future together cinched with a golden thread. What, they'd thought, could go wrong?

They were stupid in love.

She said, "We owe Cameron so much."

"We do."

"It's crazy, isn't it, all this mess?"

"And endless."

"And pointless," she said.

"Hard to think it's going to get any better."

She studied a hangnail—her fingernails were so raw-looking, he noticed, chewed down, sore—then she picked at it, saying, "What if . . . What if it gets worse?"

He'd hoped that their meeting here today would be a completely upbeat experience for her, that somehow they'd avoid talking about the situation. Not a realistic hope, obviously. Both of their existences had been consumed by the Typhon-like multiheaded monster that was the ironically named Justice System, leaving them little to discuss that wasn't related to court dates, lawyers, and their forced separation.

"I want to say 'I don't see how it could,' but I do see how it could."

"Have you thought of what it's like to be a registered sex offender?" Amelia said. "People think you've snatched toddlers from playgrounds and done awful things to them. Do you remember that movie, *Little Children*? They'd think you're like that poor man—the creepy one the ex-cop was out to get. And me, they'd see me as a sick, sex-crazed slut looking for action wherever she could find it. Cameron says sex offenders aren't allowed to use any social media, ever. No matter what. Apparently everyone convicted of a sex crime is a creeper who finds victims on MySpace and Facebook."

He laid one arm across the back of the bench, and with his other hand he stroked the smooth skin from her knee to where her shorts ended at the upper part of her thigh. She had skin like pale rose petals. "I remember the film," he said. "That's why I didn't plead out. The deal they offered was a mandatory sex addiction counseling program, four hundred hours of community service, and offender registration for five years—like they were doing me a favor by not making it more. You can't ever get *away* from that record. That's why I'm going to have to take my chances in court. If I caved to that offer, imagine what they'd want for the felonies."

"Yesterday, before my dad left, he said my lawyer's concerned I might have to go to trial—but that he's not going to let it come to that. As if it's up to him," she said, shaking her head. "He thinks he runs the universe. He can't understand how the DA could charge me when I'm obviously a victim. He's . . . He's just so *sure* he's right."

Anthony reached for her hand and twined her fingers with his. "I'm sorry. I hate that this is happening to you."

"And to you! God." She tilted her head, looking up at the top of the fountain. "I can hardly believe it's real."

"How long do you have?" he asked.

She sat up straighter and scanned the area around them, then became very still. "Not long," she said.

He followed her gaze to a spot maybe fifty yards away, where Sheri Wilkes stood, mouth slightly open, staring at them. He said, "Do you think she's been watching us?"

"I don't know." Amelia looked at him again. "She's just standing there like she doesn't know what to do. I hate this," she said fiercely. "Anthony, I don't want to *do* this anymore. I want our life back. I want our plans. Did I tell you I got a letter from Duke saying they 'could not consider admitting me at this time'?"

"You weren't going there anyway," he said.

"It won't be any different with NYU."

"No," he admitted, "it probably won't."

His phone rang: it was his mother. He answered, saying, "I'll call you right back, okay?"

"Sure," his mother said, then, "Oh, never mind, there you—"

He saw her, walking toward him with his grandmother, at the same time she saw him. Then she looked past him and stopped still. "Damn," he said, pocketing his phone. "She sees your mom. I hope this doesn't get ugly."

"My mom won't say anything, she'd never make a scene—but I better go," Amelia said, standing. He stood too, keeping a wary eye on their mothers, who hadn't moved from their spots. She said, "I thought something like this might happen," her voice thickening, "but it was worth it, to get to see you."

He put his arms around her and held her against him. "I don't want to let you leave. There has to be a way out of this. People can't really be this stupid, can they?" He pulled back so he could look at her, and laughed mirthlessly as he said, "Listen to me—it's like I'm in denial. I sound like your dad, don't I?"

She pressed her forehead to his collarbone. Her arms were tight around his waist. "Let's *go*," she said, and he could feel the warmth of her breath through his shirt. "Tonight. Before my dad gets back.

Once she tells him what I did here, I won't even be able to breathe without him knowing it."

"Go? Where?"

"Maybe New York? I have some money, and a friend who I bet will put us up for a while. I'll pick you up at . . . eleven," she said, pulling back and looking over at her mother, who still hadn't made a move to separate them and was, it seemed, now looking away. Amelia said, "She's always in bed by ten."

He watched his mother shift awkwardly and speak to his grandmother, who nodded. Despite their support of him, their generosity and willingness to see him through his ordeal, the idea of running away with Amelia, which he'd dismissed so easily that morning in the school parking lot a few weeks ago, now looked like the most sensible action possible amid the chaos their lives had become. Get away, get some relief, figure it all out then.

"I'll pick *you* up," he said, already formulating a plan that would protect Amelia if they didn't succeed.

She looked up at him, eyes bright with hope but flecked with fear. "Can we really do this?"

Could they do it? The odds weren't in their favor—but that was true regardless, wasn't it? A strange emotion, something like terror and joy combined, made him feel suddenly ravenous.

"I will if you want to."

"The fact is, now we really don't have anything to lose," she said, determination replacing uncertainty.

"What about our court dates? If we don't show—"

"We'll figure it out. Maybe once we get out of here and get a chance to think straight, we'll get some fresh ideas," she said, echoing his own thoughts. "We aren't jumping bail as long as we don't miss our next appearances, right?"

"Right." He wasn't as optimistic as she was, however. Hadn't they all been looking for a solution all these weeks, and come up with nothing? He breathed out heavily. There were so many things to consider—but either way, it would be a lot better considering them with Amelia beside him. He said, "So, okay, let's go, and see what happens."

Her answering smile was a reward in itself. "Pack warm clothes," she said.

He kissed her as if it was going to be the last time, reveling in it and at the same time hoping the display would offset any suspicions their mothers might have that he and Amelia would think they could do this again. Then he took her hands as she backed away slowly, reluctance radiating from her. Good, she'd understood that they needed to put on an act, the sad lovers parting for who knew how long, maybe forever. She turned toward her mother then, letting go, pausing, looking back at him over her shoulder, and then walking away slowly without looking back again. He watched Sheri Wilkes fight off showing any emotion, but sympathy shaped her mouth into a sad frown, and when Amelia was close, Sheri Wilkes extended a hand and touched Amelia's bowed head.

Hearing motion behind him, Anthony turned and saw his mother and grandmother near the bench. There were tears in both women's eyes. "Oh, honey," his mother said. She looked stricken.

"Come on, let's go find some lunch." He checked his phone for the time: only twelve hours to go, twelve hours of acting like nothing had changed. He didn't like deceiving his mother, but he would do it if it meant an end to living like outcasts. He would do anything if it meant Amelia might somehow go free.

ACT III

Virtue itself turns vice, being misapplied,
And vice sometime's by action dignified.

—WILLIAM SHAKESPEARE, *ROMEO AND JULIET*

26

HARLAN BOARDED THE RED-EYE OUT OF SAN FRANCISCO AT ten o'clock on Saturday night and found his seat in first class, happy enough with the results of his trip. He'd gone for the usual reasons—firsthand looks at everything the world's automakers had going, including concept cars, hybrids, and limited editions. But his main goal this time was to get a look at a 1952 Nash-Healey roadster being offered by a guy who lived in Novato and was bringing the car down for prospective buyers to view. At $195,000 the Nash was an indulgence, sure. Harlan couldn't justify it right now, what with the money he'd put out for Clem's nightclub and for Amelia's bail. He'd already planned to be here, though, so no harm in taking a look. With all that was going on at home, he felt like he deserved a little break, a day off to forget the stress and the news and the everyday grind. He hadn't bid on the car—but neither had anyone else, so it might yet be that when his upside-down life righted itself, the car would still be available, waiting for him.

The Moscone Center, where the show was still ongoing into next week, had been bustling with middle-aged men, Harlan included, along with a fair number of younger, single guys, and lots of families with small children who, just like in Harlan's showrooms, insisted on touching every part of the cars they could reach. Reps stood by anxiously, waiting for each kid to move on so they could polish away the fingerprints. This would go on endlessly for the duration of the show, and it amused Harlan to see it in action. He empathized with the reps, but still, it was funny. He'd also had a good time watching a trio of women in short-shorts or hot pants or whatever they were calling the things these days, the garments that left very little—but just enough—to a man's imagination—talk to a group of well-dressed guys standing next to a yellow Lamborghini. Prostitutes, he figured. Lonely and displaced as he felt, an island in the sea of attendees despite his having plenty to say and plenty of people to say it to, he didn't go in for that mess. He didn't, even though he could have, even though Sheri had been uninterested in getting together since that morning in the shower. Unlike some guys he could think of, some whose initials were the same as his girl's, he had too much self-esteem to go about getting sex in any dishonorable way.

"That's right, I mean you, Anthony Winter," he muttered, snapping open a copy of the *Wall Street Journal*.

A flight attendant nearby asked, "Did you say something, sir?"

Harlan smiled up at her. "I said you would save my life if you'd bring me a scotch while we wait for this puppy to load."

The plane lifted off on schedule, and for the five hours until he changed planes in D.C., Harlan tried his best to shut down his brain and get a little sleep. It would be almost ten in the morning when they got to Raleigh, and he had to go straight from the airport to a little chat he'd set up with a reporter. He hoped they'd put some makeup on him, do a little something about the bags he'd surely have under his eyes. But then again, he thought, maybe it'd play better if he looked like the wreck he was.

Harlan had scheduled this first on-camera defensive interview for Sunday at eleven, in response to five different reporters' messages requesting some comment, some response to the outcome of Anthony Winter's court appearance. Did he have an opinion? How did he think this would affect Amelia's case? Was Winter's refusal to plead on the first charge, one of them asked, a declaration of war?

Harlan liked that question, and so he'd decided he would see this reporter, a sharp young guy from the Fox affiliate, in person. The others he'd spoken with briefly by phone. He had no qualms about taking advantage of the media's interest in his reaction—which he knew full well had little to do with him and everything to do with manufacturing controversy—so word would get out even faster that Amelia was nothing like she was being portrayed in the news.

The TV crew arrived to set up at Wilkes Rolls/Bentley moments after Harlan got there himself. His flight had gotten in fifteen minutes early and still he'd had to hustle from the airport. Usually, he'd call Sheri to let her know he was in, but this time he'd told a white lie, said he was coming on a later flight because he hadn't told her about the interview and didn't want to hear from her about anything, not until after the interview was done. He wasn't happy that he felt this way. This business with Amelia was doing nothing for his marriage—which was all the more reason to strike fast and hot, and if need be, apologize later.

The news folks had asked to come to the house—makes it all more personable, the producer said—but Harlan hadn't fallen for that line. What they really wanted was access to his daughter, and that just was not going to happen. So he was having them set up in the showroom in front of a trio of the finest cars any manufacturer had to offer outside of Italy. Inside of Italy, for that matter, with the exception of Lamborghini. Harlan would love to sell those, too—the profit margin was ridiculous, but so was the insurance, and there weren't enough buyers in the area right now to justify the investment. Behind Harlan were a Rolls Phantom convertible, a Rolls Ghost, and a Bentley Continental—a million-dollar display of class and power, and if he knew anything about people, it was that they associated those things with authority. Whatever he said in this interview would be taken as gospel. Amelia's arraignment next week would then most likely turn into a dismissal of all charges against her, because there was no way Liles would want to swim against that tide.

The producer said, "Mr. Wilkes, thanks again for agreeing to do this. What we're going to do is have you seated right here, and Bobby will sit here next to you. He'll ask you a few questions, and since we aren't doing this live, you feel free to answer at length. All right?"

"You bet," Harlan said. His phone began ringing. He checked the display: Sheri. He pressed a button to ignore the call. "Sorry about that."

"No problem. We'll get you set up with a mic, a little powder so you're not shiny on tape, we'll do a sound check, and then we'll shoot it."

"Sure thing," Harlan said, just as his phone went again. Sheri. "That's my wife; I better take it. Pardon me, I'll be right back."

He walked off toward the showroom doors as he answered, "Hey hon, I *just* got in, I was going to call you in a few."

"So she's not with you," Sheri said. "I thought maybe, if you'd gotten in early . . ."

Harlan stopped walking. "Tell me the dog is missing."

"I let her sleep in while I went to church," Sheri went on as if she hadn't heard him, "so I didn't go upstairs until a minute ago. She was so moody last night. I wanted to give her time to get over it."

"Get over what?"

"I've checked the whole house and the cottage. Her car's here."

"Maybe . . . maybe she went running."

"We should have gotten her a new phone," Sheri said.

"She's just gone running, I'll put money on it. Took advantage of you not being in the house and went for a run." If he kept saying it, he might make it true. "I'll be home shortly, all right? Call me when she comes in."

As sure as he was that he'd called it right, he spent the entire interview distracted by the possibility that he was wrong, a nagging doubt that he preferred not to acknowledge, but which wouldn't leave his mind. When they wrapped things up a half hour later and he still hadn't heard back from Sheri, the doubt pushed itself to a place where he couldn't ignore it anymore. He thanked the reporter and the crew, told them to go someplace nice and have lunch on him, then got into his truck and drove home, hoping that the discomfort in his gut had everything to do with hunger and not what he would find when he got there.

27

$\mathcal{K}$IM READ THE NOTE AND SANK INTO A KITCHEN CHAIR. SHE smoothed the paper on the tabletop, a nice sheet of paper from the box of linen stationery she'd gotten from a student last Christmas, then read it again. Mexico, he said. *Mexico.* Why would they—? *How* would they—? What in God's name were they thinking?

She pushed her straggly hair back from her face and read the note yet again, hoping the words would somehow be different, would rearrange themselves into something that made sense.

Dear Mom,

    This is going to be a shock, and I'm sorry for that. You don't deserve more trouble than I've already caused you. If there were any other way for Amelia and me to be together . . . There isn't, though, so I'm taking her to Mexico. I'm broke but I made sure she has money, so don't worry about that.

*You know as well as I do that I don't have anything left to lose
if I stay. Whatever I'll owe you, I'll find a way to pay back one way
or another.*

*I still don't accept that I've done anything wrong, but until
everyone else sees it that way, this is how it's got to be.*

*It might take a while for us to get to where I can be in touch
with you. I promise, though, that I'll be careful and make safe
choices and I'll contact you as soon as I can. You're the greatest
mom ever and I love you.*

—Anthony

"I can't believe you did this," she said, shaking her head. She
stared at the paper. The words did not change.

"Pay me back?!" she said. "In what, pesos earned picking avoca-
dos?" She laughed, a delirious, disbelieving laugh, at the absurdity.
She could lose every dime she had to her name, and he thought that
his promise to somehow find a way to repay her was going to make
it all right?

This could not be happening. This could *not* be her life.

He could not *do* this to her.

How would any lawyer, any judge, any thinking person now
imagine he was anything but hell-bound guilty as charged? How
could he just run off and leave her to deal with his mess?

He gets Amelia, he gets free, and she gets *nothing*, loses *everything*. No job, no money, no William. *Oh, wait,* she thought: *I get all
the shame and embarrassment and blame.*

She never should have permitted him to date Amelia. If she'd
gone to the Wilkeses right from the start, they'd have shut it all
down and none of this would be happening. Or maybe they
wouldn't have shut the kids down, and so none of this would be happening.

None of this should be happening.

"Damn him!" she said, but the curse and the anger behind it, the black wish that she'd ignored that washstand all those years ago, felt dangerous, like a pit of hot bubbling tar she might step into at her own ruin. He was her child. How could she wish him away?

It took awhile, but when no answers came to her and the earth hadn't cracked open and swallowed her up (though she'd wished it mightily), Kim calmed down to the point of not blaming Anthony for *everything*, and blamed, too, the wine. Last night, she'd taken a bottle and a book to her room and, as the evening went on, had two glasses and then poured a third, knowing better, and drank it, too, and went to sleep a little after ten o'clock with Anthony brooding in his room, as had become his habit. She didn't think anything of it. He was in a bad mood, and no wonder, after his too-short visit with Amelia at the flea market. *She* was in a bad mood, on his behalf and hers. She'd had the wine and gone to sleep and slept hard, oblivious to his note-writing, to his taking Amelia and *leaving,* for Christ's sake, for Mexico.

She blamed herself.

Though Kim knew later that it hadn't mattered a bit that she waited two hours before she picked up the phone and called Amelia's parents, she felt terrible about it at the time. She'd showered and dressed and paced while trying to decide whether Amelia had also left a note, which, if so, would relieve her of the obligation to call— as if by obsessing over the question she'd come up with the answer. When she'd tried and failed to reach Anthony, and when the answer failed to present itself (no surprise), she'd swallowed her embarrassment (*her* son who'd sent the photos; *her* son who'd disobeyed his mother, Amelia's parents, and the court in order to see Amelia the day before) so that she could do the right thing, and called.

"This is Kim Winter," she said. "I wondered if you've heard from Amelia."

"Ms. Winter, oh. I . . . I was hoping *you* knew something. My husband, he's on his way home—he's been out of town. . . . I'm supposing she got fed up with us and has gone someplace with Anthony."

"Yes, that's why I called. She did go with him, to Mexico."

"I'm sorry? I thought you said *Mexico*."

"Yes. Yes, I did, you heard it right. He left a note—last night I guess. I was asleep. I had no idea. They . . . they want to be together, and they think this was the only way."

In the hours that followed, Kim would repeat this countless times, to various police officers and detectives, to the lawyer, to William (who returned *this* call, apologetic and supportive), to her mother, to Rose Ellen, to reporters. Disloyal as it felt, she hoped getting the news out would help bring the kids in before they actually did make it to Mexico, an act that would only heap misery on all of them.

She would discuss the note, read it, and ultimately surrender it to the authorities as evidence. She would, when the waves subsided later, battle waves of anger and fear directed at Anthony, would panic at the thought of him getting caught, then panic at the thought of him, of them, escaping successfully.

She wasn't prepared for the return of the police officers that evening with a warrant for *her* arrest.

"On what charges?" she demanded, sounding like a hysterical movie-of-the-week actress.

"Ma'am, if you'll just proceed peaceably, you'll get all your answers downtown."

As she was placed in the cruiser, taken to the jail, fingerprinted, searched, photographed, demeaned, left in a cell to protest, silently, her "contributing to the delinquency of a minor" and "failure to report abuse"—abuse!—charges until her mother came the next morning to bail her out—after she'd been fitted with an electronic "house arrest" ankle cuff, which the magistrate allowed in the hope that Anthony would contact her and she'd lead them to him— Kim understood better and better the forces that had pushed Anthony and Amelia to run. She focused on this so that the over-worn wish that he and Amelia *had just kept their clothes on* would not distract her from the matters at hand.

She was grateful to Mariana Davis, who'd argued (for no additional fee, just now) for the bail terms when the court had been inclined at first to leave her in jail. She might, after all, be tempted to join the teens if given the chance. Kim wouldn't have said it aloud, but yes, after having gotten a taste of what they had gone through, it was true, she'd have been sorely tempted.

"I hope they buy sunscreen," she told her mother later that evening, sounding pitiful. They were in Kim's living room eating on TV trays, the way they'd done so often when she was a child. Back then it was her parents and herself with their Banquet dinners steaming before them, the black-and-white television displaying the national news broadcast's accounts of the war in Vietnam. Tonight she was eating a homemade chicken and rice dish her mother had prepared for them, and the news was of a much smaller and more modern war, but Kim's reactions—loss of appetite, helplessness, and dismay—were not so different from before.

The CNN anchorwoman reported, "The case involving two North Carolina teens charged in a sexting scandal, first reported here on Sunday night, continues to draw the interest of people all around the country. Sunday also saw the arrest of Kim Winter, Anthony Winter's mother and a teacher at the elite school the teens attended, for allegedly permitting the sexting and failing to report it. The FBI has been brought in to assist in the search for the fugitive teens, who are thought to be headed to Mexico. Both are awaiting arraignment in superior court in early December. Gibson Liles, the district attorney in the case, had this to say:

" 'I am impressed and pleased with the amount of support that's been shown me as I've pursued a course of appropriate penalty for the activities of this pair," Liles said, standing in front of the court-house suited and coiffed like a young John Edwards. "Their latest Bonnie-and-Clyde behavior reinforces my initial read, which was that these are not two ordinary teenagers who made a simple mis-take. That said, some evidence suggests Miss Wilkes *may* be an un-willing accomplice this time. Further investigation is under way.'"

Kim dropped her fork. "What does he mean, 'unwilling'? They ran away together. Who could possibly think otherwise?"

"Other than her father, you mean? It's Anthony's note, I'll bet," her mother said. "He never says 'we,' only 'I.' I thought that was pe-culiar, but of course I never imagined it might mean he abducted her."

"He *didn't,*" Kim said, reaching for her phone. "You saw them— by the waterfall? Really, Mom."

"Honey, I know."

She dialed Mariana Davis while the anchor introduced a second clip, this one of Harlan Wilkes. "In this interview, which he granted before his daughter was reported missing, Harlan Wilkes, owner of the North Carolina Wilkes Automotive empire, defended his daugh-ter vigorously."

"What people haven't been seeing in the news and such," Wilkes said, looking sad and sincere, "is that Amelia was conned by this guy, taken in by his good looks and his intelligence. The fact that he's those things doesn't mean he isn't also a perverted predator of young women."

Kim pointed at the screen. "That man should be hanged for his lies," she spat, waiting while Mariana Davis's voice mail greeting fin-ished playing, then she left a message, saying, "We've got to tell CNN it's not true, he didn't kidnap her. Witnesses saw them to-gether yesterday—lovingly together. Her *mother* saw them. Oh— this is Kim Winter. Please call me back."

The anchor was saying, "He had this to add earlier today," and there was Wilkes again, this time saying, "I'm glad Liles is finally making some sense—arresting Kim Winter was a step in the right direction. I have no doubt that Amelia was taken against her will—the note they've got, that proves it. She was named after Amelia Earheart, so you can bet she's hanging tough, wherever she is. . . . My wife and I pray for her safe return and ask you all to pray with us, and we look forward to the truth being revealed and justice served."

The anchor said, "We have the text of the note he refers to—"

Kim stabbed the TV remote's power button. "I know I said I wanted to keep up with this, but how can I stand it? Bonnie and Clyde? They're not bank robbers, for Christ's sake!" She stood up and carried her plate to the kitchen, saying, "How am I supposed to stand letting them malign him this way? Why am *I* keeping quiet when he's obviously not?" She set the plate on the counter and pressed her hands against its cool surface, her head bowed, her eyes focused on the inch-wide ankle bracelet that tracked her every move via satellite.

The charges against her were misdemeanors, class 1, equivalent to Anthony's first charge—and just as ridiculous. With no prior record, she wouldn't serve jail time, but that hardly mattered now. The damage was done. She was being tried and convicted in the court of public opinion right alongside the kids. In late-eighteenth-century France they'd have all gone to the guillotine by now.

"*There's* something to be thankful for, then," she said, as her mother came into the kitchen.

"What's that?"

Kim told her what she'd been thinking, about the guillotine, then she said, "Didn't they realize this was going to happen?"

"They're so young," her mother said. "We think youth is a blessing, but sometimes it's a curse."

28

"It's one thing for them to call us fugitives," Amelia said Monday night, reading online news articles about herself and Anthony on her friend Jodi's computer. "*Kidnapping*, though— that's nuts. My dad is completely wigged out. We thought the note would just be a red herring for the local police, to give us time to get here without them on our trail."

Jodi, a long-limbed, energetic brunette who Amelia had first met several years earlier at a national singing competition, said, "So it worked better than you thought. They've even got the border patrol on alert for you two."

"We may as well be terrorists."

"Ugh, don't say the T word," Jodi told her. "We had a show canceled three weeks ago because of a bomb threat. I mean, it was nothing—probably some asshole who auditioned and didn't get a part. You forget, right, until something makes you remember and then it's 'Oh shit, I really should get a real job with my dad in Connecticut.'"

"You're so lucky to be working on Broadway. You'd never give it up."

Jodi grinned. "I know. Finally. *Fin-al-ly!*" she sang. "And so will you, one day. Your voice is *so* much better than mine. So are your legs. So is your ass."

"Jodi!" Amelia laughed.

Anthony sat across from them, watching the street scene from the fifth-story window of Jodi's Village apartment. "She's right," he said, smiling—but more dimly than he would have, if not for the turns things were taking. "You'll get here." He scratched his head and added, "Though damned if I know how, just yet."

Amelia met his gaze. There was nothing critical there. He wasn't blaming her for persuading him to leave, for catapulting them from one mess into another. Though if she was honest, she wasn't as disturbed by the furor going on now as she'd been while sitting at home, cut off from life. They'd made it here, to New York! It felt to her like an entirely different world, where nothing preceding their drive north made the slightest difference now. Life was in motion, flowing everywhere around them, and all they had to do was step into the stream.

The trip up had been long and tense. They'd started off at a Raleigh ATM, where she'd taken out the maximum cash allowed, then stopped at a nearby Wal-Mart and used her card once more, to buy prepaid Visa cards so that they couldn't be tracked later by their purchases. In order to avoid being spotted easily, they'd driven an indirect route to get to New York—almost twelve hours driving, instead of the nine it took by interstate, and taken turns napping in the car. On their arrival, Jodi had welcomed them in as if they'd all been friends forever, showed them around the apartment, pointed them to the guest room, and said, "Coffee and bagels at ten. See ya."

They'd stayed holed up since arriving, keeping track of the news and trying to decide where to go from here. As lovely as the apartment was—belonging not to Jodi, who could never afford it on her own, but to Jodi's father, a high-end interior designer who'd kept the apartment when he moved—Amelia was longing to get out and see the city with Anthony. Now Amelia wanted to see the city and then return here to the room they'd shared last night. To return to Anthony's arms, which had held her so tenderly as they'd both fallen into exhausted sleep.

He said, "So they're calling us fugitives, huh, as if we've already missed our court dates."

"I guess because we violated our bail terms just by being together . . . and by leaving our parents' homes?"

"I never should have left that note."

Amelia closed the computer and set it aside. "It isn't your fault. That's just the excuse they're using to justify more trouble."

"You know, I wrote that note deliberately keeping you out of it, thinking that if they caught up with us it would mean I'd take the heat for the idea of us leaving *together*. Why didn't I see that someone might misinterpret it and call it kidnapping?"

She put her arms around his waist. "Don't worry—all I'd have to do is say it was my idea, too, or that I jumped at the chance and you definitely didn't make me go. It can't be kidnapping if I say it wasn't, right?"

"Oh, you think Liles needs there to be a *victim* in order to charge me with something new?"

Amelia laid her index finger against his lips. "You were so sweet to try to protect me."

"It's my privilege." He put his hands on her face and kissed her. "Come on, ladies," he said, leading her away from the windowsill. "Put your coats on and let's go see the city."

Amelia brightened. "Yeah?"

"It's New York, it's dark, nobody is looking for us here. We might as well make the most of it."

The night air was biting, but filled with the scents of exotic foods and diesel fumes and a leftover dampness from recent rain. Amelia tucked her scarf behind her shoulders, then pulled her coat closed and began to do up the buttons, but stopped when a pain rippled across her abdomen. She pressed her hand to her stomach.

"What is it?" Anthony asked.

"Nothing. A cramp. Probably that salmon cream cheese stuff from this morning disagreeing with me."

"Hey, don't knock the lox," Jodi teased. "Probably you have indigestion after reading about yourself in the news. That'd do it to me—well, unless the news was a great review of one of my amazing performances."

Anthony frowned at Amelia. "You sure you're fine?"

"Absolutely," she said, nodding. "Better already." And she was. The pain had shrunk and was fading quickly, the way it had the other day. There'd been no more after it and her period hadn't come early, so she'd written it off as nothing to worry about. She'd do the same now.

"Let's go," she said, and they set off for the subway.

Amelia reveled in the rightness of the night, the company she was in, Anthony's gloved hand holding hers, the feeling of normalcy that came with being here, being away. She felt like she belonged here. Like she was an important part of something very right. She, Anthony, and Jodi were three young people walking and talking and laughing, skipping down the stairs to the train, riding it along with people from all around the world, people who knew this was the greatest city, the place where everything happened—good and bad, the place where particular kinds of dreams were inclined to come true.

Not for everyone, she understood that. Some of the people in this car with them looked as if they couldn't get further away from success. One man of indeterminate age with a greasy beard, greasy hair beneath a dirty watch cap, a once-yellow nylon jacket that had no insulation and was torn at the elbows, slept with his mouth hanging open in a seat at the end of the car. There was no way of knowing whether his plight, and that of the others here who weren't far above him, was a result of a lack of opportunity, a lack of personal capacity to achieve much, a lack of willpower, a lack of belief—or maybe they were in New York for reasons that had nothing to do with chasing a dream. They'd been born here, maybe, or had come against their wishes, or didn't accept the mythology of New York to begin with. If that was the case, she was sorry for them. She was sorry for them regardless.

She tugged Anthony's sleeve and said, "If I ever make it—"

"*When* you make it," he said.

"I'm going to give my money away. My dad is wrong. I don't want to live like he and my mom do, ever."

Anthony squeezed her shoulder and nodded his agreement. "Sounds like a good plan to me."

A good plan, and an easy one. Harder was going to be figuring out where they'd go from here. Even if Jodi was inclined to have guests indefinitely, Amelia knew they could stay anonymous for only so long. The money would run out, but even more to the point, there was no way for them to move ahead—no school, no jobs— unless something drastic put a stop to the legal nonsense. But she wasn't going to think about any of that now. It would keep. Now was for *now,* for here. The rest would work itself out; she truly believed that it would. Truth and justice, those were the foundations of their country, right? Truth, justice, and faith, none of which were serving them very well right now, but they had to get a break sooner or later.

The three of them left the subway at the Fiftieth Street station and started walking toward Times Square. Jodi said, "We'll pass most of the theatres this way, so we all can drool like starving beggars at restaurant doors."

"What are you talking about, 'all,'" Anthony said. "You're working."

"As *the* most inconsequential Tribe member in *Hair*. But yeah." She grinned, and the lights from the shop fronts and glowing signs around them made her so-white teeth appear pink. "Yeah, damn it, I am."

She took a flip camera from her pocket and aimed it at Anthony. "Okay. *The Big Adventure,* take one: the man you see before you is Anthony Winter, who's in New York City for—how many times have you been here before?"

"Twice."

"In the Big Apple for the third time," Jodi said. "He's . . . let's say he's on vacation."

" 'He's on vacation,' " they all said at once, laughing.

"Oh, we are brilliant," Jodi said. She continued her narration, "Now, Anthony wants to . . . You fill in the blank."

"Have a good time tonight," Anthony said.

"No, bigger," Jodi said. "Try again. He wants to . . ."

"Find some food. Some really good food."

Jodi cocked her head and scowled at him. "You don't take direction very well, do you? Come on. Take three: he wants to . . ."

Amelia answered. "He wants to write a show for the Ambassador," she said, seeing the historic theatre off to their right, on Forty-ninth. "The way Shakespeare once wrote for the Globe."

"Yes, that's more like it!" Jodi said, as Amelia leaned up against Anthony and kissed him. So they'd missed evaluations and couldn't reschedule; so nothing they wanted was going according to plan; still, they were here, together. Amelia looked into his eyes and felt purely happy. She felt whole. She felt loved. She kissed him once more and told him, "I'm so glad to be here with you. Thank you. This is amazing, this is perfect."

Jodi said, "Anthony the playwright, and his One True Love, Amelia Wilkes, future star of—what show do you want to star in?"

"*Mamma Mia!*" she declared. Then, thinking further, "*Phantom.* Wait . . . *Chicago?*" She laughed, then said, "Honestly, I just want to *be* here. After that, well, we'll just have to see."

"After that," Jodi said, "your name will be in lights," and she swung around to film the Ambassador's marquee and lighted feature posters, and the red "Now Starring . . . !" banner on the under-hang. The banner was not itself lighted, but light shone on it, and Amelia could envision her name being the one displayed in tall black letters. She knew it was possible. If others could do it, why couldn't she? That was what Anthony had been insisting all along this past year, and that was what she believed.

Anthony faced her and put his hands on her waist. He said, "It's going to be amazing for you."

"For us."

Jodi, camera still filming, said to a couple passing by, "Take a good look, folks, you'll be able to say you saw her in person."

"Who?" the woman asked, turning to look at Amelia.

"Amelia Wilkes, star of Broadway."

"Come on," Amelia said, pulling Jodi away from the couple. "Never mind her," she told them. "Too much crack cocaine."

When they were clear, Anthony said, "Maybe don't broadcast our names like that, huh?"

"Relax, would you? They're going to see *Chicago*," Jodi said, "not sitting around watching or reading the news about kids who are running off to *Mexico*."

They played in Times Square like tourists, riding the Ferris wheel at Toys "R" Us, crowding in with the teens who waited in front of MTV's studio for a glimpse of, someone claimed, Eminem. In Hershey's, Jodi gaped at Amelia: "You don't want any chocolate?" "I'm not really hungry," Amelia replied, surprised herself. Then they bartered for Persian scarves on a nearby corner with a pair of men whose thick Caribbean accents made a wonderful incongruity against the crisp cold and against their cold-weather wares. Jodi filmed and narrated all the while. "For posterity," she told them. "So that I can say I knew you when."

"As long as you don't post it publicly," Anthony warned, as Amelia paid for her scarves.

Jodi nodded her agreement and dug money from her purse, saying, "At least not before you've been immortalized, so I can make the most of our connection."

Amelia pushed Jodi's hand so that the camera viewed its owner. "Broadway's rising star, Jodi DeMarco!"

The vendors laughed and declared that Jodi and Amelia both had star quality. "Put those faces on da bus, everybody will ride and make da MTA rich!"

"Those guys ought to be selling time-shares for Antigua or some-place," Jodi said as they left the stand, she and Amelia each now pos-sessing three vividly colored scarves bought for four dollars apiece. "I dated a guy from there. Brilliant, great sense of humor. Amazing dancer. I should call him again." She checked the camera's battery. "Hm, I guess that's a wrap." She tucked it into her pocket and said, "Hey, so how about we get out of this cold and go for Japanese at Kodama—it's not far. Fab sushi. You guys do sushi?"

"Sounds great," Anthony said. He looked at Amelia expectantly.

"Yeah," she said, nodding. "I'm still not very hungry, though, so whatever you guys want is fine."

Jodi smiled sympathetically. "No more lox for you, got it?"

"I'm fine. Distracted by all the wonderfulness is all."

"Yeah," Jodi said, pretending to primp her hat-covered hair, "people tell me that all the time."

For two fairy-tale days, this—the city, the camaraderie—was Amelia's reality. They saw the sights, they goofed around, they went to cafés and restaurants where the food was cheap and the company was inspiring. They met actors and dancers and poets, people who intended to design the next great fashion trend or write the next great novel or build the next great skyscraper or cook the most per-fect omelets the world had yet seen. They went to Radio City for the Rockettes' holiday show. Late each night, she and Anthony climbed under the covers together, and Wednesday he serenaded her with the Beach Boys' "Wouldn't It Be Nice" before making love to her, with her, so tenderly that afterward she cried, happy, grate-ful tears. It would be nice. It would be.

Amelia avoided eating more lox, and ate little else, and the pains troubled her only once more during their stay—on Thursday afternoon, Thanksgiving, before they were to leave Jodi's and move on with the plan she and Anthony had begun to develop while sitting, bundled, in the sun at Washington Square Park the day before.

The plan they'd come up with was to leave not only New York the city but New York the state, and find an unpatrolled crossing into Canada. Anthony had lived in upstate New York for half of his life, and was pretty sure there were still back roads—not to mention fields—where they could get over the border without being seen, let alone asked to produce passports and IDs. The irony of their making this plan at that park—the center of NYU's campus— wasn't lost on either of them.

"It'll be here, waiting," Anthony had said, gazing at the buildings around the park.

Amelia nodded, saying nothing. For the first time since they'd arrived, she felt the weight of their situation bearing down on her. It wasn't that she'd forgotten there were people looking for them, or that if they were found they'd be arrested and jailed—no bail this time—until their cases were resolved. She knew, as Anthony did, that "resolved" would be no resolution, really, because there was no way they were getting out of this unscathed. As he'd said, "Fact is, we did everything they charged us with, if you look at it dispassionately—which is what the judge supposedly does. Since Liles won't let up, we have to face trial to even have a chance at avoiding prison time. Maybe a jury, if there were enough intelligent people on it, would let us off easy, but they can't exactly disregard the law."

The other part, which didn't need to be discussed, was her father, and his relentless insistence on demonizing Anthony. By the time Anthony had his trial, he'd be more likely than ever—and far more likely than she—to be convicted. Thirty years' sex-offender registration required for the felony counts. Prison time might be unlikely, but even Mariana Davis hadn't been able to say it wouldn't happen. Going back now offered no hope for either of them. They would have to take their chances in Canada.

He said, "We'll get fake IDs—even if it's not a hundred percent foolproof, it'll be close enough for us to make a new start. I'm thinking Montreal. It isn't New York, but it's a great city, you'll like it—they have a big theatre scene. We get jobs there, work our way up, and eventually come back to New York under our new identities."

"Without being recognized?"

"By who? Besides, you'll be that amazing Canadian actress who, if anyone ever put a picture of that older you alongside one of your current ones, would have a striking resemblance to the girl who'd disappeared into Mexico, and wouldn't that be interesting? But by then we'll have rock-solid creds. It can be done."

"Solid creds, but the same fingerprints."

"Then we better avoid run-ins with the law."

"Somebody would make the connection. Our parents would."

"By then, the whole thing will be ancient history. They wouldn't rat us out."

She'd been about to answer *You don't know my father,* but instead she decided that this time Anthony might be right. Her father would, by then, surely have learned his lesson and wouldn't make trouble anymore.

They knew the plan wasn't perfect. There were holes, possibly deep enough for them to disappear into with no hope of rescue. What the plan gave them, though, was a chance. It gave them hope. And most important, they would be together and not rotting in jail, alone, for the most part out of contact with each other, while the lawyers siphoned more and more money away, looking for strategies to win an unwinnable war. They would be together and not going off to prison, where the closest they'd be to each other or to the theatre world was in their memories and imaginations.

The stomach pain came when they were lounging in the apartment in the afternoon while Jodi got ready to leave for dinner with her father in Stamford. It came on quickly, as it had before, and this time hung around awhile. Anthony, who was online checking the status of "the manhunt" and researching all the things they'd need to know for their trip, didn't see her wince as the pain began. She waited for it to ebb, then went to stand behind him.

Oddly, he had Jodi's Facebook page displayed—and then she saw that he was having an instant-message conversation with Cameron. He glanced over his shoulder and said, "Jodi friended her for us—I asked her to this morning. I wanted an untrackable way to get a message to my mom."

Homesickness jolted Amelia, or rather Cameron-sickness did. "Tell Cam I miss her."

He typed her message. Cameron replied with a grimace emoticon and, *Same here. I love you, A!!!! So glad u guys r ok, and I will def get ur message to ur mom. What about A's parents?*

Anthony said, "Do you want her to pass a message to them?"

"I . . . I do, but I don't. If they find out she was in touch with us, they'll never leave her alone." She wasn't worried about his mother revealing anything to the police, but her parents, her *father,* had proven they couldn't count on him. "Tell her no. I want to wait until we're out of the country."

"I agree," he said, and typed her answer.

He finished the conversation and logged off the computer, then turned and pulled her onto his lap.

She said, "So what's the travel plan looking like?"

"Interstate 87 is the direct route—meaning most traveled. Let's go 95 and then up 91 until we're near the border, then we'll branch off to the rural areas using county roads. Eighty-one might be even less traveled, but it's only bridges into Canada that way, so that's out—I'm thinking out loud, aren't I?"

"Yes, but you're cute, doing it."

"The weather is looking pretty iffy—they're saying freezing rain turning to snow starting after midnight. How do you feel about leaving pretty soon?"

She didn't want to leave at all. The frustration that she'd been able to suppress these past few days surged again, and she took a deep breath to help push it down. Wishes were filmy, insubstantial things that had no value and no purpose. Action was the only way to make something happen. She said, "Fine by me. No one will be driving at dinnertime."

"All right, then. Let's get in gear."

29

ANTHONY HUGGED JODI AND THANKED HER AGAIN FOR HER hospitality. "We're eternally grateful."

"You're eternally welcome," Jodi said. "I mean that. If you make it back here—that is, *when* you make it back here, I expect you to stay here for as long as you need to. And if I happen to have hooked up with my own exceptionally fabulous someone by then, he will welcome you, too."

Amelia's eyes looked forlorn behind her smile. "We hate to leave. But thank you *so* much. It's been the best. You're so wonderful for risking your neck for us."

Jodi waved off the gratitude. "Please. What risk? It's New York. There are way more important criminals here than you two."

Anthony reached for the doorknob. "We'll let you know when we get there."

"I'll look for the Facebook friend requests from—who will you be? Marie and Luc?"

"Beau and Belle," Anthony joked.

Amelia said, "I like her suggestions better."

"Go on, lovebirds. You can debate it in the car." Jodi kissed them both, then Anthony led Amelia outside, where they walked in silence down the block to the parking garage. The weight of what they were doing made him feel sluggish, made every step feel like he was walking in mud-caked boots. His stomach was queasy and he walked slowly, as if anticipating that a precipice lay ahead of them after darkness fell, and he might not see it in time.

In the car, he hooked up Cameron's iPod and chose a playlist. "I uploaded a bunch of Jodi's stuff. It isn't all what I'd choose, but it's better than Cam's limited assortment. Did you know she still listens to the Backstreet Boys?"

"I guess I better not admit that I kind of do, too."

"No," he said, "you'd better not." He reached over and tickled her neck and she swatted him, smiling almost as if everything was normal.

The drive out of the city and over to where he could pick up 495 was going to be dicey. He couldn't afford to be too aggressive and risk getting in a fender bender, but he couldn't be passive either, or he'd never get the lanes he needed when he needed to. While he concentrated on driving them where they needed to go, Amelia stayed occupied watching the cityscape, until they went into the tunnel to Queens. "Goodbye, New York." She sighed.

From there, the music gave them something to focus on other than what they were leaving behind and what lay ahead. He'd mixed Pink and Beyoncé and classic Zeppelin with Green Day and the Black Eyed Peas, and some Dylan to round things out. They hadn't driven far—forty minutes, maybe, when Amelia said, "Do you think we could stop someplace?"

"You should've gone before we left," he teased, mimicking a parent's tone.

"Yeah. Sorry."

"I was kidding." He glanced over and saw her lips were pressed in a tight frown. "Is it your stomach again?"

"You know, I'm sure it's nerves. It didn't start until after all the trouble started."

"Do you . . ." He paused, then began again, "Do you want to turn around? We don't have to go through with this."

"No—I mean, do *you* want to?"

"No, I don't. This is it, this is what we need to do. Have to do." He glanced at her and she nodded. "I'll find a store and we'll get you something."

"Everything will be closed."

"Maybe not."

At the next exit, they found an open gas station and convenience store and went inside. Amelia held her hand against her stomach as they checked the offerings. "I don't think it's, you know, a digestion thing. It just *hurts*. It's worse when I'm moving."

He picked up a large bottle of ibuprofen. "We'd be smart to have this anyway. And this," he said, getting a bottle of Pepto-Bismol, "and this," he added, reaching for a bag of cheese curls from the aisle's endcap. "Sorry. I'm hungry."

She stood close to him and linked her arms around his neck. "Sorry I'm not. I love those."

They kissed, gentle, sweet kisses that made this pause in their travel plan feel like a haven. Her skin smelled of something light and floral. Honeysuckle, he thought. And something herbal, too. Her lips were warm and soft. Warmer than usual. He drew back to take a close look at her and noticed rosy spots at the top of her cheeks. "I think you might have a fever."

He scanned the aisle for a thermometer but didn't find one. She said, "I feel fine. I mean, not *fine,* but not sick. Come on, let's get going."

They chose drinks and checked out, then set off again. The sun was low, dropping behind trees already bereft of leaves. Amelia took a painkiller, then changed the music and sang along to "Aquarius," then "Blackbird," then "If I Fell," and then, turning off the stereo, she sang Sarah McLachlan's "Angel," filling the space around them with the mournful, beautiful sound, raising the hair on his arms.

"You're really amazing," he said when she finished. She shrugged off the compliment, but he felt as if he'd been given something rare and precious. "I'm telling you, one day everyone's going to know your name."

"Which name?" she said, a smile playing on her tired face. "Belle or Marie?"

She fell asleep as they got outside Springfield and into the winding eastern foothills of the Berkshires. He glanced at her from time to time, his worry counterbalanced by his admiration of her fine bone structure and the curve of her cheek. In the dim light of the dashboard, he couldn't see whether her cheeks were still flushed, but her lips looked darker than they should have.

When she woke again he told her, "We just hit Vermont. We're almost to Brattleboro. Do you want to stop?"

She stretched and as she did, she made a small sound of discomfort. "Yeah, let's stop. Maybe if I walk around some I can work out this cramp."

"You don't think you have an ulcer, do you?"

"I guess I wouldn't be surprised. It'll be fine. Quit worrying, okay?"

He took the exit for the next rest stop. After he finished using the bathroom, he waited for Amelia, and waited. Several women entered and left and still she didn't come out. Finally, just as he was going to go in to check on her, she pushed the door open and walked out.

"Sorry," she said. "And before you ask, I'm fine. Let's get some drinks and go—a woman in there was saying it was raining up at St. Johnsbury, which I guess is on our way?"

"It is, yeah." He wanted to press her for details on how she felt, but she obviously didn't want to talk about it. Maybe it was embarrassing; he got that, so he let it go.

In the car again, Amelia occupied herself with finding music, and they talked about how they'd decide which of the back roads they should try. They talked about everything except the slight breathy strain in her voice that told him she was still in pain and trying to hide it. The rain Amelia had heard about was, in fact, coming down hard as they passed St. Johnsbury and continued north.

"This is pretty miserable," she said after a while. "I wish it would just snow instead."

"Driving in snow is worse. At night especially."

"It doesn't seem as cold, though, you know?" Her voice sounded odd to him, rising extra high on "know," and then she doubled over. "I feel sick to my stomach. Pull over?"

He signaled and moved off to the shoulder as quickly as he could. As soon as they were stopped, Amelia opened her door and leaned out and retched. He kept a hand on her back while he reached for napkins in the glove box.

She sat up again and closed the door, then took the proffered napkins and wiped her mouth. "I'm so sorry. It just came over me. I don't know what that's about."

"You haven't eaten anything. . . ."

"We bought Pepto earlier, didn't we?" She started to twist to get the bag from the backseat but stopped and pressed her hands to her belly.

"Amelia, something isn't right. We need to get you to a doctor."

"It's just food poisoning," she insisted. "It's going to pass."

"Food poisoning that lasts four days? Come on."

"It's nine o'clock on Thanksgiving night and we're in the middle of Vermont somewhere. Even if I wanted to go, a doctor isn't an option right now."

Anthony put his hand up to her forehead the way his mother had always done when she thought he might be sick. "You still feel hot. It's not food poisoning."

"Then it's a virus. Let's just go. We can't be that far from the border now."

He considered their options. She was right, the border was only about forty miles away by interstate, but there was no telling how long it was going to take them to find a place to cross, and in finding one, they'd be far from anything like the kind of doc-in-a-box places he and his mother used on occasion. Suppose she got worse and they were miles and miles from help?

"We have to stop in the next good-sized town."

"Anthony, we can't. I'll have to give them my name—"

"Use a fake name. Be Marie Wilkes . . . and you lost your wallet this morning so you don't have ID. We'll pay in cash and it'll be fine."

Even in the darkness he could read the fear and doubt in her eyes as she said, "Do you think?"

"Yes. Buckle up now and let's go."

They got under way, both of them silent, the wipers slashing the rain from the windshield aggressively, as if they, too, were frustrated with this turn of events. Anthony understood them to be snapping, *Why? Why? Why? Why?* and wished he had an answer.

"Suppose it's expensive," Amelia said. "What if it ends up costing us all our money?"

"Let's just get there and have you checked out. If you're right and it's a virus, maybe they can give you some medicine and that'll be that."

The wipers again, and then he felt Amelia's hand taking his right one from the steering wheel. She clasped it in her too-warm hand and said, "You're really good to me and I appreciate it. Sorry I'm messing things up."

"Stop it. You aren't doing anything."

A dozen miles before the border, pretty much where they'd need to split off from the interstate anyway, they came upon signs for a town called Newport. "I'm taking this," he said. "If they don't have any walk-in clinics, they might have an ER."

"Okay," she said in a tight voice. "I guess you're right. The pain, it just isn't going away."

He let go of her hand and put his hand on her hair. It was damp from when she'd leaned out of the car. He smoothed it down and lifted a section over her shoulder, repeatedly stroking the path it made. She seemed to find this soothing. She closed her eyes and leaned closer so that he could put his arm around her shoulders.

A few miles farther and there was the exit. He pulled off at the first gas station, parked and left the car running while he ran inside and asked an attendant where he could take Amelia. "T' hospital," the man said. "Only other places are all closed by now. Go down-street a ways to Western and there yuhl see a sign getting you there. That out there turnin' to sleet?"

"Some. A few snowflakes mixed in, too."

"Yup. Saying by weekend we'll have snow deeper than a tall Swede. Where you comin' from anyway?"

"New York," Anthony answered truthfully.

"Well, good luck with it all."

He found Amelia in the car wiping tears from her face. "Hey now," he said, reaching for her and pressing his forehead to hers. "There's a hospital close by. We'll get you taken care of."

She nodded, then he let go of her and put the car in gear. It was a short drive to the hospital—easily found, as promised—where he pulled into the ER entrance driveway. In the light from the building, Amelia looked ghostly pale. She kept both arms wrapped around her middle, with her left laying at the spot where her right hip sloped toward her belly button, a spot he admired very much under better circumstances.

"Ready?" he asked.

"Not really. I don't think there's much choice, though."

He kissed her forehead, then opened his door onto another dilemma that he could never have foreseen.

The last time Anthony had been in an ER was when a wrong-footed leap on the soccer field at age fourteen landed him on his left arm. The radius bone had snapped clean in two, sidelining him for a couple of months. That had been when he'd begun reading the Bards intentionally, and working to make sense of their poems and plays. To understand them he'd needed to know the Greek dramas, so he read those, too, and discussed everything with his grandfather, whose probing questions made Anthony see how life now was not all that different from life then. Same stage, different players, as the saying went. Or, he thought, to be more precise, "All the world's a stage, and all the men and women merely players." Merely actors, Grandpa Phil had explained, in parts written for them at the start of time. Which role you played was not fully up to you—might not be up to you at all, he'd said.

Anthony and Amelia were merely players in this drama the Fates had designed for who knew what purpose other than their own amusement—that's what he thought as he waited. Amelia, in so much pain that she couldn't walk upright, taken away for triage while he sat, cold and scared, in a strange lobby in a strange hospital in a strange town a mere four miles away from Canada. She'd given a fake name, fake birth date, told the story of having lost her ID, and might have been discovered on the spot when asked for her address—they hadn't thought of that, what would she say?—if not for another wave of pain and nausea that encouraged the nurse to take her in first and settle the other questions later. He'd thought for a second that she was acting—but no. The panic in her eyes was about what was happening to her body, not about what to tell the intake clerk.

He held his phone as he waited, turning it end for end, then side for side, then sliding it open and snapping it closed repeatedly, until he noticed the clerk eyeing him. She looked like his third-grade teacher, Mrs. Preston, with her wide shoulders and round face and glasses that in this case sat crookedly, due, he noticed, to her having uneven ears. Standing near her at the counter was a man who might have been her brother, in an olive and black deputy's uniform, with stove-black hair that had been cut like Hitler's. " 'Specting that cold front'll be through anytime now," he was saying. "You bring thet casserole? Not turkey, I hope. Ten below, thirty with the wind, thet's what they're saying."

The three of them were the only people in the room. Noting that the deputy was armed, Anthony wondered whether the cops here in Newport (population 1,511, the sign had said) would be looking for "the fugitive teens." The deputy was watching him, too.

The wide door through which a nurse had taken Amelia ten minutes earlier swung open now and the nurse came through, without her. He watched as she stopped at the desk and got a clipboard, then came toward him. She was a tall woman around his mother's age, white-blond, sturdy-looking, wearing neatly pressed scrubs. He wasn't sure he'd ever seen scrub pants with such knife-sharp creases.

"You're Luc?" she said as she reached him.

Anthony drew a blank, then remembered that yes, if Amelia was Marie, he was Luc. "That's right," he said.

"She's doing okay. She's asked me to bring you in to keep company while she waits for tests."

He stood and followed the nurse, who said, "You're not local. Where's home?"

"New York."

"Oh? Whereabouts?"

"City."

"Mm. And where are you bound for?"

He paused again, trying to decide whether saying "Canada" was too vague and thus suspicious. And he didn't want to tell the truth, in the unlikely case that someone came looking for them later. But put on the spot this way, he was unable to think of another city's name anywhere nearby. "Montreal," he finally said, certain that the pausing before answering was itself suspicious, but she didn't call him on it.

"Business or pleasure?"

"Just a quick trip to, you know, see a friend."

"Not very good weather for a visit, until this rain here turns to snow." She glanced at him and added, "Hope you brought a warmer coat."

He was wearing his black fleece jacket. "Yeah," he said, feeling foolish. Northern Vermont in late November, icy rain outside, and here he was dressed more for Vermont spring. "This one's fine for—" He stopped, having almost said *North Carolina*. "Fine for New York," he finished.

"Boots would be smart, too."

He nodded politely. A lot of things would be smart—most of which he wished had occurred to him several months back, when being in love had made him feel as if he and Amelia were untouchable.

The nurse led him to a glass-fronted room where Amelia sat hunched forward on a narrow hospital bed, wearing a hospital gown. She smiled wanly when she saw him.

"They don't think it's a virus."

The nurse pulled the curtain across the glass wall. "We're going to need to take some blood and maybe do some imaging—a CT scan, to confirm what is presenting like appendicitis."

"You're sure?" he said.

"That it's appendicitis, or that we need to run the tests?"

"The tests."

"Oh, no question. The scan lets us see inside her abdomen—it's the most amazing tool, I'll tell you. First, though, we need a white blood count, a pregnancy test—"

"I'm not pregnant," Amelia declared.

The nurse looked at her, then at him, then asked Amelia, "No exposure?"

Amelia's face pinkened. She said, "I don't have insurance. How much will all that cost?"

"Don't worry on that now," the nurse told her. "But while we wait for the tests—which are necessary, yes—let's get the rest of your information down, all right?"

Amelia looked up at Anthony, eyes wide with questions he had no answers to either.

He asked the nurse, "What if you're right, that it's her appendix? What then?"

"Then most always it's surgery."

"We can't pay for that," Amelia said, looking at him.

The nurse was filling in information on a chart. "Maybe Mom and Dad will help you—"

Amelia shook her head and said, "No. It's just us."

She said it too quickly maybe, or maybe when the nurse looked up she saw in Amelia's eyes what Anthony was seeing, because then the nurse asked, "Tell me your birthday again?"

"February eighteenth, ninety . . . ninety-*two*."

Anthony closed his eyes briefly. *She tried,* he thought.

"And your home address?"

"I . . . It's, that is, I don't have one just now. Right, Anthony, because we're moving? To Montreal."

"Not just visiting a friend, then . . . Anthony?"

Amelia, realizing her mistake, looked at him miserably. Just then, a technician arrived with a blood-draw tray, and the nurse said, "Luc-Anthony, step outside with me?"

"Be right back," he told Amelia.

The nurse slid the door closed behind them and told him, "You pret-near had me, but I guess you two didn't have a chance to get your story on straight."

He said, "Can't you just treat her either way? It's complicated."

"Complicated how? She's underage, I know that."

"It isn't what you think. I can't really say more."

"You look like good sorts, both of you. Yes, we'll treat her, no question. But this is my one job, and my husband, he's got no work right now, so I can't go risking it all by bending rules. I have to report this."

"To who?" he said, imagining some kind of hospital authority whose job it was to verify identities, prevent fraud, that kind of thing.

"You saw him, Roger, the deputy out there."

"To the *law*? Come on," Anthony said. "We aren't doing anything wrong."

"It's procedure, not personal. And if you haven't done anything, nothing's what'll happen, right?"

Anthony bowed his head. It was all over now. The unfeeling gods and their sycophantic chorus watched them from the heights, keen to see what the poor mortals' last act would be.

He sighed heavily and asked, "When will you know for sure—about Amelia? That's her real name, Amelia, and I'm Anthony."

The nurse gave him a tight smile of approval. "Well, we got labs, then I'll set her up with something for the nausea and the pain. The doctor needs to see her, we'll do the scan, get it read—some hours. If it's the appendix, she might see surgery by two, three o'clock, depending."

"Will you at least wait—to report us, I mean? She's not going anywhere."

The nurse pursed her lips, then she said, "My son, he's about your age. I'm off at eleven, so I can give you till then."

An hour. "Thank you," he said.

The technician was leaving as Anthony returned to Amelia. He slid the door closed so that they could talk privately. "She said they're going to get you some medications so you'll at least feel better while they figure out what's wrong."

"What else did she say?"

"That we're not such good actors as we needed to be. Not in those words, but she knew we weren't being straight with her."

Amelia looked scared. "It's my fault."

"It's my fault. On the way from the lobby I flubbed my lines. I'm sure that's what tipped her off to start."

Amelia shifted, winced, said, "Now what?"

"Now we get you fixed up."

"You know what I mean."

"She has to report us, to the deputy, she said—you probably

didn't notice him when we came in, but he's hanging out right there in the lobby. I asked her to wait, and she said we've got an hour. After that . . . well, I doubt it'll be very long before he gets my ID, looks us up, figures it all out. I'll stay with you as long as they'll let me."

The door slid open and the nurse came in carrying bags of IV fluids. "These will calm your stomach and get some fluids in you. After the doctor's been in, we'll add something for the pain."

Amelia stared at Anthony sorrowfully while she held her arm out for the nurse. She was obviously exhausted, and now this burden was laid upon her as well. Redness rimmed her eyes and tears pooled in them. He wanted to cry, too. What a shitty night she was having. Pain. Tests. Surgery, probably, and then, thanks to their slipups and a heavy dose of rotten luck, a demeaning journey back to North Carolina in police custody or possibly with the FBI, and then jail for who knew how long. Thanks to capricious Fate, she was facing the annihilation of her dream to go to Tisch, to one day be the woman whose name decorated the marquee and headlined the program, whose voice delighted audiences who came to see her and who bought her recordings so that they could relive the passion, the joy, or sorrow. Thanks to Fate, his own future was an equally empty one. He loved her beyond anything. She loved him. Why wasn't that enough to conquer all? Reality was tragic and wrong.

The nurse finished with the IV and said, "The doctor should be here in a minute." She patted Amelia's knee, then left them alone again.

Amelia fingered the IV line where it emerged from the tape near her wrist. "There's still time. I could take this out and we could leave."

"Not with that deputy out there."

"I'm sure there are other exits."

Anthony took his jacket off and draped it over a chair, then sat on the bed beside her. "Yeah, okay, but suppose we do leave, and then your appendix ruptures?" He'd heard of that; his grandfather, as a young child, had nearly died that way because his home was a half day's drive from the nearest surgical center.

She said, "Okay, well . . . maybe I'll have the tests and it won't be my appendix—or anything serious—and we can still get out of here before she tells him."

"Have you been in ER before?" he asked. She shook her head and he said, "Nothing moves that fast. Even if you're the only patient they've got right now, you won't be diagnosed in an hour."

Her face crumpled. "Why do you have to be so negative?"

"I'm sorry." He put his arm around her and tipped his head to rest it against hers. "I'm trying to be real, that's all."

"I don't want real. Real sucks."

"Shh," he said, kissing her temple. "The important thing right now is you feeling better."

There was a knock, then the door opened again and a young, sandy-haired man wearing a doctor's coat said, "Hey, so it sounds like we've got some abdominal pain interrupting our plans."

Amelia said "Ha," her voice breaking, as Anthony slid from her side and moved to give the doctor room to examine her. He watched as the doctor lowered the bed and had her lie back. She looked so thin, so vulnerable as this stranger, this doctor, put his hands where only Anthony's had been in recent years—in recent days, too, a memory that felt distant and bittersweet now.

When the doctor pressed down heavily near her right hip then let up again, her entire body seemed to pull inward as she cried out in pain.

"Sorry for that," the doctor said. "But that's the one that tells us the most. I suspect we're going to need you to leave that appendix here with us before you go." He smiled, clearly a fan of his own lame humor. Amelia didn't smile. She gingerly straightened her gown, and the doctor raised the bed upright again. As he made to leave he said, "Cindy will be back with some morphine, then we'll get some-body to wheel you down to Radiology. Take care."

"So," she said when he was gone. That was all. *So.*

He said, "Yeah."

The nurse came in with the morphine. Neither Amelia nor Anthony spoke while she injected a port and told Amelia, "This will help you get comfortable. Have you thought about getting in touch with your folks? They might want to be here, 'specially if surgery's in order."

Amelia shrugged.

"Think it over. I'll be back in a bit."

Amelia laid her head against the bed and closed her eyes. "I hope the morphine works fast."

"It should."

"Lay here with me?"

"Sure." He reclined the bed and got in it, lying on his side with one arm under his head and the other wrapped around her.

"This is good," she said.

"That *was* fast."

She smiled. "No, *this* is good," she said, laying her hand on his arm. "*You* are good. And I am so, so sorry." A tear leaked from the corner of her eye and began to roll down her cheek.

"Me too," he answered softly, and caught the tear with his lips.

Her hair smelled of shampoo and rain. He kissed her where the tear had been and fitted himself closer to her side, and they lay like this, not speaking, just breathing together, her eyes closed— restfully this time. He closed his, too.

Maybe twenty minutes passed, Amelia dozing, Anthony turning their problem over and over in his mind, looking for another angle, another route, some strategy they hadn't considered that would prevent the Fates from having their way. And finally it came to him, the solution. He didn't like it—God no, he hated it in fact, but the more he thought about it, the more relieved he felt that something could be done after all. Something big. Something that, if he set it up right, would almost certainly stop the runaway train. Now all he needed was the fortitude to do it.

A noise outside the room caught his attention. He raised his head and saw a young woman in peach-colored scrubs pushing a wheelchair to the doorway. "Hey, lover girl," he whispered in Amelia's ear.

"Mm?"

"It looks like your ride to Radiology is here."

Her eyes fluttered open and she looked into his. "I love you, Anthony."

"No one could love you more than I do," he said. He kissed her, ran his hand along the side of her face, then brushed her lips with his fingertips. He put his nose in the cleft between her neck and shoulder and breathed in her scent, then kissed her there before getting up to stand at her bedside. The aide began sliding the door open. Anthony leaned down to kiss Amelia once more and said, "I'll see you later."

He stopped when he got outside the doorway, then, drawing himself up, walked away from Amelia's room. He would not allow himself to look back.

Out in the lobby, the deputy was still there, still talking with the clerk about the weather and eating something that smelled of tuna from a plastic Tupperware square. Anthony checked his phone for the time: 10:30.

Walking past them, he paused at the counter to grab a hospital information brochure, then went to the far opposite side of the room and stood facing the tall windows. Drafty as it was there near the windows, he wasn't going back to Amelia's room for his jacket. In the cones of light cast from each parking lot light post he saw sleet and snow mixed in with the rain—it was beautiful and mesmerizing.

He heard the deputy laugh loudly and say, "Yeah, but you can't blame a fool for what he doesn't know."

"Tell that to Gibson Liles," Anthony said to himself. He sat down and leaned over, elbows on knees, phone in his hands. 10:31. It was time.

30

NTHONY LISTENED TO THE LINE RING, AND RING AGAIN, FIVE times, and thought he was going to have to leave his mother a message (which he really didn't want to do), when she picked up with a tentative "Hello?"

"Hi, Mom."

She gasped. "Oh, God. Anthony! It *is* you. I saw the number but . . . Honey! Are you—Where are you? Are you okay?"

"It's okay, I'm okay. Calm down," he said. "*Sois calme*. Right?"

"Right," she sputtered, laughing. "Honey, oh, I'm so glad to hear from you. Everyone has been frantic. Cameron said you were in touch earlier, but she didn't know from where. Are you in Mexico? Can you tell me anything?"

He swallowed the stone that had lodged in his throat and said, "We aren't in Mexico, no. We never meant to go there. We went to New York. How are *you*? I saw the news—that they arrested you."

"Yes, well—wait, New York?" she said.

"On our way to Canada. Which brings me to now, and why I'm

calling. It's Amelia. We're in a hospital in Vermont. It looks like she's going to need her appendix out. They just took her for a CT scan, but the doctor seems pretty convinced already."

"Oh no! Where in Vermont? What hospital? Has she told her parents? I assume the hospital needs their consent to treat her."

"Actually, no she hasn't, and no they don't. Mom . . . we screwed up," he said, pushing his hand through his hair. "She tried using a fake name, but we weren't really prepared and they caught on. I mean . . . I don't know, probably I would've come clean anyway if she ends up needing surgery. Her mom deserves to know. Anyway, they're going to report us to the authorities. It's only a matter of time."

His mother was quiet—so quiet that he checked his phone to make sure they were still connected.

"So . . ." she said slowly, "so to begin with, I should get in touch with Mariana Davis—"

"What I need you to do is call Sheri Wilkes and tell her Amelia is here in Newport, Vermont, at the North Country Hospital. I did tell the nurse her right name, but they might still have her under the name *Marie* Wilkes." He read his mother the hospital's telephone number from the brochure, then said, "Tell her to get on the next flight to, I don't know, Montreal, I guess—I assume she's got a passport. She can drive from there. It's only about a hundred miles. I'm not sure where the next closest major airport would be."

"Burlington's probably closer," she said, then read the number back to him. "So okay, I'll do that, I'll call right away. How *is* Amelia? What happened?"

He checked the time again. 10:35. "We were going to look for an unpatrolled border crossing, but she got sick. She wanted to keep going, but she was in a lot of pain. I couldn't risk it."

"That was . . . that must have been hard. Honey, don't you think I should get Ms. Davis working on this?"

"Not just yet, okay? I think maybe I've found a way to get Liles to drop all the charges—but I can't get into it right now."

"Anthony—"

"Mom, really. You'll have to trust me."

He could almost hear her struggling with her need to know more, and her difficulty finding the willingness to trust a kid who'd abused what he'd been given—or so he imagined it. Finally she said, "All right . . . okay, well, isn't there something I can be doing? I hate to feel so helpless."

"I know, and I'm sorry. Christ, I'm sorry. . . ." He squeezed his eyes closed briefly, then opened them and blinked and cleared his throat. "Call Amelia's mom, like I said. That'll be a big help. And I'm sure there'll be other things later. Listen," he said, standing and facing the windows once more, "I . . . I really have to go now. I just wanted . . . I wanted to talk for a minute, to say thanks for everything you've done for me, and to apologize."

"Oh, honey. I only wish I could do more."

"Me too. I love you, Mom."

"I love you, sweetheart."

He pressed END before she could say anything else, and then he pocketed his phone and went out into the cold, wet night.

In the hours to come, he would get in touch with Cameron again. She would contact Jodi about the video and then begin updating their friends, and the thousands who'd begun following their story on Facebook, with news of Amelia's condition. He would trudge through the weather, icy water streaming from his hair and nose and chin, and find a garage, then a shed, then a barn from which to make calls to the hospital posing as an FBI agent in order to get information on Amelia's condition—which was surprisingly easy to pull off. People believed what made sense to them. They would think, Of course the FBI would be calling, and how exciting that they'd be able to help out!

He would be told, sometime around two A.M., that Amelia was in surgery, and in recovery, woozy, at four. He'd learn that her parents had resorted to chartering a plane—no flights from Raleigh so late at night—and that they'd be there waiting when she was brought back to her room. He'd hear that other FBI agents would be arriving in the morning to help the Newport police and the Vermont troopers in their search for the missing boy—oh, but then he probably knew that already.

Approximately three hours before sunrise, he would call Raleigh's directory assistance to get the number for Gibson Liles at the DA's office, then he'd call that number, knowing he'd reach voice mail, and tell the DA what all of this had come to. He'd text Cameron to say he'd done exactly that, and ask her to get the word out. The snow would be coming down hard by then, accompanied by a light wind. In the impossible darkness of the Vermont night, the snow would reflect almost no light. He would leave the barn, soaked through and shivering, and set out in no particular direction.

He'd thought this plan over from every angle—what people would say, how they would rally around Amelia—and knew that all he had to do now was keep walking, and the one thing he needed to accomplish before he was found would, before too long and without unbearable discomfort, take care of itself.

31

HARLAN WILKES AND HIS WIFE WAITED FOR AMELIA TO BE returned to her room, both of them doing their best to accept, or more likely ignore, the police presence in the corridor. The smug bastards, he thought. He knew how they saw it. They had her now. Now all they had to do was hang around for a day or so until she was deemed fit for travel, and then it was back to Raleigh and a small cell on one of the upper floors of the Wake County jail for little Miss Wilkes, thirty minutes' visitation allowed each week, see what happens next.

Harlan could not remember a longer night than the one he'd just spent. Beginning with Sheri finding him in the game room (where, after a turkey-sandwich supper, he had been distracting himself by lying on one of Amelia's pillows and watching rebroadcasts of NFL games from the '70s) and hearing her say Kim Winter was on the phone, to his mobilizing the people who could find them a pilot and a plane, to conversations with the FBI and the Vermont State Police—who would be ensuring Amelia's safety (a euphemism if he ever heard one), and then the long, anxious flight into this Nowheresville's tiny airport, where a local police officer met them and drove them through insanely heavy snow to "our little hospital by the lake."

"Lucky Jim stayed on to keep the runway plowed," the officer told them, as friendly as if they'd come to town for a ski vacation or some such. "Usually, they leave at five, but we knew weather was comin'. Good you got here safe. Not every pilot would be willing, nope. Much worse than this and they'd shut things down, but it's your good luck this storm's just a warm-up for wintertime. This here's hardly a storm at all, bet we won't see ten inches when it's all through. . . ." Sheri had sat stiffly in her warmest coat, gloves on, scarf on, hat on, gripping the door handle and blinking against the whiteness swirling in the headlights. Harlan had nothing to say either, except that yes, of course, they were very glad to be getting here to see their daughter, very glad to know she was safe and in good hands.

Now noise in the corridor let him know that Amelia was on her way from the recovery room. He stood and Sheri did too, a bright, ridiculous smile on her face. Who could be happy now? Relieved, yes. Winter hadn't managed to get Amelia out of the country, and she'd found medical care, thank God, before it was too late. But happy?

"Hey, baby," Sheri said, going straight to the wheelchair as it came through the doorway.

Amelia, sallow-skinned, dark circles under her eyes, hardly looked at either of them before she said, "Where's Anthony?"

God almighty, Harlan thought, unsure whether he was more upset by her appearance in that gown, lank-haired, an IV line stuck in her, or by her greeting—if you could call it that. Sheri moved back as the aide turned the chair and positioned it close to the bed. "He . . . we don't know. Didn't he say where he was going, before he left you?"

Amelia shook her head. "I already told them he didn't. Hand me his jacket, would you?"

Sheri turned to see where Amelia was looking, and took a black fleece jacket from the chair. "Well, nobody knows anything more," she said, handing it to Amelia. "How are you feeling?"

Amelia answered with a frown while the aide helped her into bed.

Harlan, displeased that Sheri would just hand the jacket over, displeased that Amelia would ask for it, came to the bedside. "Don't be ugly with your momma. We've been up all night—up for the last week, in fact, worried to death and praying that you were okay. Show a little consideration."

Looking at Sheri, she said tightly, "I'm feeling okay."

When Amelia was settled in her bed and the aide and nurse were done fussing with the IV and blankets and pillows and bed height, the three of them sat together like strangers at a funeral, no one saying a word.

The sense of unreality was so strong that Harlan felt disoriented, dizzy almost. How could they, the Wilkes family, be at the top of Vermont during a blizzard, in a hospital so small and so empty that it seemed like a stage set, with cops hanging around outside talking nothing but snow and what a damn crazy fool that Winter kid must be to have left there without his car—without even his coat! Harlan didn't like the admiration he'd heard in their tone. The kid was a renegade and a coward, leaving Amelia there, helpless and alone, so that he could escape. No doubt he was in Canada already—probably had an accomplice there, probably was sitting someplace warm knocking back a few drinks and laughing about his success. Too bad about the girl, he'd be saying, but there'll be others. Wink, nod, nudge.

Harlan decided to try again with Amelia. He'd got off on the wrong foot—understandable, but obviously not the tack to take. She was in a bad way, too. He said, "We're so grateful you're all right."

She said nothing.

"Mr. Hubbard will be doing everything possible to get you released, maybe even keep you from going to jail."

Nothing.

"If you'll testify that you went against your will—"

"Don't start, Daddy," she said, her words like three gunshots in the quiet room.

Sheri said, "Harlan, there'll be plenty of time for all that."

"How 'bout I go see if I can find me a Co-cola," he said. "Guess up here it's just Coke, though, right? Sheri, you want something?" She shook her head. "Nurse said there's vending machines in the ER—think they'll have pork skins?" He smiled, but neither his wife nor his daughter appreciated his efforts. "I'll be back," he said.

"Hold on," Sheri told him, standing. To Amelia she said, "I'll be right back. I need to talk to Daddy."

He waited in the corridor as Sheri came out and closed the door behind her. "Harlan, I have to ask you, why do you persist? Surely you can see it's not helping."

"I'm frustrated. It's . . . it's like she's out in the water about to drown, and the raft is right there next to her but she won't climb on. Makes no sense."

"I've decided, I'm going to tell her—about what happened with me and Whit Johnson."

Harlan frowned at her. "That is *not* a good idea."

"I'm not real concerned with your opinion right now. You've felt free to disregard everyone else's, after all."

"You weren't arguing too loudly, if I recall."

"You're right, and that was my mistake. None of this had to happen, Harlan. I tried to support you the way a wife should . . . but it's led us here—not *Vermont* here, but to having a miserable daughter who's under house arrest in a hospital, a boy gone missing in a snowstorm, his mother sick with worry. . . . *Here* is an awful place to be."

Harlan shoved his hands in his coat pockets and leaned against the wall, bracing one foot against it. This wasn't sitting well with him. He said, "You really want to encourage her with all that lovelorn business?"

"I want her to know that I understand a little bit about what she's been going through. Not the law mess, but a father's resistance to a man based on—well, based on nothing but prejudice and a mistaken idea of what his little girl deserves."

"Oh, so you wish your daddy would've let up so you and Half-breed Johnson could've stayed together, is that it? Wish I'd never crossed your path? Fine. But you told me yourself he was happy just running a diner. If you'd stuck with him you wouldn't have anything like the life you have now—and you wouldn't have Amelia."

"True, I wouldn't, but that's not the point. I'm not sorry for where I am. I got over the heartbreak—maybe because he wasn't really the one for me. I do love you, Harlan, but that doesn't mean I didn't love him back then."

"Fine," he said. "Have your little chat—"

"I'm not asking your permission."

"But when her *love* goes wrong and she can't ever let go and she ends up miserable and drunk and sick, don't you all blame me."

"She is *not* your mother. In fact, if anything, she's an awful lot like *you*."

He opened his mouth to argue, but before his thought made it to his mouth, he thought again. She was right, he could see it—Amelia was strong-willed and hardworking and she had a dream she wasn't willing to let go of, same as he'd been. The different part, though, was that Amelia was a girl, and girls didn't see things like guys did.

He said, "In some ways, okay, sure. But that doesn't change anything about her and Winter."

Sheri looked at him with pity. "I wish I'd never gone along with your idea that she could be talked out of it, counseled, restricted out of it—that she should ever feel like she couldn't bring *any* boy

' home to begin with. I knew better. It's *love,* all right? There's nothing to be done about it." She pulled open the door and went back into the room, leaving him there with no chance to reply. Not that he knew what he'd have said anyway.

He found his way to the ER, Sheri's words, her attitude, her *certainty* all running back and forth inside his brain, making contradictory and chaotic thoughts that he was none too happy to have. Usually there'd be a hook in there to catch these thoughts, a hook made of doubt, say, or outright rejection, his own certainty that he had a grasp of what was right and true in the world. Not this morning.

There were the vending machines. No pork skins, but he bought a soda. Outside, the day was a wash of gray light and blowing snow that seemed to be tapering off. He shivered, looking at it. Who lived in such godforsaken places as this? He wanted to ask this of the white-haired woman he saw behind the counter, who appeared to be otherwise sensible—and he would have if she hadn't already been talking to a man whose badge identified him as a Vermont State Police officer. There were two others near the door, with a deputy who looked a little like Hitler.

The officer at the desk—a trooper, Harlan thought, based on the chevron on his sleeve—was stirring a tall steaming cup of coffee with a wooden stick and saying, ". . . south of town about four miles. You know, Josiah Howell's place. Old Josiah went out to his woodpile for a few logs to stoke the fire and actually walked over part of him in the snowdrift, you know. Felt funny under his boots, he said, not s'posed to be a ridge there. Dug some, and there he was."

The woman said, "That's a shame is what it is. Betty told me at shift-change that he'd seemed like a nice, caring fella. What he could've been thinking . . ."

"Why he didn't drive, that's what we're wondering."

Harlan walked over to them. "So he'd have a better chance of avoiding the law—you're talking about Anthony Winter, right?"

"You with the news?" the trooper asked, eyeing him.

"No, it's my daughter he kidnapped."

The woman cocked her head. "You might want to think that one again."

"Pardon?"

"Cindy, she was on shift last night, she said they were no-question devoted. She's the one that had to report them, but she said she wished she didn't have to. She didn't know what the trouble was then, and when she found out, she was so sad for them. I got here at eleven and your girl was asking after him the whole time till they took her to surgery, and again after. Kidnapping, no sir, that won't wash."

Harlan tried to muster the conviction that had come so readily before. "Amelia only *thinks* she's in love. The Winter kid's a convincing actor, take my word for it. Or . . . I guess I should be saying 'was'?"

"Hypothermia—" the trooper began.

"So convincing," the woman interrupted, challenging Harlan, "that Cindy caught them out using fake names after only a few minutes?"

The trooper said, "Her statement—that is, your daughter's statement—was that their leaving North Carolina was her idea."

"She's afraid to say otherwise," Harlan insisted, feeling as if he was trying to push a boulder through a wall using only brain waves. These people didn't know the whole story. They needed to know the particulars, and then they'd agree with him. "He left a note saying he was taking her out of the country. *Taking*. That pretty well proves he kidnapped her."

"Then why would he leave a note?" the woman said.

"Right," the trooper said. "If he really was taking her against her will, wouldn't he try to just disappear without a trace?"

"Well . . ." Harlan began, but he had no ready answer for this.

"Mister," the woman said, "they were throwing you off the trail is all. I tell you, it might be time for you to stop looking at this from inside your own head. We have a saying here, 'too much for the pump,' and that's what your attitude about that boy is. Those two were in love."

"You didn't even see them," Harlan said, wanting to prevail and yet feeling his own certainty slipping, no traction in these conditions.

The woman's mouth turned down in pity for him, the poor man who was too thickheaded to understand what was plain to everyone else. She said, "I didn't even have to."

The rumble of a diesel engine got their attention. Outside the ER's entrance was a big pickup truck with a topper on the back. The trooper said, "That'll be Josiah," as a four-person team of medical personnel pushing a gurney between them went out to meet the truck. At Harlan's questioning look he added, "Calling for an ambulance didn't make sense."

As Harlan watched, the group stood at the back of the truck while someone who was crouched inside held the ends of a blanket that, Harlan assumed, was curled around Winter. They slid him onto the stretcher and what Harlan saw when they came past him again struck him as cold as the figure before him.

He put his fist to his lips. Jesus, help him, this was *real*. The half-naked blue-white body curled into a fetal position and covered, still, with a good bit of snow, was no anecdote, no subject for debate. This was *Anthony,* an actual person, a hypothermia victim, Kim Winter's son. This was the boy that Amelia had been saying all along was a good and decent person. This was who she'd asked for all night, even right out of surgery, and again when she saw Sheri and him. This boy was the one these strangers, who weren't prejudiced by wishes or fear or political agenda or stubbornness, were convinced was in love with Amelia.

But if that was so . . . why had he left there, if not to escape?

But, in leaving, why had he gone south instead of north, to the border? Could be he'd gotten his directions mixed up—that was the logical conclusion. Logical, though, would've been to put his coat on. Hell, Harlan thought, logical would've been to drop Amelia here at the door and drive himself away from civilization immediately, while he had plenty of time to do it.

The woman called to one of the team as the gurney hurried past, "Get me his ID." To Harlan and the officer, she said, "I'm gonna reach his parents myself if I can."

"Just his mother," Harlan corrected her. "No dad." If he expected the woman's expression to change based on this, he was wrong.

"*We've* got the info," the trooper told her.

Harlan wondered at the rush, and pointed toward the wide doors that were now closing. "What do they think they can do for him?"

The trooper said, "Maybe nothing. He looks pretty far gone. With hypothermia, though, there's a saying: you're not dead until you're warm and dead."

"Meaning what? They . . . they thaw him out and then they can pronounce him dead?"

"That's usually how it goes. Once in a while they can get 'em back. I've heard of it. Not here, but you see it in the national news now and again."

"Do you think . . ." Harlan began, unsure of why he was about to say what he was about to say—except that he might like to be able to ask Anthony about his motives, which weren't adding up. And he might ought to give Amelia more credit than he had been. And he'd like it if Sheri didn't look at him the way she'd done. Maybe what he was about to say was motivated by his being here at the top of Vermont, so far away from the Robeson County dirt road, where he'd grown up skinny and hungry and angry and determined, that the gravity of those memories was weakened by the distance or the setting or the blizzard. He didn't know. He only knew he had to say it.

"Do you think you can get a doctor out here to talk to me, like, right now?"

32

KIM WAS AWAKE, BUT SHE WAS NOT SHOWERED OR DRESSED OR even caffeinated to help overcome the exhaustion that came from her sleepless night—several in a row, in fact. The FBI phone call telling her that Anthony had gone missing—that he had essentially dumped Amelia at the hospital and taken off to save his own skin— had come at eleven forty-five last night. It had caught her up short, giddy as she'd been after hearing from Anthony, thinking her Thanksgiving prayer had been answered. It hadn't made sense. *This* was his plan, to run away alone? She couldn't fathom it. From that time until now, 8:20 A.M., she had waited for her phone to ring again.

The FBI agent who'd made the eleven forty-five call had wanted to know if she'd heard from him. The agent who arrived a few minutes later asked the same thing. She'd told them both that yes, he'd called, and he'd said he thought he had things figured out, and no, she'd had no indication that "figured out" meant going off in a blizzard, alone, on foot, at night, with no provisions that anyone knew of—not even his

coat, they kept telling her, driving the knife farther into her heart—
so that he might yet evade the net the FBI was casting.

Kim, baffled and afraid, had asked the people whose presence
might ease her mind to come over. Late as it was, her mother, Rose
Ellen, and William had come right away, braving the incursion of
news reporters lining the street in front of her house. They'd come,
though there was little to do besides speculate and wait. The three
of them were in the kitchen now, brewing coffee and cooking bacon
and eggs—as if she, or they, were interested in eating. What else did
you do, though, when there was nothing you could do? When you
were confined to nineteen hundred square feet and the police
would not allow you to go, by any means of transportation you
might be able to arrange, to Vermont to look for your own child—
who you were sure you could find, you, with your heart a beacon
for his—what in the name of God were you supposed to do?

William left the kitchen and sat down next to Kim on the couch.
He took her hand and held it, saying nothing. She was glad he was
there. His willingness to come when she called, his presence, these
meant something to her, they did, though she couldn't access that
color in her emotional spectrum right now. When this was over,
maybe . . . Maybe. Or maybe not. Maybe this was never going to
be over.

After a minute, William gave her hand a squeeze, then let go and
went to the desk where he'd set up his laptop. He had to leave soon,
she knew; he had family in from out of town, expecting him back.
It had been good of him to stay this long. It had been good of him to
come at all.

William said, "This is nice: only twenty-four new emails this
morning. And here's one from a parent reminding me what a fabulous teacher you are. . . . Absolutely correct." He looked at her
over his glasses and nodded. Then, reading further, he said,
"Another wrote in support of the kids."

"I'm glad to hear it," she said, trying to make her tone match her
words.

From the kitchen Rose Ellen said, "Coffee's on." Kim got up. She didn't want coffee, or anything other than answers, please God, but it would give her something to do while she waited.

"How about *that*," William said, not in reference to the coffee. Kim turned. He said, "That group, the Facebook page supporting the kids? Listen to this. There's a lot of chatter about Amelia's appendicitis . . . and—hold on, what's this?"

Kim walked over and stood next to him. The computer's screen was crowded with posts and comments and he was scrolling through them too quickly for Kim to follow. But then he stopped and said, "Here." He pointed at the screen. "Cameron McGuiness posts this last night around midnight: *'Don't believe what you hear, peeps. He did NOT kidnap her and the rest is bullshit too. The DA has a message from Anthony waiting in his voice mail and then we'll all see.'*"

"The DA?" Kim said.

"Was Anthony in touch with Cameron last night?"

"Maybe after I talked to him? I'm calling Mariana." Kim got her phone from the coffee table and was about to place the call when William said, "Hold on. Hold on," he said again. "There's a video."

Kim went to see what he was talking about. On the screen, in dim lighting but with color and with sound, was Anthony, close up and smiling.

A woman's voice said, *Okay. The Big Adventure, take one: the man you see before you is Anthony Winter, who's in New York City for—how many times have you been here before?*

Twice.

In the Big Apple for the third time, the voice continued. *He's . . . let's say he's on vacation.*

"He's on vacation," Kim heard, and Amelia appeared in the frame, the three voices now a chorus of laughter.

Oh, we are brilliant, the narrator said, and the camera moved in closer to Amelia, who was holding on to Anthony's arm and nodding vigorously, all smiles. *Now, Anthony wants to . . . You fill in the blank.*

Have a good time tonight, he said, looking into the camera.

No, bigger, said the voice. *Try again. He wants to . . .*

Kim looked at William and blinked back tears. "They were in New York—this is from there, from the other night. Look at Amelia," she said, turning her eyes back to the screen. "Doesn't she appear to be there voluntarily? It's obvious. This has to be part of his plan, whatever it is. . . . Mariana needs to see this. The DA needs to see this."

She was on the phone with the lawyer relaying all the new information when a tone told her she had another call coming in. "I'll call you back," she said, then glanced at the phone's display as she went to press the button to answer. What she read, *Harlan Wilkes,* made her pause with her thumb on the button. Her knee-jerk urge was to hand the phone to her mother or to William, who were watching her. Anything she had to say to Harlan Wilkes, or him to her, wasn't fit for right now when *he* was there in Vermont with his daughter while *she* was waiting to know what had happened to her son. Maybe she would simply say that, she thought, and drew a deep breath and answered.

"This is Kim Winter," she said, intending to shortcut the conversation—just have her say, and hang up. "I don't—"

"Ms. Winter, Harlan Wilkes here. You're about to get a call from, I don't know, several people probably, and I know you don't wanna hear from me, but give me a minute." He spoke so quickly that Kim doubted she could interrupt him. He said, "They're gonna tell you they found your son"—her heart slammed against her ribs—"and they're gonna tell you . . . they're gonna tell you that he's, that he—" Wilkes coughed. "He was outside all night in the snowstorm." Her heart plummeted. "It's hypothermia," he said. "In a second I'll put on a doctor who'll tell you all about that, but here's my part: I hired a plane, it's waiting to take you to Boston—room for four, so bring anyone you want. It's at RDU, on the General Aviation side. Go to that terminal, I got someone who'll meet you there. Go now, don't let that house arrest business stop you."

Kim held up her hand as though he could see her trying to slow him down. "Boston? Hypothermia? How is he?"

"Here's the doctor."

Kim heard the phone changing hands, and then a woman's voice saying, "Ms. Winter, your son was brought in a few minutes ago without a pulse—" Kim's knees buckled at the same time a sob escaped her. *God, no, God, no* . . . She sank to the floor as the doctor continued, "or none we can discern, and his core temp is eighty degrees Fahrenheit."

Something in the doctor's voice, or rather the absence of something, suggested hope. "What? What does that mean, none you can discern?"

"He is profoundly hypothermic. Everything circulatory slows to the point of being effectively stopped. That doesn't mean it can't work again, just that it isn't working now. It's suspended animation," the doctor said, as Kim's mother and Rose Ellen and William all crouched down near Kim, faces etched with concern. She couldn't look at them now; the doctor was saying, "People *have* been revived, and that gives us reason to think he has a chance at resuscitation. The usual procedure for facilities like ours is to try, with heated blankets and warm intra-abdominal solution, to raise the patient's temperature and then get the heart online, if we can."

"Okay," Kim said, her mouth working even as her brain scrambled to make sense of the information amid the horror of what the woman had said, *without a pulse.* "Okay—so then, he has a chance?"

"It's tricky. The rewarming process is metabolically complex and even if done carefully, the shock of it can kill a patient—often does, to be honest. But if a heart-lung machine is used, the body can be rewarmed extracorporeally using bypass. The blood itself is removed and rewarmed, which is a far more efficient strategy. Not risk-free by any means. His odds are still, I'd have to say, less than thirty percent. But that's well above what we might expect by the other method."

"Do it, then," she said, her voice rising. "Do it the bypass way. Do it now! Why are you even asking me?"

"We can't, here. We don't have the equipment. So Mr. Wilkes is arranging helicopter transport to Beth Israel Deaconess Hospital, with your consent."

"My God, yes," she said. "Mr. *Wilkes* is? Never mind. Yes, of course. When?"

"Immediately."

"Immediately. Of course, immediately," she said, moving purposefully toward the stairs. She had to get dressed. She had to get to Boston. "Of course," she said again. "I'm on my way."

By the time Kim and her mother arrived at Beth Israel Deaconess a little past noon, Anthony had a pulse and was breathing on his own. And that was all.

A nurse, perhaps thinking she was being helpful, came to Kim and handed her a heart-shaped pewter charm. "They said he had this in his hand when they found him," she said.

An hour later, his condition hadn't changed. The doctor in charge of his care came around and explained that although he was improved, it was still "touch and go." He was not "out of the woods." Kim would hear these phrases repeatedly from other doctors and nurses as the day wore on, and would herself repeat them to William, to Rose Ellen, to the FBI, to Mariana Davis, to Cameron, and to Amelia, whom she took the time to speak to at length around seven o'clock that evening.

"I wish I had more to report. They don't know when—or if—anything will change. I hope you're feeling all right?"

"I'm okay," Amelia said, though it was obvious she was crying. "I want to be there."

"I know you do. I'll tell him. They say he can hear things. He *might* be able to," she amended. "Amelia, did he tell you anything about what he meant to do?"

"I didn't even know he was leaving."

Kim understood, then, that what happened to him was no accident. He'd known what he was doing, and that's why he didn't tell Amelia, why he didn't tell *her*—they would have tried to stop him. The Facebook postings, the video, the mysterious message for the DA, all of that went together with his coatless trek out into the frigid Vermont night.

She hung up the phone and pressed it to her mouth, but the noise, the keening protest, happened anyway, a piteous whine from her throat. "How could you do this to me?" she whispered, not thinking, just then, of any of his reasoning, caring only about the black hole that had opened in her heart.

At eight o'clock his condition would be the same, and at nine, and ten, and also at eleven o'clock, when Kim left the ICU again, staying away from Anthony only long enough to check her own messages. When she saw that Mariana Davis had called, Kim had only begun to think about why the police had not yet shown up to arrest her.

The message said, "They've decided they can monitor you where you are. With Anthony in his current condition, they know you aren't going anywhere. The reporters are going to want to hear from you, so just let me know if you would like me to draft a statement. And as for Liles, regarding Anthony's voice mail, there's nothing yet, but you can bet it won't be a lot longer. The media flames are licking at the DA's door."

33

"SUSPENDED ANIMATION," THE VERMONT DOCTOR HAD CALLED Anthony's condition before the rewarming. Though his body was now a warm, pink, healthy-looking ninety-seven degrees Farenheit, he remained as suspended as before—but the wheels he'd set in motion before venturing out from that Vermont barn had begun to turn.

The neurologist, stern and serious, told the news media on Saturday afternoon that it was possible Anthony would remain in a coma indefinitely. "Reanimation is an inexact science," they reported him saying on CNN and on MSNBC and on Fox and on the network evening news reports, sparking peripheral discussions in comments trails and on blogs about the neurologist as Victor Frankenstein. That so many news sources were following Anthony's story in the first place, however, was a sign that Cameron and Jodi had lit the tinder in exactly the ways he'd intended.

Chatter of all kinds—about hypothermia, about sexting, about lovers running from the law—went on everywhere. The focus, though, was on the matter of whether Anthony would survive his ordeal, and why he'd undertaken it. Was he a hero or a coward? What kind of example was he setting for other teens in trouble?

On Sunday morning, when Anthony had lain still and quiet amongst his monitors and tubes for another night, the organ donation representative approached Kim, who could only answer with helpless nods. Yes, she believed in donation. Yes, she understood her son might be a perfect candidate. Yes, it could be that he'd intended to be a donor, if, in fact, what she suspected and what the media was now reporting was true: that he walked into the blizzard knowing he would not walk out of it. "The police reported that there were pills in his car," the woman said, "but he didn't take them, and he didn't use a weapon. He was a thoughtful young man."

"He *is* a thoughtful young man," Kim told her, choking up.

Kim remained at Anthony's side while the world outside the hospital was abuzz with speculation and suspense. Her mother was often there with her, and acted as a liaison between Kim and the media, and between the media and Kim. Sunday afternoon she reported, "William called. There are some twenty or more different videos up on that YouTube site, showing the kids onstage. It's remarkable—there's one from when Anthony was ten, doing that camp at Woodstock. They have some of Amelia singing in competitions . . . the plays they did for RLT and at school. . . . People are narrating the clips and mixing them with the one from New York, where Amelia says she wants to star on Broadway. I'm not that good with this whole computer-Internet-social-media business, but I managed to wade through some of what William told me about, and I have to say, it's a brave new world out there."

"Is it?" Kim asked, looking over at her. "Because, let's not forget, that's what got them into this state to begin with."

Throughout the day, her mother knitted or read, and Kim sat with her chair pulled up to the bed and held on to Anthony's frostbitten, bandaged hand. She talked to him, entreating him to move his arm or open his eyes. "You should see all those videos for yourself, you know," Kim told him. "Grandma says you and Amelia are the stars of the Internet right now."

Her mother added, "There's a petition circling for Tisch to let you and Amelia in, based on your past performances."

"There is?" Kim asked her.

"I thought I told you that. I'm sorry. There's so much to keep up with."

Kim leaned over and rubbed Anthony's forearm. "How about that, huh? A lot of people are on your side. So many people . . ."

"Prayer circles," her mother said. "Did I mention those?"

"No. Or maybe you did. It's a blur."

The machines clicked and beeped and whirred.

The leak came from inside the DA's office, that's what Mariana Davis reported when Kim checked in with her on Monday morning. "No telling who it was, but I'm not surprised. A lot of good defense attorneys get their start there. There's an audio link already up online—probably in a lot of places by now. But here, let me read to you from the transcript—"

"Can you play the audio, you know, just put your phone to the speaker?"

"I . . . sure. You're up for that?"

"I want to hear him."

"All right. Here we go:"

"*Mr. Liles, this is Anthony Winter. I'm hiding in a Vermont barn so I can finish getting things in order, but I'll be leaving soon, heading outside into . . . say, zero-ish temps, until hypothermia gets me, because people need to see what this has come to. I can't save myself, but maybe I'll save my mom and Amelia, who don't deserve any of this.*

"*Criminal laws are applied to people who do harm, right? Okay, so explain what harm we caused. I love Amelia. She loves me. Pretty terrible, better lock us up. You though: what about the harm you caused? Seems to me that after tonight you should be looking at manslaughter charges, if not murder. Wilkes may have loaded the gun, but you pulled the trigger.*

"You spout off about morality and examples and lessons like you're God's appointed apostle, and you wait for everyone to cheer you for sweeping trash like us off the streets.

"We'll see if they cheer you now."

Silence, then Mariana was back on the phone. "That's it. He may have gotten cut off. It's hard to tell."

At first, Kim couldn't speak. That voice, those words, they'd come from Anthony, no question, but this was a side of her son she had only ever glimpsed, a side that could one day have seen him *be,* and *do*—a remarkable side. This was a strong, mature man, a brave, selfless one. When he was backed into a corner he didn't cower and hold his wrists out for the handcuffs, he fought back, even though he understood that he had to sacrifice himself to do it. *This* was the man she'd raised.

34

Anthony's room was silent on Monday night, save for the machines that were tethered by yards of wires to almost every part of his body. Kim had been there long enough now that she knew the machines' names: cardiorespiratory monitor, pulse oximeter, IV pump, transcutaneous O_2/CO_2 monitor, blood pressure monitor, electroencephalograph. Each told her nothing she couldn't see with her eyes. Anthony had not improved. Oh, there had been a moment late in the morning when some "noise" in his EEG had gotten the nurse excited, but when it didn't repeat at all during the day, they told her it could have been a machine hiccup, some kind of interference. They said more tests would be done on Tuesday, but that if nothing changed, they'd all need to start thinking about where he should go next. "You never know," they said, their voices hopeful but their eyes betraying pity and doubt.

Kim understood doubt. She'd had plenty of time to indulge it since Anthony's first arrest. After what he'd done for her, though, and for Amelia, she felt disloyal and wrong for indulging it now.

Now she had to stay strong for him. Determined. She had to insist that everything possible be considered, tried, done. She had to stop seeing him the way she'd overheard the nurses describe his condition on arrival there. Visualization on his behalf, that's what she needed to do. Only, each time she began conjuring him alert and upright in her mind, she was overcome by memories of him. His infant self, black swirls of hair against his baby-shampoo-scented scalp. Him at three, taking corners on his tricycle tipped on two wheels. His first triumphant soccer goal at five. Her father and Anthony shelving books together, her mother serving him chicken tenders in dinosaur shapes and telling Kim to relax, some processed chicken wasn't going to kill him.

She desperately wanted the future, but she couldn't seem to find her way out of the past.

A tentative knocking drew her attention, and she turned to see Amelia at the door. "They said I can see him as long as you don't mind."

Kim got up quickly and went to her. Amelia's eyes were huge, taking in the sight of Anthony. "It's a little frightening—"

"No," Amelia said, shaking her head. "I'm not frightened. I . . . I had a dream last night." She moved closer to the bed, saying, "He was talking to me." Then, gently, mindful of the bandages, she took his left hand in both of hers and said to him, "I made it. You were right."

Kim studied her, this pale, slight girl, a wisp of a thing inside Anthony's fleece jacket. She was so calm and poised. "Right about what?" Kim asked.

Amelia, her eyes still on Anthony, said, "My dream was so vivid. . . ." She turned to Kim. "It wasn't really like a dream at all. It was more like I was having a conversation with him in my sleep. Do you believe in that sort of thing? He said Liles was going to drop all the charges—"

"Has he dropped them?" Kim asked. "I haven't heard anything."

"My lawyer says it's unofficial—but I'm here, aren't I? Not in jail."

Kim sat down in the chair she'd long since made her own. What Amelia was saying, it was awfully sweet, and Kim liked indulging her in the idea that it could be in some way real and not, say, a side effect of the anesthesia she'd been given or the pain medication she might still be on. If it could be real, wouldn't she, his mother, the person here at his bedside hour after hour, wouldn't she be the one he'd come to, if such a thing were possible? All her attempts at visualization, all her entreaties—if he was communicating, wouldn't she know?

She said, "I'm glad they let you come here—I know you've had a rough time. Our lawyer thinks that what you say—dropped charges—will probably happen, too. Liles is facing too much opposition, now that . . . now that Anthony's message is public."

Amelia put her fingertips on Anthony's lips, let them just rest there, then she smoothed back a curl of his hair and looped it around her finger. "He told me you really need to get some sleep."

Kim felt a small laugh bubble up in her. "Did he?"

"Is it all right if I stay?"

"Stay?"

"Until . . ." She shrugged, tears pooling in her eyes.

Kim swallowed hard. "Yes. Stay. Your parents—"

"They'll get a hotel room. Let me go tell them. I'll be right back."

She left the room, Kim staring after her. If she'd have thought of Amelia seeing him in this condition, she would have imagined her collapsing, sobbing at the sight. This calm, almost serene, version of Amelia seemed as unlikely to be real as the dream she'd recounted. Kim supposed it was exhaustion, supposed that Amelia, like the rest of them, was becoming resigned to the grim probability that although his rewarming treatment had restored some function, it had not restored life.

If that was the case, she thought, her throat closing at the image of it, at the thought that he might already be gone, then at least his body, his organs, could benefit others. She held on to this idea and tried, oh God, she tried hard to distance herself from thoughts of what had to be real, what had to be done in order for that to happen.

Amelia returned, holding some kind of smartphone in her hands. "My dad says we need to see this," she said, handing it to Kim. She leaned over Kim's shoulder and pressed a button. The screen filled with the image of Gibson Liles, saying, "My office— and I, personally—was saddened by the news that Anthony Winter is in critical condition after suffering severe hypothermia. It is also quite apparent that Miss Amelia Wilkes has suffered from the events of recent days. I have taken it upon myself to make a thorough re- view of all the circumstances involving these two, as well as Mr. Winter's mother, Kim Winter, and on reflection feel that the state would be well to drop the charges against each of them.

"As your servant, I am a mere instrument of justice. I did and do believe that the charges were warranted at the time they were made. However, as so many of you have expressed, these recent events suggest that justice has been done by a power higher than any of us here. My office wishes to state formally that all charges against Ms. Winter, her son, and Ms. Wilkes are dismissed."

After a silent moment, Amelia said, "So, that's it."

Kim handed her the phone. "You expected him to admit he was wrong?"

"I expected . . . I don't know." She shook her head and went to stand close to Anthony. "Liles ruins everything and he still gets to . . . And Anthony might *never* get to—"

She faced Kim, tears streaming down her cheeks. "It isn't fair."

"Life—"

"Isn't fair, yeah, no kidding."

Kim stood up and hugged her. "He did this for you—for both of us, but for you especially. To give you the future you deserve. You have to look forward now."

Amelia pulled away from Kim, wiping her eyes with the backs of her hands. "I don't want to look forward. I don't want to live without him."

"I know." Kim choked out the words.

"He knew what he was about to do, and still, do you know what he said to me? He said, 'I'll see you later.'"

"Honey, don't do this to yourself." *Or to me,* she thought. "We don't know what will happen, or when. Maybe . . . maybe you shouldn't stay. You should go home, rest, heal, finish out the school year. Take advantage of all the support you've gotten. Don't let what he did be for nothing."

Amelia was silent for a moment. Then she said, "My mom, she gave up on someone she loved, once. It was too hard to stick by him, she said. Things turned out okay, but she'll never know what might have happened if she'd toughed it out. Let me stay for tonight, at least. Please?"

Kim recalled Anthony's voice in his message to Liles. *I love Amelia.*

I love Amelia. Such conviction; how could she deny either of them anything? He'd want Amelia to stay if she wanted to.

"All right," Kim said, sitting down again.

She watched Anthony, his face slack, untroubled, as if showing them that his work was done and there was nothing pressing ahead of him.

I . . . I really have to go now. . . .

I love you, Mom.

She envisioned him standing beside Amelia in the Vermont hospital. *I'll see you later.*

You have to look forward now, she'd told Amelia.

Touch and go.

ENCORE

*Every blade of grass has its angel that bends
over it and whispers, "Grow, grow."*

—THE TALMUD

$\mathcal{A}$MELIA DROPPED THE LAST OF HER BOXES ONTO THE WOODEN floor just inside the doorway. "Done," she said. Sweat trickled down her back and along her jawline. "I had no idea it could get this hot here, even in August."

"You've been working like a dog," Jodi said. "Here." She made the word two syllables, *hee-ah,* her attempt at a drawl. "Ah made tea the way y'all drink it down home, sweet."

"Bless your heart," Amelia drawled in kind, taking a glass from Jodi. She drank deeply, then held the sweating glass to her forehead, saying, "My dad always used to do this with his beer, and he'd make a little hissing noise, like steam escaping."

"Oh, that reminds me: your mom called while you were out at the truck. They're stuck in traffic outside Newark, but she's certain they will be here by dinner. Well, she said 'supper,' but, you know."

"All right. That'll give us time to organize things a little bit, and shower. Not that it'll make them like this any better," she added. Her parents had politely suggested that she spend her first year in a dorm, rather than renting a room from Jodi. She had thanked them for their suggestion, and then politely told them that they were crazy if they imagined she was going to waste a single minute living her life on anyone's terms but her own.

Amelia finished the tea and set the glass on the counter. "Not bad for a first try. Double the sugar and you'll be closer to what I'm used to."

"Seriously? Oh well, what can I say, I was raised to know about Italian shoe designers and Swedish decorators. You'll have to educate me on how things are done in the South."

"If you want—but honestly, I'm hoping to leave all of that behind."

The sound of footsteps outside the door made her turn. Anthony came through the doorway, saying, "I hope she's not talking about me."

"Puh-lease," Jodi said. "Ego."

"Because she *did* leave me behind, to try to find a parking spot, of which there are none in all of Manhattan. I had to sell the truck to get rid of it."

He closed the door and came to join them in the kitchen. His limp, which had been very pronounced at first, was much less noticeable now. And when they'd been packing up her room and his, Amelia had observed that he used his left hand with confidence, the two missing fingertips, lost to frostbite, hardly a handicap.

Jodi gave him a glass of tea, which he downed in one long gulp. He held out the glass for a refill.

"Oh, is this how it's going to be?" she said. "I knew I should've charged you more."

"I can't believe you're charging us at all," Anthony said with mock indignation. "What was it you told us when we were here last fall—something like, we could stay as long as we needed to?"

"But not for free," Jodi said. "This is New York, kiddo. What, did you think you were somebody special?"

"Not a bit," he said.

"Nope," Amelia agreed, "he's as ordinary as anyone who's re-turned from the dead."

Jodi said, "Exactly."

"Except, you know, my eyes glow red in the dark. Oh—and I can fly."

He joked, but the truth was not so far removed from what he was saying. He'd awakened from his coma nine days in, unable to speak at all—and then when his speech returned three days later, he discovered that he was, without effort, fluent in French and Spanish. He'd always been knowledgeable about music, but now his recall of songs, bands, dates, album names, and band members was just about instantaneous. In truth, this had intimidated Amelia at first, even as he'd struggled to regain his physical mobility. He'd helped her through it, though, downplaying the change, assuring her he hadn't suddenly become a genius, joking that if they flunked out of college and couldn't find work, he could keep them afloat by working as a DJ in Europe.

Jodi raised her glass and gestured for them to raise theirs. "A toast: to my lovely new flatmates, Anthony and Amelia, may they take NYU and then Broadway by storm—and cast me well when they do!"

They drank, then Anthony put his arm around Amelia's shoul-ders and raised his glass again. "To belief," he said, looking into her eyes.

Amelia smiled and nodded. "To perseverance," she said, kissing him.

Jodi nudged Amelia's shoe with hers. "I do believe it's time for the two of you to ride off into the sunset. Roll credits!"

"Are you kidding?" Amelia said. "We're just getting started."

ACKNOWLEDGMENTS

It is my privilege and pleasure to once again be thanking the wonderful Ballantine Books team for shepherding what began as a seed of inspiration into a finished book. In particular, I'm grateful to my publisher, Libby McGuire, for her unwavering support, and my incomparable editor, Linda Marrow, for the expert ways she guides and shapes and sees and enables what it is I'm trying to do.

I'm pleased and thankful to be able to call Wendy Sherman my literary agent, my advocate, and my friend. Every author should be so fortunate. It's my good fortune as well that Jenny Meyer is the agent championing my work with publishers abroad.

So many people work behind the scenes to get a book ready and into readers' hands, and I'm grateful to all of them. In particular, however, Kristin Fassler, Kim Hovey, Susan Corcoran, Alison Masciovecchio, Junessa Viloria, Dana Isaacson, Laura Goldin, Kathleen Carter Zrelak, and Lynn Goldberg rate special mention.

I owe a lot to the amazing booksellers and librarians who are continually bringing readers to my books, and I want to extend a special thanks to my enthusiastic book-loving friends (especially Judy Lewis and Erin Hunter) and my enthusiastic readers who are doing the same. No author can succeed without people like these!

I appreciate so much the ongoing friendship and camaraderie of so many people, Pam Litchfield and Sharon Kurtzman first among them. The online writing community, which has embraced me and given me a spot at the water cooler, makes me happy to open my computer every day—and proves that the Internet is not entirely evil. (You guys rock!) And I'm thankful to have a family full of believers. It is a pleasure to be surrounded by such positive people.

My eldest son's experiences inspired the story inside this book, and I'm grateful for his willingness to see it written. Both of my boys—and my stepsons as well—informed the story by allowing me inside the world they inhabit, a world that asks more of all of us nowadays than it did when I was a young adult. I'm forever thankful to have my boys' love and support.

An author's life is rarely glamorous, and never simple. We work odd hours, go around in dazes, want to talk "story" endlessly, and sometimes become more involved in the world of our characters than in our own daily lives. I would be far less accomplished if not for my awesome husband, Andrew, who is the efficient motor that keeps everything domestic in motion. More than that, he is my Anthony.

AUTHOR'S NOTE

In 2009, my son, who had just turned nineteen, found me sitting on the screened porch working on the book that was supposed to be my spring '11 release. It was a warm day, sunny, as normal-seeming as any until I looked up from my laptop computer's screen and saw my son's expression.

"Mom," he said, "I'm in trouble. I'm going to be arrested."

When your child says something like this, time stops. Whatever you are doing at that moment, whatever's waiting on your To-Do list, whatever you had planned for later that day/week/month/year, all of it suddenly belongs to *Before*. Before my son told me he was going to turn himself in to the police for a crime neither of us had ever heard of, I was considered unusual only for being a novelist. Before my son submitted to handcuffs and a long ride in a patrol car to the Wake County jail, he was unusual only for having become a volunteer firefighter as a high-school junior. Before his mug shot and name and address appeared in the papers and on the news, our family led a normal and comfortable life, not too different from that of anyone we knew. After, it was as if we'd grown third eyes on our foreheads, making us unsavory and suspect.

In the slow, fearful, uncertain months that followed my son's arrest, when I was not supposed to talk about the case and was supposed to be finishing the book I'd been working on, my mind was cluttered with what-if questions. Some pertained to my son's safety, some to his future, some to my family's, some to my own. The story that unfolds in this book's pages comes as a result of my following those questions down the rabbit hole, setting aside the book I'd been working on in order to write this one instead.

Doing so was not an easy decision. That book was under contract and had been through the editorial cycle once already. My agent, editor, and publisher were expecting me to turn in the polished manuscript by spring. But as Maya Angelou has said, there is no greater agony than bearing an untold story inside of you. I had to tell this one if I hoped to find some measure of peace. I'm grateful to everyone on my "team" (my husband and sons included) for supporting that choice.

This book is fiction, the characters drawn completely from my imagination. But the events that inspired this tale, and the emotions that color it—the reactions and fears and possibilities—are real.

ABOUT THE AUTHOR

THERESE FOWLER is the author of *Souvenir* and *Reunion*. She has worked in the U.S. Civil Service, managed a clothing store, lived in the Philippines, had children, sold real estate, earned a B.A. in sociology, sold used cars, returned to school for her M.F.A. in creative writing, and taught college undergrads about literature and fiction writing—roughly in that order. With books published in nine languages and sold worldwide, Fowler writes full-time from her home in Wake Forest, North Carolina, which she shares with her husband, four amiable cats, and four nearly grown-up sons.

theresefowler.com

ABOUT THE TYPE

This book was set in Perpetua, a typeface designed by the English artist Eric Gill, and cut by The Monotype Corporation between 1928 and 1930. Perpetua is a contemporary face of original design, without any direct historical antecedents. The shapes of the roman letters are derived from the techniques of stonecutting. The larger display sizes are extremely elegant and form a most distinguished series of inscriptional letters.

FIC
FOWLER,T Fowler, Therese.

Exposure.

DATE			
9/04/11			

5-11